WINTER'S SUMMONERS

B. CHARLES

ᚳᚱᛟᛚᛟᚷᚢᛖ

Darkness enveloped the world, thick with billowing clouds of smoke and ash. Each crunch of fresh snow melted beneath her burning feet.

When did I first leave? Has it been days, weeks or months? I know you're out there somewhere. When I find you, I'll stop you from destroying the towers. She thought.

Flames danced along her moonlight skin, flickering in the freezing winds and providing a fragile warmth against the harsh winter cold. Guided by a faint glow in the distance, she trudged forward, the light growing brighter with each step.

"Don't stop. Your visions will help, that demon will bring ruin to all of us. Complete the task and return to us, Levanna. He must be close—end it," a charming voice whispered.

"I'll handle him, master," she replied, clutching her wrist.

The black flames crackled before surging outwards, coating her body in a mystical aura. Clapping her hands together, she unleashed a wave of fire that swept the snow from the path ahead, its heat reaching a group of demonic creatures, which recoiled, shuddering in its intensity.

Hollow eye sockets, devoid of any soul, scanned the area, letting out shrieks from gaping mouths as they spotted the girl with white hair. Their joints cracked grotesquely as they rose to attention, their long, slender bodies—towering over three metres—looming over her as she paused a short distance away. Long, claw-like fingers pointed at her, accompanied by a guttural rumbling that sounded like a threat.

"You are not the one I seek. Leave before I burn away the evil of this place," she warned, crouching into a battle stance. Blood dripped from skin that reflected the beauty of moonlight.

A quick glance at the village she could see dilapidated buildings; not a trace of life remained. Her heart ached at the loss. The demons' origins were a mystery to her, though her memories of them stretched back to childhood, when a group of powerful demons had besieged her home, destroying everything she knew and everyone she loved. Now, she roamed the lands in search of demon lord, battling to ensure they could harm no one else.

She raised her arm, black fire spreading across her pale skin before she hurled it at the demons with a wave of her hand. The resulting blast obliterated the remains of nearby buildings along with the demons. Their towering forms scattered through the village, avoiding the searing flames. Enveloped in flames, she sprinted through the crumbling streets, striking down any demons that lunged at her, her black fire magic reducing them to ash. Armoured demons withstood the dark flames, stalling her advance while others attacked from afar.

Spikes hurtled towards her, narrowly missing as she dodged to the side. She swept her arm in a wide arc, sending flames cascading over the demons. Their blood-curdling shrieks of agony echoed as the fire consumed them. She pressed on through the desolate village, amber eyes scanning for any signs of life.

"That's all of them," she murmured. "But the one I seek wasn't here either. There should be another town beyond this mountain—that will be my next destination."

Letting out a heavy sigh, she ventured forth rubbing the horns protruding from alabaster hair, leaving the destroyed village behind. In the wake of her appearance: charred remains of human bodies.

CHAPTER 1

"Astra, on me!" Lazarus shouted, his feet pounding against the snow as he raced through a thicket of trees. Hot on his heels was a pack of dire wolves, notorious for preying near villages where livestock was plentiful and defences scarce.

Using the wolves for training is our best option if we want to leave this village. The guards and village elders are more than capable of handling these wolves as a last resort, Lazarus thought, each breath forming clouds of frigid air. From a young age, he had learned to control his breathing to endure the relentless cold of the Winter Kingdom.

Breaking through the forest, Lazarus spotted the trees on the other side of the open field. His heart pounded fiercely in his chest, his blood running hot, providing warmth against the icy environment. Behind him, the crunch of snow beneath paws grew louder, accompanied by snarls as the wolves closed in. They pounced, fangs bared, but he deflected their attacks with a wooden polearm he had crafted with the help of Darius, a village elder, trying to keep them at bay.

Just as he neared the end of the clearing, a wolf lunged and clamped its jaws around his left arm. Its fangs sank deep into his flesh, dragging him to the snowy ground. Blood streamed from the wound, staining the pristine white with crimson.

"A little help would be great here!" Lazarus called out, unfazed by the pain of the wound. A fierce struggle ensued as he pried at the wolf's jaws with his free hand. Suddenly, a rustling sound came from the distance. The wolves turned, momentarily distracted by the noise—but it was too late.

An arrow whistled through the air, piercing the neck of the wolf gripping Lazarus' arm. Its jaws slackened, and it collapsed to the snow with a dull thud. More rustling followed, and a second later, arrows rained down from the sky, striking the pack.

Lazarus dropped the lifeless wolf onto the crimson-streaked snow. Two more wolves lunged at him. Tucking his wounded arm into his chest, he rolled to the side, narrowly avoiding their snapping jaws.

Out in The Glades, with its snowy mountains, dense forests, and abundant predatory wildlife, killing was often a necessity for survival. Yet Lazarus had always avoided taking a life, leaving that burden to Astra and the village guards. Instead, he relied on his polearm to fend off threats, refusing to cross that line.

Steeling his nerves, he crouched low, ready for the next attack. One wolf began circling him, its hypnotic blue eyes fixed on him, observing, waiting for the perfect moment to strike.

"I see. You want me to move towards the pack, right? Sorry, but it won't be that easy to fool me," he muttered under his breath, his grip tightening on his polearm.

The arrows had ceased. Covered in mud and snow, a female figure rose from the thicket. She wore rugged clothes beneath a white fur cloak designed to blend seamlessly into the environment. Though her appearance was far from graceful at the moment, her movements told another story. Every step, every motion of her body, was deliberate and precise. As she unsheathed a white blade with a smoky grey handle, its sharp edge gleamed in the dim light.

"I'm here to help the bait, so leave the rest to me, Lazarus," Astra said, her tone calm yet assertive.

Lazarus' eyes flickered between the two wolves circling him, his grip tightening on the polearm. "You know, I'd love to leave them all to you, but I don't think it's going to be that easy, Astra!"

"Don't worry, I'll get them to focus on me," she replied, inhaling deeply, her breath forming a mist in the freezing air.

Releasing a surge of mana, Astra exuded crackling energy that rippled through the clearing, making the hairs on Lazarus' arms stand on end. The wolves reacted instantly, baring their fangs as they turned their attention to the larger, more immediate threat.

Five wolves remained. Two veered to the left, two to the right, and one held its ground in front, its piercing eyes fixed on Astra. She smiled faintly, impressed by their coordinated formation, but her stance never faltered. Her blade was raised, ready to strike.

The wolves launched their attack, striking from both sides simultaneously. Astra crouched swiftly, evading their strikes as the next two closed in on her position. Rising smoothly from a roll, she turned to face the wolf on her right. Avoiding its claws with a deft sidestep, she raised her blade in a fluid crescent motion, slicing the closest wolf cleanly in two.

"Nice one! Four more to go," Lazarus called out, his tone tinged with admiration. Opening a pouch, he retrieved a cloth to use as a tourniquet.

"Thank you for the counting lesson," she replied in a mocking tone, her focus never wavering from the remaining wolves.

"Are you sure you're fine to handle them alone?" he asked, his guilt evident. Watching from the sidelines weighed heavily on him, but he had always resisted taking the life of any creature, even to protect the village's livestock. He had dreamed of forging bonds with all forms of life, imagining what it would be like to journey alongside them.

"I'll be fine," Astra reassured him. "You need to tend to your wound anyway. If you fight in that state, you'll just become easy prey for them."

Her blade gleamed in the dim light as she steadied her stance. "Think of this as training to become a knight. One day, I'll become one who makes everyone safe."

He'd known for years that she wanted to be a knight, but he still felt a sense of awe whenever she spoke of it. There was no hesitation in her voice when she said those words.

The pack circled Astra, searching for another way to pressure her. She encouraged them to attack. Sensing her intent, they charged at her in a staggered formation, aiming to lunge at their target without giving her room to counter. Astra quickly assessed their trajectories, sidestepped their attacks, and shifted to the offensive. The aspiring knight leapt at two of the wolves, her sword swinging like a pendulum. The thin blade sliced cleanly through their necks, decapitating the predators.

As she turned to face the remaining two, an ominous wave of energy rippled through the area, freezing everyone in place.

Cold sweat trickled down their foreheads as they exchanged knowing glances.

"Astra!" he shouted, thinking of the people in the village.

"I know. I'm on it," she said, her calm acknowledgment easing his panic as she broke into a sprint towards the village.

"I'll handle these two," he muttered, preparing to fight. But before he could take a step, the wolves fled. Something far more dangerous had their attention.

Relieved, Lazarus turned towards the village. His feet pounded against the snow, the crunching beneath him echoing as he gave chase, hoping he could catch up in time to help.

☆☆☆☆

Demons charged at the girl clad in black battle gear. She dodged and weaved through their attacks with effortless precision, grabbing their long, clawed hands with surprising strength and swinging them around before hurling them into nearby burning buildings. She continued her deliberate march through the desolate village, leaving small footprints in the snow. The demons hesitated, torn between engaging her or fleeing to avoid certain death.

Two demons cautiously approached, attempting to speak, but only guttural growls escaped their gaping mouths.

"There's no point in trying to talk. Your lives end here," the girl warned, raising her hand as flames engulfed her fingers. Just as her fiery strike was about to land, a blade deflected her attack, slicing across her stomach and leaving a thin cut.

"So, there is a strong demon among you," she remarked, unfazed. "It makes no difference. I was tasked with clearing this village of demons, and that's exactly what I'll do!" Her voice rang out as flames erupted around her.

She crouched into a battle stance, her blazing aura intensifying, eyes fixed on the small demon before her, its clawed hands gripping a blade.

☆☆☆☆

At the village of Riverfall, roofs blazed with scorching heat and billowing smoke. Children screamed as their parents swept them into their arms, dashing away from the chaos engulfing the burning village. Some villagers worked to fend off the flames, containing the fire in a bubble, while others directed streams of water from the river that split the village into two sections.

The clanging of swords echoed in the distance.

"That must be Astra and the villagers fighting the intruder." Lazarus sprinted down the main street as people ran past him in the opposite direction. He collided with a woman screaming in terror. This isn't right. No one here runs away in fear like this. I need to hurry. Lazarus brushed the dirt from his clothes and pressed onward.

"Lazarus! There you are. We were worried sick something had happened to you—you weren't with Astra when she returned," a woman cried out as she weaved through the crowd to embrace him. She was a mature woman with mahogany brown hair streaked with silver down one side, a striking feature that marked her as the village head.

"Maeve! I'm glad you're safe. It looks like Darius is safe as well." Lazarus felt a wave of relief seeing them uninjured. "You two need to help everyone to safety. I'm going to go help Astra. There's nothing we can do about the buildings now," he ordered, turning his gaze towards the fiery inferno at the edge of town.

"Lazarus, be careful. That woman is powerful. We've got people helping Astra fend off the intruder, but she still needs your help," Maeve warned before rushing away to assist a villager who had fallen. Darius wrapped his arm around the man's shoulders to help him escape.

"Alright, that's everyone. Maeve mentioned a girl. No one wanders into this village by mistake. Whatever they're here for, I won't let her get what she wants. I've got your back, Astra."

Lazarus ran towards the pillars of fire in the distance, shielding his face from the searing heat.

Astra had already confronted the intruder: a young woman who appeared to be in her twenties. Her white, shoulder-length hair cascaded in wavy locks, framing her golden-amber eyes that radiated an otherworldly glow. Two dark-grey horns jutted from her temples, giving her an aura of both beauty and menace. She wore a tight-fitting black leotard paired with thigh-high boots and gloves that stretched to her elbows.

Slap! Now is not the time to be in a trance. Astra needs help!

"Who are you, and why are you here? I've never seen a race like yours before," Astra demanded of the unfamiliar girl she was battling.

The girl didn't answer. Instead, a tail emerged behind her, whipping across Astra's chest and sending her tumbling backwards. Astra rolled with the impact and managed to regain her footing in a crouched position, clutching her chest.

"Astra! Are you alright?" Lazarus shouted as he emerged through the archway leading into the village. Around him, the snow had melted, revealing scorched earth and lifeless, blackened trees. He hurried to her side, his eyes catching the sight of her chest guard, torn where the tail had struck.

"I'll live, but this girl is strong—stronger than anyone I've ever faced," Astra said, pressing her sword against the ground to steady herself as she stood. "She's been calling everyone demons. I think she might be hallucinating, though I don't know why or how."

Several guards lay scattered on the ground—some wounded, others crawling for safety or unconscious.

Lazarus noticed the girl's expression. She looked confused, even frightened. She clutched her face and shook her head, her golden amber eyes darting between Astra and Lazarus, who stood before her.

"Help... I must find... them. They can end it," the girl said, her voice trembling with desperation.

"What do you mean by 'end it?' Are you in pain? I can help you!" Astra called out, concern clear in her tone.

The girl's gaze turned icy, her expression hardening. "No, they won't allow any interference," she replied with cold animosity.

Black mist began to seep from a gem embedded in the choker around her neck. Suddenly, a shadowy hand emerged from the gem and gripped her throat.

Lazarus realised for the first time that the girl was wearing a choker, the black mana gem at its center now glowing ominously. The hand appeared to originate from the gem itself. The girl writhed in agony, her hands clawing at the dark hand around her throat, tears streaking her face as she cried out.

"Please, Master! It was an accident—I didn't mean to mention any of you. Make it stop—it hurts!"

A chilling female voice resonated from the gem, sharp and commanding. "No one will interfere with our plans. Dispose of them now, Levanna!"

The hand of blackened mist released its grip on Levanna, retreating into the gem attached to her choker. Gasping for air as the pain subsided, Levanna's amber eyes flicked towards them, pleading for help.

An aura of blackened flames seeped from her body, making the air harder to breathe. The brief look of confusion on her face twisted into an intense, cold stare. As her gaze shifted to Lazarus, a chill ran down his spine.

"Uh, Astra, I don't like the look she's giving me."

"I thought you'd be ecstatic to have a gorgeous lady's attention," Astra teased, much to his dismay.

"Well, that would be great under different circumstances, but that stare feels more like, 'Why are you still breathing?' Wait, I've got it!" he exclaimed. "Astra, we can stop her, but it's going to be difficult!" he added before whispering his plan into her ear.

"Are you serious?! I still have no control over that technique, and you're planning for that to be the deciding factor? You're insane, Lazarus." Astra waved her hands in disapproval, rejecting his suggestion. "We need to come up with something else."

"There is no other plan. Just trust me, Astra. If anyone has a chance to defeat her, it's you. I believe in you!" He patted her shoulder before running off.

I know she doubts her technique, but it's our best shot to stop this girl and protect the village. You can do this, Astra.

Levanna's patience seemed to have run out. With legs spread and knees bent, she wore a devious smile, shifting into a battle stance. The air pulled toward her fiendish figure, creating a small vortex before an eerie silence settled over them.

All I need to do is reach the rope by the stables, and I'll be able to—

The sudden sound of a sonic boom startled Lazarus, making him flinch. It was just enough time for Levanna to close the gap, her strike poised to land. A sharp nudge to his hip sent him crashing into a haystack, which cushioned his fall.

What the heck was that? Lazarus looked back, noticing Astra had deflected Levanna's attack.

"I apologise for the interruption, but your fight is with me, Levanna. I won't let you lay a hand on anyone else while I'm still standing. On my honour as a future knight, face me!"

Sword drawn, Astra launched her counterattack with blinding speed, lowering her blade before raising it in a swift vertical arc. Though unable to deliver a killing blow, the strike drew blood, leaving a small cut on Levanna's chest.

Taking a deep breath, Astra pressed her attack, her precise slashes opening small wounds. Levanna, however, deflected the strikes with her forearms, shrugging off the damage as though unfazed.

Lazarus scrambled out of the haystack, rushing towards the rope hanging on a post in front of one of the stable gates. He quickly tied it into a hoop knot before turning back to observe the battle, waiting for the right moment to act.

The two girls clashed relentlessly. Sweat dripped from Astra's face, clear signs of exhaustion setting in, while Levanna's white-haired figure remained eerily composed.

Lazarus hesitated, knowing how dangerous the situation was, but he had no choice. He needed to restrict Levanna's movements to give Astra the chance to use her technique. Steeling his nerves with a deep breath, he shouted her name.

Levanna stopped and turned around as Astra delivered another vertical slash, forcing her to retreat just enough for the rope to land around her body. Mustering all his strength, Lazarus gripped the rope and yanked it, only for her to seize the other end and resist most of the force. That's not enough. I need to make her fall to the ground; only then can Astra destroy that black gem.

He lashed the end of the rope to a large tree, substituting his lack of strength with the weight of the rooted oak to hold her in place long enough for Astra to act.

While Lazarus struggled to keep Levanna still, Astra recognized this was her last chance. She shifted into a focused stance, closing her eyes in what Lazarus assumed was a quick prayer. Charged mana radiated from her body, causing her hair to rise with static. Revealing her sword, now coated in crackling electricity, she pointed it at her opponent, took a steadying breath, and pushed off the ground with enough force to generate a lightning flash as she leapt towards Levanna.

In an instant, Astra appeared before her target and thrust her sword into the gem attached to the choker. The sound of thunder erupted as the gem released a powerful blast of dark energy, exploding in a surge of black aura that hurled all three of them into nearby buildings and trees. They fell unconscious amid the wreckage.

CHAPTER 2

The scent of cooking meat wafted into the bedroom, stirring Lazarus from his slumber. *That smells good! Luxhorn? No, Ice Boar.*

"That's one way to wake someone up. How do you feel? I think you took the brunt of the blast," Lazarus said, looking at Astra, who was leaning over him as if checking on his condition. *Everyone's been busy—the houses are almost rebuilt. It's probably been two days since the explosion,* he thought, glancing out the window.

"I'm doing fine, all things considered. If I hadn't been wearing my chest guard, things might have turned out differently. Levanna's still unconscious; she hasn't shown any signs of waking up yet. Anyway, I'm making breakfast. Come eat when you're ready," Astra said, tying an apron around her waist.

"How are her wounds? That explosion came from her collar," Lazarus asked, worried that the gem had caused lasting damage to the girl. *That gem controlled her mind somehow, made her think we were demons. We're lucky the situation didn't spiral further out of control.*

"I'm sure she'll wake up soon. I didn't find any wounds on her body, which shows how powerful she is—her healing speed is incredible," Astra reassured him. "You should be more worried about what'll happen when she wakes up. She didn't recognise us when we were talking to her during the battle. That gem seemed to cast illusions on the wearer—we could have been horrific nightmares to her, for all we know."

Lazarus rose from his large bed and pulled on black trousers, a tunic, and a grey vest. He picked up a piece of paper bearing a crude drawing of his parents: his father on the left, with a short beard and neatly cut hair, and his mother on the right, gazing up at her partner with a big smile lighting up her face. Her curly black hair hung behind her in a lace-braided ponytail. One day soon, I'll follow in your footsteps and become a renowned adventurer. I get my mahogany hair from my father, the curls from my mother.

Snow continued to fall outside, blanketing the frozen lake and nearby houses with a fresh layer of white. Lazarus left his spacious bedroom and entered the kitchen, where Astra was busy cooking.

"I heard Maeve and Darius were the ones who found us after the explosion. They treated our wounds. We'll have to thank them the next time we see them."

Lazarus nodded and took a seat atop a stool by the circular table in the centre of the room. The walls, made from sturdy logs, matched most of the furniture in the house. A fire crackled in the fireplace, its smoke rising through a stone chimney.

A creak from the doorway behind Lazarus made him snap around. The girl stood there, her body tense with fear, a black fireball hovering in her hand.

"Who are you people... why am I here?" she asked in a panicked voice.

"That's a question we want to ask you as well. I'm Astra, and this is Lazarus. He's the one who came up with the plan to break that black gem of yours," Astra said, her tone calm and measured. "We'll answer any questions you have, but could you dispel that fireball? I'm about to serve breakfast, and if you're hungry, you're welcome to join us. Take a seat at the table, and we can talk everything through peacefully."

The girl eyed them cautiously, inching towards the table with deliberate, wary steps, keeping the fireball in her hand until she felt safe enough to let it vanish. Lazarus watched her with a hint of amusement while Astra recognised the fear in her movements, which was so reminiscent of the tension she had seen during their battle.

"Thank you. Can we start with your name?" Astra asked as the girl settled into a chair, positioning herself to keep both of them in sight.

"Le-Levanna. My name is Levanna," she replied nervously.

Lazarus already knew her name but waved at her as a greeting while Astra plated the food. Levanna eyed the succulent dishes, her stomach growling with unmistakable hunger.

"Sounds like you're hungry. Dig in," Lazarus said, gesturing to a third plate of food. "Astra's a pretty good cook, though not as good as her fighting skills."

Astra slapped him lightly on the back of the head, prompting a grin. Levanna watched them eat, trying to mimic their use of a fork and knife but fumbling as she struggled to slice the meat on her plate. Frustrated, she abandoned the utensils and used her hands instead, demonstrating much better dexterity as she ate.

Astra chuckled and set down her own utensils, switching to eating with her hands. Lazarus quickly followed suit, grinning as he joined in. Levanna noticed what they were doing and gradually slowed her pace, easing back into her chair. The fear melted from her expression, replaced by satisfaction as she let out a quiet burp.

"My apologies. I don't often get to eat food like this. I couldn't help myself," Levanna said, continuing to stare at Astra and Lazarus, who were still eating. "My masters never gave me food, I had to fight to eat." She paused.

"Fighting just to eat, what kind of life is that?" He said rhetorically, handing her a cup of water, touching her hand. Suddenly, he was overwhelmed by flashes of visions. The images vanished as quickly as they appeared, leaving him gasping for air.

"What was that?!" Lazarus exclaimed, clutching his chest, trying to calm his thundering heartbeat as sweat dripped down his face.

"I can't believe it... I found it," Levanna responded, her gaze blank as she looked up at Lazarus. "It's you. You're the one from my visions who will stop the Zodiacs. You have no idea what this means to me, what this means to all the people who have fallen at their hands. Lazarus, you'll become a champion of this world; you will prevent its destruction."

Levanna tensed, scanning the environment and searching for something.

"Champion? I don't want to be anyone's champion. My goal is to explore the Towers, as my parents did before me," Lazarus protested, his tone defiant. Levanna ignored him, her focus fixed on a single purpose, nothing distracting her from whatever she was searching for.

"What are you looking for?" Astra asked with a hint of concern, glancing at Lazarus.

"My black gem. I need to find it!" Levanna shouted in frustration.

Astra reached into her pocket, withdrawing the shattered fragments of the black gem and placing them on the table.

"Is this what you're talking about? It was destroyed when I stabbed it with my sword two nights ago," Astra explained remorsefully.

Levanna scrambled to gather the gems frantically. "Now they'll know where I am. I found my champion, but it might already be too late," she said with a tone of melancholy.

"I thought it would be a good thing for that gem to be destroyed. Now you can't be controlled by them or have hallucinations?" Lazarus asked, his hand resting thoughtfully on his chin.

"You don't understand. It wasn't just used to control me but also to track me, which means they're going to come looking for me personally."

"By them, you mean your 'masters,' the Zodiacs?" Astra asked, seeking confirmation.

"Yes, they are... were my masters, by force. Our country was peaceful but powerful. We grew strong because of the mana-rich Kingdom of Aeternalis. Naturally, our bodies absorbed mana. Those... monsters found our country, and despite our strength, we were powerless against them."

"I saw a vision of them destroying a castle. Was that your kingdom?" Lazarus asked.

"No, I don't recognise that as my kingdom's castle. The one from the dreams might belong to one of your kingdoms—an event that hasn't come to pass yet," Levanna replied after pausing to consider the vision.

"Sorry for all the questions, but we want to learn as much as we can so we know how to move forward from this situation," Astra added, pressing her hands firmly on the table. "If they're going to track you to your last location, this village isn't safe for us. We need to speak with Maeve and convince her to evacuate everyone."

"You and I both know that won't go down well with those two. We'll leave and draw the danger away from Riverfall. The Kingdom of Baylor is west of here. I've heard there's a Tower close to the city—that will be a good place for me to continue their journey," Lazarus said, thinking of his late parents.

"Levanna, there are clothes in our room if you want to put on something more comfortable. That armour doesn't look like it protects you from the freezing temperatures here," Astra suggested, her gaze lingering on Levanna's figure, which was more voluptuous than her own. The outfit accentuated her natural curves and toned physique, drawing a curious glance from Lazarus.

Levanna blushed, aware of the attention she was attracting, and nodded in agreement. After perusing their clothing options, she emerged wearing a white, strapless blouse and black pants with ankle-banded cuffs. The ash-grey hue of her skin complemented the outfit, making her golden eyes glow even brighter against the plain colours.

"That's perfect. You look stunning, Levanna!" Astra complimented her, while Lazarus couldn't help but stare.

"Do you want to join us? We'll speak with Maeve and Darius. I'm sure they'd appreciate the visit after all they've done to restore the village."

"Yes, let's go," Levanna replied, excited to see the village with her own eyes, free from the influence of hallucinations.

Snow fell on the damaged buildings, coating the charred wood in white. After Astra donned her blue cloak, Lazarus grabbed his purple one, and the two of them stepped out of the quaint home, guiding Levanna through the village. They showed her the frozen lake near Lazarus' house, the stone bridge spanning a small ravine to connect the two sides of the village, and the village entrance. The ravine sloped down into a forest of snow-capped trees surrounding the vast lake.

Levanna paused to gaze into the distance from the bridge. Far on the horizon, where the land met the water, she pointed past the edge and cupped her hands as if holding an object within her palms.

"Across the sea, far south, is Mortis, my home continent. One day, I'll return there. We will face Zodiac together, stopping them from destroying innocent lives," Levanna said quietly, almost as though whispering to a distant friend.

The trio crossed the remainder of the bridge and entered the eastern side of Riverfall. An old couple awaited them at a moon arch. The man greeted Lazarus with a firm handshake, while the woman embraced Astra in a warm hug.

"This must be Levanna. We were worried about you after the explosion. Are you feeling any better?" Maeve asked, her eyes scanning Levanna for visible injuries.

Levanna nodded to indicate she was unharmed.

"It will take a lot more than that to injure my body, but mentally, it exhausted me. All that mind control, the hallucinations disappearing—it took its toll. I realise I've caused a lot of suffering and slaughtered countless lives. I don't know how I can ever make up for that..." Levanna said mournfully, her expression sombre, weighed down by the lives lost.

Maeve comforted the young girl.

"You are not to blame for any of this. They forced you to do unspeakable things. Just know that no one in the village died this time. We're in the process of rebuilding the broken houses as well. If you want to atone for things out of your control, your aid will help tremendously, dear," Maeve soothed in a gentle tone, wiping away the tears Levanna shed.

"Maeve, is it? Is there anything I can do to help? I did cause a lot of this damage; I feel obligated to help the townspeople," Levanna asked as they walked down the village pathway. Two-storey log cottages lined the sides of the path, with a tavern towering over the other buildings. At the end of the lane stood a large, single-storey hall with a barn off to the side.

"Sure, that's a great idea. Do you mind helping those people on the right? I'll have a little chat with these two in the meantime," Maeve suggested, sitting down on a bench outside the hall. Darius took a seat next to her after clearing away the snow on top.

"Now, you two. What do you intend to do now that she's awake? There may be no lasting damage from her initial assault, but I'm sure more will come in her stead to finish the job."

"About that—Levanna warned us that the gem was a tracker as well, so you're right about others coming. There's a group called the Zodiacs who wear animal masks. As for our plan, we can't stay here. You need to evacuate everyone out of the village as well! Nothing good will come if they find people here, Maeve," Lazarus warned, hoping the elders would listen and seek safety. But he knew them better than that.

Darius refused the plea to escape, as it went against his ideals of protecting the village. "You know that's not in our nature. We're hunters, Lazarus—we never run from a predator, no matter how strong they may be. If they intend to come to our village, we will be here, ready to face them. You two should be the ones to leave. Lazarus, you have to find your parents, and Astra, you want to become a Knight of Valour. Neither of those dreams can be achieved if you waste your lives in this village."

Though he is fifty, he is strong—tougher than anyone else Lazarus had met in his life. I don't like the thought of leaving them to fight an unknown threat, but I do feel safer knowing he will do everything he can to protect everyone, Lazarus thought.

"That's right. We're going to visit the Kingdom of Baylor. I'll make sure he arrives there safely. Once we get there, I'm going to sign up as a knight," Astra said, placing her hand on her chest, her blue cloak swaying in the cold winter air.

A group of villagers gathered at the gate, parents holding their children on their shoulders. Kids waved goodbye before running off to play.

"Are you sure you want to entrust the protection of The Glades to me?" Levanna asked earnestly, responding to their request. The villagers had allowed her to stay within their community for a few days while she decided how to handle her captors—a dangerous task, but one only she could undertake.

"The village will be in danger regardless, but we would sleep better knowing someone as powerful as you acted as a town guardian," said Lazarus, hoping to boost her morale.

Levanna prostrated herself on the ground, showing her respect for those who had saved her from slavery. "I will do everything I can to ensure their safety."

"Make sure to surpass your parents, Lazarus! Astra, you keep moving forward; don't let anything stand in your way of achieving your goal!" Darius shouted as he pounded his chest. The rest of the villagers, seeing them off, began to do the same, pounding their chests in rhythmic unison.

No words were necessary as they walked away. The pride of their village swelled within them as they made their way along the mountain path.

CHAPTER 3

Lazarus and Astra slung their backpacks on and left the village behind. For the first time in their lives, they ventured out, carrying all their dreams on their shoulders. The Kingdom of Baylor, a thriving hub of adventurers, traders, and soldiers, lay west of The Glades, beyond the snowy mountain range that led to the White Forest and across a wide river dividing the two regions.

"We've got about a day's walk to get to the riverbank. What I don't get is how we're going to cross it with all this snow," Lazarus said, doubting that any ships could navigate the frozen waters of De Albo.

"You would be right about the ice stopping the ships, but I believe they have mages or tamed creatures that can make travel easier this time of year." Hoping to reassure Lazarus, Astra considered a few ways she might solve the problem herself.

A few hours passed as the duo reached the base of the mountain, following a narrow pathway down. The fields rustled with the chilly wind, and blades of teal and violet grass peeked through layers of snow. Dusk descended with the setting sun, and the two travelers decided to set up camp for the night. They found a nearby cave that showed no signs of habitation.

"We're going to need to set up a campfire. I'll gather some wood," Lazarus said, wandering into the forest to break off dead tree branches. With most of the area buried under snow, it would be difficult for them to start a fire.

Astra rummaged through her backpack, searching for her red mana crystals—tools she used to produce fire when struck together. At her side rested her prized sword, a memento from her late father. The blade reflected both the moonlight and her own reflection.

"A knight, huh? I wonder what it's like in the city. The village doesn't have a large population, so everyone knows each other. I'm sure there will be a lot of crowds there—people with talents and skills I've never seen before. It's exciting just thinking about the people we'll meet there… Lazarus?" Astra looked up, realising Lazarus had already left.

She began practising her techniques, executing each action with slow, precise movements before repeating them in faster, fluid motions. Daily training was essential for Astra if she hoped to become a famed Knight of Baylor, joining the ranks of the Knights of Valour—the pinnacle of elite knights who served as captains in the kingdom's army.

Closing her eyes, Astra cleared her mind, ignoring the creatures scurrying around her and focusing solely on the mana circulating through her body, flowing no differently than blood. Once she achieved enough focus, the mana shifted, fluctuating in zigzags as it coursed through her.

Astra released the electrically charged mana, forming a cloak of lightning. Her eyes shot open, charged with a blue spark of electricity. Resuming her training, she now moved several times faster, each motion crackling with flashes of lightning. Her gaze locked onto a tree ahead.

Target in sight, Astra assumed a launching position. A fraction of a second later, she charged at the tree, leaving a trail of scorched earth in her wake. She thrust her sword arm forward as far as she could, aiming to strike the trunk. Her blade missed the intended strike zone, deflecting off the tree and carving a chunk from its side, sending the pine crashing to the ground with a resounding thud.

I still lack accuracy in this state, she thought. Focusing on the target is simple enough with the tunnel vision, but the air pressure around me makes it difficult to strike effectively. I'll need to find a way to push through that resistance. When I fought Levanna, she moved through the air with ease. What did she do that I couldn't? Was it her movements, her strength—or her wings? Even her clothes... That's it. Levanna's streamlined clothing didn't catch on the air. She could move freely because her outfit reduced drag.

Astra leaned against the fallen tree, resting her head on the hilt of her sword, her mind racing with ways to improve her technique. An eerie silence blanketed the area. The rustling of the leaves slowed, and the soft whisper of the wind became nearly inaudible. In this stillness, she could hear the steady rhythm of her own heartbeat.

It's been a while since Lazarus went into the forest. He should be back by now. I hope he hasn't wandered too far. I'd better go check on him.

Astra got back up, brushing snow from her backside. A blood-curdling shriek pierced the air, making her stomach drop. Her muscles tensed as she instinctively shifted into a battle stance. The trees rustled with an ominous breeze, and the crunch of footsteps on snow grew louder as Lazarus burst out of the forest. Covered in snow and paler than usual, he looked distraught.

"Sky, look at the sky!" Lazarus shouted.

Astra followed his pointed finger. In the distance, a creature darker than the night sky was flying towards them.

"That's what has you terrified? A black crow?" Astra scoffed.

The black figure drew closer.

"Wait, it's getting bigger. What did you do, Lazarus?" she asked, a hint of fear creeping into her voice as she realised this wasn't a normal flying creature.

With a deafening whistle, the creature dove.

"There's no time to answer your questions—get down!" Lazarus shouted, wrapping his arms around Astra and diving into the snow.

The giant creature, its long neck arched menacingly, flew overhead, narrowly missing Astra with its talons. As it ascended back into the sky, the force of its speed generated a powerful gust of wind, blowing Astra and Lazarus into the nearby forest.

Gasping for air from the impact, Astra reeled in pain. Lazarus took cover under the canopy.

"What is that—that thing, Lazarus?! I've never seen anything like it before," Astra asked, fear swelling in her throat.

"That's a Mortesyn. Scales as dark as the night, terrorising skies everywhere they go. They bring an omen of death; those who gaze upon a Mortesyn will witness a vision of their demise. I know they appear in the Kingdom of Mortis. Luckily, this is a youngling, much smaller than an adult. Their visions aren't guaranteed," he replied.

"We don't have time to think about why it's here. Are we fighting it or running away?" she asked.

Lazarus, who took pride in his knowledge of the creatures of Aurora, held out his staff, giving her his answer.

"Running away? No. This isn't a creature you can run from. We either kill that wyvern, or we die," Lazarus said, his heart pounding against his chest. "Are you with me, Astra?"

"I'm always with you, Laz. Get me close to it—I'll give it hell," Astra said, a smile forming as she faced the challenge ahead.

The wyvern soared high into the sky until the moonlight highlighted its body—eyes glowing violet, black wispy wings with claws on their tips, talons as dark as obsidian. Its torso was covered in black scales, with glowing purple markings running along its chest.

The Mortesyn dove once more, swirling at breakneck speed with another deafening whistle. Homing in on fresh prey, it screeched. They rolled at the last second to avoid it, thinking they were safe from the attack, only for the following draft of wind to knock them back into the air. The glowing eyes fixed on a target between the two of them.

A bulbous tip bloomed, emanating a beautiful purple glow from each of its petals. Deafening whistles rang through their ears, followed by a catastrophic ray of purple light slicing through their path, obliterating the surrounding terrain.

Blasted into the rugged mountainside, Astra limped back into the open. Even covered in wounds, she was determined to keep fighting.

"That's right, come get me! You don't fear a small girl, do you?!" Astra shouted, flailing her arms with her sword in hand.

Without hesitation, the Mortesyn dove for Astra. She waited for her moment to counter, watching as it drew closer. Gathering every ounce of strength, she leapt, clearing the Mortesyn and landing on its back. With a mischievous smile, she plunged her sword deep into its scales.

Unsure of what to do to help, Lazarus looked around for an object to fight the Mortesyn. From the corner of his eye, he glimpsed a speck of red light. It became a small orb, glowing red, and grew as he watched. The glowing orb inched closer, giving off intense heat. Snow melted, and trees burst into flames. The flaming sphere paused briefly before launching into the sky. Astra clutched the scales of the dragon, frozen in place.

Fire exploded against the dragon's dark scales. It screeched in excruciating pain, the sound a spine-chilling shriek. Wisps of fire flickered, burning Astra's left arm. Lazarus glanced back to the source of the fire at the sound of footsteps in the distance. Though he strained to see, he could make out nothing yet—only the faint pitter-patter of tiny feet. The footsteps came to a stop before their owner revealed themselves.

"Were you the one who conjured that fire spell? That was an immense help, thank you," Lazarus called out to the unknown creature, but silence filled the air in response. "No reply? Whoever used that fireball doesn't want to show themselves. What kind of creature could use a fire spell powerful enough to kill a Mortesyn, though?"

A loud thud sent snow cascading toward Lazarus, and he braced for impact. Buried under the heavy snow, he held out his staff above him.

The snow dispersed as the polearm rose, letting fresh air greet Lazarus.

"Are you hurt, Astra?" Lazarus asked as he crawled out of the snow.

"I should be the one asking you. I'm just glad to be on solid ground. The heat from that fireball was intense... I was burned, but luckily, I was on its back and avoided most of the flames," Astra said as she plunged her sword deep into the Mortesyn's neck, ensuring it would not rise again.

Cold water poured over her burn as Astra rested her head against Lazarus's chest with a warm smile.

Knowing the Mortesyn is dead gives me relief. Since all creatures in Aurora have a mana core, if I can retrieve this one, we could use it to create a weapon, armour, or even high-level magic. I brought a dagger for this messy process.

Using the dagger Lazarus retrieved from the sheath at his belt, he sliced open the Mortesyn's tough skin. Dark red blood oozed from the entry wound.

"Do you have to do that, Lazarus? I've gotten used to being covered in mud, but this is disgusting," Astra said, covering her mouth and nose to block the stench escaping the carcass.

"If we're going to Baylor to pursue our goals, we'll need this core to obtain stronger equipment. We can sell what we don't need," Lazarus said, his hands moving around inside the Mortesyn's chest, the squelching sounds of blood and organs unpleasant to the ears.

Lazarus felt the core within and dragged it out through the bloody mess.

"Astra, I've never seen a core this big before. It's much heavier than I expected!" he exclaimed, rushing to the water's edge to rinse off the blood. The black gem glistened in the moonlight—opaque and pitch black.

Astra snuck up behind him, peering over his shoulder. "Ooh, that's pretty. Best to keep it hidden for now."

The two walked back to their campsite, where they had set up padded wool inside a small cave.

Lazarus and Astra awoke with the morning light, still a few hours' walk from the riverbank. They decided to cook some poultry from the

Mortesyn they had stored the night before. After a restful night and a hearty meal, the duo set out once again, avoiding any detours to reach their destination as quickly as possible. The path was straightforward, and they thought it best to stay close to it.

Halfway along their trek, they came across a commoner fending off an attacker.

"Careful, this might be an ambush," Astra whispered, causing Lazarus to tense as he scanned the surroundings for possible traps.

"Let's split up, flank the ones hiding." Lazarus suggested, glancing between two sides of the pathway. Astra nodded, unsheathing her sword.

Before the bandit could react, the two adventurers disappeared into the forest, silently stalking through the trees. They located three hidden bandits lying in wait and swiftly knocked them unconscious.

Returning to the main path, they prepared to face their next obstacle.

"Ah, I see you've found us out already. There's no need to continue with this act," one of the remaining bandits said, smirking.

Both bandits drew their daggers, ready to fight. One licked the blade with a vicious grin.

The leader was the first to move, targeting Astra. She raised her sword to deflect the incoming attack, but the sheer force of the blow sent her hurtling into a nearby tree, splitting it in half.

Lazarus stepped in to intercept the bandit, buying time for Astra to recover. He matched the leader's dagger strikes with his own, even managing to slice the second bandit in the process. For a moment, the success bolstered his confidence—but it clouded his concentration, allowing the leader to land a powerful punch to his jaw.

"A bunch of weaklings. You'll be easy pickings," the leader sneered.

By this stage, Astra had recovered enough to rejoin the fray. Focusing her mana on her feet, she increased her speed dramatically. She targeted the second bandit, who tried to parry her sword strike but failed. Her blade sliced through flesh and bone, decapitating him.

"I'm afraid you're mistaken. 'Weaklings?' Who decided that? Until one side remains standing, there are no weaklings—just opponents to fight. Do not look down on me, bandit," Astra declared, her determination unwavering.

Now the last remaining bandit, the leader sank his head as he watched his companion beheaded.

"There's no way I can let you leave now. For a youngster, you've got a lot of skill," he admitted, placing a hand over his face to hide his tears.

A sudden burst of mana enveloped his dark cloak, exuding a crushing pressure that made him even more intimidating.

"I was going to steal your belongings, but now taking your lives feels far more rewarding," he growled, his voice cold and resolute.

The bandit kicked off the ground, leaving rubble behind as he hurtled towards Lazarus and Astra. Astra intercepted the bandit's attack, but the sheer force was too much for her to handle, dislocating her shoulder. Losing strength in her arm, she dropped her weapon. The bandit laughed, setting his sights on Lazarus next.

"Your turn, fledgling."

He swung his dagger horizontally at Lazarus' neck. Lazarus managed to pull his head back in time, reactively swinging his polearm diagonally in front of himself. Instead of dodging or blocking the polearm, the bandit grabbed Lazarus by the arm, arched over his shoulder, and slammed him into the ground.

Lazarus rolled out of danger, blood dripped from his lips. Having a resistance to pain sure comes in handy.

Astra popped her shoulder back into place and retrieved her sword, gripping it with both hands to compensate for her weakened arm. This time, Astra made the first move, surprising the bandit with efficient movements and putting pressure on the enhanced opponent.

The bandit found it difficult to counter Astra's skill. Choosing to step forward instead of retreating, he halted Astra's movements. She stared up at him in disbelief.

He hoisted her up with one arm and delivered a powerful blow to her face with the other, her head snapping back from the impact. Before he could strike again, arms wrapped around his waist, and a head smashed into his stomach. The moment of distraction was enough for Astra to stab the bandit in the side.

A crashing wave surged from behind the bandit, dispersing along the path to form towering walls on either side.

"Enough, Borus. Drop the girl," commanded an unfamiliar voice. Emerging from the waves, her snow-white cloaked uniform untouched by water, was a Knight of Valour. Her cerulean hair was tied neatly into a bun.

Borus grunted, releasing Astra from his grip, though his furious gaze lingered on the young girl.

"I was stationed at the riverbank port, waiting for passengers to arrive, when I sensed a burst of aura in the distance. My instincts told me it was trouble, so I rushed over here. By the looks of it, you two didn't suffer any major injuries. Impressive, considering your opponent is a wanted criminal."

"You managed to get here that fast? If I recall, we only started fighting a minute ago," Astra said, her tone sceptical.

"Yes, I mentioned I rushed over here. One of my skills allows me to increase my travelling speed. What would normally take around twenty minutes took mere seconds," the woman explained, placing a hand on her chest. "Excuse me for not introducing myself earlier. My name is Sapphire. I'm a Valour Knight and assistant captain to Commander Morrigan. Are you two heading to Baylor?"

The pair nodded. The group continued down the path to the port, the bandits bound with leashes of water.

"It seems you've sustained injuries. May I heal them?" Sapphire offered, her gaze falling to Lazarus' leg, where a tear in his pants revealed a bleeding cut.

"Please, that would be great! We don't have the supplies to treat these wounds," Astra responded.

"Very well, let me take a closer look," Sapphire said, gently holding Astra's arm to examine the burns. A flowing bubble of water formed in her hand and dripped onto the burnt flesh. A soft glow radiated from within the water, soothing and healing the injury.

Astra gasped as the burn faded away, her skin restored to its natural state. "Thank you! That's incredible—it healed so fast."

Lazarus sat down, allowing Sapphire to assess his injury. She touched the skin around the cut and noticed no reaction. "That's strange. Touching the skin around a cut this deep would normally make someone flinch, but you don't react to the pain."

"That's because I don't feel physical pain. Most injuries don't faze me. People usually freak out when they notice," Lazarus explained casually.

"I wouldn't say freak out—I'm intrigued. I've never encountered anything like this before," Sapphire said, her tone tinged with curiosity. "Anyway, I can fix it. Give me a moment."

Water flowed from Sapphire's hand to Lazarus' leg, seeping into the wound. The faint sound of cracks echoed as the injury began to mend. Astra winced on his behalf, but Lazarus simply watched the process with a smile.

"So, you're an assistant captain to the Commander," Astra said, her curiosity piqued. "How does one become a Knight?"

"Oh, you wish to join us knights? Well, people typically train for years at an academy to become a knight," Sapphire replied. "But after witnessing your battle with Borus, I could put in a recommendation to Commander Morrigan. If she accepts, you'll be assigned to a squad and train under their regiment. Though I'll warn you—it can be... intense, to say the least." She gave a nervous laugh.

Five minutes passed before a cart pulled up beside them, led by two Frostmanes standing an imposing four meters tall, their massive forms towering over the vehicle. Sapphire ushered everyone onto the cart and directed the driver to take them back to the port.

"A few things before we reach Baylor," Sapphire continued. "First, we'll need to do an inventory check. You'll keep all your belongings, but it's to assess any risks from items entering the city."

"I'm good with that. We didn't bring much anyway," Lazarus said.

"That's good to know—it will hasten the process. Secondly, I'll give you a tour of the city. You'll learn all the key points to familiarise yourselves enough to walk around on your own. Lastly, for defeating Borus, there's a reward waiting for you at the Garrison. I'll assist you in claiming it so there's no conflict." Sapphire took a deep breath after finishing her itinerary.

"Thank you," Astra said, bowing her head. "You've made this trip so much smoother for us. We've barely set out, and we've already had to deal with bandits and a Mortesyn. Being able to relax for a while helps tremendously."

Borus shot a sharp glance at the young girl but remained silent.

"Eh?! M-Mo-Mortesyn? You encountered a Mortesyn?" Sapphire stuttered, struggling to contain her surprise. "Mortesyns are the dark element of Wyverns—one of the more aggressive and agile types. I've only ever heard of two people surviving a battle with one!"

"They bring misfortune to those who gaze into their violet eyes—a vision of death that is sure to happen. Ha! It seems I won't even have to get revenge on you two. Something, or someone else, already has it covered," Borus laughed.

"Not all visions are set in stone. This was a youngling; their visions aren't guaranteed," Lazarus replied.

"I hope so! I saw a creature made of ice about to behead me. I'd prefer that didn't happen, thank you!" Astra said nervously.

"Ice creature? I had to deal with ice, too. Mine had a spear of ice. I couldn't make out who it was, but they were massive. Even you pale in comparison to them, Borus," Lazarus said, leering at the bandit, who huffed in annoyance.

Lazarus exchanged a look with Astra and leaned in to whisper into her ear. "Should we tell her about the creature that helped slay the beast or keep it a secret for now?"

"I think it's best we keep their identity a secret for now. We don't know what they'll do with that information," Astra whispered back.

Sapphire slumped back into a seat behind them, letting out a weary sigh. "Two major events in one day... I'm scared to know what's going to happen to you two in the future."

The pair both let out a nervous laugh.

Back in The Glades, Levanna worked alongside the townsfolk, earning their favour with her kind personality. Her willingness to help rebuild what she had destroyed inspired others to join in. During a lunch break, Maeve and Darius took Levanna on a walk through the village.

"Did you want to talk about something?" Levanna asked, her voice tinged with worry.

"Sorry to make you tense; that's not our intention. We want to know what you think will happen now that the gem is no more," Maeve reassured her.

"We're also curious about the voices who spoke to you—what are their goals? What do you think they'll do now that they've lost contact with their subordinate?" Darius added.

"I'm sorry, I can't tell you much about their goals. They kept their secrets close to their chest. Whatever they're planning, I fear for the kingdoms of this continent. I'm putting my hopes in Lazarus and will do whatever I can to help him along the way. As for what they'll do now, hm..." Levanna paused for a few seconds, deep in thought, trying to anticipate their next moves.

"If I had to make an educated guess about their behaviour, I'd surmise they'll initiate a personal search for me—which could mean just one person if I'm lucky. Worst case, it would be all of them moving together. Nothing would be able to stop them from obtaining what they seek."

A look of fear crossed Levanna's face at the thought of all the Zodiac members coming for her.

"If that's the case, this village will be at huge risk, as it's the last known place you visited. I'm sure they'll come here in time, which means you'll have to leave before they arrive. We'll do what we can to hold them off, but we can't risk giving them the chance to take you back." Maeve felt guilty suggesting Levanna leave the village, but the thought of her being captured again was something she couldn't bear.

"We don't want you to leave just yet. Do you have any idea how long it will take them to arrive?" Darius asked.

Most of her time on this continent had been spent under the gem's mind control, leaving Levanna unsure of how long she'd been away from her home continent.

"I can't give an accurate answer to that," Levanna said earnestly.

"We can't pressure you, but every little bit of information you can tell us will help us deal with this situation," Darius said in an urgent tone.

"I remember two months of autumn in Mortis, so if it's the opposite season on this continent, it would have been since spring. My best guess is at least four months if they put the gem on me back then," Levanna explained, doing her best to answer their question with a sigh of relief.

Darius and Maeve exchanged a concerned look. Maeve was the first to voice her thoughts.

"Four months if they've been wandering around, searching different towns. I fear we have less time if they already know your location."

Dread washed over Levanna's face as she looked up.

"One week. Mortis is a long distance from here, but if they know my location, I believe a week is all they'll need to find me," Levanna said, her voice distant as she raised her hand to the sky as if pretending to pluck the hidden moon.

CHAPTER 4

As Lazarus and Astra neared the Kingdom of Baylor, they were greeted by the breathtaking sight of a majestic castle perched on a mountainous island. Smaller islands surrounded it in the shape of a snowflake, connected by a mix of ice bridges and manmade stone bridges.

The brigantine ship, coated in snow-white and adorned with blue sails bearing the kingdom's snowflake symbol, arrived at the eastern island port. Market vendors shouted from their stalls, fishermen cursed the freezing seas, and guards marched down the stone paths. The sprawling streets were unfamiliar to the young adventurers, their eyes lighting up with awe at the sheer number of people gathered in one place.

Snow fell on the Kingdom of White. Though Lazarus and Astra were accustomed to the cold, having lived in the Winter Islands their whole lives, this snowfall brought an even harsher chill, dropping the air to a freezing temperature.

"Does it always snow like this in Baylor, Sapphire?" Lazarus asked, his breath forming clouds of frost. Astra rubbed her arms; the cold affected her more than it did Lazarus.

"Snow is common in Baylor, though I wasn't expecting it today. While it's not the ideal weather to introduce you to the city, I'm sure you'll still appreciate everything it has to offer. We're going to be busy, so the snow won't even be an issue," Sapphire said, gazing up at the dark clouds covering the sky.

Astra spoke with Sapphire about the kingdom's defences while Sapphire took stock of their belongings. The most impressive item was the mana core from the Mortesyn. Sapphire admired the prized possession, examining its texture, the sheen of the gem, and its size—larger than a human head. Once she had finished the inventory, she placed the mana core back into Lazarus' bag.

Guards soon arrived at the ship, approaching Sapphire to take over the escort of Borus and the remaining bandits to a dungeon cell.

"Now, with that out of the way, it's time to show you around the city of Baylor!" Sapphire said excitedly, urging them to stay close so they wouldn't get lost.

In the distance, they could see the enormous castle, flanked on three sides by a snow-capped mountain.

"We use the mountains to mine resources, digging deep below sea level. That cavern connects all the way to Tower Island, providing bountiful resources to create our weapons, armour, and buildings. As other countries lack these resources, we use them to trade for valuable resources."

"If you're using that mountain as a defence, wouldn't the miners weaken it over time?" Astra asked Sapphire.

"You're right; that was a concern early in our history. Our ancestors reinforced the interior walls with barricades to ensure no miners would dig too far into the mountain. Instead, they opted to create the tunnel that goes down through the sea, reaching the mainland. That way, we can keep our protection while our workers continue mining without any danger," Sapphire explained, taking joy in teaching others about her city.

"I'll explain the island layout to you; that should make navigating the kingdom easier. We have ports on four of the islands for convenient travel—south, west, north, and back here in the east. The Adventurers' Guild, the Church of Vinter, and the library are key locations. The garrison's training grounds are up north, while merchants are based here on the east island. Every second island houses residents, with walls barricading each to protect against invasion. The only way to enter the kingdom is through one of the guarded ports or the garrison, as you can see from the squads of knights patrolling the streets." Sapphire waved at a passing squad.

"Captain Sapphire!" the squad called out as they passed.

The marketplace included a blacksmith, where several smithies were restocking shelves, an outfitter who specialised in crafting clothing tailored to customers' needs, and an alchemist further down the path who focused on potions and mana cores.

"This will be our first stop, as we need to appraise that mana core. If you wish to keep it, that's fine—I'm just curious about its rank," Sapphire said inquisitively.

"What are the ranks and properties?" Astra asked.

"Right, you might not be familiar with ranks or properties if you're from The Glades. Ranks determine a mana core's storage capacity, while properties define its elemental affinity. The amount of mana a core can provide depends on how it's used—some deplete quickly, while others last longer. You'll learn how to use them effectively in time," Sapphire replied with a smile.

They entered the store, its mystical ambience accentuated by the radiant glow of various mana cores. Potions of varying colours lined the shelves along the right wall, while mana cores of all shapes, sizes, and hues adorned the left. Behind the counter, the Alchemist toiled away, inspecting a yellow core with jagged spikes forming around its sphere.

The Alchemist had an unkempt appearance—his dark hair was scruffy, and he wore a russet sweater with the sleeves rolled up to his elbows over a half-tucked, onyx-coloured tunic.

"I'm busy. You'll have to come back later," he said in an annoyed tone, unwilling to be disturbed. He appeared to be in his thirties—older than Sapphire, who looked to be in her late twenties.

"Now, is that any way to speak to a valued customer, Byron?" Sapphire's voice carried a sweet tone.

Byron, startled, knocked over a stand holding a glowing light core that illuminated the desk. His darting eyes landed on Sapphire, and he quickly straightened up, losing his composure.

"Uh, my apologies, Sapphire. I wasn't expecting you today. I was focused on this mana core—it's a B-rank with Lightning elemental affinity. I just had a fresh trade come in, with cores of different elements—some you won't find even while exploring the Winter Tower." His voice grew more excited as he spoke about the Lightning core.

"That's great to hear, Byron, but I think we have a core that will interest you far more than this little one," Sapphire said teasingly as she poked the lightning core resting on the countertop.

Lazarus reached into his bag and retrieved the Mortesyn core, placing it on the countertop. Byron dropped his tools with a gasp, stunned by the sight before him.

"Is this what I think it is? I've never seen a core like this before." He hunched over it, examining it with intense focus while absentmindedly brushing the lightning core aside. The large, pitch-black sphere revealed blood-red swirls shifting within it with each touch.

"I knew you'd be impressed. It's a core from a Mortesyn," Sapphire said with a satisfied expression.

Byron rushed to the front door, activating runes that formed a circle around the handle, sealing it shut.

"You don't mind if I assess the core for you? Dark element cores aren't easy to come by—let alone one from a Mortesyn!" he asked enthusiastically.

Lazarus gestured towards the core, granting permission for Byron to inspect it. Without hesitation, Byron began his assessment, first weighing the core and then measuring its size. Next, he reached under his counter and pulled out a strange-looking device.

"This will give us a rank for the core," he informed them, propping the orb on top of the device. The claws wrapped around the core, pulsing with dark energy. Within a few seconds, the device stopped, and a reading was displayed above in glowing sigils: S.

"What does the rank mean?" Lazarus asked, knowing little how cores worked.

"Well, the rank determines how effective the core becomes when used for equipment or for enhancing an individual's mana reserves, E ranks will only increase by a hundred, but an S rank can increase your mana by 16000. Most people choose not to expand their mana, but for classes that rely on magic, increasing reserves is invaluable. If you decide to sell the core or use it to boost your mana, I can help you with that. Otherwise, you may want to visit the blacksmith, who can craft powerful weapons or armour for you, or see an outfitter who can create clothing imbued with runes to provide resistance or enhancements. What will you do with the core?" Byron asked earnestly, rubbing his hands together, hoping for a chance to put it to good use.

"We'll have to discuss it later; we still have the rest of the city to tour before making a decision. But thank you for your help!" Lazarus gave a quick bow, taking the core back. Astra started to leave while Sapphire waved goodbye with an affectionate smile.

The three of them took a short break to eat before continuing their tour. As they headed toward the South District, they passed through the housing area. Houses stretched across the island with winding pathways—there must have been thousands. Many were double-story structures made of wood and white stone, offering a comfortable living experience.

Along the way, they caught a glimpse of the castle entrance, which was blocked off by a guarded stairwell. Knights in golden-white armour stood watch, their uniforms distinct from those of regular knights.

"Are they a different group of knights? They aren't wearing the same outfit as you, Sapphire," Astra asked curiously.

"They are the royal guards—an elite group tasked with protecting the royal family. In our company, Commander Morrigan is the closest to them in terms of skill. She used to be one of them but resigned due to the lack of combat. The inactivity frustrated her, knowing nothing was ever going to happen while she remained in that position—much to the king's dismay. They receive their own unique armour to set them apart from us. Compared to them, we are mere foot soldiers."

"This is the Adventurer's Guild, Sapphire?" Lazarus asked as they stepped onto the southern island.

Before them stood a massive crystal dome building, its breathtaking architecture dominating the landscape. A vast square surrounded it, with a grand water fountain decorating its centre.

"Correct. This is the place you'll frequent the most, though it's not the most ideal location when you need to travel north to reach the Winter Tower. At least you can stop to prepare any equipment you need along the way," Sapphire replied. "We won't be travelling to the west island just yet, but we will stop by the garrison to see if we can enrol Astra as a knight. She may even become a Valour Knight like me."

"This is where my parents used to visit regularly. Maybe I can learn more about them," Lazarus said as he gazed up at the guild building.

The Adventurer's Guild was a colossal dome with shards of ice forming around its edges. The entrance connected to the dome by a shorter hall like building that featured a large, white, arch-shaped door. When Sapphire opened it, they discovered that the interior was vastly different from the exterior. Marbled floors stretched beneath their feet, with pillars lining the hallway leading to a large, circular reception room. Stairs on both sides of the room led to the next floor. Behind the reception desk, two women and a man were chatting; one of them focused on writing on a piece of paper.

The man had a large, muscular build and wore a winter-black suit with a crimson-red vest. His naturally black hair was combed back neatly, and he sported a well-maintained, short black beard. The girl with the wolf-cut hairstyle writing at the desk wore a beige vest, whereas the girl with wavy, shoulder-length hair wore a cobalt-blue vest. She was the first to notice their presence, greeting them with a graceful bow.

"Good evening, Aldo, Emlin, Sadie. How is the guild coming along?" Sapphire greeted them.

The two young women, both with strawberry blonde hair, were twins dressed in contrasting suits—Emlin in an elegant white suit with a beige vest and Sadie in a bold black one with a cobalt-blue vest.

"It's good to see you again, Sapphire! The guild is prospering. A lot of beginner adventurers have started forming groups to handle the Tower. The materials we've been receiving have helped the guild tremendously," Aldo replied enthusiastically. He wore a jet-black suit with red accents—far too expensive for someone like Lazarus to own.

"Oh, groups? Are there any I'd know about?" Sapphire queried.

"We have a group that formed six months ago and has risen through the ranks faster than any before them. They call themselves Arcanum. I found it odd for a group to name themselves, but they insisted. Lately, their demeanour has felt off. I'd suggest keeping your distance from them if possible," Aldo responded with a serious stare.

"Don't worry about us, sir. I'm here to find answers in the Tower." Lazarus bowed his head as he spoke, trying to be respectful—to the amusement of the two girls, who giggled. Astra shot them a warning glance, silently urging them not to pursue him.

"I admire the gusto of a newcomer. What kind of answers are you seeking, if you don't mind me asking?" Aldo asked inquisitively.

"My parents used to be adventurers. I came here hoping to explore the Towers—I need to find out what happened to them," Lazarus answered.

"Parents, huh? What do you know about them? I might be able to help. I've been here for a couple of decades now," Aldo said as he stepped out from behind the desk, leaning back against it with his hands outstretched along the surface.

"My mother had dark, wavy hair, and my father had short, umber hair. I remember hearing stories about them fighting creatures in the Winter Tower. This is the only picture I have of them." Lazarus handed over his drawn picture of his parents. Aldo examined it carefully, glancing back at Lazarus.

"These are your parents. I recognise them. Every adventurer from their time knew about them—everyone wanted to climb the Tower with those two. They were an unstoppable duo. Your mother was a summoner who specialised in spirits, while your father was a terrifying warrior. They cleared Tower dungeons with ease, rising in fame until they became legends. One day... one day, they just disappeared. Never to be seen again. I was devastated when I heard the news. I even led an expedition to find them, and believe me, we tried... but we found nothing." Aldo rubbed his eyes as they started to tear up.

Are those scars across his eyes? Lazarus thought as he watched Aldo.

The girl with peach-coloured hair looked up from her work and rushed over to comfort him.

"Thank you, Emlin. I'm okay. I didn't know they had a child together. Were they not around to raise you either?" Aldo asked after his tears had stopped.

"I didn't know anything about them. The village elders raised me— they raised Astra as well," Lazarus said, earning a nudge from Astra, who clearly didn't appreciate being included.

"Both orphans, I see," Aldo said as he ushered them forward. "I'm glad you came here, Sapphire. If you don't mind, I'll take Lazarus and get him assigned a class. You two can wait in the hall. Come with me, Lazarus. We'll do this with a crowd—I'm sure they'll love to hear about the legacy of the legendary couple. If you follow me, I'll take you through the process." Aldo gestured toward a staircase leading to a set of double doors.

Lazarus turned toward Astra, pressing his forehead to hers.

"I'll meet up with you after I'm finished, okay?" he said, gazing into her icy blue eyes. Every time he looked at her, his heart skipped a beat—

those eyes reminded him of home, of the light blue leaves caressing the snow. This closeness felt more intimate than usual. He gently brushed her hair aside, ensuring she could see him clearly.

"Yes! I mean, I'll be waiting. Do your thing, Laz." She smiled, flustered, before taking a seat on a bench beside Sapphire.

Aldo walked upstairs with Lazarus and opened the two large doors, revealing a vast domed hall filled with adventurers. Beyond the crowd, a podium stood beneath a core that nearly touched the glass ceiling. Obsidian tables were spread across the room, where adventurers gathered, drinking from chalices and eating well-prepared meals.

In a booming voice, Aldo addressed the adventurers in the main hall. "Ladies and gentlemen! We have a new prospect joining us today. You know what that means?" He looked around at the whispering crowd, all eyes glancing at Lazarus, who stood behind him. "We're going to find out what this young man's class will be! And this isn't just any regular person. As I've been informed, this young lad is the offspring of the late legends of the Tower—Adelheid the Seer and Cyrus the Crimson Blade."

The mention of these names drew the crowd's attention. Conversations paused as people gestured for silence, while murmurs spread throughout the hall as they waited for Aldo to continue.

Lazarus glanced around, noting several individuals who kept their distance from the crowd. One was a man dressed in ivory, his cloak resembling a bird's wing, with snow-colored feathers cascading down his back to his knees. He had well-maintained blonde hair and appeared tall even from a distance.

On the opposite side of the room stood a much older man with a wild, beastly appearance with salt-and-pepper hair and a thick, well-groomed beard. His muscular frame was clad in grey pants lined with black fur around the waist, black boots that appeared heavy, and a long, dark-red coat with a red fur-lined collar. His gaze, unlike the younger man's, was more curious than wary.

Standing on a balcony along the domed wall of the hall above them was a girl around his age with black hair shaved on one side. From what he could see, she wore a black top that exposed her midriff and a checkered skirt with black leggings underneath. She rested her arms on the edge of the balcony, a curious smile on her face.

On the other side of the room was a booth where three men and two women sat together, their stern gazes piercing into Lazarus as he stood in the centre of the gathering hall.

"I hope you all welcome him to the Guild! Emlin, Sadie, if you will." Aldo gestured toward the centre of the hall, where a giant translucent sphere stood. "Now, as most of you know, this core determines what class a person specialises in. We have the Offensive classes: Berserker, Monk, Assassin, Archer, and Lancer."

A cheer erupted from part of the crowd, their boots stamping the marble floor—perhaps those who were warriors themselves.

Aldo continued, "We have the Magic classes: Mage, Sorcerer, and Cleric!"

More shouts rang out, and the crowd began stamping their feet in unison.

"The Summoner classes: Necromancer, Spirit Seer, Beast Tamer, Warden, and Spectral Blade!"

The cheers grew louder.

"Last but not least, we have our Defensive classes, the backbone of any group: Knights, Guardians, and Paladins!"

The hall exploded with noise, the crowd stamping their feet and raising their fists in the air.

"Now, I have no idea what kind of class the core will choose for Lazarus, but I'd love to have another monk-class adventurer to train. What do you guys think?!"

Lazarus felt nervous under all the attention, his heart pounding against his chest. He listened as the crowd shouted different class names, none of them agreeing on a specific one.

So many classes to choose from—archer, mage, guardian. Those could be interesting choices. My dominant skill is my knowledge of creatures. I can't see myself obtaining an offensive class when I can't bring myself to take a living creature's life, he thought.

"Lazarus, please come to the podium." Aldo gestured for Lazarus to approach the core resting on a raised platform. "The process is quite simple; all you need to do is release as much mana as you can from your body. The core will assess your mana and react to the stimuli based on the type of class, and determines your stat potential by assigning you a rank. I'll list the possible reactions. If scales cover the core, it signifies a Defensive class. If it turns metallic, that means an Offensive class. If the core transforms into an element, it indicates a Magic class. Lastly, if the core glows with runic symbols, your class will be a Summoner.

"Before we begin, do you have any preference for your class?" Aldo asked after explaining the process.

"I'm not sure. People expect great things from me, but as I am now, I'm going to need all the help I can get to climb the Tower," Lazarus answered, thinking of the group he would one day have to face. His one thought was not wanting to face them alone.

Lazarus placed his hands on the core, and energy began flowing from his body. Some people outside the main crowd glanced over at the massive surge of power. His aura poured out, forming a dome within the hall, which was steadily absorbed by the core. It remained still, not yet revealing what class it would assign him.

Lazarus focused even harder, pushing himself further. The energy he released grew even stronger, whipping up a gust of wind that knocked down those standing too close. Aldo shielded his face, watching intently. The others, who had been observing from a distance, were now standing at full attention, all of them moving closer.

That's it! If you want to see all my potential, I'll give you everything I have—until I can no longer stand. This is my time to make a name for myself!

A light shone from a rune within the cube, followed by another, then more, until the crowd was forced to shield their eyes.

"Summoner! Our new adventurer has shown an impressive display of mana. The core has given an answer! As for your rank, let's see..." Aldo shouted in a booming voice before examining the core. A hologram of a runic C appeared within the sphere for everyone to see.

"C rank!"

C rank? Even with all that mana? Just how powerful are the higher ranks? I'm glad I got Summoner to make up for lower stats, Lazarus thought, disappointed that he hadn't obtained a higher rank.

The man with salt-and-pepper hair smiled in amusement while the man draped in feathers walked off with a huff. A whistle, followed by clapping, came from the balcony. The girl with half-shaved black hair smiled down at Lazarus, spurring the rest of the adventurers to join in. Meanwhile, a group sitting in a booth discussed something amongst themselves.

"That was quite a display, Lazarus! Just like your mother before you, you obtained the rare Summoner class. We've got two Summoners here, both of whom have displayed tremendous amounts of mana," Aldo congratulated him with a pat on the back.

"Thank you, but I've never used that much mana before," Lazarus said, scratching his head with a laugh.

"One thing I didn't mention before is how the core works. It doesn't just react to a person's current mana level; it taps into their full potential. Even if it takes decades to reach that level, the core will recognise it, displaying their full potential as a class. Even if someone has a lower rank, the core identifies something within them that allows them to obtain a powerful class. Lower-potential individuals tend to fall in the defensive class. From my experience, few truly excel in that class. Despite that, even someone with low potential can achieve remarkable things if they focus on developing their skills. On a side note, I have something for you—a book left by your late mother."

"You do? What is it about?" Lazarus asked, surprised that they had left something for him. He had grown up knowing nothing about them besides the tales people told of their Tower endeavours, many of which seemed too far-fetched to believe.

"Oh yes, I've kept it in good condition all these years, though I have no idea what's inside. To be honest, I was surprised by your appearance. I didn't know anything about their child, only that they would one day come here seeking information about them. They were right—here you are!" Aldo exclaimed, stretching his arms wide. "Come, it's in my office." He pointed toward a wooden door adorned with intricate gold etchings.

Lazarus walked into the office, a stark contrast to the hall outside. The interior walls were as black as night, almost too dark to manoeuvre around. Light came from candelabras hanging on each of the four walls, their red mana cores enveloped in flames.

Aldo walked around his large desk—a polished mahogany masterpiece with a black cloth covering the top—before settling into a tall leather chair, also mahogany.

"Quite ominous in here, don't you think?" Lazarus remarked as he stopped in front of the desk, earning a chuckle from Aldo.

"That is true, though it's nothing more than my admiration for the dark aesthetic. Ah, yes, your parents' book! I have it right here," Aldo said, opening a drawer on his side of the desk and pulling out a brown, leather-bound book with a binding strap. "If you're seeking answers, I'm sure this book will fill in a lot of blanks about your parents."

"Do you know what happened to them, Aldo?" Lazarus asked after taking the book. He attempted to open it, but it didn't budge.

"There's a seal keeping that book closed. I tried to open it when I first found it, but you've had about as much success as I did," Aldo said. "As for your question, unfortunately, no. The last I heard, they had gone to the Winter Tower. No one has heard from them since. We've tried sending people to explore each room of the Tower but to no avail." He lowered his head in disappointment.

Lazarus observed the man's posture, trying to determine whether he was telling the truth. He didn't know anyone here, so anyone could be an ally or an enemy.

"This is a selfish request, but I would like you to leave finding them to me. Whatever happened to them is something I must discover for myself. Maybe they're still alive, waiting for me at the top of the Tower," Lazarus said, staring into Aldo's dark glasses.

Aldo returned the stare, resting his chin on his hands. "I'll leave it… but only out of respect for them. My one condition is that you report every room you enter in the Tower so we can ensure we don't repeat history," he replied after an uncomfortable silence. "As a sign of trust, I'll give you another book to kick-start your summoning training."

Aldo rose from his chair and walked toward a bookshelf to his left, where books labeled "Vol. 1" for different classes were neatly arranged. He ran his rough-skinned hand along the spines until he found the one he was searching for. "Here it is—*Summoning Techniques Vol. 1*. Study this book, and you'll learn how to summon in no time. Before I allow you to enter the Tower, I need to know you can use summoning."

"That's fair. Thank you, Aldo," Lazarus said upon receiving the book. He placed both books in his bag, preparing to leave the office.

"Oh, one more thing, Lazarus! This will help you track your growth. Infuse mana into this sphere, and it will update your status, allowing you to grow even stronger than a regular person. You will also be able to gain knowledge about skills for your class. Make sure you always keep this close—it could help you out of a tough situation," Aldo said, handing Lazarus a black sphere. Small purple lights appeared on its surface like eyes.

"I got a C rank. What does that mean, Aldo?" Lazarus asked after examining the sphere and popping it into his bag.

"The ranks determine how many stats you receive when you level up, the lowest being the E rank, which grants four stats per level. D, C, B, A, S, and U ranks have increasing potential, with U being the highest, granting sixteen stats per level," Aldo explained. His posture was firm as he sat, one leg propped over the other.

"Do you know what my parents' ranks were?"

"I certainly do. Your mother, Adelheid, obtained an A rank, while your father, Cyrus, obtained an S rank. Let me tell you, he was powerful. Unlike his awkwardness in conversation, when he entered battle, his entire personality changed. Cyrus had a calm, calculating composure. He could find an enemy's weakness within seconds and cut them down with his signature crimson blade. Once he paired up with Adelheid, he became unstoppable while climbing the Tower."

"I used to think all the stories the elders told me as a kid were just made up, but now I'm starting to believe they were real."

"Oh yes, I'm sure the tales were genuine. They were legends among us adventurers. I'm optimistic about you, too. On that note, I'll let you go—you must think about what subclass of Summoner you want to pursue."

"You're right. I need to learn about the subclasses first. I'll figure it out today and return tomorrow once I've made my decision. Thank you, Aldo."

"Thank me for what?" Aldo asked, perplexed by the sudden gratitude.

"For the diary, for telling me about my parents. I realised there's still a lot to learn about them—this was a good start," Lazarus said as he made his way to the door.

"There's no need for thanks. The path forward will be dangerous. Make sure you prepare for the Tower—it can be unforgiving." Aldo waved goodbye as Lazarus nodded back and closed the door behind him.

"The son of the legendary duo, hm? I wonder how he will deal with an impossible task. I gave everything searching for them, yet my endeavours bore no fruit," Aldo murmured to himself, covering half of his face. "The path you walk doesn't have a happy ending... I hope you find the strength to overcome what's coming."

CHAPTER 5

By the time Lazarus emerged from the guild building, the bright sun had dipped behind the mountains, painting the sky in deep indigo and navy, with dense grey clouds drifting overhead. The snowfall intensified, and visibility dwindled. He hurried to the fountain, where Astra waited, holding a crystal that emitted a warm, crimson glow. She was now wrapped in a hooded cloak of white fur, which reflected the crystal's light. Sapphire huddled close to the crystal, her body trembling from the cold.

"There you are! This snow is becoming a problem. I don't think we should stay here any longer. Can you lead us to an inn, Sapphire?" he asked, shielding his face from the snowfall.

"Yes, I'll book a room for the two of you in the south-eastern district for the week. After that, you'll be responsible for your own payments," Sapphire said, heading toward the district entrance, now illuminated by the crimson glow of red crystals lining the pathway.

"We'll worry about that later—we need to hurry before the weather gets worse," Astra added. She jumped down from her perch on the fountain and broke into a sprint, grasping Lazarus' hand and yanking him forward due to their difference in speed.

The three of them ran along the pathway. Sapphire kept pace by skating with her water abilities, using streams of water to glide across the ground. Within minutes, they arrived at their destination—a large, three-story inn in the southeastern district nestled against the woodlands. The whimsical building, adorned with hanging light cores, offered them a refuge from the creeping darkness overhead. From inside, Lazarus could hear the murmur of voices.

They opened the door to the warm embrace of a fireplace in the reception area. Before continuing, they patted their clothes, scattering snow across the floor. The entrance was already covered in snow from other guests, making it clear that this was a common occurrence.

Sapphire made her way to the reception desk, greeting the woman standing behind it—a tall woman with a gentle smile. Wavy caramel hair draped over her shoulders, with bangs falling along the sides of her face. Her eyes, shining like a field of wheat under sunlight, peeked from behind round spectacles.

"Excuse me, Ferris, I'd like to book a room for these two for the week," Sapphire said, placing the red crystals back into her bag.

"I'm sure I can find a room for them. Please give me a second," Ferris replied, turning to a board holding dozens of hooks with large two-pronged keys. She grabbed one labeled 205. "Floor two, room five—if that's okay?"

"Perfect, thank you, Ferris!" Sapphire said as Ferris handed over the key. "This is where I leave, Lazarus. You'll want to visit the guild tomorrow after assessing your new skills. As for you, Astra, I'll stop by the garrison tonight to deliver a recommendation letter to the commander and retrieve your bounty reward. Come by tomorrow, and we'll find out if the commander accepts you."

Sapphire hugged Astra and Lazarus before leaving the inn.

They ascended the stairs to the second floor, where walnut doors lined the hallway, decorated with golden studs. After finding a door with an etched rune for five, they entered their room.

The two of them stared in disbelief at the size of the room, the elegant furnishings—not to mention the view of a forest with a creek from the rear window.

The room was spacious. A cosy couch rested near the left wall upon entering, with a rectangular mahogany table positioned near the rear balcony. A partition wall separated the bedroom area, which housed two beds. To the right of the entrance, a bathroom with a wooden wash tub completed the layout.

Lazarus stepped onto the balcony, taking in the view of the moonlit grove. Astra accompanied him.

"You know, I never thought we would make it to Baylor. I've always dreamed of coming here—I wanted to learn more about my parents—but I always thought it was a fleeting dream. I'm glad we came here together, Astra." Lazarus placed his hand on top of hers, and she intertwined her fingers with his.

"It is surreal. Compared to Riverfall, it feels like we've entered a different world. Focus on finding out what you can about your parents. Tomorrow, I will prove to the commander that I am worthy of becoming a knight."

☆☆☆☆

Flames sizzled out, consumed by a black hole the size of a fist.

"What is with this armoured knight? He's taking all of our attacks with no damage." A man in a dark hooded cloak stated, two black blades in hand shaking with nerves.

"No elite is this strong, he's as strong as a Deity." Replied a woman in a dark blue mage robe, an oversized mage hat tilted on her head.

The knight patted his armour, wiping away ash, in his right hand a wavy onyx Zweihander. Hidden behind a tattered green cloak and a horned helmet, emerald eyes leered with an ethereal glow sending a wave of black energy towards the group.

"Nox! This pressure is too much, what do we do?!" a stout man said, buckling under the waves of black energy he collapsed to the ground.

"Nox, help us…" pleaded a woman in white and gold armour, her platinum blonde hair streaked with blood from a wound on her forehead.

"Nox, is it? I have a task for you. Accept and I'll allow them to live, refuse and I end their lives. What does thou choose?" The Knight spoke with an otherworldly voice.

Nox glanced at each of them, unable to lift themselves off the ground, even he struggled to remain crouched as black mist repelled the pulsing waves. Each wave pounded against his aura, buckling his legs.

He grunted, "I accept. Leave them alone and I'll do as you ask." Nox dropped his weapons, defeated.

"Splendid choice…Nox. As requested, thou are free, thou will heed my commands." The Knight bowed, his armour shifted with a metallic drone as he walked away into the darkness. Nox rushed to his group, ensuring they were safe.

"I'm sorry, I had no choice." He said apologetically.

"You're not to blame, Nox, but I have a bad feeling about this Knight." The woman in mage clothes said.

Darkness faded away, revealing a quiet alleyway. A welcome sight after their brush with death, snow eased Nox's tension allowing himself to fall on a mound of snow.

"I think this is the worst situation I've gotten us into so far."

CHAPTER 6

orning arrived quickly. Exhausted from the previous day, they had both passed out as soon as they lay down on their beds the night before. Lazarus woke earlier than Astra, his thirst for knowledge driving him into a studious mood.

"To begin summoning, you must first obtain the necessary skill from your companion sphere," he read aloud, though quietly enough not to wake Astra.

Lazarus retrieved the sphere from his bag, examining its surface. "Aldo mentioned infusing mana into you—let's try that."

Focusing on his mana, he felt a stream of calm energy flowing within him. The orb, sensing its presence, shifted and absorbed the mana Lazarus released. Purple lights expanded, resembling a set of eyes.

"Mana detected. Processing... Name: Lazarus. Class: Summoner. Providing list of information regarding summoners," the orb spoke in an ethereal voice. A light shone above it, displaying words that detailed Lazarus' status. It spun rapidly, changing the display to a summary of the Summoner class.

"So, these are the types of summoning I can learn?" Lazarus mused. "Can you display the skills in a different way?"

"What kind of display would you like?" the orb responded.

Lazarus described a globe-like format that would allow him to view the skills more easily.

The orb processed his request, spinning rapidly before projecting a holographic sphere displaying the five summoning subclasses.

"Yes! That's better. I don't know if you have any emotions, but it feels weird talking to something without a name." Lazarus sat down at the table, placing his books beside the orb.

"I have yet to receive one. That is for you to decide."

Lazarus pondered names while scanning the list of subclasses.

What should I call it? Mana? Orby? Spheris? I also need to choose my summoning specialty. My mother was named The Seer, a title referring to the Spirit Seer subclass. The other options are Beast Tamer, Warden, Necromancer, and Spectral Blade. Necromancy sounds ominous—I don't intend to raise the dead to fight for me. Beast Tamer could be useful. With my knowledge of creatures, we could work well together. I'll look through them later. First, I should figure out a name.

"Well, I want to give you a unique name. How about something related to the moon?" Lazarus suggested.

"This world has a natural phenomenon that darkens the sky. It is called an *Eclipse*."

Lazarus repeated the word aloud several times, considering its meaning. *An eclipse blocks the light of the sun and moon from reaching the observer...*

"Eclipse? That does have a nice sound to it. Alright then, I'll name you *Eclipse*." He smiled. "Can you show me a summary of each subclass's skill preferences, Eclipse?"

At his request, the orb projected information detailing the skills a summoner could learn within each subclass.

Warden: Wardens specialise in *Totem Magic*. By placing totems, they can create barriers that deflect both physical and magical attacks. Wardens excel in defensive combat, prioritising survivability. As a summoning subclass, the Warden can summon a *Guardian Spirit* that protects the summoner from harm. High-level Guardian Spirits will also assist in battle by fighting alongside their summoner.

Spirit Seer: Spirit Seers specialise in the ethereal, summoning spirits with elemental properties to fight for them. They excel in ranged combat and can master all ranged weapon techniques, including staves, bows, and chakrams. As spirit summoners, mana control is essential to prolong the duration a spirit remains. However, Spirit Seers are not limited to summoning; they can also form a connection with the spirit world, granting them access to powerful magic. As a class that heavily drains MP, they must possess a strong spirit.

Beast Tamer: Beast Tamers specialise in forming close bonds with creatures. They grow alongside their companions, sharing Aethercite gained through combat. Excelling in close to mid-range combat, they work in tandem with their companions, utilising elemental skills, various weapons, and heightened senses. Additionally, they possess the ability to communicate telepathically with their companions. Caring for their companions is essential, allowing them to learn healing skills. As close-combat specialists, they must cultivate great strength.

Necromancer: Necromancers tap into forbidden magic to raise the dead as minions. They specialise in magic, wielding spells of elemental properties, as well as blood, bone, and poison magic. Unlike other spellcasters, their summoning drains HP instead of mana, so they have mastered the ability to siphon HP from others to heal themselves. As a class that demands a high constitution, they become insatiable.

Spectral Blade: Spectral Blade summoners specialise in all forms of combat, conjuring weapons they can control telekinetically to aid them in battle. They can infuse these weapons with elemental properties and utilise soul magic, as well as an automatic defence against incoming attacks. As a class reliant on dexterity, they must remain ever-vigilant.

"That is the summary of the summoning subclasses. Does this help you?" Eclipse stated, remaining motionless while its purple eyes scanned Lazarus' face.

"Thank you, Eclipse." Lazarus nodded. "The subclasses seem to be based on other classes. Warden is a defensive subclass, much like a Tank. Spectral Blade leans into offensive abilities with weaponry, similar to the Knight class. Necromancer focuses on magic, just like Ranged. Beast Tamers are close-combat specialists, rivaling the Warrior classes, while Spirit Seers, like Necromancers, specialise in elemental magic and ranged combat."

Eclipse mentioned that Lazarus had five skill points available for abilities, as well as ten stat points. Then, spinning around, Eclipse displayed the information again.

"I apologise. I have reassessed your mana and discovered a hidden talent called 'Champion.' After analysing this talent, I found that it grants you an additional ten stat points per level."

Lazarus peered at the talent's description. "Is this from Levanna, or is it an innate ability?"

"That's impressive. Turns out being a Champion does have its perks after all," Lazarus remarked. He found himself adjusting the holographic skill tree, carefully examining the available skills. After reviewing his status, he placed Eclipse back in his bag and turned his attention to the leather-bound book on the table.

Before I invest in anything, I want to see what you experienced, Mother.

Lazarus gripped the leather strap and attempted to unfasten the book, but it wouldn't budge. *Nothing? This isn't an ordinary book. What secrets did you have to hide to seal it?*

"Lazarus! Good, you're already up. Let's go to the Garrison!" Astra called out, rushing over to grab his arm.

CHAPTER 7

The clashing of swords echoed through the air as Sapphire escorted Lazarus and Astra through the Garrison, a training ground for the Knights of Baylor. The knights were engaged in fast-paced, intense battles, honing their combat skills through real sparring. Lazarus was impressed—they received actual combat training against one another, unlike the training back in The Glades, which had consisted of basic sword swings and deflections. He had never been interested in that, opting out of the lessons entirely.

Instead, he had studied the environment—how animals used their surroundings to their advantage, the way they hunted their prey or evaded predators. This was how he had spent his years. While not as fast as Astra, he had refined his ability to navigate any terrain with efficiency.

As they passed the training ground, many heads turned, captivated by Astra's beauty. Despite her love for combat, she had an effortless elegance—her straight black hair perfectly complemented by her icy blue eyes. She smiled as they walked, but Lazarus noticed her fidgeting with her fingers, a telltale sign of nervousness. The tension in her movements made it harder for her to walk naturally. Feeling a protective instinct stir within him, Lazarus pulled her close, wrapping an arm around her waist. Astra melted into his embrace.

Lining the edges of the grounds stood towering statues carved from marbled stone. Each depicted a different class of knight, donned in Baylor's signature armour. Their weapons varied—some wielding swords, others gauntlets, bows, spears, daggers, or even staves.

"Lazarus, look at that statue! I can see the lightning pattern my father carved into his own armour," Astra said gleefully.

"That is the former Commander, Astro," Sapphire explained as they passed the statue, its stone eyes gazing down from above. "Famed for his mastery of the lightning element, he could decimate entire battalions on his own. His death sent a ripple of loss through all of us... but I can't begin to imagine how you must have felt upon learning of his passing, Astra."

"I am here to surpass him—to make a name for myself. I want to be more than just the daughter of a legend; I want to be a legend people will tell stories about."

"Once people see you fight, your fame will soon follow, Astra," Lazarus said, gripping her shoulder in reassurance.

The three of them stopped at the entrance of a towering building as tall as the statues surrounding it. Sapphire turned to Astra, a note of warning in her voice. "The commander puts students through brutal training. This is your last chance to turn back—save yourself from the torture," she pleaded.

"I think you're exaggerating a bit too much, Sapph—" Before Astra could finish, a commanding voice cut her off.

"Sapphire! Bring her inside and stop bad-mouthing me, or I'll personally oversee your next training session!"

Sapphire gulped at the sound of her commander's voice, dread washing over her face. She moved closer to Astra and whispered, "Save yourself—it's not too late."

She then opened the door, greeting her commander with a bow and a hurried apology.

The woman standing before them was tall and powerfully built. Her attire differed from Sapphire's—white pants matched her coat, which was complemented by a dark red cloak and metallic grey boots. She stood in front of a desk, arms crossed, her wild ruby-red hair hanging past her shoulders, partially covering one of her piercing grey eyes. In the corner of the room, a rack held her armour.

Sapphire nudged Astra forward with a firm push. Astra's nerves peaked as she stumbled, unsure of how to address this formidable woman.

"This is the young aspiring knight I mentioned—Astra. The one who fought against Borus. These two helped us capture the wanted assassin," Sapphire introduced her. Lazarus remained by the doorway, silently observing.

"Yes, I was impressed with that feat. Tell me, Astra, how did you manage to fight Borus? He is no mere bandit—he's an A-rank Assassin-class fighter." Morrigan's stone-grey eyes bore into Astra with an intense stare. She uncrossed her arms and placed her hands on the edge of the desk.

"By surprise... Commander. Lazarus and I stumbled upon them on our way to the port. We suspected they were setting up an ambush, so we took the initiative and launched a surprise attack. His cohorts weren't an issue, but Borus wasn't as easy. Even though I managed to stab him in the side, if the fight had continued any longer, I doubt we would have survived." Astra blurted everything out before she could think, earning a knowing smile from the commander.

"You're honest, I'll give you that. Sapphire has already filled me in on the details. I've given her your reward for his capture. Sapphire, if you will." She gestured for Sapphire to hand over the reward, which turned out to be eighteen silver tabs—more than either Astra or Lazarus had ever seen in their lifetime. Astra turned to Lazarus with a proud smile.

"Now, as for your enrolment as a knight—I want you to fight me," Morrigan said bluntly, glancing down at her desk and wiping away a thin layer of dust.

"Fight you? I don't mean to be rude, but I don't stand a chance against you, Commander," Astra protested, her nerves getting the better of her judgment.

Sapphire looked over at Astra, shaking her head while mouthing, "Just do it."

"I wasn't giving you a choice. On the battlefield, do you think your enemy will lay down their weapons just because you say you're no match for them? No. They will come at you mercilessly. You need to prove that you have what it takes to stand against opponents like that. If you can't do this, you have no right to be here."

The commander's words stung, and Astra couldn't help but take a step back. Lazarus held out his arm, resting a reassuring hand on her lower back. This was reality—far from any idealistic vision of knighthood.

Astra's cheeks flushed as she glanced back at Lazarus, nodding to assure him.

"Okay!" she said, steeling her nerves and reaching for her sheath.

Before she could even draw her sword, Morrigan was already upon her, throwing a punch. Astra barely managed to shift her head out of the way, sliding back and unsheathing her blade in the same motion. Lazarus and Sapphire leapt aside to avoid being caught in the fight.

Astra took a deep breath, trying to steady herself. As she raised her sword in front of her, mana surged from her body, coating the blade in crackling electricity—just in time. Morrigan launched another attack, but Astra reacted quickly, angling her sword diagonally and slicing across the commander's arm, halting her advance.

"Impressive reflexes. But can you keep it up?" Morrigan asked, her voice unwavering. She released her own mana, flames enveloping her hands while her legs became encased in rocky armour.

She stayed close to Astra, unleashing a relentless flurry of jabs that forced her to retreat swiftly.

I can't keep running away like this! Levanna was powerful, too, so why is the Commander forcing me to run away? No, I need to stop thinking about this. I'm here to prove myself to her, no matter what it takes. Astra, fight back! Astra thought while locked in the intense battle.

Morrigan maintained her relentless flurry of close-combat attacks, forcing Astra to stay on the defensive. But then, Astra's aura flared to life, releasing crackling lightning energy around her body. Her movement speed surged, and her attacks became significantly more powerful.

With renewed vigour, Astra pushed back against Morrigan, slashing at her with a lightning-charged strike. The blade carved a gash across the commander's chest. Yet Morrigan didn't flinch. Instead, a devilish grin stretched across her face as she crouched low, arms spread wide.

"Now we're getting somewhere. Give me more—give me everything you've got!" she roared.

Her aura erupted, engulfing her in flames that took the form of a wolf-like creature. Then, in a blur, she lunged at Astra near the doorway.

Reacting instinctively, Astra leapt backward, her lightning-infused body flashing down the stairs as fire and electricity clashed in the air.

☆☆☆☆

"What was that technique, Lazarus? She turned her aura into electricity—just like Morrigan," Sapphire asked, bewildered by Astra's sudden display of power.

Lazarus was just as shocked, his eyes wide with disbelief, too stunned to even follow the battle.

"I didn't know she could use it properly. Astra mentioned she was learning to coat her body in lightning energy to increase her movement speed, but she hadn't been able to control it before now," he admitted, still trying to process what he was seeing.

"By the looks of it, she's learning as she fights—gaining experience in real-time," Sapphire observed, her eyes tracking the fierce exchange. "I've never seen anyone keep up with Morrigan for this long. I'd almost forgotten about her title."

"Hellhound."

"Hellhound?" Lazarus echoed, turning to Sapphire. "How did she get that name?"

Sapphire, too engrossed in the battle to respond immediately, kept her focus locked on the fight. Lazarus, sensing she wouldn't answer just yet, turned his attention back to the clash of lightning and fire.

☆ ☆ ☆ ☆

Despite her weaker physique, Astra compensated with her lightning-coated aura, allowing her to match Morrigan in combat. Sparks of electricity clashed with embers, scattering across the field as their blows met. However, the strain of using this technique soon caught up with her—her body grew heavy, her muscles burned with pain, and her lungs constricted as she struggled to catch her breath.

The knights sparring nearby quickly dispersed, clearing the training field.

"Normally, I'd scold those who lose focus during training, but this is a special circumstance. I want all of you to witness the difference between a high-level knight and a low-level knight," Morrigan declared.

She took a deep breath, shutting her eyes. The red flames surrounding her flickered and shifted to blue. When she opened her eyes again, they blazed with an even fiercer fire.

Astra attempted to strike first, but Morrigan met her halfway, delivering a powerful kick to her stomach that sent her hurtling through the air. Without hesitation, Morrigan propelled herself off the ground with a burst of flame, closing in on her airborne opponent like a predator chasing helpless prey.

From her back, flames erupted, forming additional arms that unleashed a relentless barrage of jabs, each strike dispersing fiery embers into the air. The assault ended with a devastating flaming dropkick, sending Astra crashing into the ground with a thunderous impact. Snow, dust, and debris erupted across the field, but a sudden wall of water emerged, shielding the knights from the blast.

"This is it—your limit. How do you want to end this battle, Astra?" Morrigan shouted, certain of her victory.

Astra's grip weakened as exhaustion overtook her. Her fingers loosened, and her sword slipped from her grasp. But just before it hit the ground, a sudden jolt surged through her aching muscles.

With a burst of renewed determination, she seized her blade.

"When I say it's over!" she roared, thrusting her sword forward, lightning surging through it as she plunged the blade deep into Morrigan's stomach.

The commander remained still, deliberately taking Astra's attack. Astra's sword emerged from Morrigan's back as the energy surrounding Astra dissipated. With no strength left, she collapsed, falling toward her opponent. The commander extended her arms to embrace the aspiring knight.

"Rest now, Astra, Knight of Baylor!" Morrigan declared as the audience of knights erupted into cheers, their shouts of praise rumbling across the training grounds.

"Sapphire, take her to the infirmary and treat her wounds. Tomorrow, she joins Zachariah's squad."

"Who's the girl?" a male voice asked from behind Sapphire.

Lazarus turned his head to see who was speaking, but no one was visible.

"That's Astra of Riverfall. I'm assigning her to your squad, Captain Zachariah," Morrigan said, picking up Astra's sword and examining its design. Blue flames flared around Morrigan's wounded stomach, regenerating the flesh until the wound vanished.

"That's right. Zachariah here is an Assassin-class. He uses a light-element technique to reflect light around his body, making him invisible to those around him," Sapphire added.

She took the sword from Morrigan on her way to Astra, raising her hand above the unconscious knight to create a bubble that lifted her into the air.

"Don't worry, Lazarus. I'll make sure to heal Astra. It won't take long."

The bubble floated under Sapphire's command, with Astra suspended inside as if she were submerged in water.

"I hope so," Lazarus said, unclenching his fist.

Snow danced across the grounds, coating Lazarus in pure white as he waited. He ignored the snowfall, focusing on the journal to ease his concern for Astra.

Lazarus took out a dagger and sliced pieces from an apple, his mother's journal resting on his lap. He had tried using mana to unlock the seal, but nothing worked. Lost in thought about what kind of subclass he should choose, he accidentally nicked his finger, drawing blood. He didn't notice the cut, but the blood dripped onto the book, seeping into its pages.

"What was that? The journal absorbed the blood. Okay! Let's try this again," Lazarus said triumphantly.

With the rest of the apple in his mouth, he attempted to unlock the leather strap. This time, it flew open. The book seemed to take on a life of its own, flipping through pages as a holographic figure emerged, forming the shape of a small female figure.

"If you're hearing this, my spell worked. It wasn't an easy process, and I used magic I never wish to use again to ensure only my kin can see the contents of this journal—a diary, so to speak—leading up to the reason I created this for you."

Lazarus was stunned, the apple still clamped between his teeth. *This must be her. Only kin can unlock the seal. Whatever she's hiding, I'll find the answers within,* he thought, listening intently as his mother spoke.

"Today, I became a summoner. It's all so surreal—I never imagined my life would lead me here. But he had a knack for adventure, always dragging me along with him. These past three months in Mortis have flown by. Cyrus wants to climb the Tower of Autumn, and with his sword skills, I believe he can make it to the top. I want to be by his side when he does.

My summoning magic allows me to create elemental spirits, and using the black cores I obtained during my travels with Cyrus, I summoned my first spirit—an owl of the Dark element. Shadow is loyal, wise, and trustworthy, a great first spirit for a summoner. After obtaining my spirit, I couldn't stop thinking about the mystical wonder of seeing a creature come to life. The summoning circle began appearing on everything I owned. I would later discover that Shadow was the Lord of Owls—creatures that traverse the shadows."

The journal ended after the last sentence—or so it seemed. Since it used spiritual magic to recount her experiences, it likely limited the amount of spiritual energy it consumed during the process.

"That's it? Why did it stop? Come back!" Lazarus yelled in frustration. A few knights training nearby turned toward the commotion, prompting him to force a smile and give a thumbs-up.

Just then, a flicker of light emerged from the journal.

"I am only a spirit attached to this journal. I understand that you want all your questions answered immediately, but this magic is limited. To work around this, I have entrusted my knowledge of the journal to Shadow. If you can summon him, he will aid you and explain how to unlock more of its contents. Be patient, my child. Enjoy the adventure you are embarking on. I love you."

Lazarus shut the journal, letting out a deep breath.

"Patience? That's easier said than done. I have people who want me dead, and I need to find out why."

"Lazarus? Ah, there you are. Are you okay?" Sapphire asked as she peered out from the entrance of the garrison.

"Yeah, I'm good. I just heard something I've dreamt about my whole life. Anyway, how is Astra?" Lazarus rose from the bench, his six-foot frame towering over Sapphire as he placed the journal back into his bag.

Sapphire nodded toward the door, ushering him inside. "I've finished healing Astra's wounds. She's resting in the infirmary for now. You can visit her if you'd like—she should be ready to leave soon. I have business to attend to if you'll excuse me."

Lazarus headed inside to see Astra. The wounds she had received from Morrigan had already disappeared as if the fight had never happened.

"Astra, how do you feel?" he asked, concerned about any lingering effects from the battle.

"Honestly, I don't even remember fighting her," Astra admitted. "The last thing I recall was Commander Morrigan throwing a lot of punches. I did everything I could to defend myself, but my vision went black. The next thing I knew, I was waking up in the infirmary."

She looked down at her hand, flexing her fingers even though she felt no physical pain.

"I managed to use Storm Walker this time. It gave me a fighting chance, but I don't remember how to use it properly. I've tried a few times since waking up to enter that state again, but all I've managed to produce is static."

"Astra, are you sure this is a skill issue? You fought against one of the strongest knights in Baylor—she pushed you to your limit with ease. You did the only thing you could. Your body reacted to the threat and forced you into your Storm Walker state to defend yourself. The ability to enter that state is still there, but you have a mental block."

"A mental block? What do you mean by that, Lazarus?" she asked, almost offended at the suggestion.

"Commander Morrigan is incredibly powerful—there's no denying that we're nowhere near her level at this stage, yet she still had you fight her. I think the fear of losing to her—no, the fear of not becoming a knight—has hindered your ability to enter that state again. If you do, all the memories from that fight might come flooding back at once."

"In other words, memory loss," Astra muttered, finishing his thought with a melancholic stare.

Lazarus offered a small smile. "I think we should take a walk around the city—invest in some new clothes… maybe even some new weapons. What do you say?"

At the mention of weapons—her favorite thing to spend money on—Astra's eyes lit up. Her head snapped up as excitement replaced her earlier gloom.

"I'm in!" she said, quickly grabbing her belongings before leaving the infirmary.

CHAPTER 8

A wave of warmth embraced Lazarus and Astra as they stepped into the blacksmith's forge. The massive workspace extended beneath the shop, with multiple chimneys overhead, exhaling thick plumes of smoke. Lazarus lingered near the entrance, browsing the display of weapons and armour along the racks. Everything was here—from simple, unadorned swords to intricately crafted weapons that looked as if gods themselves had forged them.

Beyond the rows of weapon racks, a stone staircase descended into the depths of the forge, its entrance glowing with fiery light. The acrid scent of burning coal and red-hot iron filled the air.

"There's no way we can afford these weapons," Lazarus whispered loudly, trying to keep his voice down. "They're in the gold range—you could buy a cottage for the same price!"

Astra, unfazed, picked up a sword with a black blade, inspecting its sharpness by running her eyes down its length before placing it back on the rack.

"Excuse me, what are your prices for weapons here?" she asked.

A stout man stepped forward, his face darkened with soot. His ragged clothes and leather apron—charred black from years of fire exposure—spoke of his trade.

"The cost of crafting weapons ain't cheap," he said. "Yer lookin' at a minimum of five silver tabs and up to two gold tabs for our highest-quality weapons. If you want to add a mana core, that'll cost an extra ten silver tabs. Those orbs ain't easy to incorporate into weapons. But if you need it done, Cryo's got yer covered."

"I'm looking for an elemental sword, Cryo," Astra said as she browsed the selection of weapons. Meanwhile, Lazarus had wandered over to the staff section.

The last thing I want to do is kill. These polearms suit my combat style much better.

"Elemental? Well, the top shelf has those—limited supply, though," Cryo replied.

Astra's eyes landed on a particular sword that caught her interest. The white blade was adorned with a cloudy grey pattern of runic symbols running down its length. It felt light in her hands as she swung it through the air, listening for the sound it made—but there was nothing. Just silence. Her lips curled into a smile as she examined the weapon in admiration.

"I'll take this one," she said, scanning the blade once more before sheathing it in a white scabbard wrapped in lapis-colored rope.

"Good choice, that one," Cryo nodded approvingly. "It's infused with an air element core—light as a feather, allowing it to slice through the air with almost no resistance. It also nullifies sound when slashing. As for the cost… 46 silver tabs." He held out a metal tray, waiting for payment.

Meanwhile, Lazarus had picked up a dark red bo staff with intricate black pommels. The moment his hands wrapped around it, a thrum of energy pulsed through his body.

Whoa! This energy… this power… it calls to me.

"I'll take this one!" Lazarus declared enthusiastically, gripping the staff as he strode toward the counter—only to nearly trip over scattered materials on the floor.

Astra sighed, pressing a hand against her forehead in embarrassment.

After paying for their weapons, the two left the blacksmith and made their way to the alchemist, Byron.

"Why did you choose a staff of all weapons?" Astra asked, perplexed by his decision. She knew he had no experience with a staff—let alone any weapon other than a dagger.

"I became a summoner. I'm not sure how well my spirits will be able to fight, so I wanted something with reach that I can also use for support spells… Also, I don't want a weapon that can take a life so easily," Lazarus replied.

After reading his mother's journal, he had given it a lot of thought. He had decided how he wanted to begin his own journey—a path he hoped would keep his hands free of blood.

"I know you don't like the idea of taking a life," Astra said, her voice steady, "but your spirits will still do that for you. Giving them the command to slay an enemy is no different from doing it yourself. You won't be able to escape that reality when you climb the Tower, Lazarus."

His face grew solemn as he considered her words. The weight of that truth settled heavily on his mind, his hand trembling slightly as he gripped the staff. But he quickly shook it off, strapping the weapon securely to his back between the straps of his bag.

"I've got a plan," he said, stopping just outside the alchemist's shop. "Taking a life with my own hands will only be a last resort."

He pushed the door open, letting Astra step in first. The noise of the bustling streets faded behind them, replaced by the quiet hum of the shop's interior.

"I can see why he spends so much time working in here—it's peaceful," Lazarus noted. He raised his voice slightly. "Hello, Byron! Are you in?"

As Astra wandered through the store, scanning the shelves, Byron emerged with a huff—clearly, they had interrupted him.

"What is it you want? Oh… it's you." His irritation faded slightly, and he cleared his throat. "I, uh, I apologise. I was in the middle of refining mana cores…"

Astra turned her head to smile at Lazarus, who could only offer a small smile in return before addressing Byron.

"Well, I'm here for a mana core. I have the Mortesyn core, but I was thinking of using it to create a dark-element spirit."

Byron reacted with a hint of disappointment but offered his assistance nonetheless.

"Spirit summoning? I once heard of a spirit summoner making a name for themselves when I first started here. She came around regularly, always wanting more cores," Byron said, reminiscing about the past before returning to the present. "If it's an elemental spirit you want to create, I can help with that. Lower-ranked creatures in the Winter Tower fall into two elemental types: Water and Ice. Do you know about elemental weaknesses?" He peered through his glasses at Lazarus.

Eclipse popped out of Lazarus' bag and displayed a chart before Lazarus could answer. The chart showed a circle of elements—Fire, Ice, Earth, Air, Lightning, Water, and Light and Dark at the centre—each displaying a weakness to another.

"As you're a rookie adventurer, the lower-floor creatures are weak. I suggest these cores—Ice, Water, and Lightning." Byron placed several cores on the counter: three Water cores, two Ice cores, and one Lightning core.

If I recall, this Lightning core was the B-rank one we saw yesterday. The others must be C-rank or lower, Lazarus thought as he observed the core.

"These Water cores are D- and C-rank, the two Ice cores are C-rank, and this Lightning core is the one you saw me inspecting yesterday— the last B-rank Lightning core I have for sale at the moment," Byron said, pointing to each mana core, giving extra attention to the higher-ranked ones. "As for the prices, from E-rank up, it's twenty bronze, eighty bronze, four silver, thirty-five silver, two gold, fifteen gold, and lastly, one platinum for U-rank."

"I'll take the Lightning core and two C-rank cores for Water and Ice as well," Lazarus said, handing over his silver tab. *Unlike weapons, these cores are much cheaper. I've never seen how these tabs work before—we didn't use currency in Riverfall.* The tab displayed runes, showing how much silver remained before shifting to bronze. Lazarus watched the exchange intently, his village roots betraying his unfamiliarity with the system.

"I'll be back to check for other high-ranked cores. Astra, let's go." Lazarus placed the cores in his bag, now stuffed to the brim with orbs of various colours and shapes, each representing a different element.

Before heading back to the inn, they took a detour to the training grounds to pick up Astra's uniform. They cut through the busy paths—carriages carting cargo, people walking through the snow as they chatted, knights patrolling the islands. Reaching the northeast housing district, the busiest area at this hour, they moved through the golden glow of the setting sun.

As they reached the training grounds, a large stone structure with statues of armoured knights flanking the gate, Lazarus was about to step into the clearing when someone turned the corner at the same time, bumping into him. Lazarus stumbled backward into the snow while the other person remained standing.

"Sorry, I didn't see you coming around the corner," Lazarus said as he got back up with Astra's help. She patted the snow off his clothes.

The stranger stared for a few seconds before speaking. "Maybe if you had a sense skill, you would have noticed my presence before bumping into me." Lazarus couldn't tell if he was being helpful or condescending.

"You're the new summoner in the guild. Have you decided what kind of summoning you're going to specialise in?"

"Spirit Seer. I saw you at the guild yesterday. Who are you?" Lazarus asked, trying to get a read on the man before him.

"Alastor. I'm a summoner as well. Though, I'd suggest not revealing your abilities to everyone you meet. You never know who lurks in the shadows around here. You picked a terrible time to arrive in this city," Alastor said, his tone pompous. "Anyway, I'm heading off now. I suggest you two go home as soon as you can. After nightfall, this city becomes dangerous."

"Why is it dangerous after nightfall?" Astra asked, positioning herself between them. Though Lazarus stood tall, Alastor dwarfed him by a foot. *He's tall! Is this what Astra sees when she looks up at me?*

"Something you don't want to get involved in. Just… don't push the topic," Alastor replied in an agitated tone.

Done with the exchange, he walked down the alleyway and disappeared into the misty snow. Lazarus exchanged glances with Astra before they continued on to the training grounds. By now, it was just past midday, though it was hard to tell with a sky full of clouds snowing over Baylor.

"You mentioned recognising him—Alastor—from the guild? What was he like there?" Astra asked, curious about their familiarity.

"I didn't interact with him there; I just saw him standing alone in the guild hall when I was about to do my class check. He had his arms crossed—I didn't get the impression he was someone who enjoyed company. It's strange that he'd go out of his way to warn me when he doesn't even know me."

"He did mention sensing aura. Maybe he bumped into you on purpose?" she suggested.

Sapphire left the training grounds, glancing at the pair standing across the street. Waving at them, she called out, "Astra! I'm glad to see you're up. I've got your knight armour set ready to go—it's in my office if you want to retrieve it. Sorry, but I can't stay; I have more pressing matters to attend to!" She clutched a few scrolls in her arms, struggling to keep them in place.

I know she's a strong knight, but she does come off as ditzy from time to time. It's kind of refreshing to see someone strong show some awkwardness, Lazarus thought.

"I'm doing a bit better now, thanks to you. Lazarus told me you used water magic to heal my wounds. You saved me from death." Astra patted her arm as they walked. As they drew closer, Sapphire nearly dropped one of the scrolls but quickly regained her balance.

"Oh... yeah, don't thank me for that. It's going to become a common thing now that Morrigan has her eyes on you. You impressed her with your skills. Anyway, I must go now. Bye!" Sapphire hurried past them, gripping a scroll by the small paper rope in her mouth.

What's her rush? Lazarus wondered as he watched Sapphire exit the training grounds on a stream of water before vanishing.

"Come on, let's go. It's getting colder; let's hurry," Astra urged, tugging at Lazarus's arm to get him to follow.

They walked down the quiet halls of the training grounds. Sapphire's office was located next to Morrigan's. Astra retrieved her uniform and left in a rush.

As they were leaving, muffled voices echoed through the halls. Astra and Lazarus quickly hid as the voices drew closer.

"...traitor amongst us. You need to find out who it is before they kill us all, Commander!" The female voice was unfamiliar, but the next voice was unmistakably Morrigan's.

"I understand your concerns. He will help us find out who killed her. I trust he won't stop until he does. The killer hasn't left any concrete evidence for us to identify a suspect yet... In the meantime, we'll continue with our normal routine until they reveal themselves."

Astra nudged Lazarus and pointed towards the stairs. He nodded and crept forward, trying not to make a sound.

A killer? The woman mentioned a traitor among them. If that's the case, Astra could be in danger. He thought as they made their way down the stairs.

Lazarus' heart rate spiked after hearing the conversation. The steps echoed through the stairwell, and his stomach dropped. They rushed out into the open, making a break for the bridge leading back to the city. Neither of them stopped until they reached the southeast housing district, their chests heaving from running through the snow.

"What was that about? There's a traitor in the Knights of Valour?" Lazarus asked as they stepped into their room. "What happens if they go after you, Astra?"

"I am a knight now—I could be a target. But I'm much safer surrounded by the other knights than I am on my own. I need to at least meet the captain of my squad and figure out if they're trustworthy or not," Astra replied. Exhausted from her earlier battle, she headed straight for the bed, falling face-first with a heavy sigh.

Lazarus, however, planned to study and was determined to learn how to use his newfound skills. He took out his journal along with a volume on summoning to grasp the basics. Sitting down, he immersed himself in the world of summoning.

"So, first, I need to create a runic circle with the symbols required for the summoning process to work. Then, I place the elemental orb in the centre of the circle marked by the elemental rune. That sounds easy enough. I should make space just in case," Lazarus muttered as he moved the furniture aside, clearing enough room to draw a summoning circle with mana.

Once the circle was complete, Lazarus took out the Mortesyn core. "Now, let's see if it works."

He placed the core in the dark element circle.

"Next, call out to the spirit you intend to summon. If it doesn't have a name, imagine the spirit in your mind before calling upon the summon."

The journal mentioned Shadow, a dark-element spirit. I should start with him. If it works, I'll have a powerful summon by my side. Not to mention, he knows how to use the journal—I'll need his guidance to find my parents.

"Shadow! I call upon you as my mother did before me—Adelheid the Seer. You aided her on her journey through the Towers; now I ask you to lend your aid once again. Heed my call, Shadow, Lord of Owls!" Lazarus commanded, raising his arms above the summoning circle.

The runes began to glow with a black, wispy aura that swirled around the room, shrouding it in darkness. Lazarus stumbled backward, nearly tripping. After a moment, the darkness receded into the centre of the circle.

"What's going on, Lazarus? I heard you chanting something out here… uh, what is that?!" Astra asked, stepping around the corner— only to freeze at the sight of a massive shadow stretching across the wall behind Lazarus.

"What do you mean?" Lazarus asked, confused by her reaction. He turned around, his breath hitching as he saw the shadow consuming the wall where the couch stood. Black mist unfurled into massive wings, stretching across the connecting walls before engulfing the room in darkness once again.

"…Shadow? Please tell me you're Shadow."

The owl matched Lazarus' height, its feathers resembling a pitch-black hooded cloak.

Its wings slowly withdrew into its body as it lowered its head in a bow. It didn't speak, but Lazarus could sense it meant no harm. When his hand brushed against its wispy feathers, they solidified beneath his touch—a comforting sensation.

"I'll take that as a yes, then. Nice to meet you, Shadow. It's strange— there's a feeling of comfort like I've been around you before. Maybe I have, but I have no memory of you." Lazarus waved his arm, motioning for Astra to come closer.

Shadow opened one of its eyes as she approached, halting her advance.

"It's okay, Shadow. Astra is a close friend of mine—you can trust her," Lazarus said, hoping to ease the owl's intense stare.

Astra inched forward cautiously, sidestepping until she was within arm's reach. She pressed the back of her hand against one of its wings, gently brushing the spirit's feathers.

Lazarus took out the journal and opened it to a blank page. Gazing up at Shadow, he called out to the diary.

"How did you communicate with Shadow?" he asked.

The book glowed as a blue aura rose from the pages, taking the shape of his mother—an ethereal figure just as young as Lazarus and Astra.

"Shadow, are you there?" she asked, looking around the room but unable to see anything.

The owl peered at the spirit in shock upon seeing its old master appear.

"I cannot see anything. Show me where you are."

The blue spirit of Adelheid reached out a palm. Shadow bowed to the spirit, resting his head against her hand.

"I am gone, my friend. I apologize that I can't be here with you, but I must ask you to take care of my son in my stead. He is new to this life and will face many dangers along the path he has taken. No matter what it takes, I trust you to do what I am unable to do myself, Shadow."

Adelheid turned to face her son.

"As for how to communicate with your spirits, you will need to learn how to use telepathy—a unique skill that summoners can obtain. It may take some time before you acquire this skill, but once you do, your bond with your spirits will strengthen exponentially, allowing you to fight as one. If that is all, I bid you farewell."

The aura of the spirit dissipated, returning to the blank pages.

"Wait! Don't go yet!" Lazarus shouted, but it was already too late. He slumped to the ground, staring at the journal. "How are you able to come and go like that?" he whispered to himself.

Astra placed a hand on his shoulder in comfort.

"I'm sorry I can't communicate well with you yet, Shadow, but I promise I'll learn soon!" Lazarus said determinedly, clenching his fist toward Shadow.

A round portal of swirling black mist appeared in the air, connecting to a dimension of pure shadow—so dark that even light failed to breach its depths. Shadow merged with the darkness, and the portal vanished.

"I'm okay, Astra. You can go to sleep if you're exhausted. I need to examine these skills and figure out which ones to learn."

Astra withdrew her hand, her expression filled with concern for Lazarus. She understood what it must feel like to watch a parent you'd never known disappear before your eyes without warning.

Lazarus remained on the floor, reaching into his bag and picking up Eclipse as Astra retreated to her room.

"Eclipse, can you bring up my skill list?" Lazarus asked the small orb. It spun around before displaying an image of a sphere, with skills branching out as interconnected nodes, representing different tiers and types of obtainable abilities.

After examining the skills beyond *Elemental Spirit Creation*, Lazarus noticed several common ones available to each subclass: increased Strength, Spirit, Constitution, and Dexterity. Elemental magic and skills included weapon proficiencies, sensory abilities, and enhancements that could aid his spirits.

One ability in particular caught his attention—*Second Wind*. It described the power to survive a fatal strike with a sacrifice. *I don't think I'll need it right now, but it could be useful!*

"Eclipse, can you explain skill points? I had some before that I used to obtain the spirit creation skill, but how am I supposed to gain more?" Lazarus asked, scratching his head as he watched the orb move across the floor.

"Skill Points: An experience-based system used to acquire new skills for each class. Skill points are obtainable upon levelling up by collecting Aethercite," Eclipse replied.

Lazarus stretched his arms along the floor until he lay on his back.

"Aethercite, huh? Looks like you and I are going to have some fun tomorrow, Shadow. We've got a busy day ahead of us—best to rest up," he said aloud as if Shadow were beside him, yet no voice responded.

STATUS

♦ Name: Lazarus

♦ Level: 1

♦ Health: 12100

♦ Mana: 3000

♦ Strength: 105

♦ Constitution: 110

♦ Spirit: 150

♦ Dexterity: 85

CHAPTER 9

The snow fell heavily around Levanna as she faced off against a crescent bear. Even on all fours, it loomed over her, standing nearly five meters tall. Its fur resembled a cloudy sky, with a white patch shaped like a crescent moon adorning its chest. As it rose onto its hind legs, its massive paws—each the size of Levanna's torso—lifted into the air in a display of strength. Now towering above the treetops, the beast cast an imposing shadow. When it slammed its paws back to the ground, the impact shook the earth beneath Levanna, yet she remained steady despite the tremor.

"You're a big one. I haven't seen any bears roaming these parts in the last few days. Must be because the Dire Wolves have moved on," Levanna mused. "You must want to take over their territory now that they're gone. But it won't be that easy." She crouched, arms outstretched, a confident smile on her lips. "If you want to claim it, you'll have to take it from me. Give me everything you've got!"

In response to her challenge, the crescent bear let out a thunderous roar that echoed across the mountain before charging. Levanna held her ground, her hands gripping the beast's thick white fur as it slammed into her. The force pushed her back slightly, but she remained standing.

"Heh, you're quite strong for a creature," Levanna said before lifting the massive bear into the air and slamming it back down with a heavy impact. The ground shook, snow cascaded from the nearby trees, and the bear roared in fury, disturbing the wildlife. It stood on its hindlegs, reaching the canopy it swung a paw with tremendous power unleashing a crescent-shaped slash of air.

Jumping over the slash, she leapt toward the bear, kicking up snow in the process. As the other paw swung toward her, she planted her feet firmly in the snow, deflecting the strike before thrusting both palms into the bear's stomach. Flames burst forth, exploding on impact. The force sent the beast hurtling through the air, toppling several trees before it crashed into the side of the mountain. It lay motionless, unable to rise.

"This is my territory to protect now," she declared. "Either leave this mountain or become my pet. If you choose the latter, I'll allow you to stay."

The bear remained still. Levanna leapt onto its belly, took a seat, and stared at its closed eyes. "I know that wasn't enough to kill you. You can quit playing dead," she said, patting iit's singed stomach as she spoke.

Suddenly, the snow around them stirred. Levanna jumped back just as the bear rolled over and pushed itself up. Shaking the snow from its fur, it sat down in obedience, placing its front paws in front of its body and sinking slightly into the snow. Slowly, it slid its massive form toward Levanna.

"This is your choice, then?"

A low rumble emanated from the bear's belly, followed by a hushed moan. In response, Levanna reached out and rubbed its head.

"Good choice… Crescendo. That sounds like a fitting name for you." She smiled. "I'll take care of you. In return, you'll help me protect the village below, right?"

The bear let out a mighty roar in agreement before lifting Levanna onto its back.

☆☆☆☆

"You're back! How did it—" Maeve cut herself off mid-sentence upon seeing the bear walking beside Levanna. "Why are you bringing that thing here? If it goes on a rampage, it could destroy the village!"

"No offense, but so could I," Levanna replied, her tone unwavering. "I've already made the bear submit to me, and in the laws of nature, submitting to another means surrendering one's territory. You have nothing to fear from this cuddly giant. He will protect you. I'll take care of feeding and training him over the next few weeks until he's strong enough to defend the village on his own."

The village elders exchanged nervous glances.

"Excuse us if we aren't as accepting as you," Maeve said. "I don't think anyone will feel safe around him unless he's by your side." She sighed before shifting the conversation. "On a side note, we've decided on a course of action regarding Zodiac coming here." She gripped Darius' hand tightly.

Levanna perked up. "What do you have in mind?"

"We're going to fight back against Zodiac," Darius said, determination burning in his eyes.

"Fight back?" Levanna's expression darkened. "You couldn't even fight against me. I'm nothing compared to them. They'll slaughter you—and everyone in this village—just for daring to resist!" Her voice rose, surprising them all.

"We know," Maeve admitted. "We've already started preparing. But we would feel more confident knowing you're by our side, Levanna. This isn't about foolish bravery—it's about Astra and Lazarus. We made a promise to protect them. For them, I would give my life to ensure they are safe." Her gaze was firm, unwavering.

"…I don't like this plan at all, but I'll do what I can to help you."

Using her strength, Levanna massaged Crescendo's belly, causing him to flop onto his back. "I named him Crescendo after the crescent shape on his chest. He'll sleep during the day, so I don't see him becoming a problem—unless someone wakes him up. I'll be training him until they arrive." She smiled at the village elders, reassuring them that nothing would happen to them.

Suddenly, fire shot up into the sky beyond the treetops outside the village, immediately drawing Levanna's attention. "If you'll excuse me, I have a personal matter to attend to," she said before leaping onto Crescendo's back. The bear wasted no time, charging toward the source of the signal.

"That fire looks familiar!" she thought, glancing back over her shoulder.

Crescendo trudged through the thick snow at a brisk pace, the trees rustling in the wind. Levanna kept her focus on the fiery beacon ahead.

"It *is* you! I'd recognise that aura anywhere."

She leapt high above the treetops, the cool breeze refreshing her skin. Landing into a roll, she came to a stop in front of a small, hooded creature with horns protruding from the sides of its hood. At the sound of crunching snow, the creature turned, greeting Levanna with a mischievous grin.

The furry black-and-white creature, with dark circles around his eyes, bounced toward her. His pointed ears twitched against the hood.

"Gamma! I missed you so much!" Levanna exclaimed, throwing her arms around him in excitement.

A thin, furry tail slipped out from beneath his brown robe and black pants, wrapping around Levanna in return. The metal horns on his head glowed red.

Red horns—he's happy!

"Miss too. Protect Champion. Champion safe." Though not human, Gamma could still speak in simple sentences. "Big Wyvern burned down," he continued.

"I knew I could trust you to find him. I'm glad you kept him safe. I'm going to need another favour. I got a letter from our friend saying he's going to a Tower tomorrow. Can you watch over Laz and help him with his Tower battles?" Levanna asked Gamma in a sweet voice.

Gamma hopped out of her arms with his arms raised. "Protect Laz. Accept request."

"Thank you, Gamma. Before you go, I have one more thing for you. Can you set up an anti-magic detection barrier for me, please?" she asked her little friend, as she couldn't use magic to hide her presence. Levanna glanced around the edge of the forest clearing, where runes marked the outer boundary, forming a barrier that encompassed the open field.

"Anti-magic, done already." His glowing red eyes stared up at Levanna, who was now gathering mana into her hands, condensing it into a small ball of energy.

"Are you hungry, Gamma? I have a tasty treat for you." Levanna focused on the ball in her palms. "Ignite."

The ball burst into flames, its glow reflecting in Gamma's eyes. He bounced on the spot, eagerly awaiting the fire. She pushed the fireball toward him, letting it float freely. He opened his mouth, ready to feast.

"You've done great. Now enjoy your treat."

The creature survived by consuming fire, which suited Levanna perfectly, as she excelled in fire magic. Sustaining him was effortless— her powerful fireballs provided ample nourishment. He devoured one in a single gulp, his body radiating an infernal aura.

"Fire delicious," Gamma said contentedly.

"Gamma, you'll find Lazarus across the frozen sea in the city of Baylor. I suggest stowing away on a ship once you reach the port. If you leave now, you should arrive in Baylor by tomorrow. I know you're just as strong as I am, if not stronger, but stay safe, Gamma." She gave him one last hug.

He waved goodbye with his tiny paws and trudged through the snow, the heat from his body carving a path as he made his way down the mountain pass.

CHAPTER 10

"Lazarus, are you awake already?" Astra called out as she stumbled into the main room, pulling a glove onto her hand.

She was clad in her new knight armour: a silver chest guard adorned with a snowflake at its centre, silver waist guards lined with white fur, and white boots with silver shin guards over ivory leather pants. Beneath the chest guard, she wore a cloud-grey coat that reached her knees. To complete the look, she draped a snow-white cloak over her shoulders, its large fur pads connected to the hood.

"Whoa! This is the armour you get to wear?" Lazarus was stunned. She had never worn proper armour before—only a leather chest guard she had received as a gift in Riverfall. Astra pulled back her cloak to reveal the shoulder pauldrons, which bore an owl design symbolising the Kingdom of Baylor. She blushed, noticing his intense gaze as he took in her new armour.

"This is kind of embarrassing. I've never worn this much armour before, but I love how it feels. It's light and doesn't restrict my movement," she said, stretching her legs.

"You shouldn't be embarrassed; you look amazing! Seriously, wow!" Lazarus circled her, admiring the full design, his eyes filled with admiration. Astra remained still but turned her head to follow his path, watching as his hands brushed over the armour. Feeling a sudden shyness, she took a few steps back toward the door.

"Enough of that—we need to go, now," Astra urged him, much to his disappointment.

Lazarus sighed but quickly picked up the journal, tucking it into a pocket inside his brown robe.

"Also, Sapphire told me that the commander wants to speak with me today. I know this is the day you first enter the Tower, but I'm not sure I'll be able to go with you," Astra said as she picked up a helmet shaped like an owl's head, its wings spread along the sides. She placed it over her head, the wings covering her ears while the owl's face shielded the upper half of her own, leaving openings for her eyes to ensure visibility.

"Alright, let's go see what she wants to discuss," she said after donning her full armour.

Upon entering the training grounds, a few knights took notice of Astra in her knight uniform, their expressions quickly turning to disdain.

"Would you look at that? The newbie's already wearing a knight's outfit—all for getting knocked around by Morrigan," one of the male knights sneered.

Another knight elbowed him in the chest plate, but he didn't take back his words.

Astra turned to walk toward them, but Lazarus stepped in, urging her to leave it for now.

"You're a knight now. Every action you take, every word you speak, will be judged. Don't stoop to their level. Keep your head high and show them why you were appointed a knight."

Astra took a deep breath, returning to Lazarus' side.

The knight who had insulted her before wasn't finished. This time, he smirked and made a snide comment about her needing protection from her "boyfriend."

That was the last straw.

Before anyone could react, Astra was suddenly in front of him. In one swift motion, she disarmed his weapon, took hold of his arm, and pivoted into a shoulder throw. He crashed to the ground with a heavy thud, gasping for air as she pressed her foot to his throat and drew her sword.

"If anyone else wants to try me, step forward now!"

The knights raised their hands and backed away.

"I may be new here, but I will not tolerate any form of harassment," Astra warned, her voice calm—though static crackled around her body.

"Well said, newbie!" a familiar voice rang out from behind them.

Lazarus hunched over slightly under the pressure of Astra's sizzling aura as Morrigan approached, her eyes locked onto Astra.

"I approved Astra as a knight because she stands her ground, no matter how strong the enemy she faces. That is what we knights strive to be. If you're expecting me to punish her for fighting another knight, you're mistaken. Astra is one of us now. Reflect on your actions and what it truly means to be a knight. Your captains will deal with you as they see fit," Morrigan reproached the group.

She then nodded at Astra, signaling for her and Lazarus to follow her into the office.

The other knights helped their fallen comrade back up before returning to their training.

"I'm glad both of you came today. I wanted to speak with you to clear a few things up," Commander Morrigan stated as the giant arched doors of her office shut behind them. "I know you overheard my conversation last night."

"How? We didn't make a sound," Astra interjected defensively, leaning forward in her chair.

"Don't worry, you're not in trouble," Morrigan reassured them, easing Astra's tension. "You're right—you didn't make a sound, as expected of a hunter from Riverfall. But you forget that we can develop sensory skills with our classes. No matter how quiet or hidden you were, I still sensed you there."

Morrigan offered wine and food to further ease the tension. Astra sipped a glass of water as Morrigan continued.

"As you now know, there is a traitor in the city. They have killed two of my Valour Knights—one just two nights ago." She paused, letting them absorb the gravity of the situation.

"Do you have any leads on the killer?" Astra asked.

"None yet. Right now, we're trying to cover as much of the city as possible. We've enlisted the Adventurer's Guild to ensure the culprit isn't hiding among their ranks. As far as I'm concerned, they're one of the few groups powerful enough to match a Valour Knight in combat," Morrigan stated, pacing behind her brown desk.

The light cores hanging from the ceiling illuminated the room, casting Morrigan's shadow against the high, arched wall. Pillars lined the space, leading toward the doorway, with arches connecting each one. The lower half of the walls was painted dark red, while the upper half was a cream colour. The floor featured black and dark red tiles, except for the centre, where a white circle bore the image of a red, wolf-like creature.

Is that creature representing her 'Hellhound' nickname? Lazarus wondered, his eyes drawn to the intricate design.

"How are adventurers strong enough to compete against your Valour Knights? Shouldn't they be the strongest if they're protecting the city?" he asked, still examining the room.

Astra patted him on the leg, refocusing his attention.

"Sorry," Lazarus apologised. "Normally, I wouldn't question the commander, but if Astra is in danger by joining your company, I want to know as much as I can."

"You're right, Lazarus. Whoever is killing my knights must be strong. I don't think they would target inexperienced individuals such as yourselves, but I don't suggest letting your guard down—especially within the city walls," Morrigan said, halting her pacing. Her smoky grey eyes peered down at them.

"I don't intend to, Commander."

"As for the adventurers, they fight against hordes of creatures in the tower. We knights don't have the luxury of spending all our time there to grow stronger. Instead, we hone our acquired skills to make up for the difference in power. You could be level 50 with high stats that make you feel powerful, but none of that matters if you can't surpass a knight's combat experience. That's why we practise active combat regularly. I want my knights to be prepared for battle at a moment's notice."

"So, combat experience would trump someone more powerful? Is that how you plan to defeat this killer?" Lazarus asked.

"If only it were that easy. Whoever is killing my captains hasn't left any evidence to reveal how they fight or what skills they use. I cannot risk my knights' lives when I don't know my enemy. I'd rather face them myself than put their lives on the line," Morrigan replied, a slight hint of anger escaping through her calm demeanour.

"Is there anything we can do to help?" Astra asked her commander.

Morrigan pondered the question, resting her face on her hands as she sat.

"I'd like both of you to stay out of this investigation. Neither of you can do anything as you are. I suspect the target has skills that allow them to infiltrate places undetected—skills neither of you have any hope of defending against. Lazarus, you're entering the Tower today, correct? Take Astra with you. Help each other grow. That's all for you, Lazarus. I'll have to ask you to wait outside for a moment," Morrigan said, nodding toward the door and waiting for him to leave before continuing the conversation.

"Is everything okay, Commander?" Astra asked after watching Lazarus exit the room.

"Astra, your lightning technique—who taught you that?"

The sudden question took Astra by surprise, leaving her momentarily speechless. Morrigan continued, "Let me tell you a story from when I was a young recruit—a knight in training. The call to arms came when the Oni army from the southern Summer Kingdom invaded the Winter Kingdom. A terrifying force known for their brute strength and ruthless combat prowess. Our squad perished during their onslaught. Even with my body battered and broken, I stood firm against them. If that was to be my final stand, I had nothing to lose. So, I strapped a dagger to one of my hands and fought with everything I had to show them hell. One by one, bodies piled up around me, drenching my clothes in crimson. Their remains were unrecognisable, the stench repugnant."

"That all sounds like a great story, but what does that have to do with my lightning technique?" Astra asked, growing impatient with Morrigan's tales of war.

"Listen, I'll tell you."

Astra slumped back in her chair with a huff.

"As I was saying, they surrounded me. With no escape, I saw that as my final moment in this life. Their commander appeared before me, wondering who was taking out her warriors. Instead of ending my life quickly, she decided to challenge me. Confident in her own skill, she handed me a healing potion so I could fight properly. Who was I to refuse? I took it, guzzling it down while her army laughed from the sidelines."

Morrigan paused, scanning her office before standing up. She moved to a chest beside her hanging armour and retrieved a pair of damaged gauntlets—standard metal armour, crushed.

"These are the gauntlets I wore during that war. They're not as tough as the armour we wear now, but they did their job back then. A memento from a time that could have been my last."

"What happened in your fight against the Summer Commander?" Astra asked inquisitively, her interest in the story now apparent.

"Oh, so you do want to hear my story after all. That's what I like to hear." Morrigan chuckled. "The fight against the commander? Well, they made a spectacle of it, forming a large circle so we could go all out against each other. I remember thinking, 'A fight against their commander? This is my chance to make a name for myself, to end this war if I can land a fatal strike.' Let's just say it didn't go as planned."

Morrigan ran her hand along the gauntlets, tracing the deep indents across the back.

"The commander gave me a vicious smile before bowing, then grabbed her rounded mace—a weapon that looked untouched but radiated power, like a massive tidal wave crashing down on me. I'll never forget the striking blue of that weapon or the way water seemed to sway along its centre.

"I returned the bow, lifting my head just in time to see her rushing toward me. In desperation, I punched the ground, sending a geyser of fire up beneath her, forcing her to leap into the air. Unfazed by the flames, she coated her mace with water, the spinning vortex around it a spectacle to behold. I stumbled backward as she descended, guarding myself with my gauntlets, igniting them with as much aura as I could muster. Despite all that, her mace smashed through my defence, shattering my gauntlets— and my hands with them.

"All of that from a single blow?" Astra asked, glancing at the battered gauntlets, which struggled to remain intact from the damage.

"Yes," Morrigan admitted. "I underestimated her power. I never imagined someone so young could be that strong. I knelt there, defeated. My hands hung by my waist while my arms trembled from the recoil. The commander smiled before grabbing me by the hair and dragging me across the ground, shouting to her army about how weak and feeble we were.

"I wanted to fight back, to scream at her, but my defeat had left me broken. The shame I felt was overwhelming as their gazes bore into me. Their laughter humiliated me further, and they spat on me as my body was pulled along the sun-scorched sand. Eventually, she completed her circuit of the circle and tossed me back into the centre. My body tumbled along the blistering dunes. 'Again!' she shouted, tapping her mace on the ground to taunt me."

Morrigan turned and punched the wall. The shock reverberated through the stones, sending a puff of dust into the air.

"I tried one more time—a last-ditch effort to reclaim my pride as a knight. This time, I focused on close combat. My attacks either missed or struck her mace, which she used to deflect blows. Each punch felt like hitting a stone wall; every kick sent a ripple into an endless abyss of the ocean. Once she had tired of toying with me, she swung her mace towards my head. I wanted to defend against it, but my body wouldn't move. Instead, the Commander froze. Her head twisted in both directions as electricity flickered through the crowd, followed by the rumbling of thunder. Shouts and cries erupted from the Oni army as they scattered. More lightning surged across the battlefield, and the Commander screamed in fury before giving chase to the one who had interrupted our fight. Emerging from the flames that had encircled the army stood a lone knight in silver armour, wearing a snow-white hooded cloak. He stared down the Commander, his presence radiating an aura that rumbled louder than any storm cloud."

"My father. It was my father who rescued you. He told me of his time as a knight, but he never mentioned becoming a Commander or having to fight one," Astra said.

"I didn't know your father personally—he oversaw the entire company and didn't have time to tend to every squad during that war. Despite that, he fought to protect as many as he could. But by the sound of it, he was modest. Not many knights hold back from talking about their achievements—the people they rescue, the enemies they defeat.

Regardless, he was the one who saved me from certain death. I would recognise that lightning technique anywhere, Astra. Though, it seems you don't have any control over it, do you?" she asked, leaning closer.

"Unfortunately not." Astra stared at her hands, tensing them. "Since my fight with you, I haven't even been able to release that lightning energy properly—just static. Apparently, out of fear from battling you."

Morrigan laughed while Astra smiled nervously. "Yeah, that'll do it. That fear is temporary—you'll learn to overcome it in time. Fear warns us of danger. Without it, we'd walk straight into death's clutches. Learn from your mistakes, and you'll become a powerful knight. You may even surpass your father one day," Morrigan said.

"Before I go, do you know anything about my mother?" Astra asked, rising from her chair.

"I didn't know anything about your mother. I am sorry for the loss of your father, though—he was a great man."

"Thank you… Commander," Astra said before leaving the room.

Morrigan watched her go, then murmured to herself, "The son of the Crimson Blade and The Seer, and the daughter of The Roaring Thunder… How will the two of you outgrow the shadows you walk in?" She opened a drawer in her desk and pulled out a sword, its blade etched with glowing runes. "I won't let you down, Commander Astro. She'll become the strongest knight of this kingdom under my watch."

CHAPTER 11

Lazarus and Astra found an open space outside the garrison where he could perform the ritual to create more spirits. On the outskirts of the city of Baylor, they had a clear view of the giant statues lining the bridge that led to the Tower. However, their sight was partially obstructed by the Mistbrook Forest and the vast chasm known as the Frozen Valley, which arched over the forest.

Lazarus drew a rune circle on the ground, placing the water core at its centre. He then added two outer lines with runes inscribed between them, ensuring the water symbol was positioned at the heart of the design. Astra leaned against a nearby tree, watching with curiosity.

"How do you already know what to do?" Astra inquired.

"When I obtained my skill the other day, a surge of energy coursed through my body, granting me the ability to summon spirits. As for the circle, Aldo gave me a book containing the necessary information on various summoning techniques, including the design for this one."

Lazarus generated mana at his fingertips and placed them around the small circle surrounding the core. In response to his mana, the runic symbols lit up with a blue aura.

"You need to either know the name of the spirit you're summoning or clearly envision its form."

A water spirit—free-flowing, gentle, yet powerful. Calm or violent. Water can take many forms in nature, but what about creatures?

Lazarus thought of home, of the days spent fishing on the frozen lake, of the various creatures he had caught.

"I know now what shape you will take. Come to me—I summon you!" he commanded.

Water emerged from the runes as the core glowed blue, reflecting the depths of the ocean. The rising water converged around the core, lifting it into the air and absorbing all its energy. The liquid mass expanded into a large sphere, swirling faster and faster—until it suddenly burst, drenching Lazarus.

From a distance, Astra laughed. "Of course, you'd get splashed when summoning a water spirit, Lazarus!"

He wiped the water from his face, glancing back at the summoning circle. The light had faded, revealing a creature resembling a small axolotl about the length of his arm. Its pale blue skin contrasted with its dark blue external gills, and its four legs allowed it to walk on water. A darker shade of blue formed the coastal grooves along its sides while its dorsal fin mimicked the surface of the water. The creature floated in the air, racing around the summoning circle.

"Mist. A fitting name for that kind of greeting, don't you think?" Lazarus called out to the spirit. It floated over to him and settled on his shoulders. Surprisingly, his clothes remained dry.

Stepping toward the circle, Lazarus placed his hand on the water symbol, releasing mana to transform it into a symbol of ice. "Alright, Mist, Shadow, let's summon another spirit," he said, placing the ice core in the circle to begin the next summoning.

"Don't forget your distance this time," Astra reminded him.

The runes froze over before a pillar of ice rose from the circle, lifting the core trapped within.

"The frigid winter has no place for the weak. This spirit will embody the strength of the frozen north. You will howl with the wind; you will conquer those who freeze in your presence. The frozen emperor. Rise! I summon you!"

The core began to crack, releasing a white light. A soft purr echoed from within the ice pillar. Claws scratched at the frozen walls until the ice shattered, sending an icy chill through the air. From the broken frost emerged a small feline creature, licking its paw with a tongue of ice. It took the form of a frost cat, its white fur marked with frozen stripes of light grey. Its pale blue eyes reminded Lazarus of the frozen waters surrounding Baylor.

"Ísarr! You and I will become unstoppable."

"Ísarr..." Astra whispered to herself, glancing at Lazarus with a worried expression.

The frost cat glared at Mist, letting out a hiss that sent her scurrying behind Lazarus' feet in fear.

"I've still got the lightning core to summon, but I need to recall these two. Keeping them out too long drains me."

Lazarus raised his hand, withdrawing mana and creating two black portals with swirling purple energy beside him. One portal had edges frosting over from the cold emanating within, and Ísarr stepped through without hesitation. The second portal rippled like still water, carrying the cool breeze of the sea. Mist peeked out from behind Lazarus' legs before quickly hopping into it. Both portals vanished once they had entered.

Lazarus switched the ice symbol to a lightning rune, preparing to summon a lightning-element spirit. He activated the summoning circle with his fingertips, causing the air above them to crackle with electricity. This time, a larger sphere formed within the circle. Without warning, lightning struck, followed by the deep rumble of thunder.

"Not only will you be fast, but you will also have the strength to charge through all enemies in your path. You will call upon the storm clouds above to strike down your foes."

The core pulsed with electricity, lifting itself within the circle before colliding with an invisible barrier. The energy it produced emitted a unique sound, almost like music. A deep rumbling followed as the core cracked open, and from within, a spirit leapt forth. It took the form of a horse, its cloud-grey body coursing with electricity while its sky-blue mane, tail, and hooves crackled with energy.

Astra's eyes lit up at the sight of the horse, and she glanced at Lazarus for approval.

"I'll call you Karah. Will you allow Astra to approach you?" Lazarus asked his new spirit.

Karah responded with an electronic-sounding whinny before turning to Astra and lowering into a bow. Astra reached out, running her hand along Karah's neck. The smooth surface tingled beneath her fingers, charged with static.

"She's gorgeous! I love her!" Astra exclaimed as Karah whinnied again. A surge of electricity ran through her hand while she was distracted, brushing against the mane.

"Ow!" She flicked her hand, trying to shake off the pain from the shock.

"I get sprayed by water, you get zapped by electricity—I'd say we're even!" Lazarus chuckled before calling Karah back. Another portal opened, this time crackling with electricity along the edges, the humming intensifying as it expanded. Karah trotted through, shaking her head up and down as she neighed.

"Ha, ha." Astra bounced on her feet. "Now that you have your spirits, what's next?"

"Before we can go to the Tower, I need to check in with the Adventurer's Guild. Are you coming with me, or do you want to meet at the bridge?"

"I don't mind walking. I want to see how the Tower process works with the Guild."

The halls of the guild were rowdy with impatient adventurers, all eager to leave for the Tower during the calm of a blizzard. Lazarus pushed through the bustling crowd, Astra holding onto his arm.

A girl bumped into him on her way out, her touch cold against his skin. "Sorry, I'm in a rush!" she called out in a rush.

For someone so small, they have a lot of hidden strength. Lazarus snapped around to identify her, but she had already disappeared.

"Oh, hello, Lazarus. Have you taken the time to learn your class skills?" asked Sadie, looking up from her paperwork as they approached.

"I have. On me, Mist."

Mist appeared on his shoulders.

"She's light. In a way, it's relieving to have her rest there, as if all my worries just wash away..."

"Doesn't she look cute! It seems you're ready to explore the Tower. If you could sign this paper? It helps us keep track of those entering the Tower. Be sure to sign again after you return," Emlin said.

"As you've just joined the guild, we can grant you access to the first ten floors on your own. It's not very profitable, but you'll be able to collect plenty of Aethercite and materials by defeating creatures on those floors. Every second month, we hold a rank-up assessment for our members, where participants are tested on their mental acuity, skills, and physical abilities. Aldo, Sadie, and I grade their performances. Although rare, some individuals can skip multiple ranks and advance significantly during the assessment. There are no prerequisites to enter, but since you'll be competing against other members, I suggest you become stronger first to achieve better results."

Emlin took a deep breath as she finished explaining everything.

The girls divided the available floors, listing the elite creatures found on each one. All were E-rank, with a reward of five silver each—the highest being for a Crescent Bear on the tenth floor and the lowest for a giant frog on the first floor.

"Do you see any good ones, Astra? If we managed to defeat Borus, I'd say that's the difficulty scale for a fifteen-silver reward."

Sadie interjected, "Actually, Borus was a B-rank assassin class adventurer turned bandit. Since you helped capture him, you received fifty percent of the reward—his full bounty was thirty silver tabs."

Lazarus glanced at Astra, both reminded of how out of their depth they had been fighting against him. They had barely survived, thanks to Sapphire's arrival.

"Well, if that's the case, I guess it's safer for us to stick with lower rewards—for now, anyway. We need to focus on collecting Aethercite to level up in the beginning," Lazarus remarked as he handed back the elites, with Astra following suit.

"We have ten options: the Meditator, the Aquatic Knight, the Dancing Mist, the Crimson, the Charging Tusks, the Ice Healer, the Drenched Venom, the Radiant Horn, the Waning Moon, and the Hunter," Lazarus read from the list of available elites.

"What do you think? Waning Moon resembles a Crescent Bear that we find roaming The Glades, but they were always too strong for us—we had to retreat on sight," Lazarus said, suggesting they avoid the bear.

"I suggest the Hunter. There's some information listed here. It's weak to ice, so Ísarr will be useful. It blends into the environment and uses ranged attacks. The camouflage could be a problem, but I'm sure we can find a way to counter it if necessary. We have experience with forest battles, so I think we should go with the safer option."

Lazarus nodded in agreement before handing the remaining elites back to Sadie.

"Okay then, I'll confirm your choice with Aldo. The floor location is listed at the bottom of the page. The elites will have others protecting them, so I suggest buying mana and health vials as a precaution," Sadie said, bowing her head as her sun-kissed locks flowed over her slender shoulders.

"We'll be sure to do that. Thank you, Sadie, Emlin," Lazarus said before exiting the Guild.

☆☆☆☆

In an unknown location, a circular room was lined with elegant marble pillars that supported a short ceiling, which led into a higher domed ceiling. Large, cream-coloured doors with an intricate design swung open. Twelve figures, each wearing a featureless white mask, entered the moonlit room. They were draped in black cloaks, each adorned with a golden embroidered animal on the back. Taking their seats in heavy, carved chairs at a round table, they positioned themselves according to the animal symbols on the table and the corresponding images above the pillars along the walls behind them.

"You all know why we are here today. Our protégé has severed their connection with us, and we must decide how to handle this situation," announced a man wearing a white mask with only eye holes. His tone was calm yet regal. He rested his hands together on the table, his gaze shifting to each of the other members of the Zodiac. "We lost our subordinate somewhere in De Albo."

"What do you mean 'we?' Snake was responsible for controlling her. Should it not fall to her to retrieve the young one?" a woman asked, a monkey symbol embroidered on her black cloak.

"You are quick to blame others, Monkey. I haven't seen you do anything helpful as of late," Snake remarked.

"Enough. We are not here to argue amongst ourselves. Our priority is dealing with Levanna. I will be sending two of you to handle her personally," Dog said, his commanding voice silencing the two Zodiac members immediately.

"I've been itching for a battle, my lord. Send me!" Ox shouted, pounding the table, causing vibrations to ripple across its surface.

"I ask that you refrain from using violence in this place of gathering, Ox."

Ox sank back into his chair.

"I have already chosen the two who will retrieve Levanna. Goat, your ability is best suited for this task. You will take Ox with you as a backup. Deal with the others as you see fit, Goat. Are there any objections?" Dog asked, shifting his gaze between each member.

No one spoke. Satisfied, he rose from his chair.

"The two of you will leave immediately. We cannot waste any more time—she will become a hindrance if left alone."

With a tap on the table, the chairs shifted. Zodiac rose in unison and exited the room one by one.

CHAPTER 12

Travelling north through the snow, which had risen to Lazarus' shins, Astra struggled more due to her shorter height, though her armour provided adequate warmth against the chill.

As they neared the gates to the bridge, they were stopped by guards on duty.

"State your names!" one of the guards grunted, his voice as gruff as his appearance—a middle-aged man with a scruffy beard, wearing the familiar owl helmet of the kingdom. He had crossed spears with his fellow guard, a younger, clean-shaven man with brown hair.

This is the kind of greeting we get when leaving the city? He seems grumpy, and this other guard looks no older than us. Though they do seem serious about their duty, Lazarus observed.

"Lazarus, and this is Astra, a new knight in Captain Zachariah's squad," Lazarus stated, gesturing towards Astra, who looked surprised.

"You already know who my captain is? I haven't even been told that yet..." Astra said, sounding disappointed. Still, she put her fist to her chest in the common salute of their kingdom's knights. "At ease, guards. We're heading to the Winter Tower today. May we pass through?"

"Ah, y-yes! I did receive word that newcomers would be passing through today. As you were!" the man replied, his voice still harsh. The two guards returned their spears to their sides and stepped aside to make way for the travellers. "We'll make note of your departure. Pray you make a safe return!" He struck his chest with a fist, producing a loud clang.

The cool sea breeze met their frosted faces, forcing them to wipe them as they walked across the bridge. Lining the sides of the bridge were gigantic stone statues of former knights. The sight of the sea was a moment they had to take in. Lazarus leapt onto the side of the bridge to admire the view, where the frozen sea met the cliffs of the mainland.

"Astra, come take a look! The sea is turning to ice around the city," Lazarus called out.

"I don't want to climb up. Can you come back down?" Astra responded with a panicked tone, holding her arms to her chest as her breath turned to frost.

The two of them glanced back at the city, noticing that the clouds forming above it looked different from those over the mainland.

"Astra, there's something different about those clouds. They don't look natural to me," Lazarus commented, noting their position and size.

"You're right... Wait, didn't Sapphire mention the snow only started recently? That it doesn't usually snow above the city like this? When we return, I'll have to discuss this with Commander Morrigan or Captain Sapphire."

"We can't focus on that right now. Let's go! I don't even know what the Tower looks like, let alone its interior," he said excitedly, already walking off on his own.

Astra glanced once more at the clouds above the kingdom before putting on her helmet and chasing after Lazarus.

The cold snow stung Lazarus' face as he ran down the path through Mistbrook Forest, past the Frozen Valley—a massive chasm of ice.

He could only trail behind Astra as she faded into the distance, the wind rushing past his body, his heart pounding in sync with his footsteps on the snow-covered ground. In the distance, he spotted a mountain where people gathered at its base. An ancient gate of howlite marked the entrance, with adventurers waiting outside, equipping their gear and checking their inventory before stepping through the arched gateway.

At the base, Astra stood watching him with a coy smile, clearly proud of beating him to the Tower. Lazarus slowed his pace until he was face-to-face with her, coming to a halt with his hands on his thighs, taking the chance to catch his breath.

"You're still no match for the Queen of Speed."

That confidence is what I love about her. I'll always push her to her limits—one day, she'll leave everyone behind with that speed of hers. I fear for the enemies who have to face her! Lazarus thought as he stepped closer to the entrance.

"So, this is the entrance to the Winter Tower? It looks ancient, almost otherworldly."

Awestruck, Lazarus took a moment to admire the Tower's exterior. A person wearing the same uniform as Aldo approached them.

"You must be Lazarus and Astra. I heard you'd be partaking in your first journey into the Tower today, with a request to do 'The Hunter' Elite battle. My name is Marv, and I'm the guild correspondent for this Tower."

His posture was formal, matching his suit. He bowed at the waist, one arm crossing his chest. A man of around forty, he had pale skin and chestnut-brown hair tied back in a ponytail. Though Marv's physique didn't appear particularly strong, being a correspondent of the Tower surely required a certain degree of strength.

"Yes, you must know a lot about this Tower if you're in charge, right?" Lazarus asked, walking back to Astra's side. "I came to find answers in this Tower."

"Is that so? Well, I'll answer any question I can. In the meantime, take a seat over here so we can log your visit."

He gestured toward a small, whimsical building. Inside, shelves lined with mana and health vials stood against opposite walls, while a heavy book lay open on a desk at the centre of the room. Marv glanced at Astra's knight uniform.

"A knight as well. Working together, you two should have no trouble clearing your first elite. The Hunter is one of the strongest elites within the first ten floors, but as long as you stay vigilant, you'll have nothing to worry about. Its strength lies in dexterity—you may find it difficult to land a hit."

"Thank you for the information. I have a question for you, Marv. Do you know anything about Adelheid the Seer or Cyrus the Crimson?" Lazarus asked abruptly.

Marv stared at him with a blank expression before snapping out of his daze.

"…I have not heard those names in two decades… How do you know them, Lazarus?" Marv stared, intense, wide-eyed, and unblinking. Lazarus leaned forward in his chair.

"They're my parents. I know about their classes. They visited this Tower, and it became their last known location. So, I plan on finding out why they disappeared."

Marv nearly fell back into the chair behind him. Astra watched with an amused smile, leaning on the back of Lazarus' chair with her arms crossed.

"P-p-parents, you say? Those two had a child together before they disappeared? Remarkable! Yes, I know about them. The last time they entered this Tower, I was still an apprentice here. They reached floors no one else has managed to since then. Whatever happened up there must not have been good. I don't suggest rushing to the top—take your time and reach it when you're strong enough. Otherwise, you too may come face to face with the Abyss."

"So, they didn't reach the top floor, then? What was the last floor they reached?" Lazarus asked.

"I believe it was past the seventieth floor, though I don't remember exactly which one," Marv answered after a moment of deep thought. "Now, as for your elite, the Hunter—it uses stealth to its advantage, hunting its prey from afar with incredible archery skills. It is guarded by Lizardfolk that spawn from a crystal inside the dungeon, each wielding spears, swords, shields, and all manner of weaponry.

"As an earth-type creature, the Hunter is a Skogjeger, and along with the patrolling Lizardfolk, they all have a weakness to Ice. I'd say that's about all the information I can give you, Lazarus. I pray you live up to—no, exceed—your parents' achievements. Create a new legend as you climb the Tower. I will be observing your efforts. May your endeavours bear success!"

Marv smiled, ushering them toward the entrance—an icy cavern lined with howlite walls.

Footsteps echoed through the hallway as Lazarus ran through the entrance, stopping halfway to gaze up at the ceiling—twenty metres high, taller than any he had seen before—dazzling with crystalline splendour. Astra followed at a casual pace, also admiring the architecture of the white interior. Streams of what appeared to be water flowed along the edges of the floor into transparent tubes that extended throughout the tower.

"Does that water reach all the way to the top, Marv?" Astra asked, glancing behind her before Marv could close the doors.

"…Oh, no, that is flowing Aether. But it does look like water at first glance—take another peek. I'll take my leave now." He bowed at the waist before disappearing behind the sealed entrance doors.

Astra examined a nearby tube and saw that it was indeed Aether. The ethereal flow emitted a glow that illuminated the walls of the tower.

"That can't be possible… The density of the Aether flowing together— where is it all coming from?" she murmured to herself, following the tube's trail to the opening of the main interior room, lighting the path with a soft blue aura.

Lazarus rushed over to her, guiding Astra into the main room.

"Feast your eyes!" Lazarus spread his arms wide as he entered the vast circular room at the base of the Tower. A spiral staircase along the outer wall ascended as far as he could see, levelling out at each floor before another staircase rose further. The stairway was supported by giant pillars that connected to each floor—pillars with cracks of transparent textures revealing the flow of Aether.

They scanned the room, packed with a huge crowd of Adventurers, ranging from scrawny, inexperienced recruits to hulking warriors, armoured knights, and powerful mages, all equipped with various weapons. Most had grouped together to venture into the Tower's dungeons, while others chose to explore alone.

"It's busy in here. I wasn't expecting so many people to gather inside," Lazarus said to Astra as they made their way to the staircase.

"By the looks of it, I'd say this is a waiting area. The guild wouldn't want everyone fighting over each dungeon, so they take turns. Though, some seem to be here just for the thrill of combat," Astra replied, eyeing a group of gruff-looking men brandishing bloodied swords, axes, and daggers.

"Best to stay clear of them. I don't want to get involved with others if I can help it."

"Make way! Wounded coming through!" shouted a guild correspondent, escorting a wounded adventurer whose clothes were soaked in blood. As they descended the stairwell, the crowd at the base dispersed.

"So it is a dangerous place after all. I wonder what elite they fought," Lazarus commented.

"This isn't a good sign, Lazarus. You have to be on high alert when we reach our floor. We can't end up like him."

The correspondent met with another as a green aura emanated from her hands, enveloping the wounded adventurer and sealing the gashes covering his body. The man looked shocked, staring at the ceiling before suddenly bolting upright, consumed by fear.

"Well, if it isn't the newest Summoner of the guild! What was your name again... Lazlo?" a deep voice called from behind them. The two turned to see a short man clad in heavy bronze armour, his thick, russet-braided beard peeking through his helmet.

"It's Lazarus," Astra corrected, stepping in front of him.

"I recognise that armour. You're a part of that group I saw when my class was selected, right?"

"Indeed, I am! I'm here waiting for the rest of Arcanum to arrive. I'm sure they'll be eager to hear how your first Tower Dungeon goes. I won't keep you. The name's Jules. I'm still deciding whether you'll survive or not. Nox thinks you will, Lucia agrees with him, while Orion and Delilah think you'll die," Jules said, polishing an axe nearly as large as himself.

"I suppose I'll be disappointing a few of you then. When they get here, you can tell them I have no intention of dying today," Lazarus replied before turning back to the staircase.

Jules chuckled. "I'll be sure to pass the message along. Until we meet again... Lazlo." His gaze never wavered as the two continued up the staircase.

"Was that the newbie, Jules?" asked a man dressed in all black, his face hidden beneath a hooded cloak. He stood a foot taller than Jules, his physique noticeably slimmer.

"It sure was. He's a confident youngster—mentioned he has no intention of dying."

"Well, we'll find out tonight if his first dungeon run is successful."

"He doesn't seem all that impressive. Maybe he'll come back missing limbs, or the girl will return with his lifeless body," interjected a tall, lanky man. His jet-black hair draped over his shoulders, and he wore a white coat adorned with grey icy patterns paired with dark grey pants.

"Always doom and gloom with you, Orion. I see this as a wonderful opportunity. If he succeeds, we could invite him into the party—his class is valuable in these dungeons," replied a tall woman clad in white armour with gold accents, resembling an angel. Her lustrous, wavy golden-blonde hair framed her face, and she held a large silver battle hammer in one arm, resting it on her shoulder.

"Hush now. We have our own elite to focus on—we can't afford to be distracted by that young runt," said a woman with an alluring tone. She wore a dark blue winter dress with sleeves that wrapped around her thumbs, plain black thermal leggings, and blue ankle boots.

"You're right, Delilah. Looks like we're all ready. Time to head up!" Nox said assertively, leading the way to the staircase. The other members of Arcanum followed closely, exuding powerful auras.

CHAPTER 13

Astra followed Lazarus up the stairway, a blue glow appearing with each step, lighting their way.

"The Hunter is located on the seventh floor, so it shouldn't take us too long to climb," Lazarus said, his gaze fixed ahead as he ascended the stairs.

"Right. It's quite a drop when you look over the railing. It's a wide staircase, but I wonder—if it ever gets crowded, would people have to wait to move?" Astra mused, following him at a stiffened pace.

"What's wrong? Usually, you'd be ahead of me, racing to our destination," Lazarus said, turning to see Astra pressing a hand against the wall, away from the railing, her body almost frozen with fear. "Oh, I get it! We never had to deal with heights in the mountains since the range surrounded the village, blocking the view. Here, Astra, take my hand."

He hopped down a few steps toward her, grasping her free hand with his own.

"Phew... I-I didn't expect this to affect me this badly. I'm sorry, Lazarus. This is supposed to be your big day, and here you are, having to look after me," Astra said, her voice rising as fear overwhelmed her. She squeezed his hand, inching forward one step at a time. "Don't stop. Please keep going!"

"Okay, okay! Wait—I've got an idea, though it might be embarrassing," he said, turning to look her in the eyes. Astra instinctively tried to retreat, but he held her hand tightly.

"Close your eyes if you have to, but this will be much quicker!" Lazarus wrapped an arm around her back and legs, cradling her in his arms. With her legs supported, he sprinted up the staircase. The air rushed around them as Astra clung to him tightly, her eyes squeezed shut.

Before long, they reached the seventh floor, passing dozens of adventurers who watched them with curiosity. Lazarus glanced down at the bottom floor.

We must be at least a hundred and fifty meters up by now! I can't blame her for being scared, but it would be great if she could take in the view.

"Oh, crap!" he thought as Astra glared at him.

Her face was tense with annoyance that he was still holding her so close to the edge of the stairwell. Lazarus quickly set her down, rubbing the back of his head with a nervous laugh. "Will you accept an 'I'm sorry?'"

"No one ever hears about this," she said, her voice a mix of anger and embarrassment.

"Well, we're here. You no longer have to worry about the height," he said, trying to smooth things over.

A woman in a black suit stood by the entrance, where mana swirled above in the shape of a humanoid chameleon aiming at its target. A seal of mana restricted access to anyone not accepted by the guardian.

"Excuse me, we're here to challenge the Elite known as 'the Hunter,'" Lazarus said, addressing the floor guardian.

"You must be Lazarus. If you're ready, I'll disable the barrier so you can head in. Are you prepared?" the female guardian asked.

Lazarus stared at the seal as it dawned on him—the weight of the world he was about to enter, the same world his parents had faced on their journey up the Tower. He hopped on the spot to shake off his nerves, flicking his hands and exhaling deeply.

Astra stepped up to him, taking his hand in a gentle squeeze. "You're not doing this alone, remember? I'll be here with you, fighting by your side. You have Shadow, Mist, Ísarr, and Karah as well to help you. Just focus on what you need to do, and we will all help you defeat this creature," she said, her gaze serious and unwavering.

"Yes, we're ready," Lazarus confirmed with determination, reaching behind his back to grab his staff.

Astra rested her hand on the hilt of her sheathed sword, ready to draw it when the time came.

The female guardian pressed her hands against a rune beside the entrance—a towering archway covered in the red mana of the seal. The barrier faded like burning paper, granting them access to the room. A menacing aura engulfed them as they stepped inside, hearts pounding, unsure when an attack might come. Guided by a white light, they pressed forward. In the distance, the sound of scurrying echoed, growing ever closer—until they reached the light.

"There's nothing else but this light... I'm going to go through it..." Lazarus stated, moving his hand into the glow. *Warmth... I haven't felt this warm anywhere in De Albo!*

Leaping into the light, Lazarus found himself in a completely different environment. The bitter cold of winter had vanished—no snow covered the ground, and the soothing sound of running water filled the air. He stood in a lush rainforest, surrounded by towering trees, exotic plants, and unfamiliar bushes. The terrain was a mix of grassy earth and muddy patches where water met land, with dirt tracks winding in several directions through the forest. In the distance, he could hear bare feet squelching through the mud, birds whistling in the treetops, and small creatures scurrying about, foraging for food. The air was fresh, carrying a warm breeze. *What is this place? It's so different from home!*

Suddenly, a sharp swish sliced through the air, slashing his backpack. Lazarus lurched forward before rolling to the side.

"Ísarr, to me!" he shouted, raising his staff.

A portal of black mist appeared, chilling the air as a low purr echoed along the creek. White paws, bound in icy manacles, emerged from the portal, intercepting Lazarus' assailant. The creature clamped down on a massive spear, freezing it, then raced along the weapon's handle to sink its fangs into the neck of the towering lizard warrior. The reptilian foe, standing three metres tall, dropped its shattered spear and lashed out, kicking the ice spirit—only for its arm to be severed in an instant. Astra had appeared between them, skidding across the mud as her blade sliced through its limb.

"Lazarus! Are you okay?!" Astra shouted, her voice raised with adrenaline. "There's one more—get back on your feet!"

Using his staff for balance, Lazarus stood up, his clothes now muddied from rolling through the dirt. "Great, my coat's covered in mud now…" He glanced over his shoulder to assess the damage, then removed his cloak and shook off the excess mud.

"Seriously?! You got attacked by a creature almost twice your height, and you're worried about your cloak?" Astra scolded him.

Ísarr had just finished off the first lizard warrior by freezing its body and was now targeting a second, launching ice spikes from the frosty patches along his fur.

"It's not just any cloak—it's one that Maeve made for me. I don't want it ruined because of a mistake I made." Oblivious to the ongoing battle, Lazarus continued shaking the cloak a few more times before letting it soak in the flowing river, rubbing away the remaining mud.

Meanwhile, Astra had joined Ísarr in the fight, ending it with a coordinated attack—Astra slashed the enemy's chest, and the frost cat followed up with an ice-claw strike, splitting the body into two frozen halves.

"That's better!" Lazarus exclaimed, pulling his cloak from the water, now free of mud. "Good job, Ísarr! Exceptional as always, Astra. Anyway, I won't need the cloak in this rainforest—the humidity alone is enough to make me sweat," he added nonchalantly, kneeling to fold it.

Astra's piercing stare bore into his back.

"Are you finished with your cleaning routine yet? More Lizardfolk are bound to investigate the area—we need to move on, Lazarus." She tried to hurry him along, succeeding only after they heard the snap of a tree branch in the treeline. They slipped into the opposite forest to evade their enemies, recalling his ice elemental spirit to conserve mana. He disappeared into his portal just as their pursuers emerged from the other treeline.

The two of them observed from a distance.

Another pair… that seems to be their patrol formation. Pairs of Lizardfolk cross patrolling routes to stay alert for invaders, Lazarus thought.

A snarl came from one of the patrol lizards, signalling the rest of the unit in the forest. In response, others began snarling as well.

Astra touched a small sphere attached to her belt, which started glowing with a cobalt aura. Lazarus did the same, pulling Eclipse from his bag.

"Eclipse, I need you to update my status quietly," he whispered, almost lying flat on the ground to avoid detection.

"Aethercite accrued. You have reached Level Three, gaining a total of ten skill points," Eclipse said in a hushed monotone.

"I don't have time to think about which ones to choose… It's in the Beast Tamer section… *Tame* looks similar to *Spirit Creation*, and *Growth* should help me in the long run."

Lazarus allocated his stat points, feeling a surge of energy flow through his body, enhancing his strength, spirit, health, and dexterity.

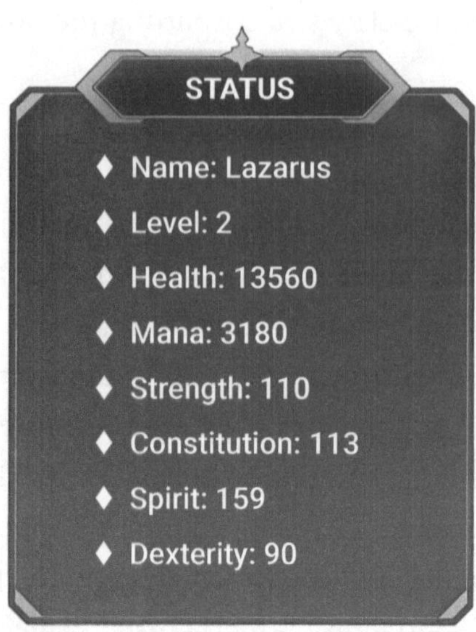

"Is that how you update your status, Astra?" Lazarus whispered.

"The orb attached to our belts—it's the same process you use. Smaller orbs are more convenient for us in the middle of combat. I can show you my status later, but now isn't the time for this discussion. We have more lizards approaching. Head behind that tree; I'll stay behind this rock. We can ambush them as they pass or take them out when they turn around." Astra refocused on the situation, creeping backward along the rock.

Lazarus moved over the moss-covered ground, but the squelching sound of each footstep made it difficult to stay quiet, alerting the lizards.

They're closing in... How should I handle them? Ísarr seems effective against them. I think the safe option is best for now, he thought.

Rain began to fall, halting the lizards' advance and distracting them as they turned their gaze toward the darkening sky.

"Rain... that's it! A perfect chance for you to stand out. Karah, strike them down!"

Several more Lizardfolk had gathered in the same spot, scanning the area. The air around Lazarus crackled with static as Karah charged up electricity from her mane, lowering her head toward the group of lizards standing in a puddle. In an instant, a bright flash erupted as a bolt of lightning surged from Karah's mane, striking the water and electrocuting six of the lizards. A low rumble followed as their bodies collapsed to the ground.

"Eclipse, how was that?" Lazarus asked, crouching back down after peeking around the tree.

Eclipse updated his status once again, granting Lazarus access to his next growth ability.

Lazarus scanned the environment, hoping to locate the Skogjeger. Instead, he spotted a strange, glowing crystal embedded in the ground, with stone forming its support.

You look interesting, Lazarus thought as he signalled Astra toward the crystal.

"What do you think that is, Astra?"

"All of this is new to me, so I have no idea, but it's worth a closer inspection," she replied, creeping toward the crystal.

Before they could reach it, the glow intensified, and a lizard warrior emerged from the crystal, letting out a guttural snarl.

"Fall back, Astra!" Lazarus commanded in a loud whisper.

She retreated to the tree line, observing from a distance.

"We found our answer. It looks like these crystals spawn those lizards, but they don't produce multiple at once. Do you think there's a limit?" she asked with a mischievous smile.

"I like where your head is at. If the Elite isn't going to show itself, we might as well use this opportunity to collect Aethercite."

"Whoever defeats the most wins!" Astra called out as she broke into a sprint toward the nearest patrolling pair.

Lazarus rose from his crouch and ran for Karah, leaping onto her back.

"At least give me a warning before you start!" he shouted from atop Karah, who began firing bolts of lightning at the Lizardfolk, heading in a different direction.

"So, you're going to use lightning? Let's see if I can use mine too," Astra said before taking a deep breath, clearing her mind to focus on the mana within. Erratic energy danced wildly inside her.

Exhaling fully, she closed her eyes. A spark ignited within, electrifying her mana. A lizard sneered at the crackling energy and rushed at Astra, spear thrust forward.

Opening her eyes in anticipation of the attack, Astra leapt onto the spear, slicing her electricity-coated blade along its arm before driving her boot into its jaw and flipping off its shoulders. She landed in a crouch and launched herself at her target, sword in hand, aiming to pierce his chest. Electricity surged along the blade into drenched flesh, frying every wet surface it touched.

"One down, let's keep this up!"

Astra took a step and zapped forward—only to crash into a bush. "Not again! It's still not ready to use… but I can't let that stop me. Keep pushing, Astra! One more time."

Sitting back up, she brushed herself off and rose to her feet, charging her aura as she locked onto a new target.

Bodies piled up around the rainforest until none remained in sight. Lazarus leapt into a treetop and checked his status.

"You have reached level five, with twenty available skill points."

Lazarus proceeded to update his stats, ensuring he stood a fighting chance against the Elite, and allocated his points to acquire new skills.

Astra was surveying the area from the ground when Lazarus jumped down behind her. She looked exhausted—sweat dripped down her face, and strands of hair stuck to her cheeks.

Lazarus placed a hand on her shoulder. "Astra, how are we doing? I don't think we can keep fighting those Lizardfolk—we need to find the Skogjeger." He had sent Karah back to conserve his mana for the decisive battle, drinking a mana vial as he sat beside Astra.

"There's no… sign of… it anywhere," she said, her breath shallow. She turned her head to glance at Lazarus before falling backward onto the ground. Lazarus huddled over her, reaching into his bag.

"Here, drink this! You've used too much mana—take it easy for now. Join me when you're ready," he ordered, handing her a mana vial. "It will restore half of your mana, but it'll be enough to get you back on your feet."

An aura of danger swept over the rainforest. Birds abandoned their perches, escaping into the sky, while other animals scrambled up trees to hide or burrowed into the ground. Lazarus felt a presence behind him— an eerie sensation as if unseen eyes had materialised in the air, piercing him with the cold stare of a hunter stalking its prey.

"Shadow! I need your help," he commanded, summoning a portal of black mist. Shadowy tendrils emerged, intertwining to form his dark elemental spirit. "Can you help us locate the Elite? It should be camouflaged, hiding in this forest."

Shadow bowed before retreating into the darkness. As the spirit faded, Lazarus observed the countless shadows stretching across the forest, realising just how many places the Elite could be hiding.

A minute passed. Astra had recovered enough energy to stand.

A whistle echoed through the treetops. Suddenly, Lazarus lurched forward. He glanced at his shoulder—an arrow had pierced it. He and Astra shifted their attention toward the source of the attack and spotted a humanoid chameleon hanging from a tall tree in the distance. Its beady eyes darted around before it vanished again—only this time, a shadow stretched from its body, spreading its wings.

"Good job, Shadow. Now we can track the Elite." Lazarus smirked. "We have our marker—I'm going after him. Ísarr... Mist!"

Breaking into a quick stride through the forest, he yanked the arrow from his shoulder, unfazed by the injury. While keeping an eye on Shadow darting around the terrain, he retrieved a health potion from his bag and drank it as he ran, the green liquid dripping from his mouth.

Another arrow whizzed past him, this time grazing his cheek.

"His accuracy improves with each shot... He's learning. This could be bad if the battle drags on." Lazarus narrowed his eyes. "Ísarr, freeze the trees—don't let him climb any surfaces! Mist, reduce visibility. I want us harder to target."

Issuing his orders, Lazarus homed in on the Skogjeger, who was now darting toward a lake with a towering waterfall—before vanishing into the safety of his camouflage.

Shadow spread its wings along the mountain, revealing the Elite's location. Hiding beside the cascading waterfall, he perched atop a small ledge, high enough to overlook the entire forest.

Idiot! I walked straight into his trap! Lazarus thought as he stared up at the Hunter, who had his bow aimed directly at him.

The creature pulled back the bowstring, aiming above himself. Its strange eyes darted around, scanning the forest below until they locked onto Lazarus as he emerged from the cover of the trees. A long finger released the string, sending the notched arrow soaring across the lake in a perfect arc toward him. With no time to dodge, the arrow struck his arm—the one he had instinctively raised to shield his chest. The impact knocked the wind out of him, and he fell backward onto the ground.

Fog rolled in from the forest. Lazarus, his gaze burning with intensity, stared at the creature as the mist enveloped his body. The Hunter peered down, searching for him, but the thick fog obscured his vision.

"Now we'll show you what it's like to fight an enemy you can't see. Come, Hunter."

The challenge was set. Lazarus had survived his opponent's bait, frustrating the Hunter.

A screech echoed from across the lake as the Hunter prepared his next attack. He loosed multiple arrows in rapid succession, bombarding the forest. The projectiles pierced trees, struck unsuspecting critters, and shattered small rocks, turning the once-still landscape into chaos.

Prowling the mountaintop, Ísarr stalked the Hunter, peering down from a rocky perch, his eyes shining bright blue. Frost filled the air around his paw, freezing the ground as ice inched closer to the Elite.

The crack of ice was all it took to alert the Hunter. Twisting his back as he leapt off the platform, he fired into the air, an arrow piercing it's paw. A painful hiss followed. Not wanting to let this chance slip by, he pounced toward the Hunter. Both fell off the cliffside, locked in a brief battle of ice shards and arrows, shattering against each other.

Ísarr homed in, leaping off discs of ice he created mid-air, catching the Hunter with his fangs. His frosty breath froze the Hunter's shoulder. In retaliation, a lengthy tail wrapped around Ísarr, twisting their positions. Using Ísarr as a foothold, the Hunter fired his arrows into it's chest until they crashed into the lake below.

Water turned to ice. Ísarr, too, became ice, forming a frozen tomb for the Hunter. Cracks spread through the ice with each thud, bubbles escaping through the fractures. Then, the Skogjeger burst out, drenched in water.

Mist confronted Skogjeger, flitting about while levitating water spheres, forcing the Hunter to dodge atop the frozen lake, his bow ready for a counterattack.

With powerful legs, he leapt into the air to evade another blast of water, aiming his arrow at Mist and firing upside down. As Mist stared at the projectile hurtling toward her, an eruption from below sent a geyser of water into the air, intercepting the arrow and sapping its force.

Mist swirled through the air, sending arrows of rain toward the elite, shattering the icy foothold. The chameleon-like creature used its tail to regain balance. Forced to retreat, the Hunter headed into the fog-filled rainforest. Unable to see clearly in the dense mist, he relied on his hearing—only to be met with an eerie silence.

The Skogjeger stalked through the forest, the trickling of flowing water and the splashes of rain against the muddied ground filling the air. Leaves rustled. An arrow pierced through the falling foliage.

"Okay, you found me." Arms raised, Astra stepped backward, revealing a snow-white cloak trimmed with fur. Whirling at the sound of an arrow being released, she deflected the tip with the flat of her blade, then thrust toward the Hunter, her sword poised to block. "I won't be an easy target."

Astra swung her sword down at the Hunter, striking against its metal bracelets. A green tail, striped black, whipped around her blade before curling around her arm and slamming her into the ground. She recovered quickly, sweeping her legs at the Hunter. He leapt over the attack, notched an arrow, and fired. The shot narrowly missed, nicking her helmet.

"Astra, fall back!" Lazarus shouted from within the fog. The elite turned at the sound and loosed an arrow in his direction. The fog began to dissipate, static crackling through the air as the hum of charged lightning energy filled the space.

"You've put up a good fight, Skogjeger, but all things come to an end," Lazarus said with a devious smile, holding an arrow aimed at the Hunter's face.

Atop Karah's back, Lazarus sat sideways, tapping her shoulder to signal the attack. Karah unleashed the immense lightning energy she had gathered, condensing it into a sphere before releasing it. Bolts of lightning tore through everything in their path, striking the Skogjeger.

His drenched, scaly skin reacted instantly, conducting the electricity across his entire body and paralysing him. His muscles seized, and his grip tightened involuntarily. The crackling of burning flesh filled the air with an acrid smell. He collapsed, smoke escaping from his lungs.

"I can't let your skill with a bow go to waste. You're going to join me—become my hunter."

Lazarus knelt beside his fallen enemy, placing a hand on his shoulder. Mana flowed from his palm, enveloping the elite warrior. Charred skin gradually reverted to its original state as Lazarus completed his **Tame** skill. When the magic subsided, a single purple handprint remained on the Skogjeger's shoulder.

The Skogjeger pushed himself into a kneeling position, using his bow—crafted from two large rib bones—for support. On closer inspection, he wore tan leather harem pants, his chest bare except for the metal armbands encircling his wrists. An animal skull mask obscured his face.

"A Radiant Horn skull for a mask? Eerie and intimidating. I'd expect nothing less from a hunter who wears their trophy," Lazarus mused. "Your name will be... Jaeger."

With that, Lazarus recalled all his spirits, including his newly tamed companion. Overwhelmed by mana exhaustion, he stumbled forward and collapsed. Astra caught him, lowering herself against a nearby tree and cradling his head in her lap.

"That was an impressive plan—using the environment to your advantage. Ísarr forcing Jaeger into the water, Mist driving him away from the lake into the fog, and Karah's lightning striking a soaked opponent. Maybe you should consider becoming a knight; you'd make a great captain," Astra said jokingly, knowing he would never want to engage in warfare.

She glanced down at Lazarus, lying on her lap, his soaked clothes clinging to his skin.

You've even put on more muscle since we came to Baylor. It won't be long before the scarred child I remember becomes nothing more than a fleeting memory, Astra pondered, stroking his hair.

"You need to rest. We defeated the Skogjeger, so we can wait until we both have the energy to travel back to Baylor, okay?" she said.

CHAPTER 14

Frosty breath escaped cherry lips, a scythe of emerald sliced through a crashing wave, freezing on contact to form a wall of ice, facing the girl wearing a checkered skirt was a man with several tendrils of water holding severed hands.

"The Collector. It seems each of your hands not only wield a unique weapon, but they also use different elemental magic." She said while observing her opponent, the way he twisted and contorted his body was inhuman.

"I'll be adding those slender hands once I'm finished with you!" he hissed, hands shot out with bursts of water, the girl jumped forwards through the water tendrils severing the link by freezing the water with her scythe.

"You and I are the same, we both collect handy skills. I'll be collecting your skill too." She stated while running along the frozen tendrils, leaping as she reached the end of their trail. The Collector shouted in frustration trying to regain his control of the hands.

Losing track of the girl, the Collector broke the frozen tendrils and brandished his own weapon, a cleaver wet with blood. "Where did you go?! Show yourself you coward!" he shouted while frantically scanning the surrounding landscape. An abandoned dam with overgrown rats scattered about the ground, sliced in half. The ground damp with water leaking out from rattling pipes, along the walls frozen water rising from a tunnel below them.

Cold steel grazed his neck, drawing blood, he escaped its embrace. Laughing echoed through the tunnels, "Let's continue our dance, come find me." She whispered, a haunting voice.

The Collector gazed at the two tunnels, running through one of them with his cleaver in hand, a red scarf flapped in the breeze along with tussled dark hair. "Who are you?!" He shouted, a leg appeared in front of him knocking him to the damp stone ground with a thud.

"I'm Krow, the rising star." She stated, pressing her foot against his throat, he gagged with a reddened face. She leered at the Elite with disdain, lifting her leg with reluctance.

"You're strong, too strong for me, but maybe I can be of use to you. Get me out of this place." He pleaded.

"Now, why would I want to do that? I enjoy coming here and fighting all of you elites, you help me become stronger."

"This place is hell, I don't want to stay here any more, I'm tired of fighting."

"Tired of fighting? But you haven't put up a fight yet, do you know what it means to fight with your life on the line?" she glared at him.

The Collector began to run, his destination unsure, led by fear, he ran as the girl gave chase enjoying the thrill of the hunt. One by one his limbs severed to reflect his way of life, an atonement for his sins.

CHAPTER 15

"The Scavengers have finished collecting the cores of the deceased. We will transport them to Byron's shop. I've also reported the quantity and element of each core," Marv stated, holding a scroll detailing all the cores they had procured.

"What happens then?" Lazarus asked.

"Byron has his own storage. He can manipulate the size of the cores, allowing him to store thousands in the back of his shop."

"Ah, Magnus! Good to see you again. Coming back for another round?" Marv greeted a burly man with salt-and-pepper hair and a short beard. He wore brown boots, thick steel-grey pants, a dark red cloak, and a red coat underneath. Magnus adjusted his silver gauntlets, ensuring they were positioned properly over his gloves.

"Sure am! I'm going to defeat that beast—I may even claim him as my own!" He thumped his chest, letting out a chuckle. "And who do we have here... Lazarus, the new summoner?" He peered down at Lazarus as he strode toward Marv, swinging his arms with gusto.

"Yes, I am," Lazarus replied, gazing at Magnus.

"Have you had any offers to join a group yet? As a fellow summoner, I think we could wreak a lot of havoc in this Tower. What do you say, son of Adelheid?"

Lazarus jolted, the sudden mention of his mother shocking him.

"Surprised, I take it? Don't fret—I was close friends with Cyrus and your mother. Of course, I'd recognise their child." Magnus chuckled, his belly shaking, as he proceeded to sign his name on the check-in forms.

"I have plenty of things I can tell you about your parents, boy. Another time, perhaps?" Magnus said, marching through the entrance with a wave.

☆ ☆ ☆ ☆

"Fall back, Jules!" Lucia shouted as she slammed a giant shield in front of herself, bracing for impact against the icy breath.

"I'll cast Resist Frost! Stay close to me, everyone!" Delilah called out, releasing mana from her hands that coated each of them in a protective aura. Jules and Nox positioned themselves in front of Delilah, while Orion stood behind her, aiming his bow at a large flying creature hidden behind the freezing breath.

"If you have the shot, you need to take it, Orion!" Nox said impatiently, shielding his face from the frost.

"I'm on it, Nox. You can't rush precision…now." Orion whispered as the frost breath dissipated, revealing an Isskala—an ice-element wyvern whose wings released frost as it flew, leaving a trail of ice in its wake.

The arrow followed the path of the frost breath, striking the Frostwing in its left eye. It let out a shriek of pain, flailing its wings as it crashed into the frozen cavern walls.

"Let's finish this while it's distracted!" Nox shouted. Arcanum followed close behind the Frostwing, ready to strike once it came closer to the ground. Another thud echoed through the cavern as the wyvern writhed in pain.

"Nox!" Lucia called out, holding her shield in place to launch Nox into the air. Jules grabbed the other side of the shield as Nox ran toward them.

"Time to finish this, Arcanum," Nox said as he leapt onto the shield. Lucia and Jules lifted it with all their might, launching him high into the air. Nox rocketed past the wyvern as it struggled to regain its bearings.

He held his daggers close to his chest until he met gravity's resistance, then twisted midair, spinning upon his descent. "It's been fun, Frostwing, but this battle was decided the moment we arrived," he whispered to himself. His daggers, infused with dark energy, transformed into black tendrils that formed rings around his body.

"Requiem aeternum."

A shadowy slice—silent, invisible, yet lethal—severed the wyvern's head in one smooth, precise motion.

Nox landed on the frozen tundra with graceful poise, sheathing his black daggers. A heavy thud rumbled behind him as the wyvern's headless body hit the ground, sending a wave of snow toward the group.

"I have to say, your technique has improved, Nox!" Jules praised as he made his way behind Delilah, who stood at the centre of a magic circle, preparing a spell.

"I've been practising the technique at home. I don't believe in perfection—that ideology limits a person's mindset and hinders their growth. Instead, I prefer to hone all my techniques, pushing them to greater heights," Nox replied as he joined the rest of the group.

"Wise words. It's a good philosophy to live by. Take my magic, for example—something as simple as a gentle breeze could become a strong gust, a destructive cyclone, or even a tornado, if you add Ice element it becomes a blizzard. Magic has a wide range of elemental spells." Delilah said as she cast her spell. A howling wind of frost swirled around the group, moving in sync with the motion of her hands. Drawing the wind towards herself, she condensed it into a ring that encircled her body.

"Here we go—another over-the-top magic spell. Do you always have to be this extreme, even after we've defeated the Dungeon Elite?" Lucia said, planting her shield once more to brace for impact.

"What can I say? I love magic," Delilah said with a proud smile as she launched her ring of frost towards the wave of snow. It expanded into a massive ice elemental blast that tore through the landscape, leaving a colossal Ice shard in its wake.

"Be thankful I grabbed the core before you used your magic. Nothing remains when you do that," Nox commented as he lobbed the core over to Delilah.

"That's why you're the leader—you think several steps ahead," Delilah replied with a mischievous smile.

Arcanum added another cleared dungeon to their repertoire. At floor fifty-nine, they were leading the climb of the Winter Tower.

CHAPTER 16

Arriving at the Garrison, Astra parted ways with Lazarus and headed to the eastern district in search of a tavern.

Lazarus continued onward, making his way to Byron's Alchemy store. The door chimed as he entered, revealing Byron toiling away behind his counter with a bright red core in hand.

"Byron! How are my cores?" Lazarus called out to get his attention.

"Bloody hell, boy, don't you know how to knock first?"

"Isn't that the point of the door chime?" Lazarus replied, glancing toward the entrance.

"Anyway, I've gone ahead and condensed your cores. They were all E-rank, but you had enough to bring them up to C-rank. I could create a B-rank core if you're willing to buy more E-rank ones, though." Byron rubbed his hands together, watching Lazarus expectantly.

"That sounds good to me. Another spirit will be helpful. What element were they?" Lazarus asked, handing over a silver tab.

"These ones are neutral cores. They don't have an element yet. I can imbue an element into your core for twelve silver."

I can choose an element, then? I've already got Dark, Ice, Water, and Lightning. Fire, Earth, or Air would be a—

"Hello? Did you hear me?" Byron interrupted his thoughts.

"Ah, sorry, I was lost in thought. Fire. I'll change it to a Fire core, Byron. Also, can you add in another Water core? Any rank will do."

"Let's see… Water cores… I have D- and C-rank ones available."

"I'll take the C-rank one, then. Another Water Spirit could be useful," Lazarus said, accepting the core with a grateful bow.

The heavy snowfall blanketed the area in pure white. Unable to see more than a few metres ahead, Lazarus hugged the edge of the snow-filled pathway, illuminated by light cores, as he made his way to the guild. The busy crowd scurried for shelter from the snow.

"It's a good thing the paths are lit with cores. I can follow this all the way," Lazarus muttered, making his way across the bridges connecting the islands to reach the southern one.

Braving the intensifying blizzard, his pace quickened into a sprint. His heightened dexterity and constitution enhanced his stamina, each step propelling him forward in powerful strides. Faces blurred as he sped past the sprawling crowds, reaching the guild steps without breaking a sweat.

"Oh, Lazarus! You're back much earlier than we expected. Neither of us thought you'd return before tomorrow. I guess having company made for an easier experience?" Sadie said as he walked towards her, brushing the snow from his clothes. "If you can sign this form, we can hand over the ten gold tabs for the reward. I also have a message for you—the Arcanum group would like to meet with you. If you have time, I suggest speaking with them in the guild hall before you leave."

Arcanum? What would they want with me?

A wave of black mist assaulted Lazarus as he stepped into the guild hall. Darkness engulfed him, leaving only a single figure sitting in the distance. The overwhelming pressure buckled his knees, sending him crashing to the floor. Clutching his chest, he struggled to breathe.

Aura Sense! Lots of blue mana, yellow, red, green... black—that's the one suffocating me.

Pulsing black waves of mist emanated from a person sitting in a booth. Dressed in black, their face was hidden beneath a hood, arms spread along the cushioned backrest.

Mustering all his strength, Lazarus rose to his feet, shooting a glance at the hooded figure, whose lips curled from a straight line into the vicious smile of a predator. His vision returned. The hall was once again filled with the laughter of adventurers, drinks in hand, the strong scent of booze wafting through the air. No one else seemed affected. *They targeted me. Why?*

"There's the son of the famous couple. You've got a strong will to resist my aura," the man in black said, pointing a dark blade at the seat across from him. "Come, take a seat."

"You know, sitting down with strangers—especially ones who greet me like that—doesn't work for me. I'd rather stand because whatever you want to discuss won't take long," Lazarus said, clenching his fist.

"Well, no need for hostilities here. We're all friends, aren't we?" A hidden threat laced his words as he offered Lazarus a chalice of red wine.

Lazarus knocked the chalice away, sending the liquid splashing onto an older man with walnut-colored hair and a braided beard. The man slammed his fists on the table, nearly jumping out of his seat.

"Watch it, Lazlo!" Jules bellowed, his voice booming through the hall. Lucia gripped his arm, trying to calm him.

"It's Lazarus, Jules," corrected a woman with light golden-blonde hair.

"The name's not important! What about my bloody drink?" Jules spat, his face growing red.

"Enough, Jules." The hooded man leaned back. "So, you didn't like the greeting. That's okay. We invited you for a reason. Delilah, you do the honours."

Delilah, dressed in a dark blue mage outfit, stepped forward. Her mage hat, almost too large for her short frame, cast a shadow over her sharp eyes.

"We are a party with the goal of conquering the Towers. Together, we've made it more than halfway up the floors. As the child of legends and a summoner, you would be a strong ally to us. We offer you the chance to join our party, gaining riches, fame, and power. What do you say, Lazarus?" Delilah asked, leaning against the table and propping her head up with her hands.

The man lifted his hood, his eyes reflecting a snowy forest under a moonlit sky—a stark contrast to his pitch-black outfit and hair as dark as midnight. "I wanted to see your potential. It doesn't matter what rank you are; as long as you have the mental fortitude to face a challenge head-on, I'd say you passed with flying colours," he said. He appeared a few years older than Lazarus.

"While our goal of climbing the Tower aligns, I do not wish to join any groups," Lazarus said.

"That may be so, but I'm sure we could be of value to you. Think about how fast you could climb the Tower with all of us aiding you," Lucia added. She picked up a half-eaten burger and devoured it.

"I'm still going to refuse. Maybe one day we can team up for a Dungeon, but I have no intention of joining groups at the moment. My reason for climbing the Tower is personal. I don't—" Lazarus began.

"Excuse me! Hi there, I couldn't help but overhear your conversation. It seems this is another failed attempt to recruit a summoner. Arcanum, how does it feel?" the woman said as she placed a hand around Lazarus' shoulder. She was short, with straight black hair, one side shaved and hidden beneath a black hood. Her eyes glowed brighter than any emerald, and a pair of skulls adorned her ears. A checkered plaid skirt swayed as she twirled gracefully around Lazarus.

The laughter stopped abruptly, and the music faded to match the hushed crowd. Silence.

All attention was drawn to them, eyes flickering between the girl and Arcanum.

"It's nothing new to us—or that muscle-brain, Magnus. But what about you, Krow? Having everyone turn their backs on you before you even get a chance to interact with them? Is it lonely, having no one to fight alongside, to share a laugh with... to fall in—"

Krow clenched her hand. She breathed out, easing the tension in her body.

"How about we see if your friends are strong enough to take me on? What do you say, little Nox?" The hand resting on Lazarus' shoulder lifted into the air as an ominous aura filled the hall, sending the crowd scattering. Krow twisted her neck to the side, glaring at Arcanum, who stood in their booth, weapons in hand. "How about a dance, Arcanum? I have energy to spare for all of you."

"Enough!"

A thunderous shout came from the entrance as the stout figure of Aldo barged into the hall. Weapons clattered to the floor, and adventurers scattered.

"Why is everyone running off?!" Aldo glared around the massive hall, veins bulging as his gaze locked onto those at Arcanum's table.

Lazarus shivered at the sound of Aldo's voice, too nervous to move.

"It was m—" He started to speak, but Aldo cut him off with a furious tone.

"Don't even think about taking the blame, boy. I know damn well you didn't instigate this, and I won't tolerate others letting you believe otherwise."

Aldo leered at Arcanum, his heavy boots stomping across the white marble floor.

"I know it has to be one of you—or Krow. Every time these halls descend into chaos, the perpetrator always comes down to one of you. Now speak!"

Nox raised his arm, commanding the other members of Arcanum to sit.

"It was me who started this, though I had no intention of it becoming such a big scene. My apologies, Aldo. I'll accept any punishment you wish to give me, but please leave my team out of this."

He vanished, reappearing behind Aldo.

"So, what's the punishment?" He winked at Lazarus.

How did he move that fast? I didn't even see him move.

The gap in power felt like a vast chasm, growing ever wider.

"For the act of using your aura on another member of the Guild outside of our rank assessment, you will be suspended for a week. That means you are forbidden from setting foot in the guild hall or exploring the Tower. Do you accept the punishment?" Aldo challenged Nox with a sharp stare as Nox began walking toward the exit.

"Thanks for leaving my team out of it, Aldo. I accept the punishment. I'll see you all in a week." He paused, glancing back at Lazarus. "Lazarus, make good use of this time. I expect to see you in the rank assessment next week—don't disappoint me."

With that, Nox bowed toward his group before departing.

"Lazarus, walk with me to my office, please," Aldo said, turning his attention back to the young summoner-in-training.

Krow cast a sideways glance at Lazarus, a mischievous smile playing on her lips.

Of all the reactions she could have after that, she chooses to smile. Did she plan to have Nox suspended? Maybe I'm overthinking this...

Lazarus waited in front of the desk as Aldo took a seat in a chair with a high, arched backrest and padded cushioning.

"First matter to attend to—I would like to congratulate you on your first successful venture into the Tower. I hope to see many more from you, Lazarus! The second matter I want to discuss is Arcanum. They're made up of powerful adventurers, all of them A-rank. You would think that's enough for them, but it isn't. Among all their classes, they lack a summoner to provide the crucial support of numbers," Aldo said, peering at Lazarus through black shades.

"They're after the summoner's ability to create an army, but why would they need that when they're already powerful?"

"Exactly right. They covet the ability to summon powerful allies to fight alongside them. Arcanum may be composed of formidable individuals, but with only five members, they lack the strength in numbers required for certain floors of the Tower," Aldo commented.

"If a group of powerful adventurers seeks numbers, what kind of threats lurk within the Tower, Aldo?" Lazarus asked, taking a seat as he became more invested in the conversation.

"Hidden within the Tower are dungeons that contain Deities. Unlike the elite monsters found in normal dungeons, these Deities wield incredible strength, possessing abilities that regular adventurers cannot hope to fight against alone. Arcanum wants to challenge these Deities to clear all the dungeons. Only by defeating every Deity can one reach the top floor."

Lazarus perked up in his seat. "Deities? So the Tower isn't just filled with wildlife and creatures, but mythical beings as well? What do you gain after defeating a Deity?"

"Keys. Each Deity holds a unique key that we believe unlocks the sealed door at the top of the Tower. I managed to obtain one of them during my days as an adventurer, though it cost me my eyesight," Aldo said, removing his shades to reveal clawed scars along his misty, unseeing eyes.

"I never noticed you were blind. How do you manage to walk around without assistance?"

"Indeed, I am, Lazarus. Aura sense is valuable—I can sense everyone's aura in and around the island where the Guild resides. Everything else comes down to my Dexterity stat. Without it, I don't think I'd be able to move as I do. Now, the Deity I tried my hand against was a warrior with eight elemental phases. I was twenty-eight at the time. That warrior killed my entire team. I was lucky it only took my eyesight. Lazarus, out of respect for your parents, I advise you not to battle a Deity without a formidable team."

"I have a reliable team of my own. I trust them to help me climb the Tower," Lazarus replied, summoning Ísarr. Its frosty aura began freezing the floor beneath it.

"Don't overestimate yourself, Lazarus. I've witnessed powerful adventurers lose their lives because of overconfidence. The Tower won't show you mercy," Aldo warned.

"I'm not going to rush into danger. The Tower already took my parents—it's not going to take anyone else away from me. You mentioned the top floor needs keys. How many?" Lazarus asked.

"There are nine Deities. I haven't been to the top, but I'd bet the door requires nine keys."

"If you don't have all the keys, that means they didn't either. They disappeared on a lower floor. The question I now have is: which one?"

CHAPTER 17

"'Winter's Embrace'—this will do," Astra commented, stumbling upon a cosy tavern tucked away on the southeastern island. Warmth enveloped her as she stepped inside. Patrons sang, danced, chatted, and drank throughout the night—exactly what Astra needed to unwind.

This music… I've never heard anything like it before. Singing tales of old, the enchanting melody adds to the mystery of the Towers. A pleasant, harmonious tune, Astra thought while striding over to the bar.

"What's a young knight doing at a bar?" a man with a quiet voice asked.

Astra turned to find Alastor looming over her—an imposing presence. He wore loose-fitting, snow-white clothes with silver wrist guards, light grey boots, and a sapphire core attached to his belt.

"Alastor? I don't visit places like this often, but after our first trip to the Tower, I thought it would help me unwind. What about you?" she asked.

Alastor took a seat beside her, ruffling his snow-white feathered cloak.

"Ah, I see. From what I've heard, Lazarus' first Tower visit was a success. I'm curious to see how he holds up against the tougher creatures as he climbs. As for why I'm here, I come for the information. You can learn a lot in these taverns. Not to mention, this melodic music helps relieve stress." His voice was soothing—no grating noise or aggressive tones, just calm and peaceful.

Astra raised her glass, about to drink. "Stress? What do you have to stress about?"

"I stress about being the strongest in this city. It's a heavy burden to bear."

"You're quite confident about that. I think Commander Morrigan could defeat you."

"Ah, yes, Commander Morrigan—the pride of the Kingdom of Baylor. Her command over Fire and Earth sparks envy in young knights." He turned towards Astra, a smile forming on his face. "She gave me a worthy fight, yet I still managed to defeat her… though I doubt she'd ever admit it."

"You've defeated her? Sorry, but I don't believe you. Also, you seem to pop up wherever I go. Is that intentional, or am I overthinking it?"

"…It might be intentional. I sense a strong aura within you two. I don't know what it is about the two of you, but you've piqued my interest. Coincidentally, other matters I'm attending to have brought me to this island," Alastor responded, staring into his mug.

At a table behind them, a group began discussing the recent death of a Valour Knight in the city, prompting Alastor to tilt his head in their direction.

"Our auras? I've no idea what you're talking about, Alastor," she said, shrugging off the comment.

"Anyway, the weather has been getting worse lately. I think we're in for a blizzard over the next couple of days. I suggest staying in and waiting it out." He sculled his drink and set the mug upside down with a cheer.

"What do you know about the clouds, Alastor?" she asked inquisitively.

He stopped after a few steps, turning back toward Astra with a knowing smile. "You've noticed them, too, then? Like I said, stay indoors tonight. You don't want to be prowling the streets after dark," he warned, his tone ominous as he walked away to join a group of patrons.

"…They say she died two nights ago—a stab wound through the stomach. Even that tough armour she always wore wasn't enough to—" whispered one of the patrons in the group behind them.

"A round for these fine gentlemen! I'd like to hear more about this female knight you speak of," Alastor interjected, squeezing in between two of the patrons.

Astra shifted on her stool to stand, hearing a faint crumple in her pocket. Reaching in, she pulled out a note with two words: Black Blade.

A voice called out to her from a table away from the music. Astra wondered who was speaking and glanced in their direction. A group of six men sat at the table, feasting on succulent meat and fruit while drinking from chalices of wine. They wore their knightly attire but had left their armour at home.

"Astra? We hear you're going to be joining our squad. Is that true?" asked a man with scruffy brown hair. None of them appeared old; most were in their early twenties, though one seemed to be over thirty.

"Yes, I'm Astra. I heard Zachariah is the captain of the squad I'm joining. Is that one of you?" she asked while memorising their features. Two of them were identical, with blonde hair, brown eyes, and slim builds. Two had brown hair—one was rotund with blue eyes and a scruffy, curly hairstyle, while the other was muscular with brown eyes and a neat, straight hairstyle. The last two had black and blonde hair, respectively. The blonde-haired man had a more mature appearance with sea-green eyes, while the black-haired man had eyes that resembled the moon.

"That would be yours truly. Pleasure," the man with red hair said, extending his hand to grasp hers in a firm handshake. *For a captain, he seems gentle,* she thought with a smile. "Meet the rest of the group. There are only a few of us here, but each squad has up to twenty knights."

One by one, they introduced themselves, getting into a playful scuffle over who would go next.

"My name is Ronan. This little runt is my brother, Konan. We're Archer-class specialists," said the man seated on the far left.

"Cut it out! We're the same height, you idiot," Konan retorted, pushing his brother away.

"The name's Theo. I'm a water specialist Guardian," the larger man said in a loud but warm voice. The man to his right struggled to silence him before he drew too much attention.

"I'm Lorenzo. A pleasure to make your acquaintance, Miss Astra. I am a mesmerising magician," a suave voice came from the black-haired man, who was doing his best to charm his fellow knight. Astra ignored him.

"Don't mind the simpleton here—he thinks he's a gift sent from the heavens. I'm the Assassin of the group, Zachariah, but my friends call me Zach." He tried to cover his fellow knights' mouths, his wavy blonde hair swaying in the struggle, while he simply smiled.

"Last but not least, I'm Tobias, a Cleric. I'll try my best not to let any of you die," Tobias said in a calm yet morbid tone, holding his hands in a praying gesture, amber beads wrapped around one hand.

"You already know my name. As for my class, I've been assigned the Knight class—a lightning specialist. I am in your care," Astra said, bowing as she introduced herself. The others exchanged glances before breaking into laughter.

"So formal—the way she bowed, 'I'm in your care!'" Ronan said, clutching his stomach as he tried to contain his laughter. Astra stared at each of them before stopping at Zach.

"I apologise for them. It's one of the few nights we get to unwind. As for you, there's no need to be so formal around us—we're here to have fun, isn't that right, boys?!" Zach pumped his fist into the air, chugging down the rest of his wine. "Astra, take a seat! There's no better way to get acquainted than with a round of drinks!" he shouted, catching the attention of the barmaid.

Outside the tavern, Alastor pulled his white hood over his head, its sky-blue eye-like patterns decorating the fabric. His feather-like cloak swayed in the wind as he walked along the quiet streets of the southeastern housing district. A familiar face passed by, muttering indistinguishable words under his breath. Unable to ignore the person, Alastor turned to follow him.

"Nox, is that you? It's rare to see you alone."

Nox leered at Alastor, his aura of darkened mist enveloping him. Alastor countered with his own aura, a swirling windstorm that blew away the mist, cancelling the mental attack. Nox came to his senses, backing away as he realised who he had attacked.

"I'm sorry, Alastor. I didn't realise it was you. I haven't been in the right mindset since Aldo suspended me. Apparently, having fun with the new adventurer is a no-go." He sat on a nearby bench, scratching his head in agitation.

"No offence, Nox, but your idea of fun never sits well with people who don't know you. You need to stop doing this to new members. You're lucky you only got suspended this time, but I doubt you'll be so fortunate if it happens again." Alastor took a seat beside him.

"Should you really be so close to me?" Nox warned, pulling out a short obsidian blade.

"Look, Nox, you can try to threaten me. We get into a scuffle, and it ends with your face pressed against the cold snow. I suggest you sheathe your weapon and go home," Alastor said confidently, refusing to look at him.

Nox rose from his seat and began walking off, turning his head once more to glance at Alastor.

"Yeah, I suppose you're right. Heading home is the best option for now," he said sarcastically, curtseying with his black cloak before vanishing into the blizzard.

Alastor watched him disappear into the heavy snowfall.

CHAPTER 18

Heavy snowfall reduced visibility—a leap into the darkness.

"It's not safe to walk around alone at night during this snowstorm. I'll help you get home safely. Where are you headed?" Krow had a powerful aura surrounding her. Lazarus would be surprised if anyone dared to attack her at night—or at any time of day, for that matter.

"I'm staying at Luna Requiem, but before I go there, I need to stop by Winter's Embrace to pick up my partner, if you don't mind," Lazarus replied.

Her smile faded.

"Oh, that's fine. The tavern is close by, so it's no trouble. What's your partner's name?" Krow asked.

The difficult path through the deep snow tempted Lazarus to summon Shadow.

"Her name is Astra. I've known her for as long as I can remember. She joined the Knights of Baylor yesterday," Lazarus responded happily. "Do you have a partner? I heard Nox's insults—I doubted you didn't have a loved one."

Krow's pace slowed slightly as she fell behind Lazarus.

"Stop… don't say any more, please. He was right. I don't have a lover—not anymore. He was a powerful man, the one who trained me when I first became an adventurer, we would fight together in the Tower, there was no one that entertained me the way he could. But we faced an opponent too strong for us at the time. He gave his life to protect me, to give me a chance to escape—so I did. I came back to find him, but it was too late. I became stronger to avenge his death. Since then, I've climbed the Tower alone, so I don't have to watch another person I care about die."

Krow's face grew sullen, her brows furrowed, and her eyes stared off into the distance.

"For what it's worth, I'm sorry for your loss," Lazarus said sympathetically. "I can't imagine losing Astra or what I'd do afterward."

Distant singing voices grew louder, and the lights of the tavern shone in the distance. Patrons stumbled out of the inn, holding onto each other, their unsteady steps crunching in the snow, the stench of alcohol lingering around them.

"Lazarus, I think I'll call it a night. My head is pounding…" Krow said, clutching the side of her head as she staggered against the stone wall. Her cheeks were flushed red, and sweat dripped from her forehead.

"Krow, what's wrong? I can escort you; make sure you get home safely." He wrapped an arm around her back to support her.

"Sorry for the trouble, I'll be fine. I used too much mana today—my body is starting to deal with the aftereffects. You go get your friend, Lazarus." Krow continued clutching her head, leaning against the side of the building for support.

That was strange. She had seemed healthy just a moment ago.

The tavern doors creaked open, and the heat inside burned away the chilly air. Lazarus shivered at the sudden temperature change.

Now, where is she? Knowing her, she'd want a spot with the best vantage point. Not the bar or the centre tables. The best view would be along the walls, where she could see the entire room, every entrance and exit. Her back would be covered if she got into a fight… or she could be drunk, where none of that would matter.

Lazarus turned to face the left wall where most of the noise emanated, and spotted her arm-wrestling the men at her table, boasting about her skill as a swordsman. Her speech was slurred, and she babbled nonsense as she waved her arm animatedly.

I should step in before things get any worse. Nothing good comes from her drinking alcohol, he thought, making his way toward her.

"Astra! I think it's time to go. Thank you for keeping her company, but we have to leave now."

Placing his hand on her shoulder, Lazarus watched as Astra shot up from her seat, drawing her blade and pointing it at him while swaying unsteadily.

"Great! Exactly what I didn't want to happen. Are you members of the squad she's joining? If so, I could use your help. When she gets drunk, she attacks anyone who tries to spoil her fun."

Lazarus tried to ask for help, but most of them laughed, enjoying the scene unfolding before them.

"What do you need me to do?" Zachariah asked, rising from his seat and reaching for his daggers—two pure white blades that reflected the light cast on them.

"We need to get her out of here first—without destroying anything in the process."

"I'll become the greatest knight, just you watch!" Astra shouted in a drunken stupor before launching the first attack—an upward palm thrust.

Lazarus tilted his head back, stumbling as Astra dropped to the floor and swept his legs out from under him with a round kick. She jumped onto his body, pinning his arms to prevent him from using any of his summoning techniques.

"Hey, big boy! Why are you—hiccup—all the way down there?"

"Alright, boys! We've got a rowdy recruit here. As recruits, we must show her how we handle these kinds of situations," Zachariah commanded.

Their laid-back demeanour shifted as six of them rose from their seats, looming over Astra while she remained atop Lazarus. She glanced up at them with a look of amusement.

"It looks—hiccup—like you want to play as well. You're all upside-down." Her words slurred as she laughed, shifting into a drunken battle stance. Her eyes, like those of a predator, darted between each of the men as electricity crackled around her.

"You lot! There will be no fighting in here—take it outside!" the barkeep shouted.

Heeding the warning, Zachariah was the first to strike, his daggers clashing against Astra's blade. In a flash of light, he dragged her out of the tavern.

Howling winds danced with soft snow, covering the island in a blanket of pure white.

"I can go fast too..." she slurred as an aura of electricity enveloped her—then she vanished.

"What's going on? You're supposed to stop her, not attack her!" Lazarus shouted, but the blizzard's roar drowned out his voice.

A rod of light pierced the snow at his feet.

"Lazarus, is it? The captain can handle her—we have to work together to restrain her movements."

"Shadow! Pin her down! We need to restrain her before anyone gets injured."

Wings spread wide across the cast shadows as Zachariah clashed with Astra—light versus lightning in a battle of speed. Another rod pierced the snow, casting long shadows toward their fight.

I see; he's creating more shadows for us to use.

"Shadow, hold your position. They're giving you more to work with—wait until it reaches them."

Another rod struck the ground, then another, until they were surrounded. Shadows stretched inward.

Shadow saw his opportunity—and seized it.

Astra tried to dodge out of the way, but it was too late. Shadows bound her arms, pulling her against the snow. Theo drew a circle with his hammer, creating a ring of water. The ring shrank around her ankles as she resisted with all her strength.

Ronan shot an arrow at the water, freezing it with a frost arrow, while Lorenzo grew vines from his palm to bind her in place.

"Get off me!" she yelled, wriggling on the ground. Blue mana seeped from her body, shifting to yellow as it crackled with electricity.

"Get back! She's using her lightning technique!" Lazarus warned, waving his arm to signal them to move away. Lightning burst forth, shattering her shackles. She glared at them, hiding her sword behind her back.

"Sorry for this, Astra, but I can't let you hurt anyone—not on my watch," Zachariah said as the pommel of his white dagger struck her solar plexus. Her eyes fluttered before she fell unconscious, right into Lazarus' arms.

"We can help. We'll make sure she gets home safe—this blizzard is dangerous!" Tobias said, shielding his face from the onslaught of snow.

"Yeah, we like her! She's fun!" Ronan shouted.

"I appreciate it. Don't worry, Astra, I've got you. I'm sorry it ended this way. Thank you, Captain—I'll take it from here," Lazarus said. "I know it's not much, but I apologise for the inconvenience. Will this do?" he asked, flicking a silver tab at Zachariah.

"It's not necessary. You keep it. For what it's worth, I'm glad to have her in my squad. Take care of her for me!" Zachariah called out.

Lazarus cradled her in his arms and sprinted through the dangerous blizzard.

"Who are you?" demanded a Knight of Valour as his diamond sword clashed against a black blade. One arm hung limp, dripping with blood, as they fought within a narrow alley. The mysterious figure uttered no words. Darkness enveloped the area, his aura overshadowed by a blackened cloud.

"What is this?!" the Knight shouted as an invisible force tugged at him, pulling him toward the centre—toward an imposing knight clad in pitch-black armour. Green plumage adorned their helmet, and a dark green tattered cloak billowed behind them. The closer he was drawn, the clearer the sight before him became. Dark energy swirled, culminating in a black hole that devoured everything in its wake. Unable to escape, the Valour Knight waited for the opportune moment to strike.

"Thy final place of rest," the black knight intoned, his hollow voice devoid of emotion.

In a final gambit, the Valour Knight stabbed the ground, and diamonds erupted in a display of colourless splendour. The crystalline formations resisted the pull of gravity just long enough for him to launch another attack. Leaping from the surface of a diamond, he aimed directly at the black hole.

"Thou dost display a brave attempt. I shall respond in kind," the black knight declared, a hint of pride in his voice.

Without warning, the black hole vanished, restoring normal gravity. The Valour Knight plummeted mid-air, crashing to the ground with a heavy thud.

The black knight sauntered over, his blade piercing the fallen warrior's back with eerie calmness. As the darkness receded, a heavy snowstorm took its place.

Carving an X into the Valour Knight's back, he watched as blood seeped into the surrounding snow, the fallen knight's tan skin fading to a deathly blue. With a flick of his wrist, the black knight flung the blood from his blade before embracing the abyss of the blizzard.

The wind howled through the night, mourning the deceased.

CHAPTER 19

Astra awoke from her slumber with a pounding headache. Rubbing her neck, she winced in pain. As she glanced around the room, her stiffened neck protested, and she realised she had no memory of how she'd ended up in her bed.

"Are you there, Lazarus?" she called out.

He popped around the corner, Mist resting on his bare shoulders as he bit into an apple. In his hand was a book labeled *Polearm Techniques, Volume 1.*

"There she is, awake at last, I see. It's already mid-afternoon—I'm surprised the blizzard didn't wake you. Anyway, how's your stomach? Zachariah sure gave you a whack," he said, handing half an apple to Mist.

Astra's gaze dropped to the scars on his chest—a glaring reminder of a tragic night.

"I have no memory of what happened last night. Why did Zachariah hit me?" She rubbed her temples with both palms, trying to recall any details.

"I came to pick you up at the tavern last night. You ended up in one of your drunken states. It was my mistake for grabbing your shoulder without warning."

"No... you're joking, right? Did I attack any of the squad? I must have made a fool of myself in front of them!" She slammed her fist into the blanket.

"Trust me, you didn't hurt any of them. They managed to subdue you easily—their coordination amazed me. It wasn't until you tried to use your Storm Walker technique that Zachariah had to step in and knock you out. They all offered to come along to see you home safely, but I decided to do it myself." Lazarus smiled. "Captain Zachariah also mentioned he's glad to have you on his squad."

"Sounds like I do, huh? I can't help but feel embarrassed regardless. I'm going to have to apologise to them," she said, lying back down. "... Lazarus, did you have another nightmare? You're up early again."

Lazarus froze. "...Please don't bring it up. You should be focusing on yourself, so rest up. We can't go outside in this weather anyway. I left some food on the bedside table for when you're ready to eat. Later, we train." He pointed at the table before leaving.

She glanced at his back, covered in more scarred runic symbols. *It still haunts him, after all these years. I'm sorry I didn't help you sooner.*

☆ ☆ ☆ ☆

"I've reached Level Seventeen just from that one floor, but I still need ten more points before I can obtain Growth Tier Three. The Aethercite I've been collecting from defeating enemies near those crystals has boosted my levels quite a bit. By now, I should be able to maintain a single summon for seventeen minutes. In my battle against Jaeger, I exhausted all my mana within three minutes by summoning all of them at once. I have to limit my summoning until I master the basics of mana control."

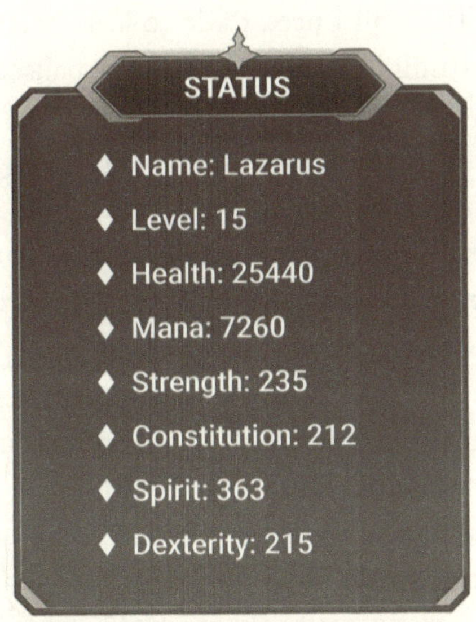

"If I want to stand a chance against Zodiac—the one Levanna believes I'm destined to fight—I need to get stronger fast. I have these books, so I can learn some basic weapon and mana skills. Using Spirits drains my mana constantly, so I need to find a skill that can counteract that drainage," Lazarus said, flipping through the pages.

Frustrated after failing to find what he was looking for, he opened the journal. "What can you tell me about mana skills?"

The page lit up with a blue aura as his mother appeared—a tiny spirit standing on the parchment.

"Mana control was one of my specialities. I had an abundance of Spirits, nearing the limit of two hundred. Using them together drained my mana within seconds, so I had to find a way to manage that weakness. I had an epiphany one day while visiting the Winter Tower. Upon closer inspection of the mana veins running through it, I realised mana could be drawn directly from the air. Through meditation, I learned to channel that mana into my body, gradually restoring my supply. It was a complicated process, but once I mastered it, I could sustain more of my summons at once. At higher levels, I assume you could prolong the regeneration process—or even increase the amount of mana you absorb."

"Meditation… That's all I need to do to learn this skill? This blizzard is the perfect opportunity to practise." Lazarus paused. "Were there any other useful skills you learned?"

"While not a skill, I did discover that strengthening my bond with my Spirits reduced the mana cost of summoning them. Your initial drain will be four mana per second for each summon, but as your bond increases, it will drop to three, then two, then one. My time was cut short, so I never learned if it was possible to summon them without mana."

"That's a lot of help. Now I have a clear direction to take while training my skills." He hesitated for a moment. "One more thing—I met another summoner named Magnus. Do you know him? He looks to be in his fifties, with short salt-and-pepper hair. I noticed he carried a brown axe with red and gold trims."

"Magnus?" The spirit let out a soft gasp. "Oh my… I haven't heard that name in a long time. He was a great man—a mentor to me when I first started out. You can't imagine how happy I am to know he's still alive! My son, Magnus is someone I would trust with my life. He may be boisterous, but he is a kind person. I'm sure he will teach you things about summoning that I never could."

"Thank you. That's all I need to know for now. Until next time… I love you," Lazarus said as his mother's spirit slowly faded away.

Closing the journal, he stared at the ceiling with an arm outstretched. *Wherever you are, I will find you.*

☆ ☆ ☆ ☆

"Sapphire, we have another dead body in the streets. Let's go!" Morrigan pulled on her dark red coat as she walked out of the office, calling out to Sapphire, who was busy filling out paperwork.

"On it, Commander." Dropping her quill, Sapphire rushed to the door, grabbing her own coat on the way.

"What do we know so far?" Morrigan asked as they ran to the crime scene. The blizzard raged on, reducing visibility, while the howling wind dulled their hearing. Morrigan used her fire aura to melt the snow in their path.

"All three victims were members of the Knights of Valour, all of them living in the south-eastern district. If I recall correctly, Hugo also lives in that district," Sapphire informed her.

"Sapphire, investigate the deceased knight while I go pay Hugo a visit. If we're lucky, our perpetrator will be in the area as well. Stay safe!" Morrigan glanced at Sapphire for a moment before leaping over a wall, heading for Hugo's home.

Sapphire arrived in an alley, the blood of the deceased knight fading with the snowfall. *Let's see here,* she thought to herself as she used her water magic to clear the snow from the area, erecting a magical barrier of water to block the falling snow.

"...Mainel…" she whispered with sorrow, closing his eyes, which had turned a misty white. With one arm raised to hold the water in place, she crouched down to examine the cadaver, searching for wounds. Following the trail of blood on his clothes, she found a wound on his back. Running her hand across it, she gauged the length of the cuts.

"This is a thin wound but deep. It doesn't appear to be from a regular blade—high quality, single-edged," Sapphire said, waving her hand to shrink the barrier around them. "Commander, come in! Commander!" she said urgently, tapping a lightning core in her ear.

"Sapphire, what did you find?" Morrigan replied after a pause.

"The deceased Valour is Mainel. He was killed with a single-edged sword, and an X was carved into his torso. One more thing—he left a note. I will show you in person."

"Bastard! Take Mainel to the Garrison and prepare him for burial. I will check the note when I return. We will find this killer. Sapphire... I don't know who their next target will be, but you are a possibility. I need you to stay alert for any suspicious activity," ordered Morrigan.

Sensing a hint of compassion from her commander, she obeyed, leaping onto a building while carrying Mainel in a dense sphere of water.

Snow atop the rooftops melted into water, trickling down the slanted roofs of the southeastern island. Morrigan raced across the rooftops, her blazing aura shielding her from the blizzard's cold embrace. Each step propelled her over two houses until she came to a halt.

Auras—two large auras converging... That light grey one belongs to Alastor; his resembles a swirling dome of air around his body. The other one appears to be black... mist. Rippling waves of mist that try to penetrate Alastor's aura—unsuccessfully. I must take a closer look and see what's happening. They're right outside Hugo's house, too!

"Alastor! What's going on here? Is this the person who killed my Valour Knights?" Morrigan demanded as she arrived in the square outside Hugo's home. Hugo lived in a two-storey estate raised above ground level, with a stairway leading to the entrance. A stone foundation supported brown walls with black tiles on top, barricading the estate.

Alastor had Spectral Blades spinning around his body, glowing with white light. The other man was clad in black leather armour with a silver chest guard, wielding two black blades. Most of his face was covered, but Morrigan could still make out black hair hidden beneath the hood of a black cloak.

"Morrigan? I see you've caught on to the murders happening in this district. Hugo is the last of the Valour Knights still alive here, so I figured he would be the next target," Alastor replied, extending one arm and pointing a white blade at his opponent. "Nox here arrived just before I did, so he became my prime suspect."

"I have nothing to do with these murders, but I did hear about Valour Knights being killed on this island. Since my suspension from the guild, I've been searching for the killer as an excuse to vent my frustrations," Nox said, raising his blades toward his chest before sinking into a sea of darkness.

Morrigan scanned the area for his aura, but even that had vanished. *A stealth technique—he must be an Assassin class.*

"Is he planning to escape or fight?" Morrigan posed the question to Alastor, who remained calm, his eyes fixed on the spot where Nox had stood moments ago.

"Nox uses shadows as his primary means of combat. He hasn't run away—he's using the surrounding darkness to move undetected. Stay on alert, Morrigan." Alastor had an analytical mind, quick to assess situations. "If I were him, I'd take this opportunity to attack from a blind spot."

As he spoke, Nox emerged from Alastor's shadow, his black blades slicing through the snow. Before he could land a strike, one of Alastor's white blades deflected the attack, casting a bright flash across the area. At the same moment, a red blade, moving with a will of its own, lashed out in a counterattack.

Surprised by the counter, Nox retreated into his shadow, preparing for another assault.

I see—Alastor is using Light-element blades to counter Nox's Dark-element blades. Nox doesn't stand a chance against him. Even I've struggled against the Spectre.

"You don't need to worry about Nox, Morrigan. I have no intention of killing him—I seek answers for the fallen," Alastor said, his gaze shifting to her. "I've determined that the killer wields a black blade. This shard was left in the body of the last victim, Grace."

Alastor flicked the shard toward Morrigan for her to examine, continuing to speak as Nox launched another flurry of attacks from all sides—each strike effortlessly deflected.

"Nox! Drop your weapons and come in for questioning. If you're innocent, we can clear you of suspicion. But the fact that the killer uses black blades like yours doesn't work in your favour," Morrigan commanded.

Nox is struggling against Alastor. I doubt he's the one who killed my knights. But the black blades are my only lead—I need to keep an eye on him in case another attack happens.

"I can't do that, Commander Morrigan. I have my orders—someone is trying to threaten thosr I care about. I can't stay here while they use me as a scapegoat," Nox replied, his voice trembling as he continued his relentless assault.

"So, why are you still in the city? We know you could leave whenever you wanted. Why stay here and fight us? That shard! It's the same type used in your weapons—I had to pull it out of my late partner's lifeless body! I am not here to play games with you, Nox!" Alastor shouted in anger, releasing a blast of aura that struck both Nox and Morrigan. They responded by unleashing their own aura to resist the onslaught of wind.

"That aura… Grace used a skill similar to this. Alastor…" Morrigan pushed through the force, reaching Alastor and placing a hand on his shoulder to calm him.

Alastor slumped. "I'm sorry, Morrigan. I didn't mean to attack you."

"It's okay. I'll make sure we find out who the killer is. You'll get your chance to fight," Morrigan said gently.

"The reason I'm here right now is to make sure my uncle is safe. I wanted to stay and watch over my team, to keep them safe, but that's no longer an option." Nox sheathed his blades and dropped to his knees. "I assure you, I have nothing to do with the murders. But if it means I can still protect my team, I'll come in for questioning. Alastor, I ask one favour in return—make sure nothing happens to my uncle or my team."

Morrigan placed cuffs on Nox, their runes glowing as they sealed his ability to use mana. "I'm sorry this has been pinned on you, but for now, we have to take you to the dungeon. Until we find out who the real culprit is, you'll remain there."

Alastor stayed behind to reassess the murders. "Framing Nox… it's possible, but I need to figure out who else uses Black Blades and has the power to slay a Valour. The only ones left are the Royal Guards and those within the Adventurer's Guild." He clenched his fists, his gaze shifting to the sky, where thick clouds fueled the blizzard raging throughout the city.

"Clouds that appear on the day a Valour Knight dies… this doesn't seem natural. It's not something anyone could do alone… Huh, so that's your game!" Alastor declared. With a sudden surge of energy, he dashed toward the guild.

CHAPTER 20

Mist raced around the room, gliding on discs of water she conjured in the air, each one vanishing the moment she stepped onto a new one. Sweat dripped from Lazarus' face onto his bare chest as he remained deep in meditation.

I can feel the mana escaping my body, filling the air around me, yet I haven't been able to draw upon it. Maybe it has to do with the position of my hands. Should my body be relaxed or tense? Is it my breathing?

Breathing... that's it! The mana shifts in the air whenever I breathe. I haven't felt it enter my body, but breathing is the key to this technique! Lazarus thought.

He opened his eyes as exhaustion took hold of his body. "No more for today, Mist. I'm too drained to continue," he said, reaching out toward her. A portal of swirling water formed beneath her feet. She leapt off her water disc, diving into the portal, which vanished in an instant.

"Are you okay, Lazarus?" Astra asked. The blizzard outside had eased, allowing moonlight to spill into the room, bathing her in its glow. Holding a poised stance, sweat glistened on her pale skin. She took a step forward, shifting her position, beads of sweat tracing the movements of her body.

"I'm fine, just exhausted. I figured out that mana regeneration has to do with breathing, but I don't have the energy to attempt it right now. Unlike regular breathing, it's as if my body has to find a way to draw in the surrounding mana. How is your training going?" he asked, unable to stop himself from admiring her physique.

With every motion she made, toned muscles surfaced beneath her skin, and arcs of electricity crackled around her. Astra crouched, ready to thrust an imaginary blade, her right arm locked behind her back.

"Stare any harder, and you'll bore a hole through my body," she said teasingly, causing Lazarus to blush. "I'm working on improving the fluidity of my movements. Storm Walker allows me to attack almost instantly, but my body stiffens under the effects of the lightning energy. It's difficult to move the way I want in that state, and I end up losing accuracy with my attacks. I'm starting to get the hang of it, though—regaining my regular flexibility."

Launching herself forward, she brought her arm into a striking position as lightning surged around it, stopping inches away from Lazarus, her fingers brushing his chin. "Phew, that's an improvement!"

"Astra? Do you mind not aiming at me next time?" Frozen in fear, Lazarus stared down at the fingers grazing his chin. Astra dropped her hand and wiped herself off with a towel.

"Sorry!"

The surge of electricity pulsed through his body. Fascinated by the sensation, he focused on each tingle.

"I'm going to extend our stay here. I'll be back soon!" he called out while leaving the room.

Upon descending the stairway into the main hall, Lazarus saw Krow talking to Ferris. As he continued through the hall, Krow, who was checking in, sensed his presence and turned to meet his gaze with a playful smile.

"Ah, Lazarus! Good to see you again! I'm going to be staying here for a couple of nights—I hope you don't mind?" she said playfully, winking at him.

"Don't worry about it. Ferris, do you mind extending our stay?" Lazarus asked, placing silver tabs on the reception counter.

"Let's see… you want one week, then?" Ferris asked.

"I don't think we'll be leaving much this week—there's a blizzard every other day."

"You're right, that is a strange phenomenon. Everyone else has had to extend their stay as well. Though I can't complain—it's good for business." Ferris giggled innocently, passing a key over to Krow, who was now stretching out her limbs.

"How's your headache, Krow? You still look pale," Lazarus asked, watching as she adjusted her shoulders.

"It's gone away for now. I came here to rest—the last few nights haven't been great for me or my shoulders. Anyway, now that the blizzard is clearing up, I'll head to the tower tomorrow. You should think about your next Tower expedition as well, Lazarus," she said before retreating to her room.

"Winter Kingdom, City Baylor."

Under the cover of the dark night sky, contrasted by a blanket of snow, a small hooded figure crept through a forest until it reached a giant bridge leading to an island.

"Find Laz. Keep safe."

The creature snuck into the city using Dark-element magic, creating portals to different spots within sight, covering great distances with ease. It stopped on a rooftop to observe the empty streets, then used its sense skill to detect auras. The entire city was lit up with tens of thousands of coloured bubbles of varying sizes.

"Use sense. Find Laz," it muttered in its short speech pattern as it scanned the city, homing in on a populated area where dozens of people were gathered in one building. The creature bounded off the roof, following a single aura.

☆ ☆ ☆ ☆

Welcoming the darkness of the room upon his return, Lazarus noticed that Astra had found a comfortable spot on the couch, the white gem in hand, as she examined her available abilities. He observed her briefly before making his way to the table and sitting down.

"I still haven't had a chance to see what your abilities are like. Do you mind if I take a look?" he asked.

Astra flicked a holographic scroll into the air, enlarging it. Tilting her head upside down, she glanced at Lazarus.

"There you go, muscles. I've decided to follow the elemental knight path. It enhances my Storm Walker technique and can boost other elements if I choose to use them. I'm level sixteen now. If I had your growth ability, I'd be closer to level twenty after all the Lizardfolk we fought. But still, I feel much stronger than I ever was back in Riverfall. It doesn't even feel like my body went through a reset. Do you get that sensation, Lazarus?" she asked, staring into his forest-green eyes.

"...Yeah, I've noticed that too. I've also realised that other adventurers here are more powerful than either of us. There's always someone stronger. We just have to keep improving to close that gap as much as possible. The rest comes down to skill—which I see you've already worked on. You've got abilities that enhance speed, plus your lightning element. Also, Mirage—what is that?" he asked, browsing through the list of abilities she had obtained.

"I haven't practised that one yet, but it should allow me to create copies of myself to fight alongside me. I thought it fitting, given the emphasis on speed—'Mirage,'" she said, excited by the sound of the name. "Just imagining the possibilities I could do with the Elem—"

Just then, a tap came from the balcony, alerting them both. A small creature landed on the balcony outside their room, melting the snow on the ledge.

"Laz, found you," he said as Astra gasped in surprise, reaching for her blade.

"No fret, Levanna sent," he continued, hopping down, his tiny feet tapping along the floor as he glanced around the room. They stood perplexed by the sudden appearance of the creature.

"Excuse me... whoever you are, how do you know Levanna and Lazarus?" Astra asked, her blade now pointed at the cloaked creature.

"Do you know Levanna?" Lazarus asked, tapping Astra's blade to make her lower it. "Is she safe?"

The creature jumped onto the bed, his tiny feet dangling off the edge.

"Levy safe, protect village." His large red eyes glanced between the two of them, unfazed by their confusion.

Relieved to hear that Levanna was safe, Lazarus went to lie down on the bed. A knock came from the door.

"Are you okay, Lazarus? I sensed a strong presence heading this way."

Lazarus got up, reluctant to open the door. Krow stood there, green mana flowing around her hands.

"It's okay, Krow. This is a friendly visit, so you can relax."

Krow eased her tense stance and peered past Lazarus to see the creature sitting on the bed. He waved at Krow, who returned an awkward wave.

Lazarus walked back into the room and stared at the creature.

"What's your name?" Astra asked, hoping to break the silence.

Turning toward Astra with an innocent stare, he pointed his small hand to introduce himself. "Gamma. Levanna call."

Astra smiled, propping herself up on the bed beside Gamma, joining him in kicking her feet while watching the other two.

"Gamma, do you use fire magic by any chance?" Lazarus asked, recalling his encounter in the forest—the moment he saw the Mortesyn and the large fireball floating through the trees.

Gamma nodded with a big smile, revealing four fangs and two rows of flattened teeth. "Levanna asked, I protect." He hopped off the bed and paced around the room, occasionally glancing at Krow before stopping to ask her, "You familiar, how?"

"Me? I don't know who you are or what you are. You must be mistaken," Krow said, a confused look crossing her face at Gamma's words.

"Just familiar," Gamma repeated before scurrying back onto the bed.

"I guess you guys will be okay. Sorry if I interrupted you. I'll take my leave." Krow bowed her head and retreated from the room.

Gamma said she's familiar. Levanna might know something—I'll have to check with her next time I see her.

"Astra, I'm okay with keeping Gamma here with us, but what will we do if someone finds out about him? I doubt they'd be happy about a hole in their security," Lazarus said nervously, eyeing Gamma.

"I hide, nobody sees." Sensing their worry, Gamma closed his eyes, focusing his mind.

"Impressive!" Astra blurted out, almost leaping to her feet before regaining her composure under Lazarus's concerned gaze.

"What is Gamma doing? I don't see any difference." Lazarus scratched his jaw, tilting his head to get a different angle.

"He's masking his aura. Anyone who senses him will only pick up a tiny aura—no more than what a regular animal would have."

"Nice! That's going to help a lot. This way, you can hide in plain sight. You're smart, aren't you?" Lazarus praised Gamma, who smiled contentedly.

"Well, apparently, the blizzard is beginning to disappear, so tomorrow, I'll be preparing for the Tower. I should get some sleep. Gamma, you can stay here as long as you don't cause any trouble for us," Lazarus said, staring at the little creature.

Gamma crossed his tiny fingers with a mischievous smile.

CHAPTER 21

The frozen beaches around the Kingdom of Baylor had vanished, giving way to waves that crashed against the high cliffs. Gazing out at the sea from atop the eastern walls, his black fur coat flapping in the wind, Lazarus steeled himself to enter the Tower once more.

"Okay! Let's go for number four—a fire-element spirit." He tapped the ledge before turning to the summoning circle, placing a dark red core with glowing, swirling flames at its centre. Gamma sat atop the ledge, observing as Lazarus began to cast the spell.

"Blazing spirit, light a path before me with your flames, leaving behind the charred remains of those who stand in our way."

The runes ignited, spreading along the lines of the circle before enveloping the core. Flames erupted into a pillar of fire, lifting the core as embers and swirling heat expanded before their eyes. Then, with a sudden burst, the core split open, revealing a small Draconian creature. Flames coiled around its nape like a collar, and its claws glowed red-hot.

Its body was blackened like molten magma, and its tail sprouted fire. As the spirit landed, the snow beneath its feet melted instantly. It exhaled short bursts of flame at the remaining snow, melting it further as the fire spread and drifted off the wall.

"Ignis! A perfect name for one who breathes fire," Lazarus declared.

Gamma hopped off the ledge, raising his arm to summon a fountain of fire.

"Gamma, stop! You can't do that here!" Lazarus shouted, watching in horror as the flames cascaded down the side of the wall, igniting the snow-covered grass below. "Mist, douse those flames quickly! We can't let it spread further!"

Panicking, he grabbed his face with both hands, hoping nothing disastrous would come of it.

"Best fire belongs to Gamma," Gamma commented as he stared at Ignis, stepping back toward the ledge.

"Yeah, yeah, you're a powerful spellcaster, I get it. But that doesn't mean you can go around destroying everything with those flames. Ignis, you too—try to hold back on breathing fire until I give the command," Lazarus said with annoyance.

Ignis stared at Lazarus with a confused expression.

Lazarus adjusted the summoning circle to a water element for his final core.

"I need a spirit with grip strength. All my other spirits are focused on offense, so a spirit that can provide support will be valuable. Come forth and help me reach new heights!"

The summoning circle glowed with an ethereal aqua light. The core bubbled as it expanded until it burst open. A ribbit greeted Lazarus as the water spirit emerged.

A frog-like creature, standing on two legs and clad in armour that gave it the appearance of a knight, stood in the circle. Its bright blue and purple skin made it stand out. The humanoid frog whipped its long, thick tongue onto the wall and pulled itself up. Its suctioned toes stuck to the stone surface as it let out another ribbit.

"I'll call you Marsh. Anyway, I'm heading to the Guild to check in and figure out which floor to tackle next. Gamma, I need you to wait on the mainland by the crossroads."

"Wait. Mainland. Crossroads," Gamma confirmed, and without another word, he bounced along the ledge until he disappeared from view.

"Ignis, Marsh, you can return for now. I'll call upon you later, I promise."

Ignis hopped around before leaping into the black portal, flames flickering as they escaped the darkness. Marsh followed, leaping into a portal with mud and water dripping from its edges.

Twirling the staff in his hand, Lazarus reflected on his newly unlocked skills, gaining speed with each spin before swinging at an imaginary target. A small gust of wind blew away the snow, briefly breaking the heavy snowfall.

I can't just rely on my spirits—we have to be able to fight alongside each other! That night... I won't let it happen again!

CHAPTER 22

A crowd of hundreds of knights gathered by the garrison, watching as the nine Valour Knights walked onto the stage, clad in their distinctive captain's armour and snow-fur cloaks, each lined with a different interior colour. They took their seats at the front of the stage, overlooking their squads and the assembled knights.

"I assume all of you are aware by now of the deaths occurring around the city over the past week. We have lost three of our Valour Knights to this unknown assailant," Commander Morrigan announced, her voice carrying effortlessly without the need for an air core to amplify it. A murmur spread through the younger knights in the crowd, stirring unrest.

"We have determined that the blizzard that has blanketed our city over the past week was not natural—it was conjured by a high-level mage," Sapphire added, standing beside Morrigan with an armful of scrolls.

"So, someone cast that blizzard spell, and either the same person or another is responsible for killing our Knights of Valour?" Zachariah asked, lounging in his chair with his legs spread and elbows resting on his toned thighs. His stern gaze locked onto Morrigan and Sapphire as they turned to face him.

"We haven't yet confirmed how many people are involved in these murders," Morrigan replied. "Once you have informed your squads, we will hold a private discussion to determine our next course of action." She hoped her words would ease the growing tension among the crowd.

"As Commander Morrigan just stated, we will inform you of what we know so far. Aside from the blizzard being a spell, we have learned that the killer uses black blades. We missed them last night, but I did find a piece of evidence—the killer wears black and silver armour. Mainel died trying to fight this person, managing to break off pieces of their armour for us to find," Sapphire informed them.

"Why haven't you informed us this earlier? Three of our squads are still without captains!" a male voice from the crowd shouted.

"Yeah! Who's next since you've all failed to catch the killer? Are we just going to sit here and die one by one, or are we going to hunt them down?!" a female knight shouted.

"Quiet!" Commander Morrigan ordered, silencing them along with the murmuring crowd. "I understand that some of you need new captains to replace Mainel, Grace, and Omak. Sapphire has been evaluating all potential candidates for each squad. In the meantime, I want you all to focus on training until we decide who will become a Valour. Today, we will be holding mock battles for the Valour Captains and their squads. I want all of you to prepare. The battles will take place in the arena. After this discussion, your captains will lead you there."

"Yes, Commander!" they shouted in unison, snapping to attention.

"Very well. Captains, with me! Back to training, knights!" Morrigan commanded as she walked off the stage, the captains following her in single file.

"What are the matchups going to be, Commander?" asked a Valour with red hair. He was tall and slim yet exuded a strong aura. The inside of his white fur cloak was lined with dark red.

"The matches will be Druinn vs. Hugo, Zachariah vs. Mars, Jacques vs. Lilith, Adonis vs. Eden, and Sapphire—you will be fighting me with your squad. Hugo and Druinn will be up first, followed by Jacques and Lilith, then Adonis and Eden, Zachariah and Mars, and lastly, our match," Morrigan stated. Her brisk pace forced the others to keep up with her until they entered the war room, where they planned to discuss their strategy for dealing with the current threat.

In the middle of the room, a rectangular desk held a model of the world. Water filled most of the hollowed-out desktop. De Albo was covered in white powder, with multi-coloured trees marking the Winter Forest and the mountainous regions of The Glades, northeast of their kingdom.

A vast desert dominated the southern region, filled with sand dunes, underground caves, and pockets of water reserves.

The eastern region was covered in swamps and a forest of undying trees in shades of orange, red, and brown. Hilltops overlooked the sea, and mana-rich fields stretched in hues of brown and orange.

To the west lay lands of abundant greenery—forests, lakes, and rivers—separated by towering mountains that blocked access from the rest of the world.

At the centre of the map sat a large island, completely unmarked—an uninhabited land no one dared to visit.

"Assassin against assassin, huh? Best friends, face to face. I can already hear everyone talking about the match," Zachariah said, spreading his hands in the air as if picturing a headline.

"We are not friends, Zachariah. 'Acquaintances' sounds more befitting of our relationship. And don't think for a second that you have a chance at winning this match," Mars replied in an annoyed tone.

"Oh, I wouldn't be so sure about that, Mars. I've got a secret weapon," Zachariah said, peering at Mars from the corner of his eye.

Mars' face reddened at the thought of someone believing they could defeat him, wounding his pride. He slammed his fist on the map, distorting the hologram.

"Enough, you two. We are not here to discuss the matches. There are people out there taking us out one by one, and it stops today," Morrigan said as she took a seat, the captains following suit.

"Do you have a plan, Commander? If we find the killer, you best believe I'm going in for the kill," asked a blonde-haired female Valour, her eyes flickering with electricity. Her inner cloak was a lemon yellow, reflecting the colour of her hair, which was styled in braided strands forming a ponytail.

"That is true. Lilith won't be able to hold back if she encounters them," added a male Valour, his inner cloak an arctic blue.

"They killed our youngest Valour—Lilith's sister. You know she's itching for a fight, and Adonis will be there, ready to back her up. I suggest we form teams and hunt down the killer," suggested a male with a midnight black inner cloak.

"Don't be so hasty, Druinn. The Commander already has a plan—let's hear her out first," said a man with a tan inner cloak.

"Jacques is right. We need to stop arguing and listen to what Commander Morrigan has to say," added a female Valour, her inner cloak a forest green.

"I know this may be hard for you, Lilith, but the plan is already in motion. I ask that all of you go about your normal routines. I don't believe they will attack us tonight. Each death happened two days apart, and with the blizzard, I suspect they were trying to hide the bodies and hinder the investigation."

"If the Commander wills it, I have no objections," an old Valour spoke, his inner cloak an iron grey. Placing his hand on the desk, he exchanged a weary glance with each of the other captains.

"I'm in," Zachariah said, placing his hand down. One by one, the others followed suit as Morrigan watched them. She stared down at the map, observing the city of Baylor.

CHAPTER 23

Lazarus approached the reception desk, where Emlin was busy filing new requests. She seemed too occupied to even notice him standing in front of her.

"Emlin?" Lazarus tapped on the desk after receiving no response. A small lightning core flashed on the surface.

"Oh! Lazarus! I'm sorry I didn't notice you sooner. Since the blizzard took us out of commission yesterday, we've had an influx of adventurers wanting to visit the Tower today." Emlin picked up the core and listened as a voice spoke through it. "Floor Fifty? Yes, I'll be sure to mark you down, Krow."

Is that lightning core how everyone at the Tower knows when people arrive before they even reach their destination? Krow is already up to fifty... she must be powerful if she's going alone.

"Is there anything I can help you with today?" Emlin asked frantically, trying to juggle her workload.

"Actually, yes. Do you know if Magnus is in today?" Lazarus inquired, recalling his conversation with Magnus before the blizzard.

"Magnus? Hmmm... he might be in the tavern hall with the others who are waiting."

"I'll have a look then. Are you okay here? Shouldn't Aldo and Sadie be helping you as well?" Lazarus asked.

"Oh, they've been dealing with other important matters. It's just me working here today," Emlin replied, her expression weary.

"It must be difficult managing hundreds of adventurers on your own. I won't hold you up. I'll see you when I return!"

With that, Lazarus headed upstairs and into the hall.

There are so many people here today. I've seen the hall filled with a couple of dozen people at once, yet now there are a hundred gathered around, Lazarus thought as he entered the packed hall.

The other adventurers had to wait to check-in, and in the meantime, they resorted to card games based on elemental affinities.

Lazarus scanned the crowd for the old man, spotting Arcanum sitting together in a booth. Their once excitable and humorous faces were now downtrodden without their leader. Lazarus almost felt bad for them.

A boisterous laugh erupted from the other side of the hall, drawing Lazarus's attention. Magnus sat at a table, playing a card game with another adventurer and winning against his opponent. The game used the eight elements, with five cards for each element, numbered one to five. Each player started with twenty cards and placed one card facedown per turn, aiming to have the highest-value card. Elemental advantages doubled a card's value, while disadvantages halved it. The match ended once all cards had been played.

"Magnus! Just the person I was looking for. Do you have time to talk?"

Magnus let out a hearty laugh. "Come, let's talk somewhere quieter." He collected his winnings in a small pouch and guided Lazarus out the back of the building into a large courtyard with a view of the horizon across the sea. Leaning against the city wall, he asked, "What do you have to discuss, Lazarus? I heard about Nox and Krow. Does this have anything to do with them?"

Lazarus shook his head. "Nothing about them. I'm here to see if you want to go to the Tower together. I have questions—questions about my mother. She mentioned you were someone I could trust."

Magnus let out a celebratory laugh. "She mentioned me? That's pleasant to hear. It has been decades since I last saw your mother." Stroking his beard, he observed Lazarus's familiar features. "You take after your parents—you get your looks from Cyrus. He was an aloof person, always preferring to be by himself—until he crossed paths with your mother. After meeting her, they soon partnered up, and he became fiercely loyal and protective of her. Those two working together were supposed to be unstoppable, so whatever they faced in the Tower can't be normal.

"Which brings me to my current dilemma. I have a special floor that I'm aiming to beat. This isn't like the other elites. As a reward for joining me, I'll even let you take the Guardian as a summon. I won't tell you what we'll be fighting—I want to test your adaptability," Magnus said, excited at the prospect of having his own small party instead of tackling floors alone.

"You'll let me take the creature? Are we going to fight a Deity?" Lazarus asked, earning a surprised look from Magnus.

"Ha! So, you already know about the Deities residing in the Tower. Then, I guess there are no surprises for you today. Yes, we are going to fight a Deity." Magnus laughed. "I've fought it a couple of times, but it's impossible for me to defeat alone—even with all of my summons aiding me."

"Even though you're a high level?"

"For regular Elites, being a high enough level makes them easy to handle. But for Deities, that is not the case. Each one requires a unique method to defeat, and they all have multiple phases. These battles demand stamina and strategy. With my summoning abilities, I lack the mana necessary to sustain a prolonged fight alongside my companions," Magnus explained, shifting away from the wall and taking a seat on a bench.

"What about mana potions? Wouldn't they help you out?" Lazarus asked.

"It's a promising idea in theory, but mana potions have a detrimental effect if you use too many in quick succession. Your body can't keep up with the influx of mana, and it begins to shut down. I wish mana potions were a viable option, but never take more than two a day if you can help it—the negatives far outweigh the positives."

"I didn't know that. I'm glad we didn't bring too many to our dungeon the other day," Lazarus said.

"Don't worry about it! You still have a lot to learn as an adventurer, and I'm happy to help in any way I can. Now, back to the Deity—it's essential never to fight alone if you rely on mana consumption during battle. I can fight solo, but this Deity attacks with relentless animosity, forcing me to use my summons to help me out."

"Do you think we have a chance of defeating it, Magnus? I'm still new and low-levelled—I don't think I can do much to help."

"Even if we don't defeat the Deity, we'll still gain experience from the other creatures we face. We can obtain new skills and grow stronger. If we're on the losing side, retreat—no matter what happens," he warned.

"Okay, one last thing before we go. How did you keep winning at that card game?" Lazarus asked.

"Oh, that? I have a small friend that hangs around the ceiling. He observes my opponent's cards, and I can see them through shared sight. A nifty skill for gathering information, if you ask me," Magnus said as he summoned a small Shadow Squirrel—pitch black with eyes of white fire. Though tiny and seemingly cute, the squirrel had a devilish appearance.

"Basically, you cheated."

"When money is on the line, I'm going to use any method I can to win," Magnus said in defence before laughing.

"Do you mind if we leave immediately? Being cooped up all day yesterday has made my body stiff." Lazarus stretched his arms and legs.

"Eager for a battle—I like your spirit!" Magnus bumped his fists together, flames spurting upon contact.

Lazarus summoned Shadow, who spread his wings as Lazarus climbed onto his back.

"Shadow? I can't believe you're here again. You managed to summon your mother's own Spirit, then! This battle is going to be fun—just like old times!" Magnus laughed before summoning his own companion, a large white bird, frost falling from its tail feathers as it flew above him. "On your lead, Lazarus."

CHAPTER 24

Braziers lined the hallway leading to the entrance of the arena, the setting for the Valour matches. Light at the end of the hall revealed a round stone platform surrounded by water, which flowed through a canal leading to the sea. Astra listened to the crowd cheering as each squad entered the arena, the stomping of thousands of civilians' feet reverberating through the ground.

"Are you nervous, Astra?" Zach asked, staring into the light as they waited for their turn to enter. The squad members were clad in armour, weapons in hand. Astra glanced at each of them—a light grey bow, one with a purple liquid at the centre of a black bow, a hammer with water flowing within its head, two blades glimmering with white light at Zach's waist, and Tobias wielding a white staff adorned with small silver rings attached to a large hoop at the top. Her heartbeat quickened, and she took a deep breath before answering her captain.

"Yeah, I don't have the experience any of you have, or the skills or talent. I feel like I'm in over my head. I know nothing about these matches, and I'm going to be participating despite that. I am nervous...

yet I feel excited at the same time," Astra said, squeezing her gloved hands. "Is that normal?"

"Nervous is good. It will keep you alert to danger, and you'll need that if we want to win this battle."

"Don't forget, you aren't alone, Astra. All of us will be fighting by your side. The captain is smarter than he looks; if we follow the plan, I trust in our victory," Theo said, smiling down at the much shorter Astra. He stood over two metres tall compared to her height of around 160 cm.

"Phew... You all talk about battle so casually. I'm used to fighting wildlife. Now I'm facing off against other Knights," Astra said, bumping her chest plate with a fist. "No, I won't doubt myself. If you trust this plan, I'll do everything I can to make it work!"

"That's the spirit! I've seen you fight—I fear for your enemies when you grow into your skills. You have a tenacity that rivals even the commanders, so when we walk out, walk out with pride." Zach bumped his chest with his fist, and the other squad members joined in, matching the beat of the crowd stomping their feet.

On the arena stage, Hugo and Druinn led their squads to their respective sides of the field. Wearing grey armour beneath a white cloak, Hugo observed the arena through his helmet.

"Let's see... large rocks for cover or high ground, pillars spanning the outer edge, water canals dividing the centre, and a pedestal in the middle—that must be the core... I see," Hugo murmured as he examined the arena.

"I won't be going easy on you or your team, old-timer," Druinn said arrogantly. He appeared to be in his thirties, with wavy black hair and grey eyes.

"I would be displeased if you did. I need something to wake these old bones up, you see."

"Now that our first participating teams have entered the arena, we will begin the first match! Are you ready, Druinn?" Commander Morrigan called out.

Druinn yelled an affirmative.

"Hugo, how about your team?"

Hugo raised an arm, giving Morrigan a thumbs-up, his weary gaze never leaving Druinn.

"Okay then! Both teams are prepared. Without further delay, let the match begin!" With her final announcement, she sliced through the air with a long, flaming arc.

Each team charged forward to claim their battle positions.

CHAPTER 25

As they travelled to the Winter Tower, Magnus clung to the legs of a giant Caladrius.

"I can't help but notice a creature has been tailing us. Lazarus, do you mind if I take care of it?" Magnus asked, glancing over at Lazarus, who sat atop Shadow. "You, show yourself!" he exclaimed, releasing his grip on his companion and drawing his battle axe, pointing it toward the dense forest.

The creature emerged from behind the trees, kicking up snow in the process. Due to the storm, the snow had deepened, making it difficult for the small figure to walk, with the snow reaching up to its waist. It lowered the hood covering its face, and Gamma began mumbling to himself as he continued kicking at the snow around him.

"You're a small one, though your aura tells a different story. Why have you been tailing us?" Magnus' tone was serious—he could sense the creature's strength and didn't want any danger befalling his new companion.

"Lazarus friend. Gamma protects," Gamma said, looking up at the hulking figure looming over him. Magnus' intense stare was met by

Gamma's own fiery gaze, the smaller figure waiting for the larger fighter to make a move.

"Very well, then. As long as you're not here to harm Lazarus, I have no quarrel with you, little one," Magnus said calmly, easing his muscles and sheathing his large battle axe. As Gamma walked past him toward Lazarus, he stuck out his tongue at Magnus in defiance.

That went smoothly. I was beginning to think it would escalate into a fight.

"The Tower isn't far from here, Lazarus. Before we arrive, I'd like to see what you're capable of first. As summoners, we can have companions, spirits, weapons, or even the undead to fight for us. I'll bring out my trusted companions, Hati and Jupiter."

Magnus continued as cracks opened in the ground, releasing flickering flames as two creatures leapt out.

Hati was a giant black wolf with yellow runic symbols along its fur, its body towering over the nearby trees. A gold and red collar encircled its neck, and a burned handprint marked its right shoulder.

Jupiter appeared to be a white fox with nine tails. Like Hati, it bore runic symbols, though Jupiter's markings glowed with an almost luminescent blue. A metal band wrapped around one of its forelegs, and a burned handprint adorned its left shoulder.

Lazarus tensed at their presence. Though both creatures appeared calm, they radiated an overwhelming aura of superiority.

"How do you expect me to fight those two? I'm nowhere near as strong as you or your companions," Lazarus stated.

"You don't need to defeat them; I know they're too strong for you. I'd like to see how you battle with your spirits—show me how you work together," Magnus said, refusing to let Lazarus back out of the fight.

Lazarus felt his chest tighten with nerves, his breathing growing short.

"Okay, I'll bring out mine. Just two, or can I bring out more?" he asked, taking a deep breath to calm himself as he sat on a nearby tree stump.

"Bring out as many as you want to show off." Magnus's interest seemed piqued now, his gaze intent on seeing all of Lazarus's spirits.

Lazarus extended his arm and called for his spirits. "Rebirth! Ignis and Karah!"

I can't bring them all out. I need to conserve my mana for the Deity battle, Lazarus thought as two portals opened.

Karah charged out of her portal to stand beside Lazarus while Ignis crawled forth, melting the snow beneath him.

"Impressive! Those are two strong-looking spirits you have there," Magnus commented. "I'll hold back my two—show me how you'd go about defeating them, Lazarus!"

Lazarus remained focused on his spirits, setting his sights on Jupiter first.

I'm going to have to restrict their movements; my spirits aren't strong enough to fight head-on.

"Ignis and Karah, don't give Jupiter a chance to retreat."

At his command, Ignis and Karah raced in a circle, forming a wall of fire and lightning. Jupiter paced within the barrier, carefully observing their tactics.

"Nice, Lazarus! What are you going to do now, Jupiter?" Magnus shouted, watching the battle unfold.

Jupiter glanced upward at the top of the pillar before leaping, bouncing off shimmering panels of prisms she conjured midair. Yellow and blue electricity crackled above them as a surge of lightning descended from the clouds with a humming strike. Jupiter couldn't dodge in time and took the full brunt of the attack on her back. She crashed to the ground but quickly shook off the hit with a cunning smile.

The Kitsune's body flickered into a mirage before vanishing, her real form reappearing on a rock behind Magnus, peering over her forelegs.

An illusion? I don't know if my spirits have any techniques to counter that ability. I'll have to focus on Hati for now.

"Karah, Ignis, return! Ísarr, Mist, and Jaeger, you're up."

Jaeger appeared first, firing an arrow at Hati the moment his portal opened. Ísarr and Mist charged in from opposite sides, closing the distance. Mist leapt into the air above Hati, conjuring dozens of bubbles that floated ominously around him.

"Mist, release the bubbles!" Lazarus commanded.

The bubbles popped on cue, releasing splashes of water that drenched Hati. He perked up with a snarl at the sudden wetness, but before he could shake off the water, Ísarr bounded toward him, flicking his frosty tail. The water began to freeze. Ísarr continued striking rapidly with his tail, expanding the frozen area. Hati's amber eyes locked onto him as he let out a roar.

Dark energy gathered around Hati's body throughout the prolonged roar until he amassed enough to trigger a ripple explosion that shattered the ice.

Arrows streaked past Ísarr as he leapt over the ripples of dark energy. He glanced at the arrows, now coated in water, and arced his frost breath to imbue each with ice.

The arrows struck their mark but weren't strong enough to pierce Hati's thick jet-black fur. Instead, their slight impact caused the water to freeze into ice across his body, halting his movement as he leered at the small creatures. A deep, rumbling snarl escaped him, sending a shiver down Lazarus' spine.

"Jaeger! You and I haven't had a chance to work together yet—let's finish this!" Lazarus shouted.

Jaeger nodded and leapt from the tree behind Lazarus, bow in hand, already prepared to shoot. Arcing over Lazarus, he released a mana-infused arrow into the sky, splitting it into several dozen as they descended.

Upon landing, Jaeger crouched on one knee in front of Lazarus, his head bowed toward Hati as the arrows rained down. Frozen in place, Hati roared furiously, shaking off the ice as the barrage of arrows pelted him from above.

"Hati, enough! Don't attack them," Magnus' voice boomed as Hati prepared to strike at Jaeger and Lazarus, his anger evident. "I apologise for his attitude; he acts as if he's the strongest creature to walk this earth and is quick to anger when faced with a challenge. I'd say you passed with flying colours. That was an exceptional use of strategy to try and take down stronger opponents. However, if this were a real battle, I fear it would not have played out as well. Hati and Jupiter focused on defence so I could observe how you wield your spirits. I think it's time to head to the Tower—don't you agree?"

Magnus recalled Hati and Jupiter before marching forward.

Lazarus returned his summons as well, pulling a mana vial from his bag to restore the energy he had expended over the past minute.

To think the combined efforts of my summons couldn't even scratch Magnus'... I still have a long way to go.

CHAPTER 26

Fireballs rained down on Hugo's team as they took cover behind rocks. His four mages erected a swirling dome of water as a barrier while he and the rest of the team waited for an opening. Druinn's team formed a structured formation of five rows, with Druinn positioned at the back: twelve archers, six mages, and six tanks and warriors forming the outer defence.

"Hold cover until I give the signal. Druinn is powerful, but he relies on basic offensive strategies. We'll wait for an opening before launching our counterattack," Hugo said, huddled with his team while the mages stood with arms raised, maintaining the barrier.

The fireballs gradually slowed as Druinn's mages burned through their mana. They attempted to recover using mana regeneration skills, but none were of a high enough level to sustain continuous spellcasting.

"There it is. Let's go, team," Hugo said as he stepped out from behind the rock, signalling his team to split. Six archers climbed nearby pillars, securing higher ground for clearer shots. As Hugo advanced toward his opponents, three clerics remained behind, guarded by four paladins. A group of four mages and four sorcerers unleashed a combined elemental beam at Druinn's team.

Unable to block the barrage of elemental spells, the warriors were the first to fall. The perched archers then pinned down Druinn's tanks and mages, leaving only the archers and Druinn himself.

"Good job, archers! Keep up the cover fire—we'll handle the rest. Everyone else, you know what to do," Hugo commanded his team in a calm voice. His pace quickened, and the defenders faltered slightly at the sight of Hugo the Unbreakable charging toward them.

He weaved through the incoming barrage of arrows, deflecting them with the flat of his sword and shield. Despite his age, he moved with agility, effortlessly reading the trajectory of each arrow. His focus locked onto the first line of defence—several male knights specialising in tank classes. One by one, they fell to his blade as he unleashed Air-element slashes they couldn't withstand.

Druinn began casting a spell, black runes appearing at his feet. Hugo's eyes widened as he recognised the markings, his brows furrowing.

"My knights! Handle the rest of Druinn's squad while I deal with Captain Druinn. Mages, cast a Light-element protective spell immediately!" Hugo's usual composure cracked as he realised what Druinn was attempting. "Stop at once! You're endangering your own squad with that spell, Druinn!"

The crowd gasped as shadows consumed the arena, a dome of darkness forming around the stage. Druinn floated into the air, massive wings of shadow unfurling from his back.

"It's too late to talk him out of this. You leave me no choice, then," Hugo whispered to himself.

"I'll prove to the commander just how powerful my dark sorcery can be! I will not yield—not even to you, Captain Hugo!" Druinn shouted in a panic as Hugo cut through his squad's defences.

"Druinn, I cannot let you harm even your own squad just to win this mock battle," Hugo said, his angry tone drawing everyone's attention.

Druinn began to rise into the air, black wings of energy forming from shadows that stretched out from his unconscious squad members. Hugo gripped his sword tightly, steeling his resolve as air-element energy enveloped the blade. Exhaling slowly, he swung his sword diagonally at Druinn.

"Forgive me, Druinn, but you leave me no choice."

The sound of the blade slicing through the air caught Druinn's attention. He quickly gathered dark energy and fired a beam to counter the attack, but it was too little, too late. The air slash tore through the dark energy and struck Druinn, leaving a gash across his chest. His wings vanished, and he plummeted back down, guiding himself into the water canal surrounding the arena. The dome shattered with Druinn's defeat, and the shadows withdrew back into their original bodies.

Hugo turned to meet Morrigan's gaze. "I apologise if I went too far, Commander Morrigan. I could not let that spell be cast and risk the lives of everyone here. It absorbs the mana of those who have formed a pact with Captain Druinn—the end result could have been fatal." He bowed, awaiting his punishment.

"Raise your head, Captain Hugo. You have nothing to apologise for. You assessed the danger to your team and others in the vicinity and acted accordingly. That is the kind of mentality I hope the other captains strive to achieve." Morrigan glanced at Hugo with a proud smile. "Sapphire, your squad will treat the wounded."

The crowd murmured amongst themselves before a wave of applause spread through the arena. Hugo left with his squad.

CHAPTER 27

The entrance to the tower loomed over the three adventurers, forcing Gamma to tilt his head all the way back to look up. His hood fell off, revealing his black-and-red fur, and his mouth hung open in awe.

"Magnus, do you know anything about how these towers came to be? Their sheer size and location can't be natural, can they?" Lazarus inquired while standing beside Magnus.

"An excellent question, my boy, but one I can't answer honestly. I believe they were created by the Ancient Ones—the four gods who shaped the seasons. The Church of Baylor worships the northern deity, Vinter, but no one has ever laid eyes upon them. Many believe they wait at the top of the tower, and those who conquer the final floor by defeating the Guardian may meet them," Magnus said, stroking his beard as he gazed up at the mountaintop stretching past the clouds. Gamma continued staring as well until they checked in with Marv.

Marv pushed against the giant arched doors, and a loud rumble echoed through the tower as they swung open. Lazarus was once again greeted by the Howlite halls and the veins of lapis mana flowing along the floor.

"We're heading to floor fifteen. I suggest summoning Shadow so we can fly up there," Magnus said as he stepped into the stairwell.

"Arctis," Magnus called out, his voice quieter than usual. The ground split open, revealing a hole engulfed in flames. A caw echoed from within, followed by the sound of wings flapping. The flames fizzled out as ice froze over the inside of the hole, and a white bird emerged.

The same bird he used to fly to the Tower. So, her name is Arctis, Lazarus thought.

"Shadow, to me!" Lazarus called out, his voice echoing through the grand hall and drawing the attention of the nearby crowd.

Magnus put a finger to his mouth, hushing him.

"...Sorry," Lazarus whispered.

A black portal emerged, its swirling purple mist fading into pitch black as shadows descended upon them. Lazarus' shadow stretched and shifted, taking the form of an owl with its wings spread wide.

I don't think I'll ever get over how cool that entrance looks. I don't even notice him leave the portal; he just emerges from a shadow.

Shadow took physical form, allowing Lazarus to climb onto his back, while Gamma's feet flared with fire, enabling him to fly. The three of them ascended the stairway, with Lazarus taking note of the creatures depicted above each sealed doorway—bears, birds, wolves, golems, and yetis.

Eventually, they arrived at their designated door, adorned with the image of a lone white wolf with red markings on its fur.

"We're going to fight a wolf... like Hati?" Lazarus asked, curious about what kind of wolf they would encounter. He raised his hand, withdrawing Shadow, and waited for Magnus to respond.

Magnus chuckled before answering. "Hati? No, this one is much bigger and fiercer. I've seen that you're capable of tactical battle, but this fight will push you to your limits. I need you to stay close to either me or my companions. One wrong move, and you'll be a goner." His voice was serious as he placed his hand on the sealed door, staring blankly.

"I know it's a Deity, but can a lone wolf really be that dangerous?" Lazarus asked.

"Oh, it isn't alone. You're a little too naïve to doubt the danger you're about to face."

"It's not that—I'm used to fighting wolves back home. Their movements were predictable; even as a pack, they would resort to circling their prey and attacking from a blind spot or flanking."

"For regular wolves, that's common knowledge. But we aren't dealing with a normal wolf. This is an elemental wolf from another world. Whether it uses its fangs, claws, or breath, each attack delivers powerful fire-element damage. It also won't try to flank you. Instead, it will charge straight at you with deceptive speed."

"Fire element, mixed attacker, frontal assaults. Don't worry about me, Magnus. When it comes to animals, no one is better than me at handling them. I'll show you."

"Confidence as well," Magnus said with a grin. "Would you believe me if I told you your parents fought this beast by themselves?" His hand tensed into a fist, steeling his nerves.

"They defeated this by themselves? How strong were they if even you struggle against it?" The weight of the upcoming battle bore down on him as he watched the sealed door fade away, revealing a raging blizzard that sent snow swirling through the doorway.

"Today is the day you clear this dungeon, Magnus." Gamma tugged at Lazarus' fur cloak. "Because it's not just you and me—Gamma is here as well, and his fire magic is powerful."

"Gamma here, no problem." His confidence in his power was somewhat reassuring, and Magnus and Lazarus both felt their bodies relax slightly, letting out a chuckle. They stepped into the snowy entrance, the force of the blowing winds and snow compelling them to cover their faces as they inched forward.

"We'll have to defeat the smaller pack first before we can fight the big bad. You should be strong enough to handle them. Take your time and defeat as many as you can before we face him," Magnus shouted over the howling wind, preparing Lazarus for the battle ahead.

Beyond the entrance, a snow-covered mountain range stretched before them, with a narrow pathway winding toward the summit. The three pressed on until they reached a clearing.

"Prepare yourself, Lazarus!" Magnus called out, brandishing his axe of mahogany and gold.

Howls echoed from ahead as wolves with snow-white fur leaped into the clearing from the cliff edges. A pack of twenty encircled them.

"Gamma, can you let me handle them? If you have any magic that can provide resistance to ice, that would help as well," Lazarus said, placing an arm in front of Gamma to stop him from stepping forward. Gamma nodded and cast a spell, enveloping Lazarus in a fiery glow that nullified the freezing air around him.

Magnus summoned his companions, and three flaming circles appeared in the snow before them.

Arctis, a white bird with light blue and white tail feathers, soared out of a flaming circle, leaving a trail of blue, mist-like energy.

Kuma, a giant crescent bear covered in snow-like white fur with a black crescent along his chest, crawled out of his flaming circle one paw at a time, towering over the snow wolves surrounding them.

Pyro, a flaming pumpkin-headed figure draped in a black cloak, with a small body hidden beneath and a flaming scythe in hand, rose from the fiery pit, a wide, menacing smile glowing from within the flames.

"Arctis will heal you and your spirits if any of you need healing. Kuma will defend you from most attacks, and Pyro will provide support or help you defeat the wolves if they're too strong."

The wolves attacked the group in unison, their fangs and claws slashing through the air as the group narrowly dodged the onslaught.

"You have to hurry and summon your spirits, Lazarus!"

"I'm on it! Rebirth... Jaeger, Ignis, on me!"

Two portals of black and purple energy appeared behind Lazarus as his summons emerged. Jaeger stalked out of his portal with a bow in hand, his eyes darting across the battlefield, scanning every direction. Ignis scoffed at the wolves as he crawled out of his portal, breathing fire onto the snow before them, melting it into a searing line of flames.

"Jaeger, hop on Kuma's back and pick your targets—we'll handle these ones," ordered Lazarus as Ignis breathed fire in a large circle around them, forming a protective barrier. Jaeger jumped onto Kuma's back, spun around, and crouched into his firing position before launching powerful shots at the wolves, aiming for their heads or necks to inflict maximum damage.

"Good job, Jaeger! Keep that up!" shouted Lazarus, standing beside Magnus.

Magnus struck any wolves that lunged at him with his fists, sending them flying toward Ignis or Jaeger to finish off. The pack's numbers dwindled—twenty became eighteen, then fourteen, nine, six—until only one remained. The last wolf bared its fangs and let out a howl.

"This is what we want, Lazarus. Don't worry about that call for help. We can do this one or two more times before they stop, and then we can move on. Use this time to train any skills you've learned," Magnus called out to Lazarus, who tensed at the sight of more wolves appearing.

Lazarus had taken several hits, sustaining wounds from claws and fangs. Arctis swooped down, shedding tears of ice onto him, healing his injuries.

"Remember what I said before—Arctis will heal you, so don't be afraid to get wounded."

Gamma began casting another fire spell, this time enhancing the wall of flames, increasing its height and width to prevent anyone from leaving or entering.

"Strong presence," Gamma said, pointing toward the top of the mountain. A thunderous roar echoed through the mountain cliffs.

"That sounds like he's appeared. He won't come down the mountain, though, so just focus on these wolves," Magnus said while looking at the mountaintop.

"Thank you for the assistance, old man. I'll take your advice and practise my mana technique." Lazarus sat down and closed his eyes. The sounds of howling, claws scraping against thick flesh, bursts of fire, and arrows piercing their targets filled the air around him. One by one, these sounds faded until only silence remained in the darkness of his mind.

Envision the flow of mana. Feel it coursing through your body. Feel it escaping your body. Reverse it.

Lazarus slowed his breathing, inhaling deep breaths and exhaling slowly. The entire process revealed itself as visible air inside his mind, with mana glowing purple as it left his body. With each breath, different-coloured strands of mana appeared around him, most of them light blue or white due to the terrain. As he breathed in, mana flowed into him—warm, radiant energy. He breathed out again, but the mana escaped.

That's not it. Try again.

He continued breathing, unaware of what was happening in the battle. This time, he held his breath. The mana coursed through his body, reinvigorating him before he exhaled.

It stayed this time! That must be the right process.

As he continued breathing in the mana, restoring his energy, his arms spread out, forming a funnel. The mana in the area began shifting into a purple hue, creating a sphere of energy that he could breathe in.

His eyes flicked open to see Ignis surrounded by wolves.

"Karah," he whispered.

A zap came from a portal by his side, triggering a chain reaction among the wolves until they crumpled to the frozen ground.

"Shadow."

Tendrils of black shadows lashed out at nearby wolves targeting Kuma, Jaeger, and Pyro, ensnaring the helpless creatures as Jaeger finished them off with a rain of arrows.

"What technique was that, Lazarus? Normally, we summoners would feel the strain of having this many out at once, yet you don't show any signs of fatigue," Magnus said, shocked by his display of control.

"This is a mana-restoring technique my mother helped me learn. It allows me to breathe in mana, restoring my supply for a limited time. I'm still learning how to use it properly, and I can't sustain it for long," Lazarus said. Staring at his hands, he felt the mana coursing through his body as if he hadn't used any summons at all.

"Well, it's a hell of a technique! You won't have much time to use that in the upcoming battle, but it'll come in handy, given the right opportunity. No more wolves are coming—your summons handled three groups well. Take this break to enhance your stats as much as you can. You'll need it." Magnus gripped his axe tightly, his fingers whitening from the pressure.

Lazarus took out Eclipse and infused mana into the sphere. Eclipse spun around as it assessed Lazarus' new status.

"I'm done processing your Aethercite. You have reached Level 27, with 950 Aethercite until your next level. You have 170 skill points and 144 stat points available."

With my current MP, I should be able to last just under five minutes with all my summons out at once. If I use my mana recovery, I restore only one mana per second—not enough to be useful in the next battle. I'll have to prioritise my summons to reduce the mana drain.

"Magnus, with my current MP, I'll last under five minutes with all my summons active. I'll have to limit myself to one or two at most. Gamma will have to cover the rest," Lazarus said.

"Summoning is powerful in short battles, but its weakness lies in drawn-out fights. You'll struggle to maintain yours while you're still new to the class, but as you and your summons develop, the mana strain will lessen, and you'll be able to summon them for longer periods. For me, they take half the mana they used to when I first started. Though I don't have any mana skills to counteract the strain, I prefer to fight alongside my companions and end battles quickly!" Magnus laughed, bumping the flat of his axe against his chest guard.

The group ventured up the snowy cliffside, all of them now resistant to the cold. The howling blizzard had little effect as they climbed higher until they reached the top.

An expansive, frozen plateau impervious to a wall of fire surrounding them, blocking off all escape routes except for one gap that led to a separate platform, which also had a wall of fire at its rear. No enemy was in sight.

Lazarus activated one of his new skills, Aura Sense, to detect any presence, but it was unsuccessful.

Where is he? I heard a loud howl earlier, Lazarus wondered. *Even in this blizzard, it shouldn't be hard to spot a large creature.*

"Don't drop your guard, Lazarus. He's here, just hiding." They ventured forward as the wind howled with an icy chill, stopping at a wolf statue in the centre.

Lazarus read the words inscribed on the stone tablet at its base. "In honour of the fallen deity, the Calamity. This is who we're facing? A Moon Wolf?" He tightened his grip on his staff.

"That's him! Once I activate this statue, it will summon a Moon Wolf and initiate the battle. I need to know that you're ready, Lazarus."

"No turning back. Whatever challenge I face, I will not back down." He said before removing Maeve's fur cloak, placing it in a safe spot away from the battlefield. "I'm ready."

Magnus stepped up to the statue, placing his hand on the wolf and releasing mana. "Good. Let's give it our all, then—no retreat!"

The ground rumbled as the cloud-filled sky dissipated, revealing a dark night sky full of stars and distant planets. A glowing sphere emerged on a floating platform at the edge of the cliff, resembling a miniature sun. An angry howl shattered the mountain's tranquillity.

"Here he comes, Lazarus! Pay attention to that sun over there—it will change with each phase. You'll need to use elements strong against the form it takes and destroy it to move to the next phase!" Magnus shouted before shoving Lazarus aside. Flames erupted from the ground, bursting into a towering pillar. Magnus slid across the scorched earth, clicking his tongue.

"Tide! Phantom! Rise!"

Two fiery pits opened in the ground, allowing a wolf-like creature with swirling water runes along its body and a mammoth with cascading water in place of fur to emerge from the depths of hell.

The rumbling stopped, but the pillars of fire continued to burst from the ground, increasing in speed until they formed a solid wall of flames. A snarl signalled its awakening. Peeking through the fire was a red-furred snout, followed by a menacing face, its massive body covered in flaming fur and white runic symbols. The beast crept forward, eyeing those who had summoned it from its slumber, black manacles rattling against the floor. The Calamity let out a bloodcurdling howl as it charged forward.

CHAPTER 28

"That's the third round of our matches concluded—an intense display of physical might. Eden and Adonis both ended up knocking each other out, with the rest of their squads lying in defeat. A stark contrast to the previous round, where Lilith and Jacques systematically eliminated each opponent before facing each other in a one-on-one duel—magic against archery. A high-speed battle designed to take down knights and weaken their overall fighting power. Every match so far has been a showcase of remarkable skill. Will our next competitors display the same resolve? Who's ready to find out?!" Morrigan roused the crowd for the next round.

"On the west side, we have Captain Mars, renowned for his mastery of fire-infused weapons and assassination techniques! On the east side, we have our second assassin knight, Captain Zachariah, wielding the power of light to deceive his opponents. Without further ado, let the match begin!"

"Do you guys remember the plan?" Zach asked his squad. Roman, Konan, Theo, Lorenzo, Tobias, and Astra all nodded, taking their positions with the rest of the team. Ronan and Konan leapt onto nearby pillars, landing smoothly and readying their bows, while three other archers perched in similar vantage points. Lorenzo and Tobias remained concealed behind boulders, prepared to provide healing and support from a distance, accompanied by three magic users and eight tanks. The second group, led by Zach, included Astra, Theo, and ten warriors. Astra brandished her sword as the mages cast a protective barrier to mitigate physical damage. Zach gripped his blades, his body suddenly radiating light before vanishing into invisibility.

"Leave the rear flank to me. Astra, you distract Mars," Zach ordered before leaving.

Astra nodded, keeping her eyes on Mars' group to anticipate their next move. Before she could react, Mars erupted in a blaze of fire, appearing within her circle and slashing through the cleric and mages, eliminating one of Zach's healers and their barrier.

That was too fast to react to. It's just like my Storm Walker technique! Astra thought.

She swung her sword at Mars, but his body transformed into flames, allowing the blade to pass harmlessly through.

"Archers, rain down on them!" Mars commanded, his gaze locking onto Astra. "You must be his secret weapon; I've never seen you before," he said coldly, thrusting his blade toward her.

Astra deflected the attack by gripping her sword at both ends, but the force of the thrust sent her sliding backward—straight into Theo's stomach.

The archers released their nocked arrows, but Theo swiftly conjured a barrier of water that caught the arrows and redirected them toward Mars. The projectiles passed through his flaming form harmlessly. Seizing the moment, Mars retreated to his squad. A magic wall materialised as the arrows struck, causing them to drop uselessly to the ground.

"Thank you, Theo! Let's keep moving. Stay together—no one strays from the group. Next time Mars attacks, I'll react faster," Astra said, coating her body in crackling lightning mana. "Group two, provide ranged support!"

Roman and Konan fired arrows into the sky, their shots raining down on the soldiers charging at Astra's team. Meanwhile, Zach's mages unleashed air and ice magic, freezing sections of the opposing side of the arena and trapping several soldiers in ice.

Nice! That's a third of their force taken care of. Now we need to break through that barrier and deal with the ranged units.

Clanging erupted from the opponents' side as an invisible force struck down the archers and mages, causing the magical barrier to dissipate. Mars noticed their plan and retreated to the rear to intercept the assassin, his aura blazing with fire energy as he blitzed toward his target, leaving a trail of flames. Sparks flew as Mars struck his target, light flaring in retaliation as Zachariah blocked the blades, locking them both in a rapid exchange of fire and light.

"Theo! We need to hurry. Knights, with me! Take out the remaining troops and advance."

Astra charged her lightning aura as she crouched, a bolt of electricity surging across the arena at blinding speed. In an instant, she cut down her opponents, their bodies collapsing to the ground as she pressed forward. Her charge brought her closer to Zach and Mars, allowing her to witness their battle in slow motion. She deflected Mars' attack on Zach and knocked the weapon from his hand. Unable to slow down, she crashed into a nearby pillar and stumbled, bracing herself against it.

Zach and Mars stared in disbelief at her incredible speed while Mars clutched his now-empty hand, his dagger lost.

"Lightning speed—that's quite impressive, newbie. But it seems you can't control your speed or trajectory. Let me show you how it's done!" Mars raised his voice as flames surged around him once more. Before Astra could react, he grabbed her and sprinted around the arena, slamming her into each pillar along the way. She coughed up blood, struggling to regain control, but her gaze remained locked onto Mars with a determined stare.

Gritting her teeth, Astra twisted her body around him, locking him in place as she held her sword behind his back. With a swift motion, she stabbed both him and herself. The two of them tumbled to the ground, rolling several times before coming to a stop.

"Astra! Are you okay? Let me heal you!" Tobias shouted as he barrelled through the arena, his massive fists smashing aside any opponent in his way.

Seizing the opportunity, Theo pinned Mars down, straddling him with a hammer poised over his head. A bubble of water formed around them, trapping Mars and preventing him from using his fire. Meanwhile, Tobias raised his staff over Astra, summoning a pillar of light around her. The bleeding from her wounds stopped, and the stab wound in her stomach disappeared. She gasped as her breathing steadied, then slowly sat upright.

"Did it work?" she asked, glancing around for Mars.

Zach smacked her on the back, revealing his presence as he lifted the invisibility.

"Did it work, she says! Of course, it bloody worked. You sacrificed yourself to deal with his experience in speed. I was banking on us winning with my plan. I thought you were insane when you proposed your idea of dealing with Mars!" Zach scolded his new knight but was relieved to see she was okay. He helped her up by grabbing her arm and raised it into the air as she stood. "Your winner!"

CHAPTER 29

"Mist, on me!" Lazarus called out, stretching his right arm to the side to create a portal. Mist swam through the air, noticing the larger water creatures beyond the giant wolf preparing to blast the Calamity with water, so she did the same. Streams of pressurised water struck the Moon Wolf from both sides. Letting out a painful howl, he glanced at the summoned creatures and, selecting the smallest one, shifted his trajectory as flames ignited from his red fur. The fiery beast tackled Mist just as she created a bubble of water to soften the blow. The bubble bounced off the ground and back into the air before the giant wolf sank his fangs into it, bursting both the bubble and Mist.

"Mist!" Lazarus shouted, running towards the Deity in anger.

"Lazarus! Calm yourself! The Calamity is aggressive and will actively target your spirits. Even if they seem gone, you can still summon them. Let me draw his attention first!" Magnus leapt onto the mammoth's back while the wolf with flowing water intercepted the Moon Wolf, using geysers as it ran beneath the larger wolf's belly.

"Keep it up, Tide, I'm on the way! Let's go, Phantom."

The mammoth spouted water from its trunk, causing rainfall above Shift. Magnus laughed as Phantom stepped forward.

Snap out of it. Like Magnus said, Mist is fine. I can't just rely on water, though—I need another strategy.

"Karah!" Lazarus ran forward as a portal emerged and leapt into the air, landing atop Karah as she raced across the terrain. "Charge up—we need to hit him with everything we have to make any kind of impact. Ísarr, Marsh! Target his legs—immobilise the Moon Wolf."

Karah charged electricity through her mane, the static humming as she galloped in a circle around the Moon Wolf and Magnus' companions. Ísarr appeared, the icy floor familiar beneath him. Moving with an agility Lazarus had never seen before, he dodged a paw strike from the Moon Wolf and lunged at its hind legs, sinking his small fangs into a damp spot where white runes remained untouched by flame.

Marsh leapt into the air with his powerful hind legs, shooting bubbles that burst into water upon contact with the Moon Wolf's flaming fur, creating an explosion of steam. As he landed, his wide mouth opened, and his long tongue shot out, whipping around the black chains. With all his strength, he pulled, trying to drag one of the giant wolf's legs.

The Calamity shook his body, pulling his hind leg forward along with Marsh and releasing a burst of flames that forced Marsh to retract his tongue and the ice spirit to retreat out of range. Unable to dodge in time, the Calamity kicked Marsh with enough force to send him hurtling into the wall of fire surrounding the battlefield. His armour burned as he collapsed to the ground before vanishing into a puddle of water.

I know I can't speak with any of you yet, but you did great, Marsh! You gave Ísarr enough time to attack!

Although tiny, Ísarr's bite managed to freeze the creature's legs to the ground. Phantom spotted the little being and sprayed water at the giant wolf's front legs, giving the spirit another opportunity to freeze more of its body. *Thank you, Phantom!*

The Moon Wolf caught on to the plan and bit into the feline spirit. Realising its mistake as its mouth froze along with one of its legs, it was left with only a single front leg free to move.

"Now, Karah!"

Hearing the command, Karah discharged her stored electricity, sending a bolt straight at the Moon Wolf's face. Tide and Phantom joined the attack with powerful blasts of water, their combined assault paralysing the beast.

"Lazarus, the core! Attack it while you can!" Magnus yelled.

The miniature sun had lost its flames, now appearing as a black sphere floating above the platform. Karah charged toward the gap in the wall, and Ísarr leapt onto Lazarus' shoulder as they passed. Magnus maintained his water assault, freezing more of the beast's body.

"Mist and Marsh, hit that sphere with everything you have!" Lazarus shouted as he jumped off her back, summoning his spirits as close to the core as possible. The two spirits leapt onto the floating platform, unleashing combined water blasts until the core cracked and shattered, revealing a second sphere—one that resembled a moon.

"Phase two," Magnus murmured.

The Calamity let out a howl as it leapt into the air. Swirling mists of freezing energy coiled around it, forming a sphere of ice that radiated an intense chill. Dark clouds rolled across the starry sky as howling winds and snow swirled into existence. In the distance, footsteps echoed toward them.

"Lazarus, recall your spirits now! Let me form a defensive line. You need to restore as much mana as possible. Gamma and I will protect you from any wolves that break through the vanguard."

Magnus recalled Phantom and Tide before summoning Sköll, Pyro, and Wrath. Sköll was another large wolf, its red fur marked with glowing orange runes. Wrath resembled a kangaroo, its hands and feet wreathed in flames.

An almost endless pack of wolves ascended the mountain, and Magnus' creatures formed a triangular formation, with Sköll at the forefront, leading the defence. As the wolves launched their assault, they charged straight at Sköll, who crouched her front legs, lowered her head, and unleashed a torrent of fire across the mountaintop entrance, scorching those who attempted to break through.

"Lazarus, the Calamity will enter its final phase after we defeat these wolves. Be prepared," Magnus said, igniting his axe and enveloping its head in flames.

If this is my chance, I might as well take it.

Lazarus sat down on the rough ground, entering a meditative state. Gamma stepped forward to assist Magnus and protect Lazarus, his small, furry hands forming balls of fire that he lobbed at the advancing wolves. Each one burst on impact, spreading flames across the battlefield. Wrath threw fiery punches, using its tail to lift itself and defend against attackers, kicking them away. Pyro swung his flaming scythe, cleaving through the pack, while fire poured from the mouth of its pumpkin-shaped head.

One by one, the wolves fell until none remained, leaving Magnus and his creatures worn out.

"Magnus, will we be able to handle the next phase?" Lazarus asked.

The chill radiating from the sphere crept along the cliffside, the scorched earth freezing over and transforming into a frozen tundra—an ominous welcome to the Calamity's second form.

"Honestly, I never made it this far. I had to retreat during that phase due to the overwhelming numbers. Without Gamma's support, I don't know if I would've been able to hold them back. Whatever happens now, we face it together!" Magnus was filled with newfound determination—one that left no room for fear, only the drive to succeed in this endeavour.

The group stepped out of the circle and surrounded the giant sphere as it began to expand. The Calamity burst through the snow sphere, sending shattered ice shards flying in every direction, forcing them to shield themselves. Upon landing on his new terrain, the Moon Wolf eyed the intruders menacingly. Now covered in snow-white fur and blood-red runes, he unclenched his jaws, frost escaping through glistening, bared fangs.

Frost breath, huh? Looks like he's switching to ranged attacks now. His focus seems sharper, too. I don't think this phase will be easy to handle. Wait... is he staring at me now?

"Watch out, Lazarus! Don't let him hit you!" Magnus yelled as he charged toward Lazarus. The Moon Wolf closed his mouth for a moment, emitting a whistling sound before firing a concentrated beam of ice at Lazarus. Just as it was about to strike, Magnus shoved him out of the way, taking the attack himself and sacrificing one of his arms to the icy blast.

The Calamity's paws thundered against the frozen earth as he raced along the outer edge of the icy arena, launching shards of ice at his opponents. Magnus intensified his burning aura, swinging his blazing axe with ferocity to withstand the relentless onslaught. A guttural roar erupted from within him, fueling his speed and destructive power as he fought back against the storm of ice.

"Magnus, your arm! Are you okay?" Panic laced Lazarus' voice as the consequences of the deity floor revealed their true form. Moon Wolf lunged at Magnus, who held his flaming axe in one hand, bared fangs snapping at him.

"Now isn't the time for idle chatter, Lazarus! Get back up and find a way to defeat the Deity!" Magnus shouted, sending a shiver through Lazarus' body. The sub-zero chill no longer affected him, but witnessing Magnus' intimidating fighting spirit filled him with both fear and respect.

Magnus kept his focus on the Calamity, matching the beast blow for blow, his movements different now—more agile, each step, arm swing, and kick serving a purpose to draw the deity's attention. He had no time to be distracted by his frozen arm or whatever Lazarus was planning. Instead, Sköll and Wrath, seeing their master fight with only one functioning arm, joined the fray. Sköll snarled and unleashed searing flames from her mouth while Wrath darted around the larger opponent, launching flaming fists and arcing fire to weaken the Calamity.

"Pyro, support Lazarus and follow his command—now go!" Magnus yelled, blood dripping from his axe arm and face.

How do I defeat that beast? Come on, think, dammit! Lazarus punched the ground with enough force to form a small crater. "Am I this strong now? Maybe I can use that to our advantage." He turned to his companion. "Gamma! I'm going to need your help. Can you create a powerful fireball—stronger than any you've made before?"

Gamma pressed a finger to his chin, considering the request.

"Big fireball, all out?" he asked Lazarus as if seeking permission to do something reckless.

"Exactly. Don't hold anything back—show us how big you can make it! I'll call you when we're ready for you to use it," Lazarus ordered, summoning a portal for Ignis to step through. "Ignis! I want you to join Gamma and stay on the floating platform. Attack that moon-like sphere with everything you've got!"

Ignis searched for Gamma and scurried across the frozen floor to join them as they made their way to the second platform.

"Old man, I've got a plan—a dangerous one. Do you trust me?" he asked the elder adventurer, closing in on the group trying to pin down the Calamity. Wrath leaned back on his tail as Lazarus jumped into the air, landing on Wrath's feet, which sent him springing back into the sky. *Make this work. Focus your mana!*

"Dangerous plan? Trust? I'm beyond that at this stage. We need to throw everything at this guy if we have any hope of coming out alive. Do what you need to do—don't worry about us!" Magnus shouted as his axe clashed against ice claws.

Locked in combat with Sköll, Wrath, and Magnus, they exchanged elemental techniques in a dazzling display of fire and ice blasts, creating a chain reaction of explosive colour. As Lazarus descended, condensed mana surrounded his polearm. The flames of the explosions scorched his skin while the ice built up frost. He forced his eyes open against the pain, tearing up in the process, determined to strike his target accurately.

I've managed to learn one technique for my polearm skills, so I have something to use that doesn't drain mana. It's not the most ideal battle to test it out, but it's all I have!

The polearm transformed as mana coursed around it, shaping into a hammer of fire.

"Moon Wolf, today you go down. I'm giving my all with this attack!"

Lazarus slammed the fiery hammer into the beast's back, crushing it against the ground. Flames spread across the snow, consuming the ice in their path.

Sköll sank his flaming fangs into the giant wolf's neck, singeing its white fur. The massive wolf roared, shaking its weakened body in an attempt to throw Sköll off. The blizzard converged on him, forming a spear of ice that pierced Sköll, making him wince in pain.

"Lazarus! Tell me your plan is ready; we won't be able to hold on much longer!" Magnus yelled, driving his axe into the side of the Calamity. The beast let out a primal howl, instilling fear in both Magnus and Lazarus. Turning to Magnus, it clamped its jaws around his frozen arm and snapped it off.

Magnus screamed in agony, collapsing to the ground and clutching his shoulder in a desperate attempt to staunch the bleeding. "Arctis! I need your help!"

Lazarus stood frozen in shock, watching the brutal ease with which Magnus's arm had been torn away. A single question echoed in his mind—*Am I going to die?*

Arctis flew over, her tears falling onto Magnus's wound, stopping the bleeding but unable to restore the lost arm.

"Magnus!" *I don't know if he can keep fighting against the Moon Wolf. What can I do to stop him?*

Lazarus examined his opponent's body, searching for a weakness—anything that could stop him long enough for Gamma to defeat him. *That's it! I can stop him if I can get close enough.*

He sprinted toward his opponent, dodging swiping paws and ducking under the wolf's head as it snapped at him. He slipped beneath the beast. "Here we go!" Gripping his staff, he thrust it into the chain attached to one of the wolf's manacles.

The struggle to hold it was intense as the wolf thrashed wildly. It bit into Sköll's shoulder, forcing her to release her grip before pinning her to the ground. Now free, the beast tried to retreat, dragging Lazarus with it, but he used all his strength to hold the chain and slow it down.

Sköll saw what he was doing and lunged at the Moon Wolf again, this time seizing another chain and pulling in the opposite direction. The giant wolf, unable to break free, collapsed to the ground once more, howling in fury, its drool freezing as it dripped from its mouth.

"Uh oh," was all Lazarus could say as the Moon Wolf opened its jaws, freezing the air to form an ice beam.

"Gamma! On me!" he shouted as the beam shot toward him.

An arm wielding a dark red sword appeared, deflecting the attack. The trajectory shifted, but the ice still grazed Lazarus' shoulder, freezing it.

Lazarus cried out, his biceps straining as he struggled to hold the giant wolf in place, the frostbite numbing his left arm.

Whatever that was, it saved me from certain death.

Before the Calamity could launch another blast, darkness gave way to the blazing light of a fireball, melting the ice walls as it descended upon the arena. Ignis collapsed to the ground, exhausted, alongside Gamma and Pyro.

You did good, you two. Rest easy.

The Calamity's eyes widened as he saw the fireball hurtling toward him. Struggling to break free, he shook Sköll and Lazarus with all his might. Lazarus held on with every ounce of strength he could muster, gripping the wedged staff until his hands blistered. Sköll sank her fangs deeper, anchoring him in place. Her body tensed, muscles taut, as she leered at the larger wolf with rage-filled eyes.

The fireball continued its descent, the melting walls vanishing in its wake. Magnus had recovered enough to rejoin the fray, wrapping a third chain around his waist and gripping the end with his remaining arm. Using every last bit of his strength, he pulled at another of the beast's legs. The creature's eyes reflected the flames of impending doom as it let out a final, bloodcurdling howl. Then, the fireball struck its mark, erupting into a fiery inferno that blasted everyone away.

Lazarus, unconscious, slid across the drenched terrain—over the edge of the plateau and into the darkness.

"You will not die here!" Magnus roared, using his remaining arm to seize Lazarus' wrist. He braced himself against the ice, but he could feel it cracking beneath him. With one last burst of strength, he hurled Lazarus up and over himself before collapsing in exhaustion.

Fire scorched the melting plateau. The Deity lay motionless, eyes closed, his body marred with scorch marks. Lazarus, struggling to stand, limped toward the Moon Wolf's unconscious form, purple energy swirling around his right hand as he drew near.

I won't let this opportunity go to waste! All of this power that you hold is coming back with me as payment for Magnus' arm!

"You may have been a deity, but to me, you are no different from any other creature. You hurt, you bleed, you rage... you feel emotions. I am not here to kill you. Instead, I give you a choice—join us. Help me prevent this world from succumbing to chaos. Join me, and you'll face foes more powerful than you can imagine, with the opportunity to unleash your full power upon them and go wild. Join me and fight against this world's so-called order," Lazarus said, blood dripping from a devilish grin as he stood before the downed beast.

The Calamity regained consciousness, struggling to rise but collapsing helplessly to the ground. His weakened gaze remained fixed on Lazarus, who reached for his neck to initiate his Tame skill.

Purple flames coiled around the beast's neck, forming a black metal collar adorned with two glowing purple lines along its edges. The flames then spread across his body, mending wounds and erasing burn marks. As the healing took effect, he fully regained consciousness and lay on his stomach.

"You're terrifying as an opponent, but as an ally, I fear more for anyone who dares to stand against us," Lazarus said, patting the giant wolf, who howled in response.

"You did it, Lazarus! Not only did you help me defeat this deity, but you also managed to tame him. I'm beyond impressed!" Magnus boomed, a proud smile on his face as he ran toward Lazarus—only to stumble and crash to the ground.

"Take it easy, Magnus! We won; you don't have to exert yourself anymore," Lazarus said with concern.

"Take your own advice, Lazarus. This was no small victory. When we return, drinks are on me," Magnus said, his eyes closed as he raised a triumphant fist in the air.

Lazarus let out a tired sigh before collapsing against the wolf's stomach, closing his eyes as well.

CHAPTER 30

"Our final round will be between Captain Sapphire and her squad against myself. Sapphire and her squad are healers and will provide support for the rest of you on the battlefield," Morrigan announced from her balcony. "Sapphire, join me in the arena and give me a worthy battle!"

She clenched her fist and pointed toward Sapphire, who smiled and leapt onto the arena grounds.

"We're ready when you are, Commander!" Sapphire responded.

Morrigan's aura burst into flames as she bounded toward the arena, taking position at its centre. "I'll give you the field advantage, Sapphire, by staying in the centre. If you manage to push me past these pillars, I'll give you the win," she stated, pointing at the pillars.

"I know very well that's not much of an advantage to us. Regardless, we will give it our all to put on a show." Sapphire readied her stance as her squad formed around her, taking positions on each side of Morrigan.

Morrigan raised her arm and shot fire from her hand into the sky. "Let the final round begin!" she shouted, eyeing the opposing team.

Sapphire enhanced each of her teammates' auras with water-element energy to counter Morrigan's fire-element strength, reducing the commander's offensive damage as much as she could.

"I'll do my best, Commander!" she said as she ran her hand along her katana, coating it in water energy. A single wave surged in front of her before she sprinted at her opponent, using water to skate across the arena and circle around Morrigan while picking up speed.

Morrigan's ember-like eyes tracked Sapphire's movements through her arms, which were raised to guard her face. While distracted by the Valour Captain, two archers fired arrows at her, while five mages used earth and ice magic to encase her legs in their respective elements. Four guardians positioned themselves around her, ready to prevent any escape attempt.

"Captain Sapphire, we've restricted her movements! Are you ready?!" one of her team members called out as Sapphire's run transitioned into skating. She slashed toward Morrigan, sending a stream of water rushing at her opponent. Morrigan blocked the attack with her flaming gauntlets, causing steam to erupt as fireballs shot from her fists in retaliation. The guardians intercepted the attack, dispersing the flames in a coordinated effort.

"Good job, guys—don't give her a chance to counter," Sapphire praised them.

Arrows of water flew through the sky, raining down on the trapped opponent. While the commander focused more on Sapphire than the others, Sapphire unleashed a barrage of water-based attacks, landing a hit on Morrigan's chest. With her body stuck in the ground, Morrigan had no way to redirect the impact into the earth. She grunted in pain, her flames intensifying as they melted through the ice and earth restraining her legs.

"If you don't mind, I'd like to have a turn to attack!" she declared. Bursting free from the ground, Morrigan leapt into the air and spun, unleashing a wave of fire at each of the guardians. Though they managed to defend themselves, the force of the flames pushed them back.

Morrigan landed and swiftly moved in front of one of them, placing her hands on their armour and planting her feet. "Rupture!" she called out, releasing a concentrated stream of fire from her palms. The flames burned through the armour and out the other side, destroying a pillar in the process. She watched it collapse, then shook her hands and feet.

"Maybe too much firepower for that one. I'll have to adjust my strength," Morrigan remarked, engulfing her boots in flames.

Witnessing the burning passion of Commander Morrigan, the crowd cheered and watched in awe as she moved through the arena like a wildfire tearing through a forest.

Morrigan unleashed a flurry of fiery punches and kicks against the remaining guardians, explosive flames erupting with each strike. Her attacks grew faster until she finally knocked them out. The mages panicked and attempted to cast water spells at her, but she conjured a funnel of fire that turned the water to steam. Leaping from the flames, she grabbed one of them, spun them around, and hurled them into another mage.

Sapphire observed the chaotic struggle against the commander and summoned a wave of water, slicing it along the stone ground. The tidal wave surged forward, engulfing Morrigan and consuming everything in the arena. Water-formed fists lifted her squad members and placed them atop the pillars.

"How do you fare being submerged, Commander?" Sapphire asked, pride evident in her voice.

"I won't lie; I'm not in a good position," Morrigan replied calmly before diving beneath the water, unleashing her flaming aura. Hounds of fire raced through the depths, causing the water to bubble.

"I see, using your fire to evaporate my water? Will you make it in time?" Sapphire mused with a smile.

Another burst of aura erupted from Morrigan, this time creating a vortex of flame that pulled the water into a spiraling tornado. "I always find a way out of a bad situation, Sapphire!"

The mixed tornado of fire and water exploded with intense heat. Morrigan collapsed to the ground, gasping for air, then rolled onto her back.

"Don't let this opportunity slip—pressure her," Sapphire ordered coldly. Her squad leapt down from their pillars and, with a combined effort, launched their second assault.

"Go—Good… this is good," Morrigan struggled to speak, having exhausted her stamina underwater. Still, she didn't give up. Rolling into a position where she could push herself off the ground, she used her flaming fists and legs to propel herself into the air, launching above Sapphire's squad just as they were about to strike.

The archers fired at their airborne opponent, but Morrigan twisted her body mid-air, avoiding most of the arrows—though a few grazed her.

Archers above, close-range fighters below. I should deal with the ground first, Morrigan thought, assessing her opponents' positions. Flames erupted from her fists, burning hotter than any fire she had used in the match until they took the form of a giant hellhound's face. She punched toward the group below, and the fiery beast roared as it descended, blanketing the sky in an inferno.

"I suggest jumping in the water!" Morrigan teased as she searched for a landing spot. Opting to use her flaming fists for propulsion, she launched toward a pillar, gripping onto it just as the Hellhound struck the arena.

Decided to face my Hellhound head-on. That's brave—but reckless.

As the flames subsided and the smoke dispersed, a few remaining knights were revealed, covered in steam and unable to stand.

"It's not over yet, Commander! My squad is tough and won't go down without a fight!" Sapphire called out as she resumed gliding around the arena on her stream of water, picking up speed.

"I'm sorry I have to do this to you, Commander Morrigan, but we have to do whatever it takes to stop you," a guardian said as he tackled the commander, locking her in his arms.

"Not at all, Creed. Do what you have to do to win!" Morrigan struggled to free herself from his grip, realising he was aiming for a boundary win. She smiled as she suddenly stopped and positioned her arms behind her, releasing a stream of fire from her palms. The pressure from the fire altered their trajectory, sending them crashing into a pillar with enough force to break Creed's hold. Morrigan seized the moment and escaped.

"That was a clever strategy, but it was executed too slowly, giving me plenty of time to break free. Think about how you can do that faster next time. Bye!" Morrigan complimented her opponent before tripping his feet and kicking him over the edge of the arena. "Now, you three."

Morrigan charged at them, flames igniting along her body. The defending knights braced themselves and intercepted her first strike, engaging in a close-quarters brawl with the commander. One wielded a sword and shield, another fought with daggers, and the last relied on his bare fists. At first, each managed to hold their ground—until one misjudged a step and fell back, allowing Morrigan to gain the upper hand.

Proceeding to take them out one by one, she clutched the shield knight and rolled on the ground, throwing him into the water. The next opponent, she tackled into a pillar with enough force to knock them out, leaving only the one who had tripped. Just as they managed to get back on their feet, Morrigan delivered a roundhouse kick enhanced by fire, knocking them out.

A vortex of water swirled around the arena as Sapphire enveloped her aura in water. Using the momentum she had gained during the scuffle below, she swept across the battlefield, slamming into Morrigan's back and pushing her toward the edge. "Archers! Focus fire on her, now!" Sapphire shouted as she continued to pressure her commander.

Morrigan braced herself by blasting fire into the water, sending steam rising from the surface as she cried out from the exertion. Two giant pillars of water formed and twisted like snakes, striking from either side and hitting her ribs with a constant stream of pressurised water.

Morrigan screamed under the barrage of attacks, and in a last-ditch effort to avoid defeat, she exhaled fire into a sphere, keeping it away from the water. As she condensed the sphere, it shrank to the size of a pebble. "You've done well, Sapphire! Against another opponent, you'd have won this struggle. The problem is... I hate to lose. So you'd better defend yourself and your team from this next attack," Morrigan said, locking eyes with her protégé.

Sapphire realised what she intended to do and quickly called off her teammates, channelling her stored water to form barriers around them. The strain weighed on her body, but she pushed herself to protect them.

Morrigan stood back up, grabbed the fire sphere, and released it into the air. "Detonate," she whispered. The sphere imploded, sending a powerful flaming shockwave across the arena, knocking everyone into pillars, boulders, and even the walls lining the river canal.

Shaking the water from her clothes, Morrigan scanned the arena for anyone who had managed to block the blast. "I take it no one avoided that last attack? If not, this is my win."

Sapphire climbed onto the arena, drenched in water, and lay on her back, breathing heavily. "Did you have to go that far to defeat us? That took everything... out of me... to protect everyone. Please don't make me do that again," she said between laboured breaths.

Morrigan strode over and helped her up. "You did amazing, Sapphire. Working in tandem with your squad to pressure me left me with no choice but to give it my all." She then turned to the knights watching from the sidelines. "Anyone want to assist the wounded?"

At once, they stood up, ready to help retrieve those floating in the water or lying on the arena floor.

The crowd erupted in cheers, the excitement growing louder by the second as they witnessed the dramatic conclusion of the final match.

"Once we've finished treatment, I want all of you to rest and reflect on these matches—think about what you could have done better and how you lost. Figure out what you need to improve, and we'll discuss it tomorrow morning," Morrigan instructed.

With her arm wrapped around Sapphire's waist, she supported her weakened body as they left the arena together.

☆ ☆ ☆ ☆

In the confines of a small, dark room stood a knight clad in black armour from head to toe, his presence illuminated only by the emerald glow of his eyes through his helmet. A dark green cloak draped over his shoulders, rustling ever so slightly in an unseen breeze.

"I see. They shall be exhausted after their training. When wouldst thou like to proceed?"

Silence filled the room as the knight awaited a response.

"As thou command, my liege. I shall deal with her first."

The glow of his emerald eyes dimmed, and the husk of a knight in onyx-black armour, gripping a massive obsidian blade, slowly faded into the shadows—leaving the room empty.

CHAPTER 31

"Your arm—what are you going to do now?" Lazarus knew it was a sensitive issue, but he was still curious about how Magnus felt about the outcome.

"Well, I won't be able to pat more than one companion at a time anymore!" Magnus laughed, pretending to pet an imaginary creature. "I'd say that's quite a loss. But seriously, I'll have to figure out how to compensate for this missing arm," he added with a sombre tone. Lazarus could see that Magnus was struggling with his loss, but he was doing his best to put on a brave face.

"Maybe Cryo or Ticy can help you with a prosthetic arm?" Lazarus suggested. Magnus stroked his beard, pondering the thought.

"Let's hear it then—you owe me an explanation," Lazarus said as they rode atop the Moon Wolf, which raced across the snowy path, weaving through the white forest.

"Yeah, yeah, I hear you. You want to know about these Deities. I'm no expert on the matter, but I've dabbled in some books that contain information about them. They are creatures and humans wielding tremendous power—beings of the ancient past."

"He does seem powerful, but I doubt that was his full strength. Otherwise, we'd be dead," Lazarus said, recalling the battle.

"That is true. I believe those shackles on his legs are what dampen his power. Right now, he's just a giant wolf, but to them, he was a bringer of chaos—a calamity." Magnus held onto the wolf with his arm as he spoke to Lazarus. "There are many more deities residing in the Tower, even more powerful than the Calamity. We've found that after the Calamity on floor fifteen, they appear every ten floors. I assume that pattern continues all the way up to floor ninety-five."

The Moon Wolf snarled in response—the thought of another creature stronger than him clearly bothered him.

If there are more deities in the Tower, maybe Aldo has more information about them. Though I doubt he'll be happy to hear I battled one so soon.

"Once we return, I'll report this battle to Aldo and let him know you were the one who defeated the Calamity—with help from your friend," Magnus said, the tunnel of wind from their speed whipping their hair back and rustling their clothes.

"About that… can you keep Gamma a secret for now? I don't want him to be known in the city and draw attention. I'm sure Aldo will believe you and your companions defeated the Calamity," Lazarus requested, glancing back at Gamma, who was clutching the wolf's fur and laughing.

Magnus peered at Gamma as well. "Hmm… very well. As thanks for defeating the Calamity, I'll make sure his identity remains hidden. Maybe he should leave us before we reach the gate so we don't attract any attention."

"Good idea. Gamma, can you meet me in our room without anyone detecting you? I don't want to leave you alone out here," Lazarus asked.

He turned to see Gamma had let go of the wolf's fur and was now staring at him.

"Fun end?" Gamma asked, looking downtrodden.

"I'm sorry, Gamma. There will be more fun tomorrow, but for now, we need to rest so we can fight at full strength."

"Need rest? Gamma goes," he replied, hopping off the giant wolf. "Bye-bye." He waved before leaping ahead, using the dense cover of the forest to sneak toward the city.

"There's this key as well. Aldo mentioned that it might be used to unlock a sealed door at the top of the Tower. What do you think?" Lazarus asked, pulling out the key. It had a unique design, with a pattern resembling the Moon Wolf engraved along the handle.

"Unlocking a door is a safe bet, though I don't know what the doors on the upper floors look like to give an accurate answer. If it came from a Deity, I suggest keeping it close to you at all times. You don't want it falling into the wrong hands, Lazarus. That includes giving it to me," Magnus said, giving serious thought to what it might unlock.

Before long, they reached the gates of Baylor, where a squad of soldiers stood with their weapons drawn.

"Halt!" shouted the captain of the guard, a tall man clad in white armour and red garments. "You will come no further, foul beast! Release!"

Archers loosed their arrows at the giant wolf, but the beast roared, exhaling an icy breath that froze the projectiles mid-air, causing them to shatter harmlessly against its frost-covered fur.

"Stand down, Captain Gerard! It's me—Magnus! And my friend here, Lazarus!" Magnus shouted from atop the wolf's back, raising his one arm. Lazarus remained hidden, clutching tightly to its fur.

"Magnus, the Beast Tamer?" the captain asked, waving his arm for the guards to lower their weapons. "Is that you?"

Magnus jumped down to the ground and walked toward the captain. The giant wolf sat down, watching the guards, who froze in fear at the sight of the beast, while Lazarus trailed behind Magnus.

"I apologise for the surprise—he just made travelling much easier on these old bones of mine. This is the Calamity, a creature that Lazarus here has tamed, so you have no need to fear him. Lazarus, would you mind recalling him before we enter the gates?" he asked, looking at the captain.

Lazarus created a giant portal of swirling black and purple energy. The wolf stepped through, disappearing into the void.

"You must have had a tough battle for someone as strong as you to lose an arm," Captain Gerard commented, gesturing toward Magnus's left side.

Magnus placed his right hand on his left shoulder. "Tougher than you can imagine. I'd say one arm is a small price to pay for defeating a deity—not many adventurers can boast about that."

Magnus and Lazarus passed the guards and headed back into the city.

Little feet scurried through the snow, searching for a hiding place. Chest heaving with each breath, clothes clung to sweat-drenched skin.

In the distance, loud voices shouted, red lights flickered from the village, and smoke rose into the sky. The young boy searched the barn.

"Ísarr, where are you?! We have to leave!" he pleaded.

Hay shifted, and a small white cat emerged from its hiding spot, purring.

"There you are. Come here."

Cradling the cat in his arms—despite it almost outweighing him—he hurried to the entrance, only to bump into a large man rounding the corner.

"I thought I saw someone run off. What do you hope to accomplish, Lazarus?"

"Who are you? How do you know my name?" Lazarus asked, shielding Ísarr on the ground.

The man smirked. "You see, we had a name for ourselves back in Baylor. Everyone feared us—it was amazing. We could walk through the streets, and people would cower. Until one day, a young girl intervened. Ignorant of who we were, she stepped in to defend a stranger, summoning a spirit owl that attacked us. Well, we made quick work of her."

"That has nothing to do with me! Leave us and the village alone!" the boy shouted, tears swelling in his eyes, lips quivering.

"Nothing to do with you?" The man leaned over him and yanked the cat from his arms with a brutal grip. "Boy, it has everything to do with you. That girl who attacked us—the man with the crimson sword who came to her rescue—they're the ones who changed everything! We had it good before your meddling mother and father interfered," he spat.

"Go away! I have no idea what you want!"

Lazarus head-butted the man's stomach, forcing him to drop Ísarr.

"Let's go, Ísarr!" Lazarus yelled as they bolted from the barn.

"Oh no, you're not going anywhere."

A tall, slender woman emerged, draped in ragged winter clothes and a tattered checkered shawl. Her hollow eyes gleamed with malice. Around the barn, a group of bandits closed in, blocking any escape.

"What's going on? Just leave us alone!"

Ísarr leapt at the woman, claws tearing at her tender flesh, raking across her eye.

"Gah! Blast it! Get me that cat, you idiots!" she shrieked.

A hulking figure lurched forward, raising a rectangular shield to block Ísarr's path. Using the shield as a springboard, the cat leapt above—only to be caught in giant hands. Trapped, Ísarr hissed furiously as the gruff, dishevelled giant stroked his fur.

"I-I caught it, L-Lady Alvara," he stammered.

A bandit beside him struck him for speaking her name.

"Lazarus, son of Adelheid and Cyrus. Tell me, where are they?" Alvara demanded, her long, pointed ears twitching.

"I don't know! Put down Ísarr—give him back!"

Lazarus lunged for his friend, but a fist struck his face, sending him sprawling to the ground.

"If you won't tell us when we ask nicely, maybe this will help."

Alvara pulled out a bloodstained dagger. With a haunting whistle, she summoned her giant subordinate. Ísarr thrashed in the brute's grip, hissing and clawing at the air.

Then, with a swift motion, the blade sliced across his neck.

A waterfall of crimson poured forth, washing away any hope of survival.

"So, you won't tell us? Maybe you don't know after all," Alvara mused, gazing at the smoke rising from Riverfall. Moonlight accentuated her pale skin, giving her an almost demonic presence. "Don't tell me they abandoned you? Left all alone in a tucked-away village. Abandoned by your friends, your village… your own parents. It seems to me no one wants you, Lazarus. How does it feel?" she taunted, waving a knife in front of him.

He could only stare, too afraid to move, too afraid to speak—his breaths coming in short, erratic gasps.

"You broke him, boss. Now, what are we going to do?" one of the bandits laughed.

"I say we kill him too—get rid of the whole family!" another blurted.

"No, we will not kill him. I want him to know what they did. I'm going to make sure he never forgets," Alvara said, pressing the dagger against his finger. Her hands clamped around Lazarus' throat in a vice-like grip as she tore his tunic away. Blood spattered as he was slammed against the ground. His screams shattered the silence as the dagger sliced into his back.

The cold snow stung his cheek, dulling—if only for a moment—the searing pain of steel cutting through flesh. His blank stare met the pale moon above before his gaze drifted downward. Leaves of lilac and teal floated in the gentle breeze. Thick bushes lay draped in a pristine blanket of white. A wild mane of hair, darker than any shadow, stood in stark contrast.

Beyond the lifeless body of a cherished familiar, past the jeering laughter hidden within the undergrowth, a child's face peeked through. Ice-blue eyes reflected the moonlight, flickering with anger and static.

"Icy..." Lazarus whispered.

☆☆☆☆

Gasping for air and clutching his chest, Lazarus woke in a violent panic, covered in sweat.

A faint pressure greeted his hands. He twisted around to find Astra holding onto him. His breathing slowed, his vision steadied, and more details of the room came into focus.

"I'm right here, Lazarus. You're okay," she reassured him, moving his hand to her chest.

Her soft touch calmed him, but more than that, it was the rhythmic beating of her heart that helped him return to reality.

He paused, catching his breath before speaking. "I'm sorry, Astra. The same nightmare. My scars ache every time I wake up after seeing their faces."

"They can't hurt you anymore, I promise. And if anyone else tries to, I'll be here to send them to the afterlife."

"Yeah, you're right. Thank you, Astra."

Lazarus held her hand to his forehead, closing his eyes to take in the moment—the warmth of her body and the icy glow of her eyes.

The sharp scent of sweat filled the lounge as Lazarus entered. Astra was practising sword strikes, her movements fluid and precise. Bandages wrapped around her chest, and her black training pants accentuated her athletic form.

"How was your Tower venture yesterday? Sorry if I passed out before you got back. We had mock battles, and I used my Storm Walker technique against a captain. I'm still recovering from the wound," Astra said, switching to lunges to refine her technique.

Lazarus sat in a chair by the couch, holding a journal in his hand.

"That's okay. I'm proud of you for winning. That couldn't have been an easy battle for you or your team."

As for my day..." He let out a huff, recalling the arduous battle against the giant beast. "We managed to defeat a deity..." he said slowly, watching for her reaction.

She straightened, turning to him with a stare of disbelief.

"Deity? As in beings capable of vast destruction, omniscient knowledge, and immortality? Those deities?!"

Lazarus nodded with a faint smile.

"How are you even alive right now, you idiot?! Deities aren't something you can fight and walk away from unscathed," she scolded, though he knew it wasn't out of anger but relief that he was still here, in one piece.

"Well, I have Gamma and Magnus to thank for that. Without them, I wouldn't have stood a chance—I wouldn't have lasted five seconds against him," he admitted, clenching his fist.

"We fought the Calamity, a ferocious, giant wolf with immense strength, wielding both Fire and Ice magic. At one point, he even summoned a massive pack of wolves to attack us. Magnus and his companions took the brunt of the onslaught, allowing us to draw his attention while Gamma charged a massive fireball for the finishing blow—the same fireball magic that defeated the Mortesyn."

Lazarus finished his explanation and relaxed back into his chair.

"I'm just glad you're alive!" Astra pulled him into a tight hug before pulling back to gaze into his verdant green eyes.

"Anyway, how do you know about the deities? I only learned about them yesterday," Lazarus asked, his curiosity piqued.

"Well, I don't know what they look like. All I know is that when I was a child before I even met you, my mother would read me stories about powerful beings and creatures from other worlds. I would ask her to read them every night. The sad part is I don't remember what my mother looks like. Did I get my looks from her—my hair, my eyes?" Astra recounted, reminiscing about her childhood memories.

"Don't you think it's odd that there are stories about these deities? How would they know about them unless they fought them in the tower?" Lazarus asked.

"Maybe they did fight them, or maybe these stories existed before the towers. We don't have enough information to truly understand all of this. I'm just glad you're safe after having fought one."

"I'm not going anywhere, Astra. We've both lost our parents, but I promise I'll be right by your side when you need me. Even the organisation I'm meant to face will have their work cut out for them trying to kill me. I'll give them hell before I take my last breath," Lazarus said as he gazed into her gleaming sapphire eyes.

"There's no way I'm letting you face them by yourself. I'll fight by your side, and we'll defeat them together. Promise me you won't fight them without me!" Astra demanded, her voice tinged with frustration.

Lazarus grabbed her hands and pressed them to his heart, letting her feel his steady heartbeat. "I promise you, I'll make sure you're by my side so we can give them hell together."

Astra nodded, and he could tell she knew he was speaking the truth. She rested against his chest for a while before they had to leave.

CHAPTER 33

Byron finished processing the cores Lazarus had obtained from the dire wolves, leaving him with two B-rank dark cores and two C-rank dark element cores.

There's an ability I can get that will allow me to rank up my summons using cores. I don't need to summon another dark element spirit, but I can use these to make Shadow more powerful. I'm sure he'd love it. But for now, I'm going to get one of each element first.

"I'm looking for air, earth, and light cores. Do you have any of those?" Lazarus asked, touching a light grey one that appeared to contain mist.

"The one you just touched is an air core. Generally, the colour of the core determines its element. Sometimes, they share a colour but have different shapes. Take the lightning core you bought—it had a yellow colour but was spiky and had surging electricity inside. A light element core will be spherical and emit a bright glow. They're commonly used as light sources around the city or in dungeons. Air element cores come in assorted colours, ranging from light grey and sky blue to green. For the ones you're looking for, there's a B-rank earth core, an A-rank light core, and an A-rank air core. The total cost for those will be four gold and 35 silver tabs. Is that all?" Byron explained, his tone patient but brisk.

Lazarus proceeded to buy the new cores.

Thankfully, Magnus already shared his half of the reward, so I can afford this now. I can create three new spirits. I'll have to think about what I want to summon.

"I'm going to need to buy more healing vials. Do you have anything for frostbite and poison?" Lazarus asked as he glanced at the potion racks, having not examined them before.

"Frostbite? This one will take care of that within seconds. As for poison, you'll want these antidotes—they cure just about every type you might encounter in the Tower," Byron said, procuring several vials. The frostbite remedy glowed an icy blue while the antidotes shimmered in various shades of purple.

"This will do. I'll need them for my upcoming Tower battle. Thank you." Lazarus paid for the items and left the dimly lit alchemist's shop.

Before heading to the guild, he stopped by Ticy's outfit store to buy new clothes. Knowing the Tower's diverse environments required preparation, he selected warm black attire to match the fur cloak Maeve had made for him.

Seems like the others have already gone off to the Tower, Lazarus thought as he stepped into the quiet guild hall.

Sitting in their usual booth, Arcanum relaxed with several drinks. Seeing an opportunity to strengthen his relationship with them, Lazarus took the initiative and sat down, catching them off guard.

"Good morning, Arcanum. You seem a lot quieter than usual. Are you doing okay?" Lazarus asked sincerely.

"Don't patronise us, Lazarus," Orion replied, his cold, dark eyes locking onto him.

"Wait, Orion. He didn't do anything wrong, so calm down," Lucia interjected, grabbing Orion's arm before he could act impulsively. "It hasn't been a good few days for us. We visited the Tower, but it's not the same without Nox. So we've decided to wait for him to return."

"Why did he even use his aura on me? Doing it as a 'test' doesn't make sense. He could have waited for the guild rank assessment next week to test my skills," Lazarus said.

"I'll admit, he didn't think that through. He's a strong adventurer, but sometimes he acts before thinking. It's gotten us into several bad situations before, though we don't hold it against him because he always makes up for it," Delilah said as she created a small ball of water in her hand and began spinning it, carefully containing its shape so it didn't splash anyone.

"That's right. Even if our plans don't go the way we want, we always come back together and work through the battle as one. Anyway, Lazlo! I heard you and Magnus defeated the Calamity yesterday. How was it?! I bet he was a handful for you, right?" Jules said enthusiastically, slapping Lazarus on the back.

"Do you mind not touching me? Yeah, we defeated the Calamity—at the cost of one of Magnus' arms. I can't call it a victory when we lost something in the process," Lazarus replied with regret.

"Aye, don't be so hard on yourself. You're new to this experience. Mistakes are bound to happen when we visit those dungeons. Remember, it could have been a lot worse. Each of us has lost someone to the tower. We came together to support each other. Take this as a learning experience and do better next time!" Jules added.

"That's right. All of us expect to see you at the assessment next week to test your skills. If you're getting depressed over Magnus losing an arm, you won't be focused when we battle," Lucia said. Her demeanour was that of the group's mother—tough yet gentle.

"Also, the Deities only drop one key each. Magnus has been going to the same one every day to stop us from collecting his key. We've managed to gather one key ourselves, while the others belong to Aldo, Krow, and Alastor. We heard your parents obtained a key as well, but there's no clue about its whereabouts. I'm sure it has to be on one of the floors, though—that was their last known location, according to the rumours. We're hoping to collect the rest as we climb the Tower. Whatever is at the top is the ultimate test of skill and courage, I'd say," said Delilah as she flung her water ball at Lazarus, who picked up an empty chalice and caught the water before it could hit him. "By the looks of it, even you have some skill to take on the challenge."

"Are you challenging me to collect keys?" Lazarus asked as he placed the chalice down.

"Would you accept if we were?" Delilah responded, leaning against the table teasingly.

"I'm all for a challenge, but how do you expect me to catch up when all of you are already on floor sixty?" Lazarus asked, uncertain about how the challenge worked.

"We won't be going to the Tower until after the rank assessment. We'll be practising our skills until then—catch up to us by that time, and we'll start on even ground," Delilah suggested.

"The rank assessment determines how high up the Tower you're allowed to go. So, in other words, you want me to score high in the assessment so I can reach the same floors as all of you."

"Smart lad. That's the goal we're setting for you. Most of us are around level 200, so you've got a long way to go in a short period. I'd say we have quite the head start at the Tower," Jules said with a laugh.

"I've got ten days to close the gap, then! Don't complain when I leave you in the dust, Arcanum!" Lazarus said excitedly, a burning passion to surpass his competition evident in his voice.

"May Vinter bless you," Lucia said as Lazarus left the booth.

"Ah, Lazarus! I just received a message from Aldo—he wants to speak with you. Magnus came by and notified us about your request. Please head straight up, if you don't mind," Emlin called out as she exited Aldo's office.

"That's who I wanted to see. I'll be on my way then, Emlin," he said, hastening toward Aldo's office.

The door opened before Lazarus could even grab the handle.

I'm expected if they're sensing my presence.

"Come, sit," Aldo gestured toward the chair in front of his desk.

Lazarus sat down and watched as Aldo took a seat as well.

"I see you've been waiting for me. You know why I'm here, then?" Lazarus asked as Aldo rested his head on his hands.

"I do. Magnus told me about your encounter with a Deity—an impressive feat for a new adventurer such as yourself. The only ones who have defeated a Deity before you are me, your parents, Alastor, Krow, and the group Arcanum. I wasn't happy to hear that Magnus took you to fight one so soon—you could have lost your life! I was disheartened to learn that Magnus lost an arm, but when he and I spoke about the Deity, he mentioned he had no regrets about it. His only concern was making sure you were safe and that you didn't suffer for his recklessness. On top of that, Magnus wants to take a break from the Tower to figure out his next steps. I don't blame him—it's a tough business taking on the Tower, especially the Deities. At least he got some closure with the Calamity."

"Magnus mentioned that they appear every ten levels after floor fifteen. Is that true?" Lazarus asked.

"That is true. However, we have restrictions on entering those floors. The entrances bear a red seal marked with the identity of each known Deity. This book contains all the details." Aldo passed him a red, leather-bound book with a seal on the front cover. "Since you have defeated a Deity, I'm entrusting you with this information in the hope that you can defeat the others and collect their keys."

"You will need to unlock it with your mana. Only those who have defeated a Deity can do so, as the seal only acknowledges those who hold a Deity Key."

Lazarus ran his hand across the smooth leather and sensed the presence of mana. Releasing his own mana through his fingertips, he brushed against the seal. The seal spun and expanded until he heard a click, and the strap flicked open.

"Quite the display just to open a book, Aldo. Did you make this yourself?" Lazarus asked as he flipped through the pages, revealing detailed records of Deities he had never seen before.

"Indeed. I fought a Deity when I climbed the Tower, back when your parents were adventurers. If you want to battle them, you'll need to advance your rank in the monthly Guild Assessments."

"I just heard from Arcanum about the rank assessment next week. How does that work?" Lazarus asked, continuing to flip through the pages. He came across a section on the Calamity, which detailed the environment, the fire techniques he used, and even the wolves he summoned—including his weakness to water—but there was no mention of his Ice phase. Other pages depicted a woman with black hair wearing a snow-white kimono, a man drenched in water with tentacle-like hair, and a woman wielding a katana.

"The assessment is a tournament where all participants engage in combat with other guild members. The more members you defeat—along with the skills and tactics you display in battle—will determine your new ranking," Aldo explained.

"So, the odds are stacked against me."

"What do you mean by that, Lazarus?"

"Well, Arcanum challenged me to see who can collect the greatest number of keys. They're only continuing their climb after the tournament."

"To do that, you're going to need to reach S rank quickly. The members of Arcanum are all S-rank adventurers," Aldo stated.

"I figured they would be high-ranked. Somehow, I have to defeat them in the tournament as well to score higher."

"Arcanum aren't your only hurdle. There are plenty of adventurers with higher ranks and levels than you at the moment. Alastor is the strongest in the guild, followed by Krow, Arcanum, and Magnus."

"I'd be the lowest rank then. Which is?"

"I assigned you E rank after obtaining your class, though I doubt you'll have any problems rising through the ranks. We have ranks E, D, C, B, A, and S. Only after reaching S rank will we allow someone to face the floors above ninety."

"When is the rank assessment?" Lazarus asked. He knew it was the following week but was unsure of the exact day.

"It will be held ten days from now, at the end of the week. Do your best to prepare in the meantime. I've seen matches end in seconds while others last an hour."

"Ten days. I'm going to be busy then. I'm heading to the Tower today—would it be okay if I stopped by occasionally to check this book out? I'd like to battle these deities in the future," Lazarus said as he placed the red leather book back on the desk.

"Of course you can. I do hope you become strong enough to face them before walking into their dungeons next time. If you want to get stronger faster, we have certain floors where some of our staff or adventurers clear out the boss so others can focus on gaining Aethercite. These floors contain crystals that summon creatures. If you need assistance, I suggest visiting one of them—Marv will be able to guide you to the appropriate floor. They're open to everyone, so you don't have to worry about ranks or inexperience," Aldo said as he sealed the book and placed it in one of his desk drawers.

"I'll be sure to do that. I haven't asked before, but can we take on multiple floors when we visit the Tower, or are we only allowed one floor per trip?" Lazarus asked inquisitively.

"At your current rank, we only accept one dungeon request at a time. As you rank up, the number of floors you can visit per trip will increase," Aldo explained, tapping on his desk while pondering something. "Actually, I have a request for you."

"What kind of request?" Lazarus asked.

"I want you to train with an adventurer today. They'll be overseeing a dungeon, so you'll have the opportunity to gain Aethercite in the process. What do you say?"

Lazarus considered the offer for a moment. "Why are you asking me to train with this person?"

"I've seen you interacting with them lately, and I think you could learn some new skills from them. I'm sure they'd appreciate seeing a fresh face, too."

"Someone I've interacted with? There aren't many people I've spoken to, but sure, I'll do it," Lazarus said, rising from his seat and heading toward the door.

"That's great. I'll be sure to let Marv know you're going!" Aldo called out just before Lazarus left. Then, gazing out the window, he muttered to himself, "He's a very peculiar individual—from completing his first-floor dungeon to defeating a deity on the next. I'm curious to see how far he can go." Dark clouds loomed overhead. "I have a feeling today won't be a pleasant one," Aldo said wistfully, clenching the windowsill.

"Lazarus, I heard from Magnus about your encounter with a deity yesterday. It's good to see you're still alive," a voice called out before Lazarus could turn around. Across the courtyard, Alastor leaned against a pillar, his arms crossed, his golden hair layered to resemble the feathers of an owl.

"Alastor, right? I was surprised to be battling a deity. I would have died without Magnus' help," Lazarus replied.

Alastor pushed himself off the wall and walked toward Lazarus. Standing a few inches taller, he looked down as he spoke. "You and I are cut from the same cloth. Since I started, I've only ever fought opponents stronger than myself. Those weaker than me don't give me the same thrill of combat. As you gain more experience, you'll come to feel the same way—just don't let it go to your head." His voice was calm but carried a tone of superiority that irked Lazarus.

"Is there a reason you stopped me, or do you just enjoy boasting?" Lazarus asked, trying to keep his annoyance in check.

"Yes, there's a reason, but with that attitude, I might just walk away. Boasting? That's a first. Do I really sound like that?" Alastor took a step back, placing a hand on his chin as he considered Lazarus' comment.

"You do. Though I must admit, you give off a powerful aura, so it's to be expected," Lazarus admitted.

Alastor crouched, letting out a breath as he looked up at Lazarus. "I see you've heeded my advice and learned the Sense skill," he said with a smirk. "Anyway, I need to warn you. I've narrowed the list of suspects for the killer down to a few at the guild. Today, I'm going to find out who it is and apprehend them. I came to advise you to stay away from the city in the meantime. Someone with your potential shouldn't get caught in the crossfire."

"You want me to leave the city because of the killer? What about the Valour Knights? Shouldn't they be handling this? Will Astra be safe?!" Lazarus demanded, his voice rising in intensity as violet mana emanated from his clenched fists.

"I'd advise against lashing out in anger. I only came to warn you because I see potential in both you and Astra," Alastor replied, standing back up and pacing. "As for Astra, if she stays with the other knights under her captain's protection, she'll be fine. I'll be watching the suspect in the meantime."

Alastor fixed Lazarus with a firm gaze. "Make your choice. You don't have long to decide, but know this—I won't let the killer harm Astra." With that, he turned and walked off through the trees lining the pathway.

How can I just leave the city knowing Astra could be in danger? I need to see her first and let her know!

Lazarus raced along the island pathway, heading for the training grounds on the northern island. His heart pounded in his chest as countless scenarios of what could happen with the killer ran through his mind. Upon reaching the grounds, he walked inside and used his senses to pinpoint Astra's aura. He found her sitting in an office with Sapphire. His fist slammed against the door.

"Astra, are you in there?! I need to speak with you—now." His voice was urgent, and a moment later, the door unlocked as Astra appeared.

"What's wrong, Lazarus? You sound worried." She pressed a hand to his chest, feeling his heart racing. "Come, sit down."

"It's Alastor—he says he's narrowed down the identity of the killer and is planning to apprehend them today. He warned me to stay out of the city in case a fight breaks out. I couldn't leave without warning you first, Astra," Lazarus said, his eyes filled with fear—the fear of losing her.

Astra and Sapphire exchanged aghast looks.

Sapphire rose from her seat and retrieved her armour. "I'm going to notify Commander Morrigan. She needs to know if Alastor is planning a battle in the city."

Astra's expression darkened with concern. "What's going to happen if Alastor fights in the city?" Her voice wavered with worry.

"If he intends to fight, this opponent is stronger than we thought. When Alastor fights, destruction follows. We need to ensure everyone is ready to fight at a moment's notice… or evacuate," Sapphire said, equipping her armour and cloak.

"Is there anything I can do to help, Sapphire?" Lazarus asked, his eyes filled with fierce determination.

"It's good to know you care a lot about Astra, but she'll be fine with us. I'm sure Captain Zach won't let anything happen to her. As for you, Alastor asked you to leave the city. It might sound like a strange request, but coming from him, I'd take his advice. Whatever reason he has for asking you to leave must be important." Unable to stay any longer, Sapphire rushed out.

"Lazarus, he warned you to stay out of the city. Can you think of any reason why?" Astra asked, her expression betraying her fear of what was to come.

"I'm not sure, but I couldn't leave without telling you what was going on. I needed to know you're safe. Stay on high alert—I'll notify Gamma in the meantime. If you need help, send lightning into the sky so he can see it. I'll let him know that's your signal, okay?" Lazarus held her shoulders as he spoke, then let out a breath of relief. Their shadows flickered and intertwined as they embraced, uncertain if this would be the last time they saw each other.

"I won't give anyone the opportunity to slay me, and you will do the same and return to me," she said softly, leaning into his chest to feel his elevated heartbeat.

"My opponent today won't stand a chance. I won't hold anything back, Astra. I'll be back as soon as I can," he said, taking a moment to gaze into her icy blue eyes before departing.

"I love how much your eyes remind me of home—and the fierce determination you have. Survive, no matter what happens."

Astra embraced his arm with her own, and a simple touch of their foreheads was all they needed to know they would give their all to overcome whatever challenge lay ahead.

☆☆☆☆

Now that Astra knows what's happening today, I can breathe easier—though I won't be stress-free until I know for sure she's safe. I can still feel the sensation of her lips—another reason for me to return alive.

"Gamma! Are you here?!" Lazarus called out as he barged through the entrance of his room.

Gamma appeared from behind the couch, a pile of food in his hands and sauce smeared around his mouth.

Seriously, you have the most carefree friend, Levanna.

"Problem?" Gamma asked, stuffing his face with spicy food.

"Not yet, but I need you to watch over Astra today. If she's in trouble, she'll send a signal into the sky, and I need you to be on the lookout for it, okay?" Lazarus said urgently.

"See signal, protect Astra," Gamma repeated, pointing at the balcony.

"Yes! That's it. Wait on the rooftops. I don't know when or where it will happen, but I do know the Knights of Baylor are in danger today."

Lazarus summoned Ignis. "By the looks of it, you enjoy eating hot things. What about magic?" he inquired.

"Eat fire," Gamma replied, peering at Ignis.

"I had a feeling you did. Ignis, can you give Gamma some of your flames to eat?"

Ignis nodded at Lazarus, then turned to face Gamma with blazing ruby-red eyes.

Gamma stood up quickly, dropping all his food to the ground. His mouth opened wide as he stared at Ignis, his eyes glowing crimson.

Ignis took a deep breath before exhaling a stream of fire. Gamma spread his arms, guiding the flames toward himself and drawing them into his mouth. When he finished, he let out a small burp, releasing a puff of smoke.

CHAPTER 34

Three rune-summoning circles surrounded Lazarus in a triangular formation. The cold air flushed his cheeks red, frosted his brows, and formed icy tips on his lashes. Before beginning, he took a moment to calm himself, inhaling deeply with his eyes closed and exhaling a frosty breath a moment later.

"Okay, last three spirits: Earth, Air, and Light. I wonder what you three will become," he murmured to himself. Placing the Cores into their respective circles, he turned to face the Earth summoning circle first.

"Earth. Resilient mountains, bountiful plant life, sturdy ground beneath our feet. You will become an immovable presence—one that can take hits and dish them back. Watch as the ground shakes in your wake!"

Green energy pulsed from the runes as Lazarus activated the summoning. The ground trembled, shaking the trees as snow fell from the cerulean leaves. Rocky spikes emerged from the snow-covered earth, converging at the centre above the Core until they completely obscured it. The rumbling intensified, accompanied by a primal growl. A tail thumped against the spikes, knocking them back, but not strongly enough to break free. The thumping grew faster, striking each spike in turn. Lazarus couldn't make out what was inside—only glimpses of leathery skin in pale brown and green tones.

"You got this, just a bit more!" Lazarus encouraged. Hearing its summoner, the creature's tail struck the spikes with enough force to shatter them, sending debris flying. Lazarus ducked just in time to avoid a piece.

Emerging from the remains was a prehistoric bipedal creature, standing about a metre tall, with a pale green cranial dome and stubby spikes trailing down its neck, spine, and tail. It stared at Lazarus with a fierce gaze, pawing the ground as its tail flicked.

"It's okay, Arco, you're safe with me," Lazarus said, crouching and sitting on the ground.

Arco watched cautiously, his tail flicking as his pawing stopped. He inched closer to Lazarus until he stood right before his lap, bowing his head.

"See? Nothing to fear."

Without warning, Arco head-butted Lazarus in the stomach, leaving him retching and gasping for air.

"Ow…"

Gently placing his hand against the leathery skin, Lazarus rubbed Arco's back until the creature relaxed, recalling him.

"Strong but cautious. This one may take some time to bond with, but I've got a good spirit!"

Next came the Air element spirit.

"Air. You have the gentleness of a breeze, the force of a hurricane, and the power of a tornado. Gracefully floating in the air, embracing everything with a gentle touch, escaping the clutches of violence."

Air swirled within the circle, forming a miniature tornado. Lazarus covered his face as the gusts blew away the surrounding snow. A girl with pale skin, wearing a flowing dress of white and light blue, emerged, levitating above the ground. Her snow-white hair, streaked with shades of blue, danced in the breeze.

"Nimbus… dancing with the air," Lazarus said.

Nimbus smiled as she floated to his side, holding onto his shoulder, her feet reaching only to his waist. She glanced at the remaining circle, aware of what the runes would conjure next.

A blinding pillar of light shot up from the runes, separating into nine beams that converged at the centre. The beams twisted around each other, forming a glowing sphere of white light. As the glow dimmed, a small fox appeared, its white fur adorned with ethereal blue markings that glowed softly. Its nine fluffy tails swayed with the breeze.

"You're majestic—otherworldly, even. I'll call you Lumen," Lazarus said, awestruck.

He glanced around to ensure no one else was nearby before summoning the rest of his spirits. "Now I have a full team. With all of you by my side, I'm sure we'll grow stronger together! Let's go hunting!"

The spirits released elemental energy in unison before Lazarus recalled them.

The next floor mentions a Nagi—a female serpent-like creature that wields weapons and poison. I have no resistance to poison, so I'll have to rely on these antidotes if I get afflicted. In the worst-case scenario, I have Second Wind… though I don't know how to activate it or what it means by requiring a sacrifice.

CHAPTER 35

A tear cracked open in the cloudy sky. Two figures emerged, descending toward the snowy mountain below.

"Is this the place she was last seen?! I don't sense her anywhere!" a burly man shouted, his voice deep and boorish. He was clad in dark grey pants with fur lining the waist, barefoot and bare-chested, gripping a large black axe with a brass handle.

"It appears so. Though her presence is gone, this is the last place Snake lost communication with Levanna. We will start by asking the villagers about her whereabouts," replied a shorter man, his gruff voice matching his shaggy, curly white hair. His woollen black robe swayed with the motion of the trees as they descended.

Landing with a heavy impact, they sent a wave of snow cascading toward the entrance of Riverfall. Maeve and Darius stood waiting at the village entrance, blocking the wave with their own auras—one resembling a mighty tree, the other a flower of flames.

"We've been expecting you. The Zodiac organization isn't welcome in this village. I suggest you leave," said a woman with short brown hair streaked with silver. Her voice was stern as she stood her ground against the intruders.

"Yet here we are anyway. I ask that you show us Levanna. We know she is in this village. If she is handed over, we'll leave," said the man with white hair, his eyes hidden.

A dozen villagers emerged behind Darius and Maeve, wielding swords and shields, spears and bows—anything they could find.

"Who are you to be giving us orders?" an old man demanded.

"No one here goes by that name!" shouted a young woman.

"Have you no respect for people who just want to live in peace?" asked a man standing behind Darius.

"Peace? Is that what you all desire? Peace cannot exist when opposing ideals clash. None of you could possibly comprehend our higher understanding of this world. Your so-called peace will shatter and crumble when we usher in our new world order." He asserted his voice, ensuring the crowd backed away.

"I don't care what order your organisation plans to bring to this world—we want no part of it!" Darius' voice rose, breaking from his usual calm demeanour as he listened to their nonsense. A vine shot out from the ground beneath the shorter Zodiac, wrapping around his torso and arms.

"I suggest you release these vines, peasant." His voice turned cold, his gaze shifting between the villagers.

"I won't let you do as you please!" In a fit of rage, Darius yanked the skinny man away from his protégé, dragging him across the ground.

"What are you doing, Goat?! Are we here to play, or are we here to find Levanna?!" shouted the burly man.

As Darius stopped, something invisible severed the vines, allowing Goat to stand up again. He wiped the dirt away nonchalantly.

"Patience, Ox. We came for answers, and I will obtain them," Goat said, his eyes locking onto Darius, who stood before him, his hair and face sullied by snow and dirt.

"We don't know this Levanna you speak of. Now leave!" Darius yelled before covering his arm with vines, forming a lance and aiming it at Goat.

"Where is Levanna?" Goat demanded.

The Vine Lance pierced straight through Goat and emerged on the other side. He flicked a finger, and an invisible blade sliced through Darius' arm.

Maeve was the first to gasp in horror as Darius' vine-covered arm fell to the ground in a pool of blood. Dropping to his knees, Darius clutched his shoulder and let out a pained yell. The villagers charged at Goat—whether out of foolish pride or comradeship, it was a hopeless act.

Ox stepped in front of Goat, his lips curling into a vicious smile. The villagers swung their weapons at him, but he shrugged off each attack, their blows failing to even graze his thick skin.

A thunderous sonic boom halted their assault as Levanna burst through the forest, landing a punch covered in a dark aura against Goat. The impact sent him crashing to the ground, blood dripping from his mouth.

"There she is!" Ox said, his grin widening. "Your punch has improved, Levanna. Now it's my turn!" He started toward her.

"Hold on, Ox. We still need to know why she deserted us—and who disrupted Snake's signal."

"Maeve, take Darius and treat his wounds. Everyone else, please leave the area," Levanna ordered, black aura surging around her body. "I have nothing to discuss with you, and I'm not going back to Zodiac. You and Ox need to leave this village—now!"

Her anger peaked as she launched herself toward the duo, preparing to strike Ox. Standing his ground instead of dodging, he seized her arm and slammed her into the ground, the impact driving the wind from her lungs as she coughed up blood.

"As I mentioned before, we have issues to discuss. You will listen," Goat said as Levanna cried out in frustration, powerless.

"I understand you refuse to return with us, so that choice is no longer available. I believe you were tasked with finding the champion and killing them. Am I correct in assuming you found them, hence your desertion?" Goat asked as Levanna lunged at him again.

"I don't have a champion! I never found them!" Levanna shouted, punching Ox once more. Tendrils of flame erupted from her fist, wrapping around his body and singing his skin.

"Ugh!" Ox cried out as scorching pain shot through him, forcing him to flinch in agony.

"I see you're still weak to my fire, at least," Levanna said mockingly, bouncing back to create some distance between them.

"Lies. Very unfortunate. I had hoped you would make this easy for us, but it's only natural for you to rebel." Goat sighed. "We bear no hatred toward your actions, but actions such as these require appropriate punishment. If the champion is not here, we'll have to send them a message." He shook his head in disappointment, wiping the blood from his lips.

"What do you mean, 'send a message?' You don't even know the champion's identity." Levanna's voice wavered with confusion and fear of what they had planned.

"Oh, don't worry about that. You will be the message." Goat's eyes were unreadable as he gave the order.

"Ox."

Grinning, Ox lifted his bloodied axe. "Finally! Now I get to have fun!"

Levanna raised her arm and hurled a fireball into the air. It exploded, showering the battlefield with burning embers.

The ground shook as Ox broke into a charge, deflecting the falling embers with the head of his axe.

Levanna stepped back, pressing her hands together in front of her chest as fire energy swelled between them. "I won't let you harm anyone in this village!" she shouted, thrusting her hands forward and launching the amassed fireball at Ox.

"Another fire attack? You're too predictable, Levanna. Ox can just knock it away," Goat remarked, settling onto a stump by the lake.

Ox did just that, slamming the fireball with the flat side of his axe and redirecting it back toward Levanna.

"I've learned new techniques since our last fight, Ox," Levanna said as she leapt toward the incoming fireball. A fiery arm extended from her own, catching the blaze and swinging it back around, striking Ox in a violent explosion of scorching flames.

"Is that all?" Ox's voice rumbled through the thick smoke. As it cleared, a slab of hardened magma stood beside him, shielding him from the blast. He remained unscathed.

"How?! That should have killed you!" Levanna gasped, dropping to her knees in despair.

"Don't underestimate my strength, little one," Ox said, standing before Levanna once more. He gripped her snow-white hair and lifted her with ease.

A foot landed against Ox's face with a heavy thud, blood splattering from his mouth before she delivered another kick to his ribs. This time, he caught her toned leg with his free arm and leapt into the air with a mighty jump. The full force of his body slammed against her as they crashed to the ground together.

The impact folded her body in half, her legs and upper half almost wrapping around Ox.

"As we were saying, you're going to be the message," Goat reiterated.

Ox knelt beside her defenceless body and delivered a punch infused with his own aura. Unconscious, Levanna took hit after hit until a deep crater marked the entrance to Riverfall.

CHAPTER 36

"Lazarus! Good to see you again. Aldo has already informed me that you'll be training with another adventurer today. Let's see..." Marv said, checking a list of members in the Tower. After scanning a scroll, he paused at one name. "Here we go. They're already up there waiting. I do warn you—others who have trained with them have described the experience as a nightmarish ordeal. Do you still wish to proceed, Lazarus?"

"They can't be that bad!" he said, glancing at the arched doors.

"Very well, a response I'd expect from the son of Adelheid and Cyrus. Head to Floor Thirteen," Marv commented as he pushed the doors open, stretching out his arm to let Lazarus pass. "Good luck!"

Lazarus climbed the stairwell, passing other adventurers along the way.

"Here we are—a skull above the entrance. Does that mean I'm going to fight skeletons?" he wondered as he approached the floor guardian.

"Skeletons? The crystal inside spawns more than just skeletons, though all the creatures will be undead," a woman in a black suit said, bowing at the waist as Lazarus approached. "You may proceed at your own peril."

That wasn't ominous at all, he thought as he walked through the doorway.

As he entered the dark hallway, Lazarus' eyes took a moment to adjust. Armoured statues lined the corridor, large swords in hand. Braziers illuminated the entrance to a giant, circular room. Pillars supported a smaller ceiling, which led into a domed, glass roof, glowing under a white crescent moon surrounded by a constellation of bright stars.

What is this place? he wondered. *It's my first time seeing a building instead of different landscapes.*

"It's a breathtaking view, right?" a woman said, startling Lazarus.

A fresh yet familiar face this time. Brave of you to show up to my training of all places... Lazarus," she continued, sitting on a balcony on the upper level of a dance hall, cloaked in a dark hood. She leaned forward and flipped gracefully to the floor, raising her hands along her torso and above her head.

"Krow? You're one of the trainers?" Lazarus asked, surprised by her appearance in this dreary dance hall.

"The one, the only. Tell me, Lazarus, do you fear the dead?" She lowered her head to meet his eyes.

"The dead? Not particularly. I just heard about these types of rooms. Is that the crystal that spawns the creatures?" Lazarus asked, glancing at an emerald crystal in the centre of the room.

"Indeed, it is, Lazarus. Are you sure you want to fight these ones? If you are, I'll activate the crystal for you," Krow said while stretching her arms. "I've already defeated the Lich King, so you don't have to worry about any interference."

Lazarus gripped his Bo staff firmly. "Let's do it."

"Very well then. This room may be used for training, but you can still perish if you're not careful." Krow walked to the crystal, placed her hand on its surface, and released her mana. The crystal lit up with an ethereal green glow.

The dance hall distorted as the picturesque maroon walls and golden pillars faded into damaged black columns and grey walls. Cracks appeared along the floor.

"What's going on? This doesn't feel right..." Lazarus muttered, observing the changing setting. Skulls, spinal cords, ribs, and other bones filled the walls, creating a macabre theme.

Krow leapt back onto the second-floor balcony as swirling green smoke rose from the ground, pulling bones together until a skeleton emerged—then another, and another—until dozens of skeletal warriors, archers, and hounds surrounded Lazarus.

"This crystal spawns a skeletal army. I'd advise you to destroy them before they overwhelm you." Krow rested her head on her palms, watching Lazarus with amusement.

"In the coming darkness, light shines brightest. Come forth, Lumen!" Lazarus called, summoning a portal. Soft taps of furry paws followed as a light shone through the darkness, blinding the grotesque horde before releasing a pulse of energy that burned through their bones, splitting several skeletons in half.

"Nimbus, help her out!" he commanded.

Nimbus drifted through her portal like a wandering cloud, nodding at Lazarus with a confident gaze.

"Impressive spirits you have there. Let's see what they can do," Krow remarked with a playful smile.

"Nimbus, stay close to Lumen and provide air support. Lumen, I'll leave the front to you—I'll handle rear support," Lazarus instructed, positioning himself back-to-back with Lumen.

Krow observed his tactics and fighting style with keen interest.

Lazarus used his staff to strike down any skeleton knights that advanced on him. Bones shattered and collapsed around him, evaporating into Aethercite, which flowed into Lazarus.

Nimbus appeared to be gazing at the night sky. She pointed to the ceiling as she called out to Lazarus—no words, just a whisper of the wind.

"What are you seeing, Nimbus?" he asked, confusion etched across his face.

Nimbus twirled, gathering a gust of wind before kicking toward the ceiling. A powerful slicing current struck the glass, shattering the entire ceiling. Krow giggled.

Shards of glass rained down until a swirling breeze caught them, forming a tornado around the group. Unable to defend against the onslaught of shrapnel, the whirlwind of glass tore through the surrounding horde of skeletons as Lazarus shielded himself.

"Nimbus, you brilliant spirit! That makes this a lot easier," Lazarus called out, though his voice was muffled by the howling winds. Lumen picked off spawning skeletons before they could be swept away.

"Enough!" Krow's voice rang out. Her commanding aura halted the battle below, stunning Lazarus and his spirits. They turned to her, uncertain of what to do.

"What's wrong, Krow? Why are you stopping us?" he asked.

"I've seen enough of your spirits to know you can handle more than just these skeletons. Will you indulge me instead?" Krow asked sweetly.

"You want me to fight you?"

"What happens when you face an opponent with unfathomable power? When death's gaze stares back at you, what do we do in that situation? We welcome Death—laugh with our dear friend as we dance together on the battlefield. We embrace their presence, wondering when our next encounter may come."

Krow twirled along the banister on the upper level, her aura of frost seeping out, freezing the floor beneath her with each step. "Come, Lazarus, show me how you dance with Death." She laughed with pure joy as her movements became livelier.

"If that's what you want, I could use the practice against another adventurer!" Lazarus said, leaping toward Krow to initiate the fight.

Lumen and Nimbus followed close behind, supporting him with their Light and Air magic.

"Good. Come at me with the intent to kill. You'll learn fast when you're battling for survival," Krow said ominously.

Lazarus thrust his staff at Krow, but she caught the end in defense. With a sharp twist, she forced Lazarus to flip, sending him crashing to the ground.

His eyes widened as a scythe materialized in her grasp. He rolled to the side just as the blade came down like a guillotine toward his neck. *What the hell?! She's trying to kill me! And she summoned that scythe—I didn't think she was a summoner!*

Krow laughed as she danced around him, swinging her scythe in fluid arcs, narrowly missing fatal strikes.

"Are you just going to dodge, Lazarus, or are you going to dance with me?" she asked, tilting her head, her eerie gaze locking onto his.

"Fighting isn't my strong suit, Krow! Plus, I don't like all this murderous intent you're giving off!" Lazarus shouted, jumping onto the balcony.

Krow closed the distance instantly, creeping along the banister toward Lazarus.

Lumen and Nimbus exchanged glances. Lumen lit up the hall with a flash, blinding Krow, followed by several blasts of wind that sent her crashing into the wall, causing her to drop her scythe.

"Nice! But I need to switch you two out. Shift and Jaeger, come to me!" Lazarus yelled, jumping back down to the floor below to escape Krow, who now wore a bloodied smile.

Arrows whizzed past Lazarus, aimed at Krow. She picked up her scythe and deflected each of them with its blade.

"How fun! You have a Deity summon!" Krow exclaimed, laughing as she chased after Lazarus.

Shift caught her mid-leap and flung her around in his frozen fangs. Ice shattered as she reappeared behind him. He spat out the fake Krow and snarled, his growl rumbling through the hall as frigid air rolled in, freezing the ground and walls.

"This lady is crazy powerful. If she wants me to go all out, I have no choice!"

"Shift! Stop her!" Lazarus ordered, his heart racing, his body drenched in sweat from the fear she instilled in him.

Shift shook his body, releasing more ice energy. A deep, guttural roar followed as ice shards spread across the room toward Krow.

"Ice type—who is the better Ice user?" she murmured, holding her scythe in front of her face, eyes closed. Just before Shift's ice shards could strike, she opened her eyes. With a blast of her aura, she swung her scythe at the incoming attack.

A giant scythe made of ice materialised, slicing through the shards with ease before continuing toward Shift. It slashed through him, cleaving him in two. The giant wolf dissolved into ice before vanishing completely.

"Shift!" Lazarus shouted, reaching out for his spirit.

"Master, don't worry about Shift—he'll be fine. But this opponent is too powerful for us. If you don't escape, she'll kill you," Ísarr whispered.

"Ísarr? I don't know what to do. I don't think she'll let me escape… She's obsessed with this dance with Death," Lazarus replied in his mind.

"Send us all out. We'll hold her off long enough for you to escape. Forget about fighting her—this isn't someone you fight," said Marsh.

"Okay, I'll leave her to you guys. Do your best!" Lazarus replied.

"I don't know what your obsession with Death is, but I can't fight you anymore, Krow. Someone I care about is risking their life outside—I need to return as soon as I can! Everyone, hold her off!" Lazarus yelled as eight portals opened. His spirits and companions emerged, united by a single goal: to stop Krow.

Moving as one, they combined their elemental powers to create stronger forms of magic. Jaeger, Marsh, and Ísarr focused on restricting her movement with their techniques.

A haunting laugh escaped Krow, sending a shiver through Lazarus' body as he sprinted toward the dungeon entrance. She released an aura resembling a grim reaper, composed of dark mist and chilling frost.

As they clashed, Krow and her grim reaper aura tore through the first line of spirits. Jaeger fired arrows to hinder her movements, Marsh parried her scythe with his short sword, bouncing around to avoid her attacks, while Ìsarr conjured ice shards to trap them within.

"I like the tactics, but you're still weak! They can't hold me off," Krow warned. Enveloping herself in a veil of energy from her reaper aura, she shifted her stance. No longer aiming at the spirits, she transformed her assault into a graceful, calculated performance. With a sweeping motion, tendrils of dark energy erupted, shattering the ice wall and scattering the spirits.

With no more spirits to hold her off, Krow's dance carried her toward Lazarus, who had just reached the hallway leading to the entrance. Pouring every ounce of energy into escaping, he couldn't react in time as Krow slipped past him, her scythe slicing through the air toward his neck, forcing him to halt abruptly.

A sudden buzzing sound echoed in her ear, disrupting her attack. Holding the scythe to his throat, she paused to respond to a message.

"Is that so? Well, if you say so, I'll make sure to be there to help you out. I'm sorry to ruin our little dance, but I have another business to attend! Do keep up with your training—I'm sure we can have more fun together in the future, Lazarus."

With that, Krow withdrew her weapon and skipped toward the exit of the Dance Hall, a strange whistling tune fading into the distance.

I should not have come here. She almost killed me and then acted like nothing happened. Now I see why people avoid her, Lazarus thought.

CHAPTER 37

A blanket of dense clouds rolled over the city of Baylor, turning the midday sky into night. All the squads of Valour had gathered at the training grounds, seating themselves in the stands overlooking the snowy field. Statues of past Valour Knights lined the large, oval-shaped arena, watching over Baylor's knights in training. Commander Morrigan stood on the field, surveying her knights before turning her gaze to the looming clouds above.

"I'm glad to see you all here after yesterday's matches. I'd like to congratulate each of you on your efforts! None of you faced easy opponents, yet you demonstrated strategies that would be invaluable on a real battlefield!" Morrigan announced.

I'm still reeling from my victory yesterday. The tingling from the electricity feels like it's still coursing through my body, Astra thought, glancing over at Mars to see how he was faring. His intense focus remained on the commander.

"Captain Hugo, our most experienced knight, displayed remarkable composure while facing a dangerous threat. His quick thinking not only prevented his squad from sustaining injuries but also halted the casting of a devastating spell. I'm grateful to have him on our side rather than as an opponent," Morrigan said, gesturing toward Hugo. He waved the praise away with a weary smile.

"Captain Sapphire demonstrated a perfect balance of offence, defence, and support tactics, working seamlessly with her teammates. If I hadn't gone all out against her, I would have lost that battle—though I hate to admit it. I have no hesitation in placing my life in her hands, and neither should any of you if you fight by her side." Morrigan's expression was one of pride as she glanced toward Sapphire's squad.

"Next, I'd like to commend Eden and Lilith on their victories, both facing opponents with similar combat skills. Eden's elegant display of evasive and energetic techniques allowed her to defeat our powerful brawling monk, Adonis, despite having an elemental disadvantage. Lilith countered Jacques' swift elemental magic with her own lightning-based ranged techniques, overwhelming her opponents with a relentless barrage of lightning bolts.

"Lastly, we have Captain Zach, who managed to overcome Captain Mars' intense fiery aura—with the help of a new recruit, Astra, of course.

"For the next week, I want all of you to focus on training in an area of weakness. As an example, archers should learn how to defend themselves in close-quarters combat. Today, you're going to be doing regular training. Are there any questions?"

Now that I think about it, my control needs improvement. I'm not quite sure how I'm going to do that, though… Mars seemed to use a similar technique with fire. Maybe I could ask for his guidance? Astra thought while looking over at his squad.

"Commander Morrigan?" Astra asked, raising her arm into the air.

"Yes, Astra. What do you want to say?" Morrigan replied, shifting her attention to the young knight.

"Are we allowed to have tutors? During our battle yesterday, I realized a few Captains use techniques that could help me improve. Captain Lilith utilizes lightning element techniques, Captain Mars uses an elemental technique similar to my Storm Walker, and Captain Eden shares the Elemental Knight class." Astra's cheeks flushed red with embarrassment as the crowd of knights focused their attention on her.

"I am not opposed to anyone asking for help if they need it, though that's not a question directed at me. What do you say, Captains? Are you willing to accept her as a pupil?" Morrigan posed the question to them.

"It leaves a bad taste in my mouth losing to a recruit, but if that's my penalty for defeat, I'll accept it. I'll make sure she knows how to control her elemental surge by the end of the week," Mars said, his fist igniting with fire.

"Of course you'd try to save face like that, Mars. I'm glad you're so willing to help! What about you two?" Morrigan replied.

"She sounds fun. I can show her a few techniques to help her improve," Lilith said with a smirk.

"I'm happy to help," Eden added with a pleasant smile.

"Good! On a side note, experience outweighs familiarity. You may not always know the enemy you face on the battlefield—they could have a lifetime of experience or be stepping into their first fight. We always enter battle expecting our opponents to be stronger than us. That mindset ensures we remain cautious and alert to their movements and attack patterns.

"Though each of you has different strengths, weaknesses, and levels of experience, the deciding factor in battle is one's desire to win—the tenacity to persevere in the face of death. Sometimes, all it takes is one mistake from the opponent to turn the tide in your favour. Now, all of you, get down here and begin your training!" Morrigan commanded, her aura blazing red-hot with the thrill of growing stronger.

Captain Lilith zipped across the field, appearing next to Astra in a flash of electricity. "You want to be my pupil? Show me your lightning technique," she said.

Astra nodded, focusing on her mana as electricity crackled around her body. "This is as much as I can do without running."

"Hmmm, you've got the basic gist of mana control at least. But you need to become one with the electricity—you're trying to fight it, to control it. If you want to master this technique, let it flow through you freely. Don't resist the pulse you feel," Lilith commented, observing Astra's flow of mana as she paced around her. Her cool demeanour reflected confidence earned through hardship and experience.

Astra closed her eyes, breathing slowly. *This tingling sensation… it feels like a heartbeat dancing through my body. Every tingle moves in rhythm with my pulse. Surging. Erratic. I can feel it all flowing within me.*

She swayed her body—her arms, her hips—moving in sync with the electricity's flow. The rhythm revitalised her senses, and energy swelled within her. For a brief moment, her body flickered, transforming into pure electricity.

A startled gasp escaped her, breaking her focus and cancelling the electricity.

"Impressive! Remember that feeling and practise. You'll be able to enter that state at will in no time," Lilith praised, nocking an arrow and shooting it toward the tip of a pillar. In an instant, her body released electricity, transforming into a ball of lightning that flickered toward the arrow at breathtaking speed.

"Wow!" Astra exclaimed excitedly, tracking the captain's movements as she darted between the pillars.

From the corner of her eye, she noticed thick vines sprouting from the ground, carrying a knight toward her.

"A pleasure to make your acquaintance, Astra. You put on an impressive showing in yesterday's matches. Reckless. Brave. It was admirable," Captain Eden remarked.

"Thank you, I guess?" Astra replied, slightly dejected by the reckless comment. "I've never learned how to use lightning with my sword techniques."

"After witnessing your skill with Storm Walker, it shouldn't be difficult for you to learn how to channel that energy through your weapon,"

Eden commented. "Your weapon is an extension of your body. Using this understanding, we've learned to infuse our weapons with different elements."

Captain Eden's pale green sword glowed with a violet hue. "I can manipulate my energy to give my sword the properties of earth elements—stone, sand, crystal, vines, plants. Each of these serves different purposes, from increasing durability and sharpness to inducing paralysis, poison, or even sleep."

"I could stun opponents with a touch using electricity, then," Astra said thoughtfully.

"Basically, yes. The possibilities depend on the creativity of the individual. You'll need to figure out what kind of knight you want to be—one who protects, one who kills, one who shows mercy. Your motivations will shape the techniques you choose to master," Eden replied, planting her sword into the ground. Mana pulsed through the blade, and barbed vines sprouted from beneath the snow, swaying in unison to form a protective barrier around her.

What kind of knight do I want to be? Astra wondered. *I've never really thought about that. My goal was always to surpass my father… but maybe that isn't worth following if I don't even know who I want to be.*

"You always come to my rescue. When I'm staring down danger, I take a breath and relax because I know you'll be there to help me."

Lazarus' voice echoed from the deep recesses of her mind—a memory from long ago.

He relies on me. He doesn't show fear because he knows I'm there for him. I can be that person for others. Even if just one more person feels safe because of me, that could make a difference.

"He fought to protect as many as he could."

Morrigan's voice rang in her mind next, recalling her father's unwavering dedication to defending others.

I know who I want to be! Astra's resolve burned within her. *A defender for those who can't defend themselves, a beacon of light to guide them and ensure their safety. But more than anything… I want to be by his side. I want to be his Sword.*

She gazed at her weapon, its blade gleaming faintly under the overcast sky. *I will be his Sword.*

Electricity surged around her hand, fusing with the metal as she raised her blade toward the clouds. "I'm going to become a beacon of light. I'll make sure no one has to fear the dark."

"That is a great ideal to work toward, Astra," Captain Eden said, kneeling on one knee in a gesture of respect. "If you don't mind, I'll take my leave for now. I have my own squad to train, but in the future, I'll look forward to training alongside you."

A throne of vines rose from the ground, carrying her away as she returned to her squad, who were engaged in intense physical training.

"I see you're making an impression on the other Captains. You're going to make me jealous," Captain Zach smirked, draping an arm around her shoulders. "Next up, the final boss—Captain Mars! Will she succeed in gaining his favour, or crash and burn? Let's find out!" he teased, dramatically waving his free hand forward as if to welcome Mars.

Astra giggled at his antics.

"Well, if it isn't my dearest friend, Mars," Zachariah said mockingly. "How was my new recruit's welcome gift?"

"It's fine, Zachariah. I'm here because I want to get this training over and done with so I don't have to deal with you," Mars snapped.

"Okay! I'll leave her in your capable hands," Zachariah responded, raising his hands in surrender.

"I'll be fine, Captain Zach. Go join the others," Astra insisted.

"I don't enjoy this situation you've put me in, but at the same time, I'm impressed with your lightning surge technique. You've already figured out the basics—generating elemental energy through your mana circulation," Mars admitted, though his praise was reluctant.

"It's not easy. I've been trying to master this since I was ten. Generating that surge comes naturally now, but I can't maintain it for long. Changing directions while using it is the real problem," Astra explained.

"Maintaining your surge while controlling your movements is a difficult hurdle to overcome. I'll try to make it easier for you," Mars said. "You should know that elemental techniques affect the body in different ways. Your lightning supercharges your motor neurons, enhancing your speed and reflexes. For me, my flames heat up my body and increase blood flow, boosting my physical attributes in a similar way to your lightning."

He pointed to the far side of the field. "I want to see you enter that state again and run across the field."

"Are you sure that's a good idea, Mars?" Zachariah asked, gripping one of Mars' shoulders. His tone was laced with suspicion at the younger captain's sudden willingness to help Astra.

"If she wants to learn how to use her technique, then she needs to show me how she handles it, Zachariah. Now take your hand off my shoulder," Mars replied, his eyes flickering with embers of fire as he glanced toward his fellow captain.

"Please go, Captain. I can handle this," Astra reassured Zach.

With a nod, Zachariah stepped back.

Astra focused her lightning energy, willing it to flow through her body. Electricity crackled across her skin as she activated her enhanced state.

First part done... now the hard part—keeping this state active as I run across the field. Even the split-second bursts I've used before take a toll on my body...!

Astra kicked off the ground, launching into a sprint as her vision narrowed. The only clear image was the wall of the stands on the opposite side. The other knights in training became a blur as she sped past them. Her gaze remained fixed on the wall, but she had overlooked one crucial detail—how to stop once she started running.

"There she goes. You did this on purpose, didn't you? You couldn't handle losing to a recruit, so you took this opportunity for payback. I don't think she'll forget this, Mars," Zachariah said, watching his subordinate crash into the sturdy barricade.

Mars laughed at the new recruit's fumbled attempt, only to receive a punch to his arm.

"Ow!" he yelped, rubbing the sore spot.

"Take this seriously, Mars. You know who you're training, don't you?" Zachariah said, his eyes boring into Mars' head.

Astra rose to her feet, brushing the snow off her armour. Sparks of electricity flickered from her body as she made her way back to Captain Mars and Captain Zach.

"I am aware of her lineage, Zachariah. You don't have to worry about her around me. I looked up to him as well, so seeing someone else with the potential to rival his prowess is something I'm eager to witness."

"Well, as long as that's clear, I won't have to take matters into my own hands," Zachariah warned before striding toward his squad.

The knights who had paused their training to gawk were promptly met with a blast of embers from Commander Morrigan, forcing them back to their drills.

By now, the clouds had cast their shadows over the training grounds, and the soft sunlight of dawn had faded into a bleak darkness. Light cores positioned around the area illuminated the grounds with artificial rays.

"The same result as usual. When I'm in that state, I can't control my body the way I want to. I can only run forward until I crash into something," Astra ranted as she neared the captain.

"I noticed. The first lesson will focus on how to stop. With lightning energy surging through your body, controlling your movements will be difficult at first. When I started, my body would burn up—no one could touch me unless they wanted to be burned. I had to learn how to focus the fire on specific parts of my body, control the amount I released, and, finally, do all of that at once," Mars remarked, igniting flames on different parts of his body one by one. "I want you to run across the field again. This time, try to stop before you reach the other stands."

Astra nodded and crouched, preparing to sprint. Electricity crackled around her body, lifting her hair from the static. The hum of energy reverberated through the arena before she bolted across the field.

Stop, stop, stop! she thought, willing her legs to respond. Her muscles tensed, one foot planted firmly into the ground—but the other missed its mark. She lost her balance, tumbling across the ground before crashing into the stands with a heavy thud.

Darkness. What was that feeling? Astra wondered, scanning her surroundings for the source.

Footsteps echoed from the arena entrance. She pushed herself up, wiping dirt and snow from her armour, only to see her captains drawing their weapons, their respective elements flaring to life.

"What's wrong?" she asked.

"Astra! Get out of there, now!" Zach shouted, charging toward her with his blazing daggers.

Astra turned her head toward the entrance, where a knight clad in polished onyx-black armour loomed before her. His imposing figure radiated an unsettling presence. Her gaze drifted upward, locking onto the knight's helmet, where eerie, glowing emerald eyes stared down at her. A tattered cloak draped over his dark armour, shrouded by a hood that only deepened his air of mystery.

Zweihander in hand, the blade absorbed all light, reflecting nothing.

Black blade? The note Alastor gave me—move, Astra, or you're going to die!

The cold grip of death seized her, paralysing her with dread. She stumbled, desperate to flee.

A single word was spoken—ethereal, commanding, absolute.

"Collapse."

What is this pressure? I can't move. I can't see. Everything is collapsing in… or is it me?

All she could see was white—blinding, suffocating—accompanied by an unbearable weight.

Mustering all the strength she could, she forced her head up, her body lying motionless in the snow. Her eyes darted around frantically.

What's going on?! It's like I'm paralysed—I can't move!

Auras flared across the training grounds, one after another. Valour Knights, momentarily crushed under the immense pressure, steadied themselves and forced their trembling bodies upright, fury burning in their eyes as they fixed their gazes on the enemy.

Zach's aura erupted in pure light, radiating warmth and brilliance. His body glowed with an ethereal sheen, his speed second to none. In an instant, he cleared the field, scooped Astra into his arms, and launched his own blade of light at the knight. The Black Knight merely tilted his head slightly, effortlessly dodging the attack.

"Astra, are you okay?!" Zach shouted, panic thick in his voice.

Knights lay strewn across the field, their bodies limp, groans of agony escaping their lips. The crushing darkness had overwhelmed the inexperienced, leaving them helpless.

"I can't see—it's so dark!" Astra trembled, struggling to break free from Zach's grip.

From the abyssal shadows, tendrils resembling clawed hands slithered forth, creeping like living nightmares. They latched onto those of weaker minds—those unable to resist the dreadful aura seeping from the blade of pure darkness.

Amidst the panic, a whistle cut through the terrified screams. A single arrow, crackling with powerful sparks of electricity, whizzed through the air and clashed against the black blade. Disrupted by the surprise attack, the blade released its hold over the knights.

Sweat dripped down Astra's face, now devoid of colour. Even her naturally pale complexion would have been vibrant in contrast. She gazed at the Zweihander, its emerald runes glowing along the blade.

"Now, Astra, escape!" a female voice called out, wielding a bow of pure electricity. Heeding the knight's warning—whether out of obedience or fear—she entered her Storm Walker state, blitzing across the arena.

Turning briefly, Astra caught an expression she had never seen from Zach before. Beneath his jester-like persona lay a hidden side of her captain—wrath.

Furrowed brows, eyes colder than a frozen tundra—Zach stared up at the knight before him. Unflinching. Unfazed.

Is that you, Zach? The real you? I don't know whether to be afraid or sad. I don't like that expression—the hidden pain you must be feeling, Astra pondered. *I won't be a distraction. Where is a safe spot… is there a safe spot?*

By his side, one dagger glowed with blinding luminosity.

"You made a mistake coming here. It's not because you killed my friends… no, it's much worse than that. An unforgivable act. For pointing your blade at one of my knights, I will be your executioner," Zach snapped.

A pillar of light shot through the clouds, reaching the heavens above and enveloping the two of them.

Two daggers. That was all he needed.

One blink—he appeared by his second blade, embedded in the wall behind them. A second blink—and two daggers pierced through flesh and bone, twisting to find the right melody.

The knight groaned in agony; each twist of a dagger produced a different, painful howl. Flashes of light glimmered through bloodied armour.

The grinding of daggers against armour screeched through the training grounds, a deadening echo that lingered until Zach had enough. Mustering his strength, he hurled the knight into the stands, shattering several rows of flattened stone seats. A thick shroud of dust obscured their view of Zach's rage.

"A valiant display. One would expect no less from a Knight of Valour such as yourself," a voice chimed—eloquent, devoid of animosity.

As the dust cleared, the knight stood unscathed.

"Even after all of that, there's no damage?! What are you?" Zachariah spat, his voice laced with anger.

"I am a bringer of darkness, of death. I am the end of the journey you call life."

The weight of the blade cleaving through the air shattered a barrier of light, slicing through flesh. The knight had aimed to do more damage, but his attack was foiled by a rain of charged arrows intercepting his strike. Zach collapsed, writhing in pain.

Electricity crackled from fingertips along a notched arrow. Perched atop a statue of a female knight wielding a lightning bow, Lilith took aim at her sister's killer, her eyes surging with sparking energy.

"Valour Captains, do your duty! Squad members are to retreat immediately. Those petrified are to be assisted by any able body!" ordered Commander Morrigan, cloaking herself in red flames before bursting toward her enemy. The knight turned its gaze to the flaming hound charging toward him.

"Serenus Aqua," whispered Sapphire. Tranquil water flowed around Zach, washing away the blood and restoring his wounded arm to normal.

"I'm sorry, Sapphire. I let my guard down... it won't happen again," Zach apologised, picking up a bloodied white dagger.

"Good. This doesn't look like an opponent we can take down by ourselves," Sapphire remarked, gripping her sword handle so tightly that her fingers whitened.

"I'm going against orders, Astra. This may be an opponent you can't defeat, but I want you to witness how we Valour Knights battle together. You may find an answer to your technique in this fight, so stay safe and watch carefully!" Zach said before rising to his feet, glowing daggers in hand.

Mars arrived beside them in a trail of fire, his aura shaped like a flaming bird of prey.

Frozen footsteps marked Adonis' arrival, pounding in unison. Veins bulged on his thick neck as a freezing aura took form, creating a towering ice replica of himself.

A throne of vines carried the Knight of Thorns, his form enveloped in the blooming aura of a flowering rose.

Wings of shadow drifted in silence as Druinn descended, his otherworldly eyes scanning the area, shrouded in the abyss of his aura.

An arrow of lightning struck a pillar behind them, followed by Lilith emerging from a ball of electric energy, sparks flying in every direction.

Orbs of different elements juggled in the air as Jacques hovered above the ground, his aura clashing with a raging storm of elemental forces.

Quiet footsteps drifted with the wind as a howling gale surrounded the Unbreakable Knight's sword, ready for action. An endless tunnel of wind spiraled around Hugo.

All the Valour Knights together... their aura is overwhelming! Astra thought, her heart racing with excitement at the sight of them standing united. A smile spread across her face as the scene unfolded before her eyes.

"Okay, Captain! Do what you must to win!" she called, turning on her heel and sprinting toward the stands. With a swift leap, she cleared the arena, ensuring she wouldn't be in their way.

"Captains, just as the commander predicted, our killer has revealed themselves this day. As a final send-off for our fallen brethren, let us dispose of this heinous criminal," Hugo boomed.

Unfazed by the lightning arrow piercing his eye, the knight calmly retrieved the bloodied arrow.

"I have been tasked with eliminating thou Valour Knights. Retreating is not an option," he declared, his voice echoing with an ethereal resonance.

Intercepting the flaming hound with a dark-element-imbued blade, wisps of fire and black mist clashed. Picking up the pace, Morrigan and the knight exchanged blows—deflecting flaming fists, dodging dark slices, and countering with relentless precision.

"I'm glad you took the bait. I figured you would show yourself before all of us if we appeared weaker."

"Trap or no trap, mine master wishes to obtain pawns. Thou Valour Knights make the perfect sacrifice."

"Pawns? You think so little of us as to call us mere pawns?" Morrigan fumed, her aura blazing like an inferno.

"Indeed," the knight replied. "Mine master has a grand plan. Pawns are necessary to achieve our victory."

"What does this master of yours plan on achieving?" Morrigan demanded.

Glowing emerald eyes flickered behind his helmet.

"Yes, it shall be done. Thou have heard too much. Thou must die."

Dark energy gathered around the black blade, a void of bleak, crushing dread forming around the knight. Raising his weapon toward the cloud-filled sky, he unleashed the amassed energy. Orbs of darkness shot upward before raining down in a devastating cascade, each blast of dark energy aimed at the captains.

But the captains stood firm, intercepting the attacks with their own unique skills:

A flash of light from glowing daggers.

A crushing tidal wave.

A gaping mouth of shadow.

A hand of ice catching a ball of darkness.

A flaming geyser erupting.

A crystal spike emerging from a sword stabbing the ground.

A lightning arrow discharging an electrical sphere.

A powerful gust from a sword thrust.

Orbs of light forming a triangular barrier.

"As you can see, it won't be easy to take us all down," Morrigan smirked.

"Ah, yes, it appears so," the knight taunted. "Thine female Valour died without resistance. Fear gripped her by the throat, crushing her delicate neck."

Morrigan's focus wavered, panic creeping in as she realised this was exactly what they wanted.

"Don't do it, Lilith!" Morrigan shouted, but it was too late. A thick, onyx blade punctured her stomach. Morrigan coughed up blood, her body flung into a mound of snow, staining it crimson.

A flash of lightning struck a statue, drawing the knight's attention. He darted around, searching for the source—Lilith, now surging with a powerful lightning aura.

Lilith screamed in guttural rage, firing rapid lightning arrows at the knight. He deflected them, his pace quickening with each arrow he batted away.

"I'm going in!" Lilith yelled, firing another arrow as she gripped the edge of a pillar, preparing to launch herself.

"Lilith, don't!" Hugo shouted, but it was too late. She had already landed before the taller knight, meeting his gaze with electricity flickering in her eyes. Another lightning arrow pierced through him, transforming into a ball of electricity that travelled with the arrow, reappearing behind him.

Lilith stood back-to-back with the knight, muscles tensed. Clutching the arrow with a tight grip, her knuckles whitened as she waited. Time stood still for her as her chest rose and fell with each breath.

"You killed my sister. There is no way out for you—none that doesn't involve your death," she whispered coldly.

"Thou hath an impossible task. Thou cannot slay me," the knight responded calmly.

"You haven't fought me!" Lilith thundered. She dropped low, sweeping his legs before he could react. As he lost balance, she seized the moment, pinning his arms behind his back and delivering a spine-crushing blow with a lightning-enhanced knee strike.

Instead of falling to the ground, tendrils of shadow wrapped around the armour, lifting him back to his feet as he dusted himself off.

"Dost thou require another attempt?" he taunted.

Anger reddened her cheeks, igniting her aura as she launched another assault. This time, she refused to let up, striking his armour with relentless flashes of lightning. The surging electricity paralysed the knight, leaving him unable to move, unable to defend himself.

"You're not so tough! I'll make you pay for killing my sister! She didn't deserve to die—you do!" Lilith screamed, firing a barrage of arrows from every direction as she darted back and forth.

"Thou art wrong, Lilith. My master willed her death, and I obliged. As for myself, thou canst no longer end a life that hath already been stolen," the knight replied. His helmet fell off after bearing the brunt of her relentless attack, revealing a man with white hair and stubbed horns.

Lilith landed in a backflip, her body freezing as fear took hold.

"Lilith, what's wrong?! Get out of there!" Eden called out, commanding her vines to travel through the ground in an attempt to retrieve her.

"Thou hast witnessed too much!" Clenching his fist, a thrum of energy pulsed within his palm, drawing darkness toward him.

The vines stretched toward Lilith in a last-ditch effort. She clawed her way forward, reaching for them, but an invisible force blocked her attempt.

"What is this?" Lilith gasped, struggling to free herself from its pull. The Abyss refused to let anyone escape.

"This is the darkness that consumes all. However much thou may try to resist, the black hole I hold shall pull everything in," he answered.

Standing ankle-deep in what appeared to be water, surrounded by an endless black void, Lilith came to a realisation.

"If it consumes everything, then I'll give it all to you."

A spark of aura dissipated. With no other option, Lilith gave her entire being for one final attack—a raging storm.

She glowed brighter than ever before, lightning returning to the heavens above, determination unwavering, unyielding, unable to be swallowed by any black hole. Lilith pushed her aura beyond its limits. Sweat poured from every pore, evaporating into steam as she exhaled.

"Take. It. All!" she roared, her voice thunderous. A single clap of her hands sent out a deafening boom, shattering the sound barrier. A bolt of lightning struck the black hole, disrupting the energy within. It imploded, blowing everything away—nothing, not even the dark mist, remained safe.

Lilith tumbled across the ground, rolling an ankle and dislocating a shoulder. Pain shot through her body. Gritting her teeth, she grunted to push past the agony and hobbled towards the Black Knight.

The knight, having taken the brunt of the damage, crashed into a colossal statue, shattering his armour. Beneath the broken metal, his features glowed, starkly contrasting his dark aura. No older than Astra or Lazarus. Just a young man.

"...No, that can't be..." Lilith whispered, fear seizing her. "You're young. I wasn't hallucinating. Why? Why do you kill without remorse, without shame?!"

"For her... for her, I would do anything," he replied, his bloody smile unwavering.

"Who is she? Tell me!" Lilith seized his collar, lifting him off the ground.

Unafraid, he laughed. "She's almost here. I was just the opening act."

With a sudden motion, he reached out with his onyx gauntlet and crushed her throat. Lilith's eyes widened in shock as her grip weakened, and she dropped the knight. Clutching at her throat, she tried in vain to staunch the bleeding. Desperately, lightning seared her wound, an instinctive attempt to cauterize it.

"She requested you to be the next target—a splendid choice, I must admit. I bid thee farewell."

Reaching out for her friends, fearing for her life, thoughts flooded her mind—all possibilities fading before her eyes. "I'm... sor-ry... Com-der." The broken knight struggled to speak.

Her body remained limp as the electricity flickered within her eyes before fading.

"No!" Astra screamed, covering her mouth, aghast at the events she had just witnessed. A flicker of a spark turned into a powerful surge.

Hopelessness took hold in her grief, but one thought glimmered within the darkness consuming her mind. "Send lightning into the sky."

She glanced upward, searching for a solution—a way to ensure their small ally could find them. Deep breaths escaped her trembling body, daunted by the sheer climb ahead.

Astra gulped. "This isn't the time to be paralysed with fear. They need help, and I'll do what I can to support them."

The weathered pillars supporting the arena's walls bore natural cracks from years of wear. Tapping on a crack with her sword's pommel, she secured handholds and footholds.

Wind and snow pelted her face. Embracing the cold breeze, her eyes watered and froze over.

I'm almost there. If I can leap to the next crack, I can reach the top, Astra reassured herself.

Upon jumping, she punched into the crack, holding on with one arm as her body dangled. No, no, no! Panic set in as vertigo overtook her. Her eyes locked onto the ground below, and fear threatened to grip her entirely.

Mustering her strength, with her heart pounding against her chest, she swung once—just enough to reach the top.

Covered fingers gripped the edge. An armoured leg climbed over, dragging the rest of her body up.

"I did it!" she shouted triumphantly, raising her sword toward the sky. "I need your help, Gamma. I hope you're watching because I'm giving my all to signal you. Please hurry!"

Energy gathered around her sword with a crackling noise.

"Come forth, Lightning!" Astra shouted, discharging a powerful bolt into the gloomy sky.

The surge of energy drained her mana excessively. Her arms lost strength, her legs buckled, and her vision blurred until she could no longer continue. She collapsed atop the arena walls, unconscious.

Unbeknownst to the knights locked in their struggle with death, on the other side of Baylor, a light flickered in the dim, dreary city.

CHAPTER 38

"I have telepathy now; I wonder if they can hear my thoughts or if I can hear theirs," Lazarus whispered to himself as he neared floor 18.

"We hear you, Master Lazarus."

"Who was that? You can hear my thoughts now, then? It's great to hear your voice finally. You said 'we'—are you all in the same place on the other side of the portal?" Lazarus asked.

"It's Shadow. I've been wanting to speak with you properly. All of us are here in the spirit world. We each inhabit a different environment, but it all belongs to one realm. I have information that Lady Adelheid left for me to pass on to her child," Shadow replied, his voice wise despite his small appearance.

"What did she have to say, Shadow?"

"The answer lies in the spirit world," Shadow answered.

"The answer lies in the spirit world? That's vague. Can you sense her presence there, Shadow?"

"I do not sense her presence. While I can sense all spirits within this realm, there is a place I cannot break through—a place shrouded in darkness. I am sorry I can't help her in my current state."

"Darkness you can't breach in your current state... Is it to do with mana? Maybe if I can make you stronger, you can access that darkness."

"The shroud is dense. Whomever it belongs to does not want anyone entering their domain. I fear Lady Adelheid is trapped within it."

"Thank you, Shadow. That's helpful. I'm one step closer to finding her now," Lazarus thought as he reached floor 18.

"Lazarus, I take it? I've confirmed your check-in today. Proceed through the entrance when you're ready," a young man said while undoing the seal on the doorway. The red seal faded.

"I'm ready," Lazarus said as he rummaged through his bag. Potion vials clinked together—*Eclipse*, the journal, all inside. Lazarus slung the bag back over his shoulders and walked through the doorway.

"Everyone, we need to make this a quick battle. I'm going to Tame The Widowmaker once she's been weakened. There were no elemental weaknesses listed; she might specialise in physical attacks as a result."

"If it is a physical battle, may I make a suggestion?" asked Shadow.

"What do you have in mind?"

"All of us summons are connected through you. I think Shift, paired with Arco, would be the perfect candidates for a physical battle. Many of us spirits are suited for elemental opponents, though our abilities may come in handy if you think the situation calls for it."

"Noted. What do you say, Arco, Shift? Are you up for a fight against a giant snake lady?"

"I want to play." Arco said innocently.

"A giant snake, you say? I've fought a giant snake before—larger than a mountain!" Shift added, excited about facing another massive creature.

"Oh yeah? How did that battle end, Shift?" asked Shadow, a hint of amusement in his voice.

"Neither of us won! We both lay on the ground, exhausted from the thrilling battle. I will face this foe again if fate allows us!"

"I'm sure you would. You always think about fighting—I'd say there's nothing else on your mind. Simple brutes think the same." Shadow said with a huff.

"I'm stopping both of you there. We're here already. Be ready to attack, both of you. The rest of you, wait for my signal to join."

Lazarus entered a moonlit ravine, where a riverbed stretched as far as he could see, cradled by sheer mountains. Thrones of ivory, adorned with sapphires, rubies, and amethysts, gleamed atop a ritual dais. Glancing around, he spotted a lone walkway floating above the tranquil water below. Removing his cloak, he found a dry spot by the entrance to keep it safe.

"Nagi!" he shouted, waiting for a response. Ripples spread across the calm riverbed.

"NAGI!" he called again, this time hearing movement beneath the water in the distance.

"There you are... Arco, you'll go first. I want you to stop her movements—Shift," Lazarus commanded. "On my signal."

A wave burst from the riverbed, shattering the serene silence. Two emerald sabres pierced the water's surface, refracting the moonlight into Lazarus' eyes, momentarily blinding him.

Standing his ground, he closed his eyes and focused on her aura. A colossal, serpentine form lowered toward him until she was face-to-face with him, rain cascading around them.

"You dare intrude on my home and shout my name like that, you pathetic little… human," she sneered, eyeing him with disgust.

"I don't have time to waste searching for you. The best way to draw you out was to make sure you knew I was here," he replied calmly, unflinching.

"You wanted to lure the great Nagi out… now, why would you throw your life away like that?" Nagi said, using her elbows to lift her upper body onto the dais, where she took a seat.

Lazarus knew he was stronger than when he had left Riverfall, but even now, he hesitated as he sensed her aura flare. Meeting her glare with unwavering determination, he declared,

"You're going to become one of my summons. Though I may be looking up at you now, by the end of this battle, you will be on your back, struggling to move, while I stand victorious over your weakened body."

Nagi laughed, rising into the air with her snake-like body. Her cackling echoed through the ravine, filling the silence.

"You? Defeat ME?! Oh… the confidence, the SHEER AUDACITY…" Nagi boomed. Surpassing her limit, her anger erupted, and murderous intent seeped from her swaying form. A poisonous mist crept along the ground, thickening into a cloud of toxins.

"Wrong choice," Lazarus stated, his glare sharp.

Nagi brandished her two emerald sabres, slashing at him in a cross pattern. Lazarus backstepped to avoid the attack and whistled.

Out of the corner of her eye, Nagi caught sight of a clubbed tail swinging toward her. She raised her arm to block, but the impact crushed it. Reeling in agony, she hissed at the tiny earth-element spirit.

"Shift," Lazarus called out, leaping into the air just as Shift lunged through his portal. The fiery beast sank his flaming fangs into Nagi's shoulder, drawing red ichor. She cried out in searing pain as they tumbled into the water, her long, powerful tail coiling around Shift in an attempt to pry him off.

The water bubbled and hissed against Shift's scorching fur, steam rising as flames reacted with the surface. Amidst the chaotic underwater struggle, Lazarus glimpsed a light reflecting in the distance.

"Arco, keep guard until I return," Lazarus ordered, sprinting along the path leading to a glistening metallic-black door with crimson indents.

"No one will get past me," Arco responded.

During their death struggle, Shift pierced Nagi's opposite arm. In an instant, he switched into his Ice state, rapidly freezing the water around them. Forced to break away, Nagi slashed at Shift with her sabres, hacking at him until his fangs loosened.

Escaping the frozen trap, she emerged from the water, blood leaking from both shoulders. One arm dangled uselessly at her side. Narrowing her eyes in anger, she clenched her jaw as she spotted Lazarus running off.

Nagi let out a furious scream. "There he is! I'll kill you!" she roared, giving chase through the dense rainforest along the mountain.

Shift surfaced from the river, limping as purple liquid mixed with blood dripped from his wounds. He collapsed to the ground, letting out a faint howl before his body turned to ice and shattered into shards.

"Shift… you did great. Rest easy," Lazarus whispered, now approaching the steps to the doorway, leaping four at a time. "Shift, are you okay?"

"I was poisoned by her blades, but don't worry about me! Once I've healed enough, I want another shot at her!" Shift growled inside Lazarus' mind, excitement flickering beneath the pain.

"I want you to rest, Shift. Leave it to the rest of us, please," Lazarus replied.

His gaze shifted to the doorway before him. "What is this door? I've never seen one like it before. No connecting walls… it's as if it appeared out of thin air." Curiosity got the better of him, and he pushed the door open, revealing a dark cavern.

"Master, this is dangerous. I have never seen a door appear in a Dungeon before—not even when I was with your mother," Shadow warned.

"I understand your unease, Shadow, but we need to investigate this. The guild needs to know a second door has appeared. Maybe Aldo will have some insight," Lazarus replied.

"I need your help, Lumen. Can you find out what lies beyond this cavern? I'll stay here and handle Nagi," he said. The dense mana in the air set him on edge, warning him of the danger ahead. Trusting his instincts, he turned back toward the steps.

Nagi appeared behind him, her face mere inches from his own, swaying slightly with the breeze. She greeted him with a devilish grin.

"I found you."

"What the hell?!" Lazarus' body stiffened in shock, every muscle tensing. "I thought you were handling her—how did she get behind me so easily? …Arco?"

"I did chase after her, but she was too quick for my little legs, Master," Arco replied, sounding dejected.

A heavy thump caught Lazarus off guard, knocking him back slightly.

"Huh… I thought that would send me flying. Looks like I can fight on even terms with her after all. Don't worry, Arco—we can handle her together."

Lazarus grabbed hold of Nagi's tail, preventing her escape. Arco followed up, ramming his head into her stomach.

"Jaeger!"

A menacing presence emerged from a swirling portal as Jaeger crawled out, his cold gaze locking onto Nagi.

"Leave her to me."

Drawing his bow, Jaeger took aim at the massive target before him. His eyes flickered as he assessed his new prey, a slow smile creeping across his pale face.

Nagi hissed, struggling to break free from Lazarus' grip. She slashed downward, aiming to force him to release her, but before she could strike, arrows embedded themselves in her wrists. Her hands snapped open from the sudden impact, and her sabres clattered to the ground.

"Two hands down. Two shoulders injured. One crushed arm," Jaeger muttered, analysing his opponent.

Bursting into a sprint, he leapt onto her swiping arm, using it as a platform to continue his run before launching himself into the air. A volley of arrows rained down—two struck her elbows, and the last pierced her chest.

As Nagi collapsed with a thunderous crash, several trees splintered beneath her weight. Jaeger descended onto her motionless form, standing victorious.

The crimson ichor blended into her tan scales, transforming her beauty into a haunting presence. Nagi wiped the blood away, running her bloodied fingers through her ebony hair.

"Playtime is over, Nagi. It's time to end this battle. Shift, to me!" Lazarus shouted, still pinning her tail. "I've got her pinned down—finish this, you two!"

Summoning the last of her strength, Nagi flung her tail, sending Lazarus crashing into the surrounding trees and rocky formations. Shift lunged at her, tackling her onto her back and pinning the giant with flaming paws.

With the massive wolf taking over, Lazarus found himself free to act. Clutching his wounded arm, he climbed up her body until he met her furious brown eyes. She lashed out in anger, nearly knocking him off.

"Marsh, restrain her."

A portal opened, and a tongue whipped out, wrapping around Nagi's neck.

"As I said earlier, you'd end up on your back with me on top. Now… I can still feel you resisting." His gentle hands grasped her jaw, tilting her head back against the steps of a dais. Nagi stared wide-eyed, her expression full of rage.

"You will become mine, Nagi. You are strong—never forget that. But with my help, your fury will become a force to be reckoned with. At my side, you will face opponents stronger than you can imagine."

"Blast!" Nagi blurted. "A puny human could never tell me what to do or who to fight!" Her lungs burned with rage.

"This puny human is the one who took you down—don't forget that, okay? All I care about is having your combat prowess on my side. However, I can just as easily leave you here, in this quiet, lonely place where nothing exciting ever happens."

Her muscles relaxed as she let go of her anger. "I'm listening. What do you want to do with me?"

"Master, it's Lumen. I've located the one inhabiting this cavern. I'll be there in a second..."

"What do you mean, in a second? Whatever it is, don't bring it here... Lumen... hello..." Lazarus panicked, but it was too late to stop Lumen. The cavern became illuminated by a clash of red and blue light shining through the doorway above them.

"Sorry, Nagi, I don't have time to explain the situation. You'll just have to come with me," he stated, pressing his hand against her collarbone. A purple handprint appeared on her tan skin, and a choker materialized around her neck. Nagi touched the choker, which gleamed in the moonlight.

"It feels... soothing," Nagi commented, rising from the steps as Shift retreated through his own portal.

"I'm not here to enslave everything I meet in battle. It's the opposite. I want to see everyone free from their shackles, from these places of solitude. Outside, there's a world teeming with wildlife, races, and cultures—"

"No time for idle chatter, Master. We're already here—she's right behind me... she's powerful!" Lumen interrupted, leaping out of the doorway and down the steps onto the platform below. Turning to face her pursuer, she flared her tails toward the doorway, a protective growl warning of an imminent threat.

Footsteps echoed inside the cavern, slow and deliberate. Light taps against the cavern walls unsettled them, and the sight of a crimson glow filled them with unexpected discomfort.

"This is quite interesting," a voice echoed. "A spirit entering my domain, interrupting my slumber... and bringing me to this luminescent place. Oh... I see she was not alone. It seems I have plenty of food to wait out this cold."

The female voice was eerie yet seductive. Long, glossy black arachnid legs reached out, wrapping around the doorway as a slender woman stepped through, greeting each of them with a ghastly smile. Her hair, as black as obsidian, was styled in a bun and secured with a webbed string. Two black eyes fixated on those standing on the steps, their bodies frozen in shock at her sudden appearance. A jet-black leather outfit clung to her form, complemented by a regal black dress adorned with web-shaped pauldrons on her shoulders. A pair of black and red ankle boots completed her ominous ensemble.

With a flick of her wrist, webbing shot from her fingertips, encasing Nagi in a cocoon of silk.

"Who are you?!" Lazarus demanded, shifting into a defensive stance.

"Ignis, Nimbus, you two switch with everyone else. Nagi, I haven't given you a name yet... but I'll call you Karava. You will return as well—rest easy while we take care of this enemy."

"Who am I?" she echoed, amusement lacing her words. "I am the one who waits in the shadows for my next victim to stumble into my trap. I am the ruler of all arachnids—Arachne. And all of you... will feed my kin." Her tone carried undeniable authority.

A net of webbing rose behind her, launching toward Lazarus and binding his arms and legs.

"You made a mistake entering this domain. This place no longer belongs solely to Karava. This is our realm," Lazarus declared, locking his piercing gaze onto her.

In a sudden burst, Ignis emerged from his portal, spewing fire to burn away the webbing. Nimbus followed, summoning a gust of wind that hurled Arachne across the riverbed. Now free, Lazarus descended the steps.

"You passed through that door assuming you could defeat whoever was on the other side. I have seen my future—it does not end here. This battle is insignificant in the grand scheme. I will admit you have impressive skills; for that, I will grant you mercy... if you accept my offer to join me."

Arachne had returned to the main path just as Lazarus reached the bottom of the stairs. Her breathing was shallow after having the wind knocked out of her, and she gasped for air as she collapsed to the floor.

"I-I will not… join you..." Arachne said breathlessly, struggling to lift herself off the ground.

Lazarus pinned her down with his polearm, its ice-infused blade freezing her in place.

"I'm sorry, but it wasn't a choice. You will help me, Arachne, Queen of the Arachnids."

He raised his arm, signalling his two spirits to attack. Nimbus conjured a pillar of wind energy, which transformed into a fiery vortex as Ignis breathed into it. The stench of burned flesh assaulted the senses, and Arachne's shrieks were deafening. Lazarus, sitting on the bottom steps, clutched his ears in a futile attempt to drown out her agonising screams.

Why am I doing this? he thought. *I know I need to end this quickly, but this is torture!*

"Do not fear your capabilities, Master. You are not the one harming her—that is our job. Focus instead on how you can help Astra," Marsh reassured him.

"I can't just distract myself—she's in pain. Enemy or not, no one deserves this."

"That means you are compassionate. Remember when we defeated Jaeger together?" Karava added.

"Or the time you pushed your body to its limits to defeat Shift," Frost said.

"We will take on the burden of defeating your opponents, so you don't have to worry about that," Shadow said.

"I'm lucky to have all of you by my side. Thank you for all of your help," said Lazarus.

"Enough. Return, Ignis and Nimbus. I'll take care of her," he said as he knelt in front of the weakened Arachne. Her charred arms hung limply by her sides, and only fear remained in her blackened sclera and crimson eyes. He gently lifted her chin, a faint glow reflecting around him.

"Will you join me, Arachne? A queen should not hide herself away from the world—she should revel in her freedom to do as she pleases. Come with me, and I'll give you that freedom."

Arachne stared at him for a moment, judging whether he was sincere. Pale hands with red fingernails pushed his hand, moving it to her chest.

"Do it. Show me this freedom you speak of. I'm going to hold you to your word."

Violet mist seeped into her charred skin, leaving a handprint between her bosom. A wave of energy swept away the burnt flesh, restoring her moon-touched, pale skin. The black crown atop her head transformed into a deep, bloody red.

CHAPTER 39

Hellhounds emerged from a flaming aura, latching onto the wounded knight, who slashed relentlessly at the creatures.

"I will never forgive myself for Lilith's death. My lapse in judgment cost her life—I will not let that happen again!" Commander Morrigan raged, her body blazing with a fiery inferno. Snow melted away, revealing muddied ground. "Did you think a stab wound would be enough to kill me? My fire burns away all injuries inflicted on me. Do not drop your weapon. Do not lower your guard. Most importantly, do not drop to your knees! I am your hell; I am your punishment. You will not have an easy death!" Flames swirled around her limbs.

"Lilith!" Zach cried out, sliding across the ground and cradling her lifeless body. The other Valour Knights split up to support their commander and ensure Astra's safety. Zach held Lilith in his arms as Sapphire attempted to heal her, only to realise it was too late. He gently eased her back to the ground, covering her with her bloodied cloak before rejoining his fellow Valours. Together, they formed a protective circle around Sapphire. Morrigan, Mars, Adonis, and Zachariah took the front, while Eden, Druinn, Hugo, and Jacques stood at the rear.

"Sorry for the late arrival. I'm not too late, am I?" a female voice called out.

Perched atop a giant statue, Krow gazed down at the battlefield.

"You shouldn't be here, Krow. Leave this knight to us!" Morrigan shouted as the knight released a fog of aura that clashed against her fiery blaze.

"Now, now, no need for hostility, Commander," Krow said, pulling a sharpened bone from her arm, its surface enveloped in frost energy. She launched herself at the knight, forcing him to retreat from the group. "Let me have this dance!"

The knight charged at Krow, who twirled on her feet, keeping the bone blade close to her body. As his massive sword swung toward her in a horizontal arc, she flipped into the air, landing deftly atop the weapon and pointing her blade at his neck.

Tilting his head back to avoid the strike, the knight countered by dropping his sword and grabbing her leg in one smooth motion. With immense strength, he swung her overhead and slammed her into the ground. Krow coughed up blood but rolled with the impact, landing beside Lilith's lifeless body.

"Ugh… not a smooth landing at all. Excuse me," Krow muttered, using Lilith's body to steady herself.

Before she could regain her footing, a flaming blade whizzed past, slicing her arm. Clutching the wound, she turned her gaze toward her attacker.

Alastor knelt atop a statue of a knight, spectral blades glowing with ethereal blue energy forming wings on his back. His silver-white armour gleamed under the stormy sky.

With a graceful flap of his spectral wings, Alastor descended to the battlefield, towering over Krow.

"Krow! Long time no see. Sorry if I interrupted your dance, but I needed your attention," Alastor said. "It seems my plan worked, though I had hoped he could delay you a bit longer."

"What plan? What are you talking about?" Krow asked, her confusion evident.

"All these murders of Valour Knights, the sudden blizzards appearing on clear days… That couldn't have been a coincidence, right, Krow?" Alastor summoned a flaming sword in one hand and a glowing shield of light in the other.

"That does seem odd. I've been too busy to notice. What have you learned?"

"I'm glad you asked," Alastor said. "Normally, I wouldn't meddle in the affairs of knights. But the killer made one critical mistake—they killed my love, my Grace. Oh, that was a big mistake, because now? It's personal." He flared his fire sword, the blade growing in size.

"So, your lover died? All of us die eventually. It is the one certainty in life—no one can escape death."

"That may be true, Krow. But death doesn't come for those who still have a life to live. She had a life to live! Not anymore—it was taken from her!" Alastor's anger swelled. "So, I dug around. I waited for the next death, and sure enough, two nights later, another body turned up—the same day the clouds appeared over the city."

He tightened his grip on his sword. "I figured out that this couldn't have been the work of just one person. I asked Aldo for help, making sure Delilah stayed at the guild to see what would happen. Nothing. She had no part to play."

Alastor raised his blade, pointing it at Krow.

"You are the last remaining piece of the puzzle—the one summoning these clouds, trapping everyone in the city so your knight over there could do as he pleases. I asked Aldo to train Lazarus with your help, just to keep you out of the city long enough for them to defeat your knight. He wasn't successful in delaying you for long, but it makes no difference now. Morrigan will kill your knight, and as for you…" His eyes burned with fury. "I will deal with you personally, Krow."

"Are you done talking, Alastor? You may have put a plan together to stop me, but I'm afraid it's all for naught. You cannot stop what I've started. Come, Alastor, let's dance!" Krow said, pulling her scythe from a spatial pocket. She spread her arms wide, inviting a challenge only Alastor could accept.

"If it's a fight you want, I'm more than happy to oblige!" Alastor declared, swinging his sword and sending a slash of fire toward Krow.

"I've wanted to play with you… Spectre. When I'm done with you, you can join your lover in death."

"It is a tragedy that both sisters died," Alastor responded, his expression darkening as he glanced at the lifeless body beside Krow. "I'm going to have to ask you to step aside so I can ensure she's no longer involved."

"Not going to happen. I have plans for her."

Krow's eyes flickered with emerald energy as she cleaved through the air with her scythe. Alastor deflected the strike with his shield, countering with his flaming sword and scorching her thigh. She attacked again, but he parried once more, this time cutting her other leg.

"A physical fight against you won't work," Krow admitted, placing her scythe back into the pocket. Her fingers glowed green as she slammed them into the ground.

"A perfect opportunity for my new friends to take the spotlight. Let the curtains rise on their opening performance! Rise from your slumber— fight once more!"

The ground shook as cracks spread across the surface, ethereal emerald energy seeping from below. Several hands emerged, clawing their way out of the earth. Two male knights, clad in brown and blue Valour cloaks, loomed over a shorter female knight wielding a sword infused with wind energy and a shield that shimmered like a mirror of water.

Beside Krow, the lifeless body twisted unnaturally, bones cracking as it rose. Lilith's vacant eyes flickered with unnatural light as she grabbed the bow at her side, nocking an arrow and aiming it directly at the man staring at Krow.

"So, you're a summoner… Necromancy?" Alastor's expression darkened. "I see now. I can't let you roam free in this kingdom any longer, Krow. Every dance must come to an end, right?"

He launched a barrage of spectral spears, but Lilith retaliated, loosing charged arrows too fast for his defensive weapons to block. The arrows tore through his loose-fitting clothes, slicing through flesh in their wake.

"I bid you farewell, Alastor. My dance is just beginning. The main stage awaits my grand entrance—bye-bye!" Krow waved mockingly as she retreated.

☆☆☆☆

A circle of Valour Knights surrounded the Black Knight and Morrigan, a wall of flame separating them to prevent interference. Their auras clashed along with their fists, while the black blade lay shattered on the ground, broken into several pieces after Morrigan used a technique to sever the bonds holding the metal together.

"Don't get distracted. I need to vent all of my anger on you," Morrigan yelled, driving her knee into his stomach, flames bursting through the back of his armour. An elbow to his face erupted in embers. The knight tried to block the third attack, only for Morrigan to seize his arm and swing him into the air.

Fire channelled into her feet, melting the ground as she crouched. An impact crater formed beneath her as she launched herself like a rocket. Her speed increased drastically, allowing her to blitz her opponent mid-air, leaving a fiery trail that shaped a pentagram around him. Flames engulfed the knight until his flesh melted away, his charred bones collapsing to the ground.

"Crowley!" Krow screamed from the sidelines, alerting the Valour Knights. Morrigan landed outside the flames, collapsing upon impact. Enraged, Krow unleashed powerful ice magic, bombarding the knights as he leapt from frozen waves and slid along the slopes while they moved to defend their commander.

The next minute felt like an eternity for the Valour Knights.

"Valour Knights, protect your commander!" Hugo shouted, leading the knights into a defensive formation against Krow.

Light clashed against skeletal soldiers.

Thick vines lashed at blood sickles.

Fire halted the advance of ice spikes.

Blades of air sliced through Spectral Wraiths.

Orbs of darkness collided with ice shards.

Ice melted into water, weaving through the chaotic battle to aid the other knights.

Fists of ice hammered Ice Golems.

Throwing daggers, glowing like lasers, pursued Krow as she danced around her battlefield.

"One by one, all who live must come face to face with Death," Krow declared, relinquishing her summoning and elemental magic, opting instead to wield her scythe once more. "Death is the final act for all."

The Valour Knights advanced on her. In a breathtaking display of agility, Krow danced past each of her opponents, slashing their chests with precise movements—like a dandelion swaying in the wind.

Until she reached Morrigan. A frozen hand seized her by the throat, lifting her off the ground. Weak and unable to resist Krow's grip, Morrigan raised her fist into the air, sending fiery strikes into the clouds above.

"The mighty Commander of Baylor, renowned throughout the world of Aurora as the Hellhound who escaped purgatory. What a joke. You are nothing without your captains by your side," Krow spat in disgust.

Laughter escaped the weakened Morrigan, blood dripping from her mouth as she leered at Krow, sending a shiver through her opponent's body.

"Hellhound... I never liked... that name," Morrigan struggled to speak, her breathing laboured.

Krow punched her in the stomach, forcing more blood from her lips. Yet Morrigan only laughed again.

"Why are you doing that... why are you laughing?!" Krow yelled, slamming her against a pillar.

Morrigan seized Krow's wrist, squeezing with what little strength she had left. Krow flinched from the sudden pain, instinctively releasing her grip. Morrigan dropped to the ground but landed on her feet, her arms hanging limply at her sides, her head lowered.

Frustrated, Krow struck her again and again. But even as consciousness faded, Morrigan remained standing, her blazing aura unyielding, her devilish eyes locked onto Krow.

Above them, flashes of lightning tore through the sky, followed by the deep rumble of thunder and the onset of rain.

Locked in battle with the four deceased Valour Knights—commanding the elements of earth, water, lightning, and air—Alastor weaved through the onslaught of their attacks. Arrows remained the only true threat, shredding his clothes and piercing his flesh while narrowly avoiding critical wounds. Four swords floated above his shoulders, each imbued with an element to counter the four Valour Knights.

"I apologise, Knights of Valour, for what has happened to you. I am sorry I could not help you before this tragedy. Now, I can give you a swift death," Alastor said, pointing a white blade at them, an axe with a blue handle gripped in his left hand.

A cloudburst drenched their clothes while Alastor's torn shirt hung at his waist, revealing his shredded muscles.

"Enemy. Of. Master. Die," Lilith said, her twisted mindset persisting even in death.

She aimed her bow at Alastor—but that was not her true mark. Instead, she targeted the stormy clouds above, firing a charged arrow into them. The energy returned in the form of a massive bolt of lightning, striking Alastor—only for his image to disappear in a mirage.

"No time for idle banter, then. I'll have to end this quickly."

Alastor charged at the knight with a brown cape—Mainel—who wielded a black spear with a diamond tip. Thrusting the spear forward, Mainel unleashed shards of diamond at Alastor. Mid-air, Alastor twisted, switching with the icy blue sword floating above him, slashing through the shards until they shattered. He then dove toward the summoned knight, his swords charged and ready to strike.

The swords fired condensed beams of ice and air energy; the howling of the freezing ice grew louder as the expanding air increased the beam's size until it struck the knight. Mainel attempted to shield himself with a pointed diamond barrier to divert the energy, but it shattered under the freezing temperatures. With no other protection, he froze within seconds—only to be shattered completely by a single strike from Alastor's axe.

Alastor could feel his blood pumping, riding a high. Mid-flight, he turned to find his next opponent—the Valour of blue, Omak, a dwarf of the berserker class.

Arrows rained from above in a relentless barrage, hindering Alastor's advance.

Brandishing two battle axes, Omak leapt toward him, water energy swirling around his weapons. Each swing sent powerful waves of water crashing toward Alastor. He raised a shield to block the attack, but the secondary splash of acid burned through the defence and splattered onto his skin. Pain seared through him as the corrosive liquid ate into his flesh. With a yell, he thrust a lightning spear into Omak's chest. Soaked by the heavy rainfall, the dwarf's body conducted the powerful surge of electricity, frying the berserker instantly. The charge crackled and flickered across rippling puddles.

"Two down. The two sisters remain…" Alastor whispered to himself. "Air and Lightning."

He switched out his weapons, bringing forth spears of ice and earth. Metallic wings beat with a powerful, resonant rhythm—reminiscent of an angel. From his vantage point in the storm-lit sky, he observed his fallen opponents.

Their battle had led them to the bridge. Guards had fled to the opposite end, seeking refuge from the collateral destruction.

Blending seamlessly with the dance of lightning, a lone arrow honed in on Alastor but struck a shield instead. The barrier deflected the charged arrow back at its owner, who caught it in her bare hand.

An electric yellow aura swelled around her, mirroring the rage-filled expression glaring at Alastor.

Alastor glanced at Lilith. "No patience? You were always the one to shoot first and ask questions later. Let's finish this!"

Grace moved to shield Lilith, her older sister, conjuring a violent gust of wind that spiraled around them. She planted her shield firmly, its size towering over her short stature. Testing her defences, Alastor used telekinesis to hurl several weapons at her, but each one rebounded with twice the force.

"Excellent defences, my love. It broke my heart to hear of your death, so I made it my mission to find the one responsible. I promise to grant you a peaceful respite," he said solemnly.

Alastor dove toward Grace, the wind rushing past him as he descended. Twisting midair, he dodged a barrage of arrows. Summoned blades floated around him like flowing water, aiding his assault. From the stormy sky, blades rained down, bombarding the bridge below.

Using Grace's shoulders as a springboard, Lilith launched herself toward Alastor, flinging a charged arrow to the side of the descending blades. Electricity crackled around her body as she stretched midair— then vanished.

"Oops! Not this tech-" Alastor braced for impact.

Lilith teleported beside Alastor, pressing her palm against his stomach. Electricity surged through her arm as it transformed into a spear, piercing him. The barrage of blades halted, clattering to the ground. Before he could fall, Lilith grabbed hold of him, watching as he coughed up blood, his eyes locked onto hers.

"Heh... beaten by... speed..." Alastor rasped, his voice strained by the damage to his lungs.

"Strike. Fast," Lilith replied, her expression hollow as she prepared to pierce him again. But before she could make contact, his form flickered and vanished, leaving only an afterimage.

"You're right—ending a battle swiftly has always been your greatest strength. But it's useless against someone who can evade every strike," Alastor said, reappearing beneath her. As he advanced toward Grace, his body shifted between multiple copies, each moving in seamless unison.

Grace raised her silver mace high, unleashing a powerful gust of air that expanded into a swirling dome of wind around her. She spun the mace, amplifying the barrier's reach.

"I'm sorry, Grace... this nightmare will soon be over," Alastor murmured through the howling wind. His afterimage phased through the defence, materialising behind her. A spectral blade emerged in his hand, slicing through her neck without leaving a single wound. A calm serenity washed over her, freeing a restless soul.

Delicate hands cupped his chiselled jaw, welcoming him with a radiant, affectionate smile.

"I'm sorry, Alastor. I wanted to do so many things with you. I wanted to visit the sprawling desert sea of Solaris, the mystical forests of Floratum, and witness the haunting beauty of Mortis by your side." Tears rolled down her face as she choked on her own words.

"We will. I'm going to show you everything this world has to offer; you'll be by my side every step of the way." Alastor trembled, his heart breaking at the sight of her, knowing she would leave him so soon. "I won't let her have you. If you let me, I can free you. Together, with me— for eternity."

"Eternity? That sounds... nice," Grace whispered, the light in her bright blue eyes fading into darkness.

Alastor glanced up at Lilith as she descended to the ground. She let out a painful, blood-curdling scream as her lightning aura exploded, sparks flickering and destroying everything they touched.

No time to hesitate. I didn't want to do this—not to you. But I can't bear another day without you in it. I need you, Grace.

Alastor matched her power, summoning a destructive tornado that pulled every weapon into its spiraling winds.

He placed a weapon in Grace's hands, wrapping her fingers around it—a silver blade with sky-blue runes etched along its surface.

"Across vast fields, oceans that surpass the horizon, peaks that reach the heavens above, an endless expanse of stars and planets—none of that could ever keep me from you. You are my one true love. In this lifetime and the next, I bind thee. Stay by my side until my final breath. I grant this blade a name, soul-binding in its execution. Return to me, Grace," he whispered softly.

Ethereal blue energy flowed into the blade as Alastor cradled her hands around it, then plunged the ethereal weapon into her body.

A spectral blue aura enveloped Grace in a warm glow. The runes detached from the blade, floating in a circle, joined by her spirit. She gazed at the blade with longing before her eyes met his sea-blue ones. A knowing smile formed on her lips. The spirit reached for the blade, merging with the runes before they returned to the weapon.

"*Grace?*" Alastor called internally, waiting for a response in the vast, empty white room of his mind.

A silent, ethereal figure stepped into the space. Draped in a flowing white dress, golden locks glistened in the radiant light. A smile, brighter than anything he had ever witnessed, welcomed him.

"I'm here, Alastor. You used your soul-binding skill, right? It feels... tranquil. I remember everything I experienced on the outside, yet none of the pain, turmoil, or sadness. It's all gone," Grace said.

"It's a peaceful respite. You don't have to worry about anything in here," he reassured her, gently grazing her cheek with his rough hand. "I can change the scenery to whatever you want—rolling fields of green, a sky filled with clouds, a home overlooking the city."

"Show me the place where we first met."

The white room shifted, transforming into a bustling town square with a fountain at its centre. Sunlight bathed the scene in a warm glow.

"Where you and I first bumped into each other. I tried to catch you, but you pulled me down with you into that fountain. I'll never forget that day."

"It's beautiful, Alastor. Now that I'm one with you, I can sense your unease. She's still out there—she's in pain too. I know she wouldn't want you to do this to her, but I want you to free her from Krow. Please."

"It will be done, I promise."

Auras continued to clash as they walked toward each other. Electricity spiraled around the raging tornado, charging the weapons caught in its grasp. The surge lashed at Alastor as he pressed forward, enduring the pain.

"Lilith, the pain you've endured this past week is beyond my imagination—not even this electricity coursing through me could compare. I pray Krow does not twist your afterlife as well. For now, let me give you a peaceful end. I cannot break you free from this torment yet, but I swear I will find a way to release you from those shackles."

Alastor's afterimages closed in on the grief-stricken Lilith, lost in her own rage and sorrow. An ethereal blue sword formed in his hand as he faded past her, granting her a death befitting her sister.

Lilith's fury ebbed. The electrifying aura dissipated, and her body vanished into the unknown.

"That's it. Rest easy now, Lilith... Until we meet again."

Waking to the sound of a raging lightning storm, Astra felt a wave of dread wash over her. As she took in her surroundings, the sheer height of the walls struck her. She paced along the edge of the arena wall, 150 meters above the ground, scanning the destruction below. Her muscles tensed—she had always feared heights.

The battlefield beneath her was in ruins: massive craters from elemental explosions, jagged walls of ice, vines scattered about, scorched earth, puddles crackling with electricity, and broken pillars reduced to rubble. Bodies lay motionless across the battlefield.

"What the hell happened here? Everyone's passed out on the ground... including Commander Morrigan? Is that Krow?" Astra whispered to herself.

In the heart of the wreckage, Krow crouched beside Crowley, her hands clutching her knees. The rain masked the tears running down her face.

"I need to get down. I don't know what happened, but maybe Krow can help," Astra muttered, scanning her surroundings for the shortest drop.

Rubble shifted, and pillars crumbled as Astra leapt down, the sudden movement alerting Krow. Instinctively, Krow drew a bone sword, pointing it toward the noise.

"Who's there?! Show yourself now."

"It's just me, Astra. Is that you, Krow? I passed out... What happened? What caused all this destruction?" Astra asked, her cloak drenched by the rain along with the rest of her clothes.

"The Valour Knights defeated this knight. As for the storm, Commander Morrigan shot flames into the clouds, bringing this upon us," Krow said, motioning toward the bleak sky.

Astra's gaze drifted to the unconscious bodies scattered across the battlefield. Her eyes narrowed as she studied their wounds. *These don't look like injuries from the knight's blade... These were caused by a different weapon.*

Suspicious, Astra reached for her sheathed sword, catching Krow's attention.

"Terrible decision, Astra," Krow warned, her gaze shifting towards Crowley.

Bone met flesh in an entangled struggle. Astra's eyes widened as Shadow appeared before her, his shadowy flesh wrapping around the bone sword and Krow, trapping her in place.

"Shadow! Are you okay?!" Astra shouted as he hunched over the blade, his strength fading.

Electricity crackled around Astra. Thunder rumbled, following bursts of lightning.

"No... more..." she whispered, as the energy around her surged exponentially.

Krow tightened her grip on Shadow, who turned his head toward Astra. He cooed softly, attempting to speak through her distress.

Dark tendrils wrapped around Krow, engulfing her in darkness.

"I don't want anyone else to die!" Astra screamed.

A bolt of lightning struck her, supercharging her aura. Unable to contain the massive surge of stored energy, stray strands of lightning flickered violently, searing through her own flesh.

I can't hold it any longer... Please, let this work!

Pulsing electricity thrummed like a heartbeat, converging on her sword.

Bolts of lightning burst forth, forking into chaotic zigzags and striking both Shadow and Krow. Shadow vanished with the first surge, but Krow endured longer, encasing herself in a shell of ice. With each strike, fragments chipped away.

Astra let out a thunderous roar, doubling the radius of the lightning and shattering the icy shell.

Exhaustion took hold—one knee buckled, her breathing ragged, sweat drenching her skin. Blurred vision clouded her final gambit.

"I can't... hold... on..." Astra whispered breathlessly. Her arms, weakened by relentless strain, fell to her sides, and her sword splashed into a puddle.

She collapsed onto a mound of snow, the chill refreshing her senses. Gazing upward, a giant, warm light welcomed her.

"That feels nice..." she murmured before passing out.

"Don't worry, I protect," Gamma called from above, cradling a massive fireball that shrank in his tiny palms.

Krow instinctively jumped back, her gaze snapping upward. "You! You're the little creature from Lazarus' room!" she shouted. Summoning all the energy she had left, she conjured a massive iceberg.

"That's me. They're friend," Gamma replied, bouncing between descending magic discs. Though the fireball in his hands appeared harmless, its aura was overwhelming, freezing even Krow in fear.

Desperation flared in Krow's eyes as she growled and hurled the iceberg toward Astra and Gamma.

"Astra stays," Gamma declared, aiming the fireball at the oncoming ice. Scorching heat shimmered in the air, creating mirages that reflected both fire and ice along the ground. The iceberg was no match—the fire melted through, turning ice to steam.

"How?! That ice freezes everything! Nothing can melt it!" Krow shouted in frustration.

"My flames of purgatory consume all. You had the misfortune of involving my friends," Gamma said, now standing before Krow. She stared in disbelief, exhaustion overtaking her as she stumbled backward and collapsed onto the ground.

Gamma hopped onto her stomach. "Astra safe. We win."

With a devilish grin, he pressed the miniature fireball into Krow's abdomen. A contained explosion erupted, launching him into the air while avoiding the blast. Krow let out one final cry before the explosion engulfed her, shattering the ice shell and knocking her unconscious.

In the aftermath of the battle, bodies lay defeated, strewn across the battlefield. Faint auras flickered in the darkness. *They're all alive!* Alastor thought as he sprinted from a devastated bridge toward the ruins of the garrison.

The crunch of snow alerted him, drawing his attention to Astra, who lay motionless, wracked with pain at even the slightest movement. Beside her stood a small, hooded creature, metallic horns protruding from its hood.

"State your name and intentions, creature," Alastor commanded, raising his blade toward the figure. His body was covered in wounds, the rain washing away the excess blood.

"Gamma. Astra safe," the creature replied, draping her fur coat over Astra for warmth.

"Gamma?" Alastor echoed. "You mean no harm to these people?" His grip on the sword remained firm, uncertainty flickering in his gaze.

"No harm. Protect Astra," Gamma affirmed.

"Okay then. As long as you mean us no harm, I won't bring any harm to you."

Alastor recalled his blade in a flash of ethereal blue light and lowered himself to the ground beside Astra. As Royal Guards rushed into the collapsed grounds, calling out for survivors, he exhaled heavily. *I kept my word, Lazarus,* he thought, wondering how his friend fared in the tower.

A guard clad in ivory and gold armor hurried over, reaching out to help Alastor to his feet.

"Are you okay, Prince Alastor?!" he asked, concern etched into his face as the young man struggled to stand.

"I'm fine. Take care of the others, please. Just let me rest—I think I've earned it," Alastor replied, waving a tired hand toward the fallen knights. "Also, make sure to use the magic seals on Krow. She caused all of this… and murdered four of the Valour Knights."

"Very well, Prince Alastor!" the knight responded before rushing off to aid the wounded.

On this dreary day, another Valour Knight had fallen in battle—a younger sister who only wished to protect others, a dwarf with an insatiable thirst for battle, and a man whose resolute sense of justice was tougher than any diamond.

Victory? No, this tragic battle could not be a victory, with the loss of four of their Valour Knights, Krow had won even in her defeat.

CHAPTER 41

Shift raced through the Mistbrook Forest, the rushing air pressing against Lazarus as he clutched the snow-white fur, holding on for dear life.

"Are you okay, Shadow? Is Astra safe?!" Panic set in as they sped back to Baylor.

"I am unsure, Master. A woman called Krow tried to attack Astra. I did what I could to hold her in place, but I was struck by lightning that Astra cast. Master... she was angry. I am worried about her well-being, too."

"Krow?! I was just with her! What happened? What did Krow do, Shadow?"

Shadow recounted the events from Lazarus' last encounter with Astra up until the moment lightning struck his body.

"You went through all of that, Astra? I'm sorry I couldn't be there with you. We're meant to face threats together. Next time, we will!" Lazarus said, his gaze fixed ahead, waiting for the bridge to appear.

"One more thing—Queen of Arachnids—do you have a name?" Lazarus asked.

"I won't stop you from using that title, but yes, I do. My true name is Aravelle."

"Aravelle, it—"

All of Lazarus' spirits alerted him at once as a woman suddenly appeared before them, standing in their path, covered head to toe in blood. The girl limped forward, one arm clutching the other.

Shift came to an abrupt halt, nearly launching Lazarus off his back. His fur bristled as he snarled at the figure before them.

The forest, once teeming with wildlife foraging for food, had fallen into an eerie silence. Now, the only sound was the distant murmur of running water from the brook.

"L-L—I am sor-ry, Lazarus... I couldn't protect them..." the girl rasped, her voice strained by her bruised throat. Lazarus recognised her voice but struggled to discern her features through the bruises—until he noticed the horns hidden beneath her blood-stained white hair.

"Levanna!" He rushed to her side, catching her as she collapsed to the ground. Quickly, he removed his coat and draped it over her trembling body.

"I-I tried... we all fought together... but it wasn't enough. They tore through us like we were nothing—like toys." Levanna's blurred vision barely allowed her to focus on his emerald-green eyes. "Lazarus... they want you to return to Riverfall. They're waiting there... to kill you. Don't go—I don't want you to die too."

Rage swelled within him—an anger he had never felt before, one he could not contain. A powerful aura erupted from within, unleashing a shockwave that sent nearby trees toppling.

The silence shattered. Animals fled in every direction—some darting through the undergrowth, birds scattering into the sky, while others burrowed desperately into the earth.

"Levanna, you once said I was your champion—that I would be the one to defeat Zodiac. Do you remember any of your visions?" He exhaled sharply, trying to steady himself. "I see glimpses of them—randomly. It all happens too fast for me to hold on to it. But in one of them... I saw my own death—facing a man in an ox mask." He clenched his fists. "Was he the one who slaughtered everyone?"

Regaining his composure, Lazarus sat heavily on a fallen tree, resting his head in his hands.

"I see... flashes. When I'm in the environment of the vision—moments before it comes true." Levanna's voice wavered. "Don't even think about trying to fight him. Nothing you do will have any effect on him."

Shift sat beside Lazarus, allowing him to run a hand through his fur before recalling him.

"It's about time I met them. They need to understand that I am coming for them."

Levanna's hand struck his cheek. "You're going to die if you fight them!" she shouted. "I will not let you walk into a trap. I can stop—"

"Levanna!" Lazarus boomed, silencing her. "Enough! They sent me a message—I intend to repay the favour. A message I will carve into their very souls."

Intrigued, she rose to her feet. "And what message would that be?"

Lazarus dropped to one knee, bowing before her.

"I will be your Champion. Zodiac will learn to fear me."

CHAPTER 42

An eerie silence settled over the mountain pass, each step on the icy snow cracking beneath their boots. Every step was another pounding beat against his chest as anxiety swelled within.

"So much has happened since we left. I'm nervous about returning. Are you sure you want to be here, Astra?" Lazarus asked, his footsteps slow and deliberate as the rolling mist descended from the peak.

Beside them, Levanna tensed as the realisation dawned— they had returned to Riverfall. Forced to confront the regret of every death, she carried the weight of the lives she had failed to protect.

"You promised you wouldn't fight them without me. I'm not leaving your side," Astra replied, standing firm, clad in armour and ready for battle.

The deep wounds she had endured had healed, leaving only a scar across her throat. Flames danced within her palm, providing warmth as they ascended the chilly staircase leading up the mountain.

"We're going to need information about them, Levanna. Who are the ones in the village?" Lazarus asked, retrieving his journal.

"There are two of them—Ox, with his unparalleled strength, and Goat, who can manipulate space, creating tears that act as portals," Levanna said, patting down their cloaks to clear away the excess snow.

"I need your help, Mother. We're about to face Ox and Goat of the Zodiacs. Please tell us you have information about them."

The journal glowed, and the small spirit figure of Adelheid appeared.

"Zodiac? Your father and I have fought against them before, but we did not have the power to stand against them. Despite being outnumbered, we managed to pressure them, learning their favoured elements, classes, and skills."

"What can you tell us about Ox and Goat, Lady Adelheid?" Levanna asked, leaning past Lazarus to peek at the spirit.

"Ox takes pride in his strength, wielding a great axe that splits everything in his path. I remember him utilising Earth-element techniques. If you fight him, don't get close—he is slow and will struggle against anyone faster than him. Specialising as a Berserker, he focuses on Strength and Constitution."

"My spirits could work against him. If they can't do anything, I'll need your help, Levanna."

"I'll do my best."

"Goat, on the other hand, is agile, intelligent, and specialises in spatial magic. His weakness is his lack of Strength and Constitution. Please don't make the same mistake I did. I trust you will find a way to defeat them."

Adelheid faded back into the journal.

"One uses speed and magic; the other uses strength and endurance. Is that right, Levanna?" Lazarus wondered as he glanced across the footpath and saw the arched entrance to the village.

A strong aura, solid as a mountain, surrounded the village, making it hard for them to move closer. Dried blood stained the archway. Buildings lay in ruins, reduced to rubble and piles of timber. Adult bodies, clad in shredded leather armour and gripping shattered weapons, were scattered throughout the village, attracting scavenger rats hungry for food. The stench of rotting flesh filled the air, and Lazarus retched.

"I see the older villagers. What happened to everyone else, Levanna?" Astra asked cautiously, manoeuvring around the dead bodies and witnessing the horrors of the Zodiacs' brutal siege.

"They all escaped; I do not know where, though. I thought it safer for them that way," Levanna replied.

An aura of golden splendour clashed with crimson flames, creating a small pocket for them to breathe.

Across the stone bridge, Lazarus spotted two figures waiting on tree stumps, gazing out at a lake that glistened with crystalline resplendence. Cradled by the stump, their hair matted and their clothes stained with dried blood, lay Maeve and Darius.

"Astra..." Lazarus whispered. Blood boiled beneath his skin, but instinct forced him to remain calm.

"It has to be them..." Astra murmured, a flicker of electricity zipping along her fingers, inches from a sheathed sword.

A boisterous laugh greeted them as Ox loomed above, standing three metres tall.

"You took your time coming here, champion. I hoped our message would have sufficed for a hasty return," Goat commented, gesturing to the aftermath of their visit.

"I received it loud and clear. I have my own message for Zodiac," Lazarus glared.

"A message for us? And that is?" Goat asked. Trees rustled with a wild breeze, disturbing leaves of violet and sapphire.

"I know you have been searching for me. I cannot even begin to comprehend why I am a threat to your organisation—a nobody who couldn't fend off a wolf attack a week ago. Do you truly see me as a danger to your existence?

"Whatever your reasoning, you made a big mistake. You came to this village and murdered the people who raised me. Now, that is unforgivable," Lazarus threatened.

Ox pressed a finger into Lazarus' chest, pushing him back. "Unforgivable? I see a bunch of dead people—idiots who thought they could go up against Zodiac. Their pathetic attempt at resistance didn't even serve as a warmup."

Ignoring the behemoth's taunts, Lazarus made his way to the elders—the couple who had raised him in place of his parents and taught him everything he knew.

Maeve... Darius. I am sorry this happened to you. None of you deserved any of this.

Lazarus adjusted their bodies so they lay properly on the ground. As he did, a thin chain with a locket slipped from Maeve's hand.

What is this? he wondered, opening it to reveal a hidden note. A single word was written inside—a name.

Is this my true name? If that's the case, all of you have protected me in ways I never considered. This name carries a burden—one I cannot dwell on now. But when the time comes, the world will know. Thank you, Maeve, for everything you have done for me... for Astra.

Out of respect, Lazarus draped his fur coat over the couple.

He locked eyes with Ox, a sudden flare of radiant light blinding him.

"Words are not enough to describe the hatred I feel towards you," Lazarus said coldly, frost escaping with each breath. "No, I need to deliver my message another way." He exhaled sharply. "Ísarr."

Bo staff in hand, Lazarus and Ísarr charged at their opponent. Shards of ice formed where the staff dragged through the snow while Ísarr leapt across discs of ice, reaching Ox first.

Using his icy breath to blast away at the giant foe, he moved swiftly, running circles around him.

Ox remained unfazed by the attacks, smirking at Lazarus. "Is this the best you can do?"

Provoked, Lazarus launched into an attack, hurling a barrage of ice shards. He batted away at the fragments, sending them flying toward Ox. Yet, Ox remained rooted, refusing to defend himself.

"Why isn't he attacking?" Astra asked Levanna from the sidelines.

"This is a test for Ox," Levanna replied. "If Lazarus can't deal any real damage, Ox won't retaliate. It's a blur between hopelessness and false hope. He's always enjoyed breaking his opponents' spirits."

"Ísarr, time to swap with Karava. We need to try a different approach," Lazarus commanded.

His largest summon arrived, shielding him while smoothly wrapping her tail around Ox.

"Now you're speaking my language!" Ox boasted, using his monstrous strength to break free, much to Karava's dismay.

Brandishing her signature sabres, she slashed at Ox with terrifying precision while lifting Lazarus onto her shoulder with her tail. Matching her speed, Ox deflected the strikes with his axe.

With a hiss, Karava exhaled a poisonous mist, forcing Ox to step back.

"What's the matter, Ox? Not strong enough to handle poison?" Lazarus taunted from his perch.

Laughter echoed from within the mist. A sudden jolt sent Lazarus off balance as Ox grabbed Karava's tail, swinging her through the air before slamming her into the ground. Her weapons clattered against the cold earth.

"Swap, Nimbus!" Lazarus called out.

A gust of wind swept the poisonous mist into a swirling funnel around Ox.

"Good thinking, let's keep it up. Ignis, give it everything you have!"

Arriving in a fiery blaze, Ignis unleashed a torrent of flames, turning the funnel into an inferno.

"Ox, enough games! Hurry and finish him off before he can do anything else!" Goat yelled, rising to his feet.

"You shouldn't worry about him," Astra suggested, her blade crackling with electricity as she pointed it at Goat's neck. She was joined by Levanna, who radiated a blazing aura, a fireball in hand.

"I was content observing from this comfortable stump. Are you sure you wish to do this, Levanna?" Goat warned.

"Yeah, I'm pretty sure I do!" she said confidently, hurling the fireball.

"Very well," Goat replied. A sudden elbow strike sent Astra crashing into the frozen lake. The ice shattered on impact, plunging her into the icy depths. Electricity surged along his body, but he remained unfazed by the jolt.

"Look at him indulging himself over there. I don't get what it is about fights that he finds so thrilling. I detest them. Levanna, let's finish this so I can go relax."

With her legs ignited, her speed surged, allowing her to land a single unguarded strike to his jaw.

"That's my intention," Levanna declared. A stream of fire flowed from her hands, engulfing Goat in an infernal tornado. Air sickles tore through the flames.

☆ ☆ ☆ ☆

"Swap, Shift! Freeze him in place," Lazarus ordered, recalling Ignis.

Shift leapt out of his portal with a rumbling howl, frost escaping through bared fangs as he bit into the fire, freezing the flames.

Shadow emerged along the ice, tendrils of darkness enveloping Ox. Enraged by the cheap tactics, Ox burst through the icy prison, swinging his axe into the ground. A fissure split open, shaking the earth beneath them. He pursued Lazarus into the woods, cleaving through trees and boulders. Every time he aimed for Lazarus, a spirit took his place.

"Enough games, Champion! Show me how you fight!" Ox roared in anger.

"You asked for it," Lazarus whispered into his ear, striking Ox in the back with an ice-tipped staff. Blood seeped onto the ice, staining it crimson. Ox retaliated with a backhand, but Aravelle appeared in Lazarus's place.

"Manners, darling. You mustn't strike a lady," Aravelle chided, a web shielding her from his heavy fist. Despite her proximity, she evaded every attack, spinning a web around his body.

"Marsh, on me!" Lazarus shouted, soaring high into the air. The two descended in a spiraling surge of water—a crushing wave. Ox raged beneath the cascading torrent, tearing through the webbing.

"Champion!" Ox bellowed. Marsh landed on his bare chest, driving his sword into the giant's throat.

Nearby, hoofbeats thundered, accompanied by the crackling hum of electricity pulsing through Karah's mane. She waited.

"Just a little more, Karah. He's right where we want him," Lazarus murmured, ice gathering along his Bo staff.

Three... two... one!

Ox stood up, swiping away the excess webs, oblivious to his surroundings.

"Karah!" Lazarus shouted. Ice continued to grow, forming a massive spear tip.

Karah fired a bolt of lightning, striking Ox square in the chest. His muscles tensed as electricity coursed through his drenched skin, leaving his body rigid with paralysis.

Ox grunted, unable to speak, his gaze fixed on Lazarus pacing toward him. The ice spear had grown to twice Ox's height. Planting his feet, Lazarus mustered all his strength and thrust the spear into Ox's bare chest, drawing blood.

"Unmatched strength? I don't care how strong you are—I'll use every tactic at my disposal to counter that strength." Blood stained the ice piercing his chest. "I am weaker than you. I have less experience than you. I have nothing to my name... yet here I am, drawing blood from someone who claims to be the 'strongest.' Tell me, how does it feel?"

Lazarus locked eyes with Ox, a cold smile forming as he drove the spear deeper into his flesh.

A bloody grin spread across Ox's face. His stone-grey eyes leered down at the Champion.

"Bloody amazing!" he said ecstatically.

With a sudden motion, he pulled the spear deeper into his own body. Giant fingers wrapped around the shocked Champion's throat, yanking him closer.

"Let's see how you handle an attack from the 'strongest,'" Ox growled, head-butting Lazarus.

Idiot! You had him, and you fumbled.

Dazed and confused, arms and legs hung limply. The chill of the air brushed against Lazarus' skin as the world began to spin—white, blue, grey, white again.

What's going on? The ground looks so... distant. My head is spinning. I can't tell up from down.

"Not yet," Ox muttered.

Hands that felt like an iron vice gripped his ankles, spinning his world around once more.

This strength... I don't even have time to react. The snow... I can almost touch—

Thud!

A wave of snow and dirt exploded outward, crashing against trees, ice, and buildings.

Lying in a deep crater, a broken body twisted unnaturally. Blood spattered from his mouth, bones protruding through torn flesh.

Bare feet stamped down on shattered ribs.

Coughing up blood, Lazarus lay motionless.

My insides are on fire. I can't talk. I can't move. Every breath is a painful struggle to survive.

"All that bravado—for what?!" Ox roared. "Is this what you want me to remember? The pathetic champion sprawled on the ground, nothing but shame on his face?" His hand trembled with rage.

"The Champion should be someone who stands even when he *can't* stand anymore—someone who fights until his last breath."

A shimmering light reflected off an icicle spear. Bulging muscles raised it high, preparing to bring it down like a guillotine.

A crimson blade flashed through the air, slicing Ox's arm—just not enough to stop the killing blow.

This is it. This is death... death from Mortesyn. I'm sorry, everyone. I couldn't help you. If I were stronger, it wouldn't have ended like this... I would be able to hear you all laugh again, hear your voices one more time, tell you that I love—

Sharp ice pierced his chest, the force behind the spear immeasurable.

Blood pooled around the lifeless body—a husk of a fallen champion.

A mortified, agonized scream shattered the haunting silence.

A geyser of rage erupted, spewing flaming embers that rained down upon the devastated village.

☆☆☆☆

Light and fire blended beneath the lake's surface. Rising from her watery tomb, Astra clawed her way onto solid ground, drenched and shivering. Frozen lungs heaved between gasps for air.

I made it! Darkness almost took over... but those embers guided me back to the light.

"Lazarus!" she called out, scanning the area.

"...he's gone..." a voice whispered.

"Where is he?" Astra asked, stumbling upon Levanna, hunched over molten lava.

A grim expression met her, tear stains marking Levanna's face. Silently, she pointed toward the destroyed forest.

Panic surged through Astra. Wind and snow pelted against her skin as she sprinted toward Lazarus—until a crater in the corner of her vision halted her dash.

Goosebumps confirmed her worst fear.

No... please. If I turn and look at you, you're going to be resting. Nothing else.

She inhaled deeply, knowing all she had to do was look—perhaps the hardest moment of her life.

She turned.

A pool of blood surrounded him, his usual colour drained away.

No…

Her weapon slipped from her grasp, strength vanishing as she collapsed.

"Why? We were meant to fight together, stay together. I was supposed to protect you… don't you remember?"

She slid down the edge of the crater, crawling toward him, each step breaking another piece of her heart. Astra clenched his hand to her chest.

"This was Ox's doing," Levanna murmured, appearing cautiously beside her. "They refused to finish me off… said it was more punishing to let me live, knowing I keep failing to defeat them."

She exhaled shakily.

"They're right. Everything I try to do just crumbles before them.

Astra rose abruptly, her hands tightening around Levanna's throat.

"Where did they go? Tell me!" she demanded.

"T-That… way," Levanna gasped, choking out the words. She coughed violently as Astra released her.

Lightning crackled around Astra's body, raw and uncontrolled. Stray tears sizzled on her skin, but she remained unflinching. The sting was nothing compared to grief.

Then, in a flash of lightning, she bolted away in the direction Levanna had indicated.

Rubble, trees, bodies—all blurred as she ran. Her grip tightened around her sword, poised to strike at the first sign of her enemies.

She prowled through the mountain pass, descending snowy steps until she found them—two Zodiacs walking casually, not a care in the world.

Unforgivable.

Goat was the first to sense danger—too late.

Astra plunged her surging sword into his back. Again. And again. Each strike fueled by agony and rage. Goat's screams tore through the frozen air.

Ox turned abruptly, his gaze locking onto Astra.

Launching off Goat's shoulders, she propelled herself at the giant—the one who had taken everything from her.

"You're mine," she said coldly.

Burning-hot metal tore into his thick neck. Lightning crackled and fizzled out as the blade lodged deep. She yanked, but it wouldn't budge.

"Big mistake, little lady," Ox said, a wide grin stretching across his face. A fist as large as her torso crashed into her, forcing the air from her lungs. Blood splattered across his face.

"You shouldn't have followed us. Now, it's your turn to suffer," Goat sneered, clutching his bleeding wounds.

Ox slammed her into the ground. A sickening crack—ribs shattered. Her cries echoed through the valley of ice.

Two attacks? Not good enough! I want to make you suffer. I want you to feel this pain.

"I went easy on her. Pathetic," Ox scoffed. "I was hoping for more." Disdain twisted his expression as he turned to Goat. "I need to go before this sour taste gets worse."

"Are you okay?" Goat asked.

"What kind of question is that? Of course, I am!" Ox gloated.

"But your hand is trembling. I've never seen you tremble before."

Ox clenched his fist tightly.

"Anyway, we did what we came for. He'll be happy to hear of our success. We can move forward with our plan now."

"Finally! I'm excited—it's about time I get my revenge," Ox boasted, his voice booming through the cold mountain valley.

Stop! I can still fight…

Astra reached out weakly toward the Zodiacs as they vanished into the spatial rift Goat had created.

Darkness crept into her vision.

Then, she collapsed, unconscious in the frozen tundra.

ᛗᚲᛁᛚᛟᚷᚢᛗ

Trees fell one by one, clearing a space in the small forest outside Riverfall. Sweat dripped from Levanna's forehead as she placed a log atop the funeral pyre.

"There are a couple more, Astra. I'll retrieve their bodies. Will you be okay?" Levanna asked.

Covered in bandages, Astra pushed through the pain, carrying logs to the pyre.

"I'm fine. It's a short distance to carry them. You've done most of the work anyway," she replied, glancing toward the village. Her mind drifted to memories of loved ones—happy faces appearing one by one, only to fade into nothingness.

Levanna stepped forward, her tone soft but firm. "You need to take it easy. You don't heal like I do. Your ribs are fractured. Let me handle the rest, okay?"

Dark blue mixed with violet as the sun dipped below the horizon. A blazing fire roared to life, joining the last fading light of the day.

"Are you sure we should leave him there?" Astra asked, cradling her arms as she welcomed the bonfire's warmth.

"Before we came here, he mentioned a plan—one that sounded crazy. By the looks of it, everything played out exactly how he wanted. All he said was, *'Leave me where the axe falls. If it works, I'll come back. I need to die so they'll leave us alone.'*"

"Sounds like he planned to die," Astra murmured. Her voice faltered as she stared at the glistening lake. "I never imagined he'd give his life in battle like this."

She wrapped her arms around herself.

"This hollowness... I just want him back. We were always together. I don't remember a life without him in it."

"You loved him, didn't you?" Levanna asked, idly picking at her food while Astra's gaze remained fixed on the lake.

Astra took a deep breath.

"You know, when we were young—before either of us knew how to fight—bandits raided our village. At the time, Lazarus had a frost cat—a young one. They were inseparable," she said, pausing to collect her thoughts.

Levanna's eyes widened. "What happened?" she asked, horrified.

"During the raid, they trapped Lazarus and his cat. I hid in the bushes. I *wanted* to run to him, to help him, but I knew it would only make things worse. So I watched... helplessly."

Astra's hands clenched the stump beneath her.

"I watched as they killed Ísarr. I watched as they carved symbols into his back. And I saw his eyes stare at me—pleading—before rage erupted inside me."

She exhaled shakily.

"What they did to him left scars—physical and mental."

"What did you do?" Levanna asked gently, taking Astra's hand to offer comfort.

Tears welled up in Astra's eyes. "I—I did what I had to. A bandit stood close by; the dagger on his belt screamed at me to steal it, so I did. I had practised with a wooden sword before but never in real combat. The rage overcame me. With a flicker of electricity, blood stained that dagger and drenched my clothes. I sliced at ankles and slit throats—two of them died before the others even realised what was happening.

"The leader lunged at me, wide-eyed and angry. I fought her off like a wild animal, but it wasn't enough. Her attacks drove me toward a giant bandit who caught me with a gentle smile. I struggled and screamed in primal rage, trying to break free, reaching out for Lazarus. Vines sprouted from the ground, forcing the giant to drop me while others were impaled. They broke Lazarus, and I wanted to break them—but they escaped..." Astra's hands trembled.

"What happened to the two of you is terrible. No one should experience that at such a young age. As children, we are weak, vulnerable, and innocent to the dangers that lurk in this world. Did you ever find the bandit leader?"

"No, they escaped and never returned. The elders sent regular patrols to ensure they never came back. Levanna, from that night on, I knew he meant everything to me. I never wanted to see him suffer like that again. I trained every day after that, hoping I could protect him from anything. Tonight is a reminder that I can't protect him from everything. Out of all the things to fear in life, there is one thing he fears."

"Now that I think about it, he never flinched or froze when facing Zodiac—and they're the strongest people I know."

"Lazarus had no fear of people, despite his past. What he fears is losing those around him. He's protective and would put his life on the line for anyone he cares for without a second thought. Losing those precious to him—he never wants to experience that again."

"You share a bond that's rare to find," Levanna said softly. "I can see it in the way you glance at each other. We're young; we have all the time in the world to grow stronger, to learn from our mistakes." She lay down on the ground, raising a hand to cover the moon. "I've never been in love before, but I've imagined what it would be like. In my twenty years working for Zodiac, I knew nothing but combat. When I returned from searching for the champion, I had little reprieve from the haunting visions. Dreams of a better life were all I had to keep me going."

"I'm glad you escaped that place," Astra said, her voice carrying a hint of hope. "We'll find a way to defeat them in the future, but for now, I think it's best to enjoy the time we have."

"You're right. My life in this village was short, but it showed me there's a better life for me out there. I want to find where I belong. When you return to Baylor, can I go with you? Maybe there's something for me there."

"Someone with your strength could fit in as a Knight," Astra replied with a faint smile. "Or you could explore the Tower."

A sharp pain shot through Levanna's head. "Tower?"

"Are you okay?" Astra asked, placing a hand on Levanna's back.

"I think so, but when you mentioned the Tower, something flashed in my mind—a memory of a conversation I had with the leader of Zodiac, Dog. He used to talk about four towers, one in each kingdom. Each comprised of a hundred floors, filled with creatures of all shapes and sizes. But what interested him most was the inclusion of Deities—he would tell stories about them every night. There's something I'm missing, though. He also spoke about special items in the Tower, ones that were important to him."

"Do you think those items are what Zodiac is after? Now that they've... killed the champion, they can go after them without worrying about a threat," Astra replied.

"That's a possibility. I'm sorry—I don't remember more about what they were. But I do believe the Towers will be their next target. Whatever is at the top of those Towers is pivotal to their grand scheme."

"If that's true, I'll report to my Commander. We need to ensure the Tower has increased security. We can't let them succeed."

"If only it were that simple." Levanna sighed. "Enough of that—we can discuss it later. I just want to relax. The last couple of days have worn me out."

"I'm with you there. We can leave for Baylor in the morning."

Flames burned throughout the night, the crackling fire fending off the eerie silence of Riverfall. The once joyous life of the village had vanished in a single tragic day.

"Accepting sacrifice; activating Second Wind," Eclipse droned.

Ethereal light enveloped Lazarus, lifting his body into the air. Pulsing waves of energy quickened in rhythm, radiating outward. Luminescent rays of glimmering violet pierced the dark, cloudy sky, ushering in a new dawn. Fingers twitched, eyes fluttered behind closed lids. Then, with a sharp gasp for air, shock set in—before a haunting, anguished howl escaped his lungs.